MW00462626

THE BONE SCROLL

It's a secret lost in time, a myth among immortals, a relic of such power that vampires around the world have quietly harbored the hope that it doesn't really exist.

It's a mystery that Tenzin and Ben cannot resist.

But to obtain the bone scroll, they'll need leverage over the most powerful and mercurial vampire in the known world. Saba, oldest of immortals and mother of the vampire race, has returned to her homeland in the highlands of Ethiopia, searching for the scroll with a cadre of elders. In order to outsmart them, Ben and Tenzin will need to walk a literal and figurative ledge through a maze of vampire loyalties, shadowy motivations, and ancient secrets.

If Saba wanted them gone, she could command the earth to swallow them whole. But the mother of vampires is playing her own game, and both Ben and Tenzin are no more than pawns.

Can they outsmart and outmaneuver the most primeval beings in their race to find the bone scroll before it lands in the possession of those who care only for their own selfish gain?

The Bone Scroll is the finale of the Elemental Legacy series by Elizabeth Hunter, *USA Today* best-selling author of the Elemental Mysteries, the Irin Chronicles, and the Glimmer Lake series.

PRAISE FOR ELIZABETH HUNTER

This book was exciting, mysterious, suspenseful, and romantic, with several sides of wry humor to make it a perfectly delightful read from beginning to end.

— Beautiful Chaos Reviews

For everyone who has been on this ride of Ben and Tenzin's adventures, this one will not disappoint you at all. It has all the adventure and the complications that come with it.

— The Blue-Haired Reader

You feel the night in Addis Ababa pulse around you as Ben and Tenzin step off the plane or you feel awed by the sublimeness of the rock churches in Lalibela, even as our protagonists are in a race to find the Bone Scroll first.

— Monadh, Goodreads

Ms. Hunter draws you into the story with her lush descriptions of the Ethiopian landscape and people and Ben and Tenzin's adventure keeps you enthralled.

— Bookhoarder

THE BONE SCROLL

AN ELEMENTAL LEGACY NOVEL

ELIZABETH HUNTER

The Bone Scroll
Copyright © 2021
Elizabeth Hunter
ISBN: 978-1-941674-68-0

All rights reserved. Except as permitted under the US Copyright Act of 1976, no part of this publication may be reproduced, distributed, or transmitted in any form or by any means, or stored in a database or retrieval system, without the prior written permission of the author.

Cover: Damonza
Content Editor: Amy Cissell, Cissell Ink
Line Editor: Anne Victory
Proofreader: Linda, Victory Editing

If you're reading this book and did not purchase it or it was not purchased for your use only, please delete it and purchase your own copy from an authorized retailer. Thank you for respecting the hard work of this author.

Recurve Press LLC
PO Box 4034
Visalia, California 93278
USA

To all the scientists,
The researchers,
Protocol watchers and data-junkies,
For all the healthcare workers,
The doctors and nurses,
Lab techs and therapists,
And for all of their families who have sacrificed countless hours
without them,
For the people who held the hands that we could not,
Looked in the eyes of the lost,
And mourned with each family,
Thank you. We cannot say it enough.
Thank you.
Thank you.
Thank you.

1

The water vampire wanted to meet at a self-storage yard near the airport, which didn't instill a sense of confidence in Ben Vecchio. The damp night air over San Francisco wrapped frigid fingers around his throat and slid down his collar as he hovered over the appointed meeting place. In the distance, the seemingly endless queue of jumbo jets circled, waiting for their turn to land at the airport by the bay.

The storage yard off Old Bayshore Highway was like any other anonymous industrial complex in the United States. Painted a dull, salt-speckled taupe, it sat under the evening fog in a half dozen neat rows. Nothing about the yard would have seemed off to a human, but Ben could scent multiple threads of amnis, the immortal power that animated their kind, drifting in the air.

Vampires guarded the place. Not wind vampires like Ben—not that he could detect anyway—but multiple immortals were present, which meant the Trader wasn't alone.

Not necessarily a threat. The vampire was known for doing business with legitimate and slightly less legitimate businesspeople, which meant that security was prudent.

What Ben wasn't sure of was if he fell under the "legitimate" or "slightly less" label these days.

Probably slightly less.

He descended from the darkness and landed under the cool glow of a streetlamp, deliberately making himself visible. He saw a guard behind the chain-link fence emerge from the darkness, nodding toward a narrow gate next to the car entrance. The guard took a device from his pocket and pressed a button, speaking into it.

Ben stood at the gate, waiting. He knew he was on camera; he could feel the electronic waves emanating from the building. It was an erratic ability that had emerged in the past few months that was both useful and annoying.

Being a fairly new vampire, Ben was still developing his amnis. Having been sired by an ancient wind vampire, that also meant that when new abilities emerged, they often came on full blast. It was a little like dropping into a vehicle going one hundred miles an hour. Sure, you could get used to it, but it would be a lot nicer if you were there for the buildup.

The guard got the approval he needed and opened the gate for Ben. Neither one of them spoke the obvious: Ben was a wind vampire. He could have flown over the gate as easily as breathing, but he was showing the Trader respect.

See? I will respect your rules even if I don't have to.

The silent guard walked into the anonymous maze of storage units, and Ben followed. They turned right, then left, following no obvious landmarks other than painted numbers on units. When they reached C-201, the guard opened a smaller door next to the large garage door and pushed it open, motioning Ben to enter.

The interior of the unit was pitch-black, and Ben could scent two vampires inside.

Okay, here goes nothing. If he had to beat up his hands

tearing open the roof of the unit to get out of a sticky situation, he was going to be pissed. But Tenzin had vouched for this trader, and she was his partner, so he trusted her.

Mostly.

Ben stepped through the doorway and heard the door shut behind him. A light flipped on, nothing harsh enough to blind an immortal, but it still surprised him, as did the view.

In front of Ben, there was a very comfortable and well-appointed office. A thin, pale vampire in a business suit was sitting at the desk, his hand on a switch.

"Mr. Benjamin Vecchio?" The vampire spoke with a slight French accent, and if Ben hadn't known any different, he would have thought he'd walked into the offices of a fashion magazine.

The art on the wood-paneled walls was modern with a distinct Asian flair. The concrete floors of the unit had been covered in thick, polished wood and wool rugs so luxurious he could feel his feet sinking into them.

"I'm Ben Vecchio." Ben stepped toward the desk, close enough to be polite but not close enough to be a threat. "I'm here for a meeting with the Trader. My partner called a few days ago."

"Of course. She is expecting you." The man nodded a head of wavy brown hair. He motioned to a set of leather chairs on one wall. "If you'll give her a moment, she'll be right out."

Ben sat and examined the space. How many exits? It was an old game he'd played with Tenzin for years. One, the door behind him. Two, the window in the back that probably led to another storage unit, which would have another door. Three, the vent over the head of the fashionable secretary, easily ripped out to access the sky. Four, the door leading to the neighboring storage unit on the left. Five, the door leading to the storage unit on the right.

Five exits was acceptable. It was quite ingenious when he

thought about it. No one from the outside would ever suspect the offices of an international antiquities trader were veiled by an industrial storage unit. The units were light safe and only accessible from single points unless expanded.

A few minutes later, a thin woman with Southeast Asian features emerged from the office on the left. She was wearing a black top that wrapped around her slim figure and a flowing skirt in black with striped floral panels in what looked like traditional silk fabric. Her jewelry was simple: gold hoops in her ears, a gold chain around her neck, and a thick jade bracelet on her left arm.

"Mr. Vecchio?"

Ben rose, trying not to show his surprise. He'd been expecting something different. He wasn't sure what, but it wasn't a seemingly young vampire who looked like she'd be running a high-end gallery, not a sometimes-illicit antiquities trade.

He stopped a few feet from the Trader and bowed his head slightly. "It's a great pleasure to meet you. Tenzin speaks highly of you."

The woman smiled. "That is very flattering." If she wasn't a native English speaker, you'd never know it—her accent was impeccable. "I've enjoyed working with your partner in the past. We share an appreciation of directness."

Ben smiled. "Yes, she does appreciate that."

"Tenzin told me you were looking for something quite specific for a client." She motioned to what he assumed was her office door. "Please join me and we'll talk. Gregory can get us something to drink if you'd like. Blood-wine? Coffee? Tea?"

Ben turned to Gregory. "Blood-wine would be great. Thank you."

"Of course." He murmured a brand label in French, and the Trader nodded.

Ben kept on alert as he walked into the Trader's office, but he wasn't feeling uneasy. So far the meeting had gone as expected.

You can't distrust everyone, his aunt would say. Then again, his aunt was a librarian. A vampire librarian and protector of rare books, but a librarian nonetheless. She didn't deal with quite as many unsavory characters as Ben did in the course of his business.

He looked for a desk but found only a sitting area in front of a wall of books and objets d'art. Thick coffee table books were stacked along the wall, interspersed with brilliant orbs of glass, shiny porcelain, and carved wooden pieces.

"Your collection is diverse." He turned when he sensed her behind him.

"The world is full of beautiful things." She spread her hands. "In my business, I aim to facilitate the right buyer finding the right seller." She motioned to the sofas in front of the bookcases. "Please have a seat and tell me what you're looking for."

Her power was a low thrum calibrated to set clients at ease, which was exactly what was happening to Ben. He was still working on his own ability to muffle the startling ancient power that blasted through him, and he was feeling good so far that neither the Trader nor her secretary seemed intimidated.

"I'm looking for tenth-century African artifacts."

The Trader furrowed her eyebrows slightly. "Can you be more specific? Benin? Ghana? Egyptian?"

"Ethiopian," Ben said. "Specifically, ceremonial or imperial headdresses or crowns from the late Aksumite Empire."

The Trader pursed her lips. "Very specific. You do realize that much of the Aksumite treasury was raided in the late tenth century?"

"I do."

"And many of the later antiquities, which likely contain the remaining Aksumite relics, were taken by the British."

"Unfortunately, yes."

The Trader said, "I know of an excellent collection of Aksumite gold coins that is available. Finest quality, and the seller is quite motivated."

Gold coins? He could always interest Tenzin in that.

Keep on track, Ben.

"I realize I'm looking for something very specific." He shifted slightly. "We are also more than happy to trade for information."

"I see." The Trader's chin tilted up. "I can definitely reach out to contacts and possibly see what might not be on the market yet."

"But for the right price...?"

She smiled. "For the right price, one can often obtain things that are not strictly for sale."

"Thank you. We appreciate your discretion and your connections. I do have one other inquiry."

The Trader spread her hands. "I am at your service."

Ben kept his eyes on the woman and relayed the information exactly as Tenzin had told him. "What do you know about the collection of Trevor Blythe-Bickman?"

One eyebrow went up. "I know Mr. Blythe-Bickman's family collection is quite extensive, and I do believe much of it was acquired in the Horn of Africa. His collection of Somali jewelry and gemstones is well known."

"I've heard that. I also have reason to believe he has quite a good collection of Aksumite manuscripts."

"It's possible." She took a moment to examine Ben. "I have not worked with Mr. Blythe-Bickman. His social circle and mine do not overlap."

Meaning: I am not a billionaire tech bro with an overblown ego and an elevated opinion of my own IQ.

"I see." Ben smiled. "We may have an interest in some of Mr. Blythe-Bickman's collection."

"Even those not currently on the market?" The corner of the Trader's mouth turned up.

Trevor Blythe-Bickman was the heir to a massive British fortune who had made his home in San Francisco and also considered himself a technology guru. To his credit, he'd started some minor companies that had quickly been gobbled up by the titans of Silicon Valley, leaving him with both old *and* new money, a massive ego, and an enormous Tudor mansion in the exclusive Pacific Heights neighborhood of San Francisco.

Ben definitely wanted to rob him.

"As you said, for the right price, one can often obtain things that are not strictly for sale." He leaned forward. "I think what we might be looking for is... information."

The Trader smiled. "You're in luck. I also deal in that."

Tenzin leaned against the white-painted lighthouse on the tip of Point Reyes, waiting for the earth vampire to appear. She tucked her small frame into a shadow of the old structure and listened as the ocean crashed beneath her. The damp sea air permeated her shoulder-length hair; it hung like a heavy curtain around her face.

Tenzin remained on alert despite the cover of darkness. The location was only a short flight north of San Francisco, and she'd come seeking information from a problematic source.

Lucien Thrax appeared in the distance, steadily descending the many steps leading to the rocky promontory that jutted into the Pacific. The presence of another ancient progeny caused her feet to lift from the ground, the air drawn to her as her senses went into overdrive.

The earth vampire reached the base of the stairs and stopped, searching the darkness for her shadow. "I'm here, daughter of Zhang."

Tenzin emerged from the dark fog. "Son of Saba."

Lucien sighed, stuffed his hands in his pockets, and furrowed his eyebrows. "We've never been enemies, Tenzin. Why the formality?" He looked like a harried intellectual, not an ancient warrior turned modern healer. In reality, he was all those things. His stone-grey eyes, pale skin, and dark hair told humans he was a tall European in early middle age, but he was the last son of Saba, most ancient vampire known to their kind, mother of their race, and the woman who had manipulated Tenzin's partner into losing his human life.

"You are aware of the current status of Benjamin?" she asked.

Lucien looked annoyed. "I know Ben is a vampire now, Tenzin. It's been... What? Three years? We were at his aunt and uncle's house for Christmas. My mate and Ben's aunt are practically family."

She flew closer. "And do you know how that came about?"

Lucien's eyes grew wary. "I have heard... whispers."

"From your mother's people?"

"From Alitea. I wasn't certain what was true or not. You know how rumors can fly in vampire courts."

Lucien's mother was head of the Council of Alitea that ruled the Mediterranean, much of Europe, the Middle East, and North Africa. Tenzin's father was the oldest of the Eight Immortals who ruled East Asia from Penglai Island. They were both children of power and politics, who knew that rumors could carry lies as easily as truth but were more often somewhere in the middle.

"She orchestrated it, Lucien. I heard it from her own soldier's mouth. She gave the order; she took his choice from him." Tenzin had always had every intention of persuading Ben into immortality, but she'd wanted him to choose it. In the end, he had not, and Tenzin had made the choice for him. The rift it had caused led to over two years of resentment they had only recently overcome.

Lucien took a deep breath. "I'm disappointed but not surprised. You know I have little to no influence over my mother, Tenzin. I don't know what you want me to—"

"She *wronged* him. She stole his life after he saved yours." Ben had once pulled Lucien from the sunlight, saving his immortal life and allowing Saba to heal him.

"I know." Lucien looked more than embarrassed; he looked pained. "I'm sure she doesn't see it that way," he said. "Saba doesn't think like us; you know this."

Tenzin said nothing.

"Does Ben know?" Lucien asked. "About my mother?"

"No."

"He needs to know, Tenzin." Lucien shook his head. "Don't make the mistakes I have. Don't try to hide the truth from the ones you love, even if you think it's for their own good."

"He can't..." She took a breath. "He's powerful, Lucien, but compared to Saba—"

"There is no comparison."

The ancient mother was more of an elemental force than an individual power. No one knew when she had come into being, not even Saba herself. Her elemental force could literally reshape the earth and wipe out their kind if she wanted it.

"Give him a little credit for wisdom," Lucien said. "Ben is the son of Giovanni Vecchio; he knows what discipline is, and he deserves to know."

Tenzin let the subject lie. It wasn't the true reason she'd come. "Something is happening in the old world," Tenzin said. "My father came to give me a message in New York."

Lucien blinked. "Zhang came to New York?"

"He told me Arosh had found the bone scroll in Aksum." Arosh, the ancient Fire King of the Near East, was one of the Council of Alitea and Saba's consort much of the time. As such, Lucien knew him about as well as any living vampire Tenzin could think of.

"Zhang thinks Arosh has the bone scroll?" Lucien closed his eyes and shook his head a little. "Your father thinks the bone scroll is *real*?"

"He says he knows it is. He says he saw it in the possession of a Manichaean missionary in the sixth century."

"And he didn't take it?"

"He didn't realize what it was at the time. It was just an old scroll written in a language no one could decipher. I'd heard about the bone scroll, but only as a myth. Zhang had no idea."

"It's practically a vampire urban legend," Lucien said. "I don't think it exists. And if it did, why would it be in Aksum?"

Tenzin spread her hands out. "How did the Hebrew Ark of the Covenant end up there? I don't know, Lucien. People like to hide things in Ethiopia." That wasn't how it ended up there, but she didn't have any obligation to share her research with Saba's son.

"The Ark..." Lucien waved a hand. "Longer story. Tenzin, *if* the bone scroll exists, and *if* it does what the stories say it does, then I am confident that Arosh does not have it. He probably put out that rumor for political reasons or something. It's petty posturing."

"How are you so sure?"

Lucien pursed his lips. "Has he overtaken the immortal world in the past few months and no one told me?"

Tenzin narrowed her eyes. "No."

"There you are." Lucien shrugged. "He doesn't have it."

2

Ben didn't wait for Tenzin to arrive at the restaurant to place an order; he'd known the woman for over a decade, and he knew what she'd want to eat. He ordered a bowl of noodles and a bowl of polo from the dark-haired waiter, then settled into the corner booth, sipping a glass of Coke and soda water. The older he got as a vampire, the more he disliked how sweet most sodas were. He found most flavors intense, but sweetness bothered him more than most.

The Central Asian restaurant was open twenty-four hours, owned by a grumpy Kazakh earth vampire, and served an eclectic clientele. Most of the patrons that night were young vampires like Ben, taking advantage of a discreet location to meet humans or fellow immortals without dishing out the money for pricier vampire clubs.

One of the things that Ben had learned quickly was a lot of vampires—especially young ones—were remarkably cheap. While some immortals came from wealthy families like Ben did, a lot of them were what his father would have called "working stiffs."

Kind of literally, in a vampire's case.

If you were newly turned and under the aegis of a powerful vampire, you weren't likely to have a lot of money unless your sire was particularly generous. Those who ascended the hierarchy in clans gained power, influence, and cash. Those just starting out had to earn their keep.

Unlike Ben, most of these younger vampires didn't have to consciously put a mental blanket over their amnis so they wouldn't start a fight when they went out for middle-of-the-night noodles.

Ben was watching the two a.m. traffic pass when he felt her approach. Tenzin and he had shared blood a few times, but Ben was cautious. He didn't know what all was involved in a blood bond, and he didn't want to form one without talking to Tenzin, who didn't seem interested in discussing the subject.

Rock, meet hard place. They hadn't shared blood in months. A bed? Absolutely. But not blood.

As Tenzin walked through the door and headed toward him, he thought about an old joke he'd heard from his uncle's butler, Caspar.

Question: How do porcupines mate?

Answer: Very carefully.

She sat down, and she was soaking wet.

Ben blinked. "Did you go swimming in the bay?"

"No." Tenzin leaned over and wrung out her hair on the floor next to the booth. The Kazakh in the opposite corner started muttering at her in a language Ben didn't understand. Tenzin turned and said something in the same language before giving the man a gesture Ben didn't need to translate.

"Are you trying to get us kicked out? I like the food here."

"I know him." She shrugged one shoulder. "His wife is wonderful and likes me. She's too good for him, and I remind him of it regularly."

"Vampire or human?" He shoved a half-full glass of tea toward her. "Do you want a towel?"

She reached for the tea. "For what?"

He shook his head. "Never mind. How did the meeting go?"

"Lucien doesn't think he has it."

Mindful of vampire hearing around them, Ben kept things vague. "Really?"

"Really." She sipped her tea, then added sugar. "He says if he'd had it, he'd have used it by now, so he must not have it. I don't think Lucien even believes in it."

Ben reached for the sugar before she could go overboard. "But you do?"

"Of course. If my father says it's real, it's real."

Ben still didn't have the full picture on this scroll made of bones, but he knew enough to know it was considered a magical artifact, and Ben treated anything purporting to be magical with a huge degree of skepticism.

Sure, he was a vampire, but that was all explainable when you understood amnis.

And where amnis came from? Maybe they didn't quite understand that yet, but what animated any kind of life really? Magic scrolls of power, on the other hand, seemed about as realistic as werewolves, zombies, and witches who flew on broomsticks.

"Tenzin?"

"Hmm?" She sipped her tea, seemingly lost in thought.

"Do you believe in witches and werewolves?"

"Witches? Of course. Werewolves are biologically ridiculous."

He smiled but didn't ask more. He was sure she'd have an explanation if he asked, but their food was coming; he could smell the lamb and cumin from the kitchen. He set a plate in front of her, along with some chopsticks and a large spoon.

Their food arrived, and he spooned some of the polo onto her plate, then a portion of noodles. Tenzin was still staring into space.

"Hey, good-lookin'." He nudged her foot with his. "You come here often?"

Tenzin blinked and refocused on him. "What?"

Ben picked up his spoon and started on the polo. "I was just wondering if you ate here often. It's my first time at this place. Do you live in the neighborhood? I just moved here. We could go for coffee sometime if you want, get to know each other." He winked at her confused expression.

Tenzin cocked her head, staring at Ben as if he'd grown two heads. "Did something happen to your memory?"

He couldn't help it. Ben broke into a grin. "I'm teasing you, Tenzin."

"How is that teasing?"

He reached across the table and cleaned the corner of her mouth with his napkin as she frowned at him. "You had a piece of parsley—"

"Did you sustain a head injury of some kind? If you have, we need to contact—"

"Tenzin, I'm *teasing* you." He leaned his chin on his hand and didn't try to stop the smile. "I was pretending you were a pretty girl in a restaurant I was just meeting. I was playing with you. There's nothing wrong with my memory."

"You were playing?"

"Yes." He reached for the chopsticks their waiter had set on the table. "The noodles are good here. You should have some." He couldn't wait; it had been ages since he'd had hand-pulled noodles cooked this way.

Tenzin was still staring at him. "Is this your way of suggesting we incorporate role-play into our sexual practices?"

Ben nearly spit out the mouthful of noodles he'd just stuffed in his mouth. He tried to swallow as quickly as possible while simultaneously reaching across the table to cover Tenzin's mouth.

"I don't have any objections to that, though there are some scenarios that I would not find arousing, such as—"

"Oh my God, please be quiet." Ben finally managed to speak. "No, this was not a suggestion to incorporate... You know what? Let's change the subject. I should tell you about my meeting too."

"Props might be fun, but we'd want to be careful with any fully functional weapons, because we both tend to forget our strength sometimes when we're—"

"Blueprints! I think I can get them for the house. Good news, right?" Ben had to get her off the subject before all of immortal San Francisco had a clear picture of Tenzin's particular sexual proclivities, which were wide, varied, and none of their damn business. "Remember the meeting I had?"

Tenzin frowned, then nodded. "Right. And we didn't finish talking about Lucien."

"He doesn't believe in it and doesn't think the guy has it, right?"

"Right." She opened her mouth, then closed it. "Yes. I suppose those are the main points of the conversation."

She was keeping something back, which exasperated him, but he was learning to be patient. Since they'd reunited, Tenzin had been learning to open up, but she was a five-thousand-year-old creature who'd survived by secrecy and evasion; hiding things was second nature. She was making an effort to share more with him, but it took some practice.

Ben let the silence hang for a moment. "So that was it? He doesn't think the guy has it?"

"Yes. That was what we talked about." She ate some polo. "And they were at Giovanni and Beatrice's for Christmas."

He glanced at her since it was a sore spot. "We were invited."

"Your aunt is very... polite." Tenzin focused on her food, very deliberately not looking at Ben. "I'm not going to do that."

"B is going to get over it." His aunt, who had once been like family with Tenzin, had been furious when Ben had turned. He knew Beatrice had been angry that Tenzin had taken the choice of turning away from him, but he thought things had been getting better. "One step at a time. She smiled at you in Rome."

"Because Sadia was there." Tenzin was concentrating on her noodles. "Beatrice can carry a grudge longer than you or Giovanni. It will likely be some time before we are friends again." She turned her head. "Aldiyar, your noodles are better than ever."

The brooding vampire in the corner grunted but didn't say anything.

"So you think she's going to avoid the house all next week?" Ben asked. "That doesn't sound practical."

"No, she will be very" —Tenzin bristled at the word— "*polite.*"

Since they were working on the West Coast, they'd planned a visit for Ben to see his family in Los Angeles. His aunt, uncle, and their adopted daughter Sadia—who was Ben's baby sister in all ways but blood—were excited to see him. Giovanni and Sadia were also excited to see Tenzin, but Beatrice was notably silent when Ben called to tell the family they'd both be coming.

Ben tipped up her chin and forced Tenzin's eyes to his. "Hey."

She met his eyes with her own stormy grey ones, incongruous in a face that hailed from Northern Asia. "Benjamin."

"She loves you. We'll get past this."

Her ever-present fangs appeared behind her lips. "I want to leave now."

"I'll have them pack up the food." He nodded toward the door. "Do you want to head out first?" Two vampires flying were considerably more noticeable than one, even at night.

She nodded. "Don't take too long." She stood and headed for the door. "We will try the role-playing sex later."

At least everyone in the diner waited for Tenzin to leave before they chuckled.

As Ben was leaving, the gruff Aldiyar waved him over.

Ben smiled. "Everything tasted great. Thanks for—"

"They warned you, yes?" Aldiyar nodded toward the door. "About that one?"

Ben struck an innocent expression. "Warned me about what?"

Aldiyar narrowed his eyes and waved a dismissive hand at Ben, who smiled and headed out the door.

SINCE TENZIN HAD COLLECTED a wide variety of residences in her nearly five thousand years of life, when she told Ben she "had a place" in San Francisco to stay, he simply assumed he was going to find out about another real estate purchase.

In fact, Tenzin's "place" was the attic of an enormous Victorian house off of Alamo Square, owned by an elderly woman who didn't realize the attic window was easily accessed by someone flying outside.

While Ben couldn't complain about the spacious attic or the light-safe modifications Tenzin had made over the years, he felt distinctly uncomfortable with what was basically a squatting situation.

He was lying back on the comfortable king-sized mattress she'd somehow gotten into the place. "I just don't know how you believe she'd be comfortable with this arrangement if she found out about it. She doesn't even know about vampires, Tenzin."

"I realize that, but I've met her. I pretended I was a new neighbor once, and she invited me in for a glass of wine." Tenzin lay next to him, snuggling into the crook of his arm. "Mavis is very generous, and I wanted to get a look inside the house."

"Are you warm enough?"

"I'm completely dry." Tenzin leaned in and kissed his neck. "Stop fussing."

Kiss, don't bite. He felt his body react to her. Like an electrical current, all it took was a moment of contact. Ben closed his eyes and enjoyed the feeling of Tenzin's hand sneaking under his shirt. It would be gone shortly, but he'd discovered that she liked to disrobe him and take her time.

"Mavis is generous because she thought you were her new neighbor, Tenzin, not because you wanted to steal her attic."

"I contributed to the foundation work several years ago, Ben. I made a deal with the contractor and paid for most of it. Don't insinuate I'm a leech. If you want to talk about parasites, those are her children." She muttered something in Mandarin that would likely make the old woman's ears bleed. "They're waiting for her to die. I hate them."

"You are not allowed to kill them, Tenzin."

"I knew you were going to say that." She rolled on her back. "I have considered insinuating myself into Mavis's life in order to disinherit them though. They don't deserve her money. She and Walter worked very hard for it. I know what her favorite charities are. I would keep the house, obviously."

"Tenzin, you're not allowed to disinherit Mavis's children. That's not the kind of con we do."

She pouted. "We could do it just once though."

"No." It was the kind of thing his biological mother had liked to do, and Ben had made a vow long ago not to poach from the vulnerable. He wasn't like her. He worked hard to create his own identity, even in eternity, and now he belonged only to himself.

Well, himself and the tiny, slightly sociopathic vampire he loved.

"I'm just saying that there is an argument to be made to remove the second generation." Tenzin clearly wasn't ready to let the subject go. "The grandchildren seem quite nice and visit her regularly. There are five of them, and they are redeemable. The oldest girl is studying to be a teacher, which is a very honorable profession."

He had to distract her somehow, otherwise Mavis's unsuspecting grandchildren might end up orphans. "So what did you have in mind for role-playing sex?"

She popped up and looked at him, her eyes alight. "I read something on the internet that sounded highly erotic. It's probably good Mavis doesn't hear well."

Ben bit back a laugh. "I absolutely adore you."

"I know."

3

Visiting Ben's family should have been simple, but it wasn't. They landed a few blocks away from the house so as not to trigger the extensive electronic surveillance that surrounded the compound in San Marino. The exclusive enclave in Southern California was home to more than one immortal—along with business leaders and celebrities—so the patchwork of human and immortal security was a minefield for wind vampires. It was really best to just walk a few blocks and avoid the drama.

Tenzin dressed in her regular uniform of black leggings and a body-hugging tunic that moved with her. She and Ben had left their weapons at Tenzin's warehouse in nearby Pasadena, so while she might have been covered in clothing, she still felt naked.

"I don't know why you're being like this," Ben said. "You're acting like we could be perceived as a threat."

"This is the first time we have visited your family home as... whatever we are now." She glanced up at him. "I do not want to put Beatrice on edge."

Ben stopped in the street, and she paused with him. He

stared at her. "You're not planning to stay with me, are you? You're going to go back to the warehouse for the day."

"Ben, it is not my territory."

"It's my family home. You're my... person. You are staying there with me." His face was mulish. "They wanted a family visit, you're part of the family."

"Your aunt—"

"Beatrice." He took her by the shoulders. "Beatrice. Who loves you even though she's angry right now. Beatrice, who loves me. Beatrice, who is as much of a mother as I've ever really had. Beatrice will understand that I want you with me. Giovanni said they planned to put us in the guesthouse anyway."

Tenzin considered it. Giovanni was one of her oldest and dearest friends, one of the few who claimed her loyalty. He was also a fire vampire of enormous power, which meant that distance between them was usually preferable.

But the guesthouse was distant.

"The guesthouse is acceptable. I've stayed there before."

"I know." He leaned down and pressed a firm kiss to her mouth. "Will you relax a little now? Please?"

They reached the gates of the compound, and the guard immediately recognized them. He opened the pedestrian gate and waved them in. "Ben! Good to see you, man." The guard held his hand out. "Is this my first time seeing you since the change? I kind of think it is. I was gone the last time you came."

Tenzin watched as Ben considered it. She recognized the man. Eddie had been on the security team since Ben had been in university.

Ben finally said, "I think it may be. Man, it's been a while since I've been home, huh?"

"You look good!" Eddie cocked his head. "The eyes are different, right?"

"Yeah. They still catch me off guard sometimes."

"Hey." Eddie shrugged. "At least you're not getting old. I catch myself in the hall mirror sometimes and wonder when that old man with wrinkles and grey hair moved into my house." Eddie turned to her. "Miss Tenzin, how are you doing tonight?" He didn't hold his hand out to shake like he had with Ben, but his polite nod set her at ease.

"I'm doing well, Eddie. Thank you." She glanced at the others at the gate. "Beatrice and Giovanni should be expecting us."

"Hey, the instructions we have? You're always welcome." Eddie put a hand to his ear and winked at Tenzin. "I think I hear the welcoming committee now."

Tenzin heard it as well. Ben's small sister Sadia had learned to ride a bicycle the year before, and she delighted in telling Tenzin about it. The churn of wheels on concrete grew louder as the girl raced down the long driveway.

Ben took Tenzin's hand and gripped it. She could feel his amnis in a riot. The mix of emotions—love, protection, fear, excitement—they were a vivid aura around him.

"Beeeeeeeeen!" The girl's excited shout echoed in the night. "You're heeeeeeeere!"

Sadia Vecchio whooshed around them at top speed, turning in a wide circle as Tenzin smiled. The girl was a force of nature despite being only six years old.

Dema, Sadia's nanny, appeared in the distance. She was a former Special Forces soldier, and Tenzin approved of her cautious nature.

"Dema." Tenzin nodded.

"Tenzin." Dema nodded back, then turned to Ben. "How you convinced Tenzin to give you a second glance will surprise me eternally."

Ben put a hand over his heart. "Dema, I know you're heartbroken that we can never be together and are putting on a brave face, but try not to let disappointment steal your joy. Stay strong. You will find your lobster."

Was she amused or annoyed? With Dema, it was often difficult to tell.

Sadia abandoned her bicycle and leaped into Ben's arms. "Let me see your teeth."

"Sadi—"

"Pleeeeeeease," she begged. "I want to see if they changed yet." She put her hands on Ben's cheeks and pressed his lips together.

He was the child of an ancient warlord, a being of unspeakable power, and defenseless against his baby sister. These were reasons why Tenzin loved him.

Ben opened his mouth and forced his fangs down. "See?" His mouth was half-open. "They're the same."

Sadia sighed deeply. "But I thought you were married to Tenzin now. Aren't your teeth going to change to curvy like hers?"

Tenzin's eyes went wide, and Dema hid her laugh with a coughing fit.

Ben grabbed Sadia's hand from his mouth. "Who told you that? Tenzin and I are not married."

"But Baba said you love each other special like Baba and Mama love each other." She wrinkled her nose. "Do you kiss Tenzin on the mouth?"

"Sadia, that's none of your business."

The little girl giggled. "You do." She flipped back in Ben's arms and looked at Tenzin upside down. "Tenzin, why didn't you come visit me before this?"

"We've been very busy, *habibti*." She pinched Sadia's belly. "You're getting very fast on your bicycle. Are you going to start driving race cars soon?"

"No." Sadia giggled and her belly shook. "Are you going to marry Ben? If you marry Ben, I think then we would be sisters."

"Sadia," Ben protested, "will you stop asking if we're going to get—"

"Marriage is a patriarchal social contract designed to commodify women's sexuality and reproduction," Tenzin said. "I don't ascribe to it."

Sadia righted herself and frowned at Ben. "What does that mean?"

Ben shot Tenzin a dirty look. "Marriage is also a very special promise that people like Baba and Mama make when they love each other and choose to be a family forever."

Sadia immediately looked at Tenzin for confirmation.

"Yes," Tenzin said. "And that as well."

AFTER GENERAL GREETINGS and updates from Sadia about her school, her friends, her dog Percy, and her trampoline, the little girl was supposed to go to sleep. They had created an unusual school schedule for her, allowing her to keep to more of a nocturnal life, but she still attended traditional classes a few days a week. Instead of bedtime, Sadia led them to the kitchen, where a meal had been prepared.

"You promise?" Sadia sat on Tenzin's lap and stared into her eyes, pressing her small hands to her cheeks as she bid a reluctant goodnight. "*Promise* promise."

"I will be here when you wake up in the morning," Tenzin said. "And you can come visit me."

"I know you wake up in the day like Mama."

"I do."

"So I'm gonna see you in the morning? You're not flying away?"

"I swear on my favorite sword," Tenzin said. "I will be here when you wake."

Sadia's head fell back. "When are you going to teach me sword fighting? It's been foreeeeeeever since you told me."

Oh dear. She could almost feel Giovanni's accusing gaze. "I think I hear Dema calling for you."

Sadia turned to look, and from across the large kitchen table, Tenzin could feel Beatrice's cold eyes on her.

Throughout the light meal, Tenzin had deliberately kept her distance from the water vampire. Ben was sitting next to his aunt, speaking quietly with his arm around her as he ate the traditional Mexican food Beatrice and her grandmother had prepared.

SADIA SLID off Tenzin's lap and went to Dema, the dreaded bedtime enforcer.

"Sweet dreams, *habibti*."

"Sweet dreams, Tenzin!"

Conversations hummed around her, friends and family catching up and enjoying the occasion of guests to talk about news, family gossip, and interesting bits of life. Tenzin was among the conversation, but still hovering on the outside; it was a familiar position.

Despite Beatrice's coolness, Tenzin could feel her own blood living in the woman, feel the ancient tie. Tenzin had been mated to Beatrice's sire, though it wasn't a love match; it had been a practical and political arrangement. Nevertheless, the blood was there, an eternal link with someone who now burned with anger at Tenzin for making an impossible and inevitable choice.

This was why Tenzin was trying to be cautious with Benjamin. Blood bonds were tricky things, and there were few rules to them. She could feel a nascent mating bond forming between them, so she'd pulled back.

They had enough changes to deal with; a blood bond was a complication at this point in their relationship.

The greedy part of her wanted it, wanted to bite into him, steal his amnis and life, devour him and captivate Benjamin until he was in her thrall.

But the new path Tenzin had turned down when Ben's immortal life started kept her from trapping him. He was still painfully young. Though he'd always been an old soul, his immortal character was still emerging. Ben loved her, but would that love turn and change over decades? Who would he be in fifty years? One hundred years? A thousand? What did "choosing to be a family forever" mean when you *actually* lived forever?

"Tenzin?"

She looked up and saw Giovanni standing in the doorway. She was sitting at the table alone; everyone had left while she was lost in thought. "What did I miss?"

"We're going to the library to review what I've found so far about the scroll," Giovanni said. "Join us?"

"Yes." She stood and followed him out of the kitchen and up the stairs where they had turned most of the second floor of their mansion into a large research library, half with traditional collections of books and the other half with vampire-specific technology that could handle Beatrice's amnis.

"It's good to see you." Giovanni put an arm around her. "My son looks happy."

"He should be."

Giovanni smiled. "And so does my friend."

Tenzin paused on the stairs. "I would kill anyone who threatened his happiness or life. He would not approve of that, but I know you understand."

Giovanni hung his hands in his pockets. "I do."

"Is there peace between us, Giovanni di Spada?" She used the name he'd gone by when he was an assassin sent to kill her. The vampire's startling blue-green eyes had reminded Tenzin of her own child's, and she had spared his life, forming an unusual and unbreakable bond over three hundred years old.

He looked at the ground, then back at her. "You don't have to explain yourself to me."

"To her then?"

"She understands."

"In her head perhaps, but not in her heart."

"The one will catch up with the other. I promise. Come on." He nudged her toward the landing. "Let's go talk about an urban legend."

"The bone scroll, if it exists, dates back to an ancient vampire known by the name Ash Mithra." Giovanni projected an image on the wall that looked like a long-haired monk or holy man drawn in a flat, medieval style. "This is an artist's rendering, of course. No one knows what he looked like, though some stories say that he originally came from Eastern Africa, in a territory along the Red Sea."

"How old?" Ben asked.

"No one knows. He would have been contemporaries of Kato, Ziri, and Arosh but likely predates them all."

"So old," Ben said.

"Very old." He clicked a button and another picture appeared. "And this is an artist's rendering of the bone scroll."

"It looks like a bamboo scroll to me," Ben said. "Like most of the ones in Penglai."

"Only this one was made from polished vampire arm bones." Giovanni was frowning at the screen.

Ben blinked. "What the fuck?"

"Do you know what happens to our bodies if we die?" Tenzin asked.

Ben frowned. "We turn back to our element within days."

"True." Beatrice spoke for the first time from the back of the library table. "But there is one odd quirk. If we lose a limb—any body part really—it will usually decompose normally. The amnis seems to... abandon that limb, and it becomes just another human relic."

"So Mithra cut off vampires' arms to make—"

"Oh no, he used his own arm," Giovanni said. "Reportedly. He cut it off, waited for it to grow again, then cut it off again."

Ben blinked. "I'm sorry, that is so messed up. Why would he—"

"No one really knows, but he was trying to accomplish a unique goal," Giovanni said. "Mithra believed that he had discovered the secret for a single vampire to control every element and, for some reason, that was how it needed to be preserved."

"Holy shit." Ben sat gape-mouthed, and the thought churned Tenzin's stomach.

She had cultivated power in her lifetime, learned to master her element and bend the air to her will. She knew others of similar skill with their own elements and respected them highly even if they were enemies.

But no one vampire needed that much power. No one good. No one bad.

No one.

"That's why we're here," Tenzin said. "I have decided that we need to find the bone scroll and keep it from Arosh or steal it back if he has it already."

4

Ben was stunned by the revelation, so he wasn't expecting the quiet snort from Beatrice.

"You *decided*," she muttered. "Yeah, you decide a lot, Tenzin."

Ben turned to his aunt. "Hey. I told you—"

"You told us that Zhang came and laid this all out, but I'm not getting a lot of facts here." Beatrice's voice cut through the silence of the library. "I hear a lot of rumors and a lot of fairy tales, but no one knows if this actually exists, Zhang has only heard rumors, and now Tenzin wants to drag you to the other side of the planet—again!—on a wild-goose chase that could put you in a hell of a lot of danger, Ben."

He was stunned by the bitterness in her voice. "Beatrice."

Tenzin stood. "Why don't we go outside and talk."

"Talk." Beatrice rose as well. "Yeah, that's a good idea. Why don't we go *talk*, Tenzin?"

The two stormed out of the house, and Ben could almost see the electricity between them. He tried to follow, but Giovanni grabbed his arm.

"Wait."

"They're going to go kill each other."

"No." He frowned. "Not kill. Possibly maim, but they'll recover."

Ben's eyes went wide. "And you're okay with that?"

Giovanni patted Ben's shoulder. "You still have a lot to learn about women."

~

TENZIN FOLLOWED BEATRICE AT A DISTANCE. The cool, polite mask was gone, and the anger she had been repressing had simmered over into a raging boil. Beatrice walked to their sparring studio at the back of the house, next to the indoor pool.

"I understand why you're still angry with me," Tenzin said. "If you want to—"

"Angry?" Beatrice reached for a dagger off the wall and pivoted, flinging it close enough to Tenzin's head to gust her hair off her neck. "You do not understand what I'm feeling if you think it's anger, Tenzin."

The sensation of the knife whispering against her skin set Tenzin's teeth on edge. "Feel free to thank me anytime."

Beatrice grabbed one of the hook swords she favored and didn't wait for Tenzin to grab a weapon before she swung it in a circle over her head. "You think I should *thank* you?"

"Absolutely." Tenzin flipped heels over head, grabbing a pike from a bracket on the wall as she landed. "We both know you wanted him changed too."

"Only if he wanted it!"

"Bullshit." Tenzin parried another strike from Beatrice's blade. "If he'd been dying in your arms, what would you have done?"

"I would have protected him," Beatrice yelled. "He wouldn't have been in a situation where—"

"You and Gio put him in that position when he was a child!" Tenzin knocked her blade off-balance and thrust the head of the pike toward Beatrice. "He had to kill a man when he was sixteen years old! Were you there? *No.* I was."

"Fuck you!" Beatrice grabbed the second sword and hooked it on the first, creating a lethal, whirring orchestra of blades coming ever closer to Tenzin's neck.

The wooden shaft of the pike cracked; Tenzin tossed it aside and reached for a blade of her own. The steel clashed between them, and sparks flew in the darkness. Beatrice was an expert swordswoman, and since Tenzin was keeping to the ground, they were evenly matched.

The clanging ring of steel filled the air, and every instinct in Tenzin's body went on alert. She had to focus everything she had on not killing her opponent.

That would be bad.

"He cried in my arms," Beatrice said. "He kept saying, 'I might have lived. I might have been okay, B.' Did you even once consider taking him to the *goddamn hospital?*"

Tenzin nearly tripped. "And let the human butchers gamble with his life?"

"Well, what were you doing?" Beatrice reached for the handle of her second sword and gripped it in her left hand.

"I *saved* his life." Tenzin locked her sword in Beatrice's handle and pulled up, dragging the woman closer. "I refused to gamble with his life. I had to be sure; I didn't have any other choice."

"So you took him to your father?" Beatrice was crying bloody red tears that tracked down her face. "After everything Zhang did to you, you gave Ben to *him?*"

Tenzin locked Beatrice's swords in position and pushed. Her face was inches away, and Tenzin could smell the salt-and-copper tang of grief and anger.

"I took him to the most powerful vampire I knew," she said quietly. "The only one I knew I had leverage over. I could not gamble with his life or his eternity. Even when I had to crawl across stone on my hands and knees to *beg* for him." Tenzin pulled the swords closer. "You, of all living beings, know what that means to me."

Beatrice's face was blank. There was still anger, but there was also pain and confusion. "Why?"

"Why do you think?" Tenzin asked. "He is mine." She shoved Beatrice back, releasing the tension holding their swords hostage. "You are my dear friend and Stephen's own blood, but if you try to drive a wedge between us, Beatrice De Novo, our friendship will end and your eternity will be forfeit to my rage."

Tenzin threw her sword on the ground and left the room. There was nothing else to say. She had no other argument, no silver tongue. Beatrice would cool her anger or they would have war. Ben was standing on the edge of the practice arena, leaning against the wall.

She walked out the door, and he followed her in silence.

WHEN BEN LED her to the guesthouse, she followed him. Though Tenzin's instinct was to take Ben and fly to safety, she fought it. This was his home. This was his territory. He would stake his claim to it—and to her—or he would become a stranger.

When they walked through the door and into the light-safe quarters, she spoke. "Benjamin, I was not trying—"

"No." He turned and put a single finger over her lips. "She provoked that. You did nothing wrong. And honestly, that was like a year of passive-aggressive bullshit boiling over."

Tenzin rose to him and took his mouth with hers, capturing his lips as he wrapped his arms around her. Her hands found the dark hair at his nape, and she twisted her fingers in the curls, tangling herself into his body; she wrapped her legs around his waist.

He didn't carry her but rose in the air with her, floating them through the unfamiliar house and into a room muffled by heavy drapes and deep carpets. She heard the door shut behind them, and sound became muffled and thick. They were in a cave-like room designed to hide sound and light.

Ben came to rest on the wide bed piled with pillows and down blankets. She felt cool cotton touch her back. His hands slid beneath her tunic and lifted up. She fell back into the pillows and looked at him.

He was so beautiful to her. She found herself staring at the pattern of muscle across his torso, the defined dips and curves. She imagined the muscle beneath the skin, the blood coursing through his human body that had filtered down to every cell, building him into a creature of light until the darkness—

"Stay with me." His fingers on her jaw. "Tenzin, stay with me."

Her eyes refocused on his face. "Do you see the space within us?"

"I don't think anyone sees things the way you do." Ben's smile was soft as he lowered his body over hers. "No space now."

The temperature of his skin matched hers, and when his fingers touched her body, stroking along her skin or delving into corners that made her senses shudder, she felt the infinite space of his amnis twisting within hers.

He took her mouth again, and the pleasure of flesh touching flesh made her fangs lengthen, nick his skin, where the blood welled and reached for her tongue.

"Mmmph." His groan was only pleasure. "Take it."

She wanted it.

"Take it, Tenzin." Ben slid his full lower lip along the length of her fang, piercing the skin until the scent of his blood overwhelmed her mind.

She latched onto his lip and pulled hard, feeling his erection rise and press against her thigh. She twisted as he removed her leggings, aching for his penetration. Fangs, cock, blood. She wanted him *in* her. The need to consume overwhelmed her self-protective instincts.

You are mine.

You are mine.

You are my own.

She pulled away from his mouth and sank her fangs in his neck as Ben penetrated her body. Tenzin bit harder and he cursed, pressing her teeth harder into his flesh as his hips drove into her. Sensual pleasure and bloodlust took over her mind; she was a creature of touch, sound, and taste, twisting under him as he drove them both toward climax.

"You didn't take my blood." She lay in the curve of his arm, languid with pleasure and thrumming with the energy from his blood. "Are you hungry?"

"I'll drink before dawn." His fingers were busy braiding a strand of her hair. "Are you going to grow your hair out again? I miss your braids."

"I will, but it will take a long time."

"I can wait."

He was avoiding the topic of her blood.

Tenzin supposed she was also avoiding it.

"Beatrice is going to forgive you," Ben said. "She loves you. She loves me. She knows I'm happy with you."

Most of the time. He still went into dark periods every now

and then. She still had to distract him from staring into eternity too closely. Ben was wrestling with the same question that plagued all new vampires at some point in their life: What did life mean when it lasted forever?

For most vampires, they didn't hit that point of self-reflection until decades into immortal life, but Ben had always been precocious. He'd also had more than ample time as a human to debate the question.

He never wanted this.

The sly, whispering voice that haunted her often reared its head in the most peaceful of times, like now, when her lover was caressing her shoulder and trailing kisses along her skin.

"I love you. And I will learn to love this life."

When the voice came, she remembered Ben's words from months before, when he'd finally embraced her and embraced immortal life.

She turned in his arms and faced him. "I believe Beatrice will forgive me. I told her you were mine and that trying to drive a wedge between us would end our friendship."

Among other things, but Tenzin decided to leave those out for now.

He brushed his fingers along her cheek. "I'm happy with you. I'm excited about the new project. Life in New York is good. She'll come around."

"We may need them for this project. I just don't want everyone to be uncomfortable or walk on toadstools while the two of us are around."

Ben was trying not to laugh. "Do you mean walk on eggshells?"

"It's not toadstools?"

He shook his head. "Eggshells."

"But what difference would walking on eggshells make? Eggshells would already be broken."

"But toadstools makes sense?"

"They are mushrooms and would be crushed if you stepped on them. Obviously that makes more sense." Ugh. English was so annoying.

"I'll let everyone know." He lifted a strand of her hair. "And no one is going to walk on eggshells or toadstools. I'm telling you, I know my aunt. She's going to get over this."

"I am glad you are so confident." She glanced around the room. "This is a vampire sex room."

Ben blinked. "Excuse me?"

"Look at all the soundproofing. This is where they put the guests so they don't have to hear them having sex."

Ben closed his eyes. "And let's be eternally grateful for that."

"I don't know why you care. It's not like the two of them don't copulate like rabbits every chance they get."

"Shhhhhh." He closed his eyes and pushed her face into his chest. "Don't you feel the dawn coming? Pretty sure I do. Let's get ready to sleep. Night night. Or... day day? That sounds so wrong."

Tenzin still hadn't told him she was sleeping some days. With the amount of blood she'd taken from him that night, she'd definitely sleep for an hour or two at least.

And she'd tell him about it. Eventually.

She knew why she was reluctant even though she'd resolved to be more open with him. Keeping secrets felt safe. Baring them felt like a leap in intimacy that could threaten everything: Ben's happiness, her new life, the delicate balance they had reached.

He needs to know, Tenzin. Don't make the mistakes I have. Don't try to hide the truth from the ones you love even if you think it's for their own good.

5

The following night, Ben and Tenzin walked to the house at nightfall. He felt rested and newly refreshed. It wasn't only his body but his mind. The conflict between Beatrice and Tenzin—the two women he loved most in the world—had been festering. And while nothing felt healed, Ben thought that perhaps the wound had been lanced.

"You feel better," Tenzin said. "You rested well."

"I did."

"You've been restless while you're sleeping, which is unusual for a new vampire."

"I'm not that new anymore." Ben didn't like thinking about it, but he'd been dreaming. And lately, most of his dreams featured him and Tenzin dying violently in a burst of flame flung from the Fire King's hands.

So they were much closer to nightmares than dreams.

"You know, sleep can be weird and I've had some of your blood, so maybe that changes things." He wanted to change the subject. "Did Sadia come to visit you during the day?"

"Yes. She brought a makeup set and sunglasses so we could" —Tenzin frowned at the memory— "take 'fancy pictures.' I was very unsure of what she meant and made the mistake of agreeing."

Ben barely kept from laughing. "Please tell me someone took pictures of that."

"I am fairly certain Dema took many, despite my threats."

Task one for the night: find Dema and obtain Tenzin's *fancy pictures*.

"So does Sadia have a future as a makeup artist?"

"I have worn various cosmetics over the years for different cultural and court reasons. I was confused by her choices, but I am probably not the best person to judge. There was a lot of glitter. And she had trouble putting it on my eyes."

He bit his lip hard. "I'm sure it was beautiful."

"I'm sure it was ridiculous, but Sadia was delighted and that was the important thing. Do you know her father has her memorizing Virgil already?"

Ben opened the french doors leading to the living room. "I'd like to say I'm surprised, but I'm not." He could hear the family gathered in the kitchen, as per usual. "Do you want to go in for dinner or go up to the library?"

"Library." She rose and brushed her fingers over the rise of his cheekbone. "You need time alone with your family."

"They're your family too." He caught her fingers before she floated away.

"Which means I understand that certain members of it might need space." Her smile was fleeting but content.

Ben let her go and entered the dinner chaos that erupted at nightfall in the DeNovo-Vecchio household. He jumped in with no fanfare, cleaning Sadia's face, taking out the garbage, and setting dishes on the table. He listened as disparate factions shared details of the day and waited for opinions, questions, and ideas.

As the meal wound down, he made his exit with his uncle next to him.

"I'm going to get the slides ready," Giovanni told his wife. "Maybe ten minutes?"

"I'll get Sadia to bed then," Beatrice said. "She has classroom in the morning."

Ben escaped before Sadia's whining could gain volume. "Tuesdays?"

"Tuesday, Wednesday, and Thursday." Giovanni climbed the stairs with Ben following. "She needs human interaction with other children."

Ben nodded. He'd already been savvy enough to keep secrets by the time Giovanni had adopted him at twelve, but small children must be a different challenge entirely. "So her whole school—"

"Designed for day-people only," Giovanni said. "She'll transfer to your alma mater when she's older, but for now she assumes everyone has vampire family. There's no way she could go to a typical school."

They entered the library, and Ben saw Tenzin lounging on a sofa near the fireplace.

She turned her head to look at them. "No Beatrice?"

"She'll be joining us shortly." Giovanni walked over and sat near Tenzin. "You realize she knows how much you care for each other?"

"Of course."

"And this is mostly a function of maternal—"

"It's completely expected, my boy." Tenzin sat up and waved a careless hand. "Don't feel like you need to apologize."

"I'm not apologizing." Giovanni glanced at Ben. "She loves you both."

"I know that." Ben sat next to Tenzin, desperate to change the subject. "What do you think about Tenzin's proposal?"

"About finding the bone scroll and keeping it in our library?"

Ben said, "You already have Geber's alchemy manuscripts. What's one more dangerous threat to the vampire world?"

Giovanni and Beatrice had a secure and discreet library in central Italy, off the beaten track and guarded by a crusty ex-priest from the Vatican, a research librarian, and numerous human, vampire, and electronic guards. It was available for scholars who petitioned for entry, but only at Giovanni and Beatrice's discretion.

"It's not a bad idea," Giovanni said. "But I'll be honest: if this thing actually exists—and it actually does what the myths say—I don't want anyone to have it. Not us, not you and Tenzin, not the Elders at Penglai."

Ben said, "You think it should be destroyed?"

"Vampires are powerful enough. I know immortals who can pull water from the cells of a living human, leaving them a writhing husk. And that's one powerful vampire controlling one element. You think someone like Saba or Arosh needs control over all four?" Giovanni shook his head. "Some things shouldn't exist."

"I don't agree," Tenzin said. "And I will tell you why: I don't think it's as simple as we are thinking. I think there is another key to this myth. Otherwise, I believe it would have been found before."

Giovanni said, "Are you talking about the blood of Mithra myth?"

Ben asked, "What blood of Mithra myth?"

His uncle raised a finger. "Let's wait until Beatrice gets here. I don't want to have to explain all this twice."

"That reminds me, I was supposed to video-connect Chloe so she's not in the dark." Ben rose and walked to the large desk with various electronics that had been modified for vampire use. "I gave her a summary of what's going on last night, and she wanted me to beam her in if we went over more stuff."

"Beam her in?" Tenzin frowned.

"I'm just going to put her on video, Tiny. I'm not actually going to transport her here. Though that would be convenient."

"Though possibly a bit shocking for her," Tenzin said. "And Gavin would likely have issues with you manipulating Chloe's molecules."

~

FIVE MINUTES LATER, Ben and Tenzin's human assistant, Chloe Reardon, was visible on a computer monitor from New York, Beatrice was back in the library, sitting marginally closer to Tenzin with significantly less glaring, and Giovanni was back in professor mode.

"I'm so excited!" Chloe's voice chirped from the computer. "This is the first time you guys are doing a big project in Africa. We're going, right? I am so excited. You better be going and you better be bringing me."

Tenzin stared at the computer. "Are you excited because your ancestors were African?"

Chloe cocked her head to the side. "Really? Did you put that one together yourself?"

"But as a Black American, you are far more likely to be related to people in West Africa, and we are going to East Africa."

"Whatever, Tenzin. I won't be the only Black person in the room for once. Hush and let me have my joy."

Ben coughed to cover a laugh. "Chloe, I can't lie, most vampires not in Saba's clan steer clear of the continent to avoid pissing her off; that's the only explanation I have for taking this long to visit. But did I hear Gavin is going to be in that neck of the woods anyway?"

Chloe nodded, her curly dark brown hair bouncing around her ears. "Yes. He's going to be in Nigeria though. He's opening a club in Lagos with a new partner. He's cautiously optimistic and said something similar about not pissing off Saba, so I know what you guys are saying, but I'm still excited."

"Then let's get to the details." Giovanni was eager to start class. "Chloe, Ben gave you a summary?"

"Creepy scroll made from vampire bones that's supposed to make the owner capable of controlling all four elements," Chloe said. "Did I get that right?"

"Yep." Ben pointed to Giovanni. "And you just mentioned something about a blood myth."

"Yes." He put the picture of the old man with the beard up again. "There are some stories related to the myth that say Ash Mithra created this scroll so that only his own children could use it. That's why you'll hear sayings about the blood of Mithra in some circles. It's kind of vampire shorthand for saying someone was sired into a lucky situation."

Beatrice frowned. "I've never heard that before."

"Neither have I," Ben said.

"I have," Tenzin said. "But it's a really old saying."

Chloe asked, "So what does the blood of Mithra mean though? Does that mean vampires this guy sired, or like his human bloodline?"

Giovanni smiled. "Very good question, Chloe. We don't know. We don't even know if this is true, but if it were talking about his human bloodline, that would probably be quite vast. Much like Beatrice's great-grandfather, Ash Mithra was renowned for the massive clan of human family he kept to serve him. They were rumored to be originally from the Land of Punt, which was an ancient trading partner of Egypt on the Horn of

Africa. Stories say they were wildly wealthy gold traders who moved north, becoming prominent in Arabia, then Assyria and Persia."

"And they were related to this vampire? So he moved with them?" Beatrice asked.

Giovanni nodded. "It's not unheard of. Many vampires bring their blood family into the immortal world because they don't trust anyone else, and it wasn't uncommon to hear about arrangements like that in the ancient world. The myths around Ash Mithra vary some but are surprisingly consistent for such an old character."

"So if the bone scroll can only be used by someone with the blood of Mithra, that could still mean a lot of people," Chloe said. "I mean, in theory, his human descendants could have had lots of children. There could be thousands and thousands in the modern world, right?"

Giovanni nodded. "That is correct." He flipped to another slide. "For instance, this Sasanian noble was the governor of Sidon in Lebanon under the Romans and claimed to be part of Mithra's line. He had twelve wives and concubines and sixty-three children."

"Holy shit," Ben said. "Okay, so half the Middle East and Central Asia could be related to this guy in some way or another?"

"That might be a slight exaggeration, but yes."

"None of this matters," Tenzin said. "Because we're going to find the scroll and safeguard it from anyone who might want to use it for bad reasons."

"If this scroll was so powerful," Chloe asked. "Why would this Ash Mithra guy ever let it out of his possession? Did someone kill him?"

"No one knows for sure," Giovanni said. "Though obviously that's an excellent question. But one of the myths is that Mithra sired an immortal son named Rutha, and unlike Mithra's other children, he was more thirsty for power than wisdom. In that legend, Mithra disowns his son and hides the scroll so that Rutha could never use it."

Chloe nodded. "Okay, so there's this superpowerful and dangerous object floating around the world now, but it can only be used by Mithra's descendants."

"According to legends," Tenzin said. "No one knows that for sure."

"But it's not out of the realm of possibility," Giovanni said. "After all, only Mithra's descendants would have his amnis, which could be a component of how the scroll works."

"How would it have gotten to Ethiopia?" Beatrice addressed Tenzin directly for the first time that night. "Why are you so sure it's there?"

"According to sources I trust, the scroll was in the possession of a Manichaean missionary who was on his way to visit the court of the Aksumite emperor in the sixth century. And now rumors are saying that Arosh found the bone scroll in Aksum. I don't think that's a coincidence; I think the relic is in Ethiopia."

"In Aksum?"

"Possibly. Or possibly in some other undiscovered Aksumite treasury."

"So you're potentially looking at a lot of sites," Beatrice said. "Have you figured out a way to narrow them down yet?"

Tenzin narrowed her eyes. "Not yet."

"Hey." Chloe piped up from the computer. "I was just thinking that everyone seems to be afraid of Saba, right? And she rules Ethiopia and like, North Africa and most of the continent, right? She's the big, big boss?"

"Yes," Beatrice said. "She's the oldest vampire anyone knows of, and Ethiopia is where she is originally from. So she kind of considers the entire continent of Africa her territory."

"And so we're going in there," Chloe said. "And hopefully finding and taking a superpowerful object from her territory."

"Yes," Ben said. "That's the basic idea."

"And no one thinks she might have a problem with that?"

Ben and Tenzin exchanged a look. "Oh, she won't like it," Tenzin said. "But we have an idea."

"More like a distraction," Ben said. "We have an idea how to distract her."

"Shiny objects," Tenzin said. "We're going to trade the bone scroll for something she wants more."

Beatrice looked skeptical. "There's something she wants more?"

Ben nodded. "Yes. And we think we know where it is."

6

B en sat on the balcony of a vacant house that was perched across the road from the private club where Trevor Blythe-Bickman was dining. He was lounging on an easy chair that hadn't seen company since its owner had left the city for his villa in Thailand the month before.

One after another, shiny new electric sports cars and hybrid SUVs arrived at the club and were swiftly whisked away by the ever-present valets. The club was not a typical bar or a restaurant but an extremely expensive social club that catered to the city's young, hip, and ridiculously wealthy.

Hidden behind immaculately trimmed hedges and high walls, the club was hard to surveil from the ground, but Ben had found a clever workaround for observation on the balcony. Finding his way *into* the private club should have been a bit more difficult, but he'd managed to find a side door.

Though it wasn't advertised, the club had twenty luxurious guest rooms available to book for a small fortune. If you knew the right person to talk to—and he would find out—booking a room at the club would give you access to the lounges and bars where Trevor Blythe-Bickman lorded over his social clique.

The only problem Ben was running into was demographics. To be blunt, he was far too young and far too male to garner any kind of attention from Trevor Blythe-Bickman. He'd blend right in with approximately eighty percent of the people he saw entering the place. Normally Ben would be ecstatic to be so anonymous, but for this job he actually needed to gain Blythe-Bickman's attention, which wouldn't be easy if he didn't stand out.

From his profile, the Englishman seemed like a people collector. He sponsored artists' talks and gallery openings for a number of ex-girlfriends. He hosted film screenings for up-and-coming directors he was dating and used his shiny, glass-decked lobby downtown as a venue for a noted Japanese performance artist... whom he'd also been sleeping with.

So no, Ben had nothing Trevor Blythe-Bickman would find interesting.

At two in the morning, the Englishman exited the building on the arm of a laughing woman wearing a designer coat and holding a pair of red-soled heels in her hand as she leaned into Blythe-Bickman's side. She was beautiful, with a tousled black pixie-cut, fair skin, and typically Korean features.

She was also the fourth Asian woman Ben had seen on Blythe-Bickman's arm in the past week.

Tenzin strolled up to Ben and sat on the bench across from him. "I told you."

"I still don't think it's a good idea."

Tenzin had been proposing a honey trap for days. As soon as she'd noted Blythe-Bickman's "type," she volunteered to be the target, which had annoyed Ben on two fronts.

One, he didn't want her honey-trapping Blythe-Bickman.

Two, Tenzin would have to pose as someone other than herself, which was... not ideal.

"Okay." He turned to her. "What would be your cover?"

She shrugged. "Chinese tech heiress."

Fuck, that was a good start.

"Okay, and why are you in San Francisco?"

Tenzin pursed her lips. "None of the women we've identified so far has been an actress, model, or any kind of high-ranking courtesan, so I am going to assume he's not with these women only for status, looks, or sexual skills. He likes smart women. Therefore, I would be visiting San Francisco in order to accompany contract negotiators for... semiconductors?"

Ben muttered, "Damn it. Make it microprocessors and that's a fucking good cover story. You're not heading up the negotiations—that's ridiculous for someone so young—but you're in the business and you're learning."

"Yes." She motioned toward him. "With my personal security, of course."

The corner of Ben's mouth turned up. "Good thinking. Any substantial heiress would have a security team, especially if she was in the US for business reasons."

"Exactly. We'll need to book two rooms at the club then." She shook her head. "I'm not sleeping with my bodyguard; my father would be appalled."

"Is this one of the role-playing scenarios you wrote down the other night?"

"Possibly. Now that we have figured out how we're going to get into Blythe-Bickman's mansion, can you come back to the house? I think Mavis is having trouble with the water heater. There are strange sounds coming from the basement."

Ben narrowed his eyes. "We are not tricking this woman into leaving us her house."

"I'm just trying to be a good neighbor, Benjamin."

～

He watched her slip into a dress that should have been illegal. Tenzin had a subtle figure that she usually hid under practical clothes, but when she dressed up, her ass was lethal. And not only because she was sliding ceramic daggers into custom designed pockets in her dress.

"Is that another Arthur original?" He motioned for her to turn, which she did. "Can't see a thing." *Except a really fabulous backside.* "You're sexy as hell, Tiny."

She smiled and her fangs peeked out. "It is an Arthur original. He has stopped asking questions now, which is very good."

Arthur was one of Chloe's oldest friends in New York, a professional costume designer, and he must have either believed Tenzin was a serious cosplayer or he had no issues with violent criminals, because this was at least the fourth garment he'd designed for her to conceal weapons at formal events.

"Okay, Zhang Ming, why are you staying at the club?" Ben busied himself packing Tenzin's handbag, which he would probably be carrying as her bodyguard.

"My friend, Li Yan, recommended it after her stay last year."

"Excellent." The young Chinese socialite was not only known for her fashion designs but her business acumen. She was also widely recognized as very private and used no personal social media. A friend of Li Yan's might also prefer similar anonymity.

"I'll be there the whole time." He checked that her lipstick was in the bag and hoped she would remember to actually use it. "I already made the reservation and told them you'd be arriving at midnight."

"I'll try to remember not to smile."

"Closed mouth only unless you're with me, Ming." He sat on the edge of the quilt-covered mattress in Mavis's attic and ran a finger down the back of Tenzin's thigh. "How are you feeling?"

"It will be fun to fool a bad person." She turned to look at him and raised a single eyebrow. "Don't be so forward, Mr. Rios. My father would not approve of our liaison."

Ben's cover identity was as a bodyguard by the name of Amir Rios. His room would be adjoining Ming's, and he'd accompany her everywhere. Including into Trevor Blythe-Bickman's mansion if everything went according to plan.

It still annoyed Ben that he couldn't find a hole in the electronic security around the Englishman's house. It was almost as if the man knew he had millions of dollars' worth of art and antiquities sitting around. Which, of course, was the reason they needed to break in.

Blythe-Bickman came from a long line of minor aristocracy who served in the British foreign service in one capacity or another. Consul of this and ambassador to that. And in every posting, the Blythes and the Bickmans had collected a few more trinkets and smuggled a few more treasures away, all under the auspices of the British Crown, of course.

What Ben had noticed in the background pictures of the slavishly fawning profile in an architectural magazine wasn't the antiquities hanging about the Blythe-Bickman mansion. No, it was the manuscripts.

"You ready to go?" He stood and straightened the collar on his simple black shirt. Black shirt. Black suit. Black sunglasses, even at night.

"Ready." She threw on a black gabardine trench coat and slipped her feet into sleek flats, all sensible choices for someone just arriving on a private jet from Shanghai.

They'd be picked up at the airport in a car and arrive at the club just shy of midnight. Tenzin looked around the attic. "I'm going to miss this place."

"Tenzin, we're going to come back. We've left our real luggage here."

She slipped on her sunglasses and headed for the window. "Amir, I never look back, I only look forward."

Ben rolled his eyes and followed her.

IN HER REAL LIFE, Tenzin hated bowing people. She hated the formality and hierarchy of Penglai, where her father ruled and others served. She hated the idea of power equaling authority, as if strength and wisdom had anything to do with each other.

But when it was in the service of stealing shiny things from an egotistical, aristocratic asshole, she could play the game as well as anyone.

She stepped out of the car and ignored the valet holding her door. He was for Amir to deal with. She paused to take stock of her surroundings as her bodyguard dealt with the bags and tipped the driver.

Foggy night. Crescent moon. She could hear people talking in the distance and the tinkling music of dishes moving around a table.

"Ms. Zhang?" A hostess carrying a discreet portfolio joined her on the sidewalk.

Tenzin took her time looking toward the woman. "Yes?"

"Welcome. We've been waiting for you. I hope your flight was comfortable."

"It was fine." She flavored her English with a southern Chinese accent and a little bit of British thrown in. Ming had likely learned English from a British tutor. "Is my room ready?"

"I'm sure you're very tired. It is all ready and the adjoining room—"

"I'm not tired." She pouted. "I'm hungry. I want a steak."

She turned her face. "Amir" —she continued in Mandarin— "I want a steak. Tell them to make me a steak."

Ben stepped forward, carrying a briefcase and a small handbag he handed to Tenzin. She took it as the hostess responded in fluent Mandarin.

"Ms. Zhang, if you will give me fifteen minutes, I will arrange to have our best steak prepared to your liking. Would you care to eat in your room or in the Icarus Bar?"

Tenzin glanced at Ben. Interesting that the woman was fluent in Mandarin, but not a challenge. They knew they'd have to stay in character unless they were alone.

"The bar." She affected a bored expression and switched back to English. "I am tired of only seeing his face."

"Of course." The hostess offered a slight bow, and within minutes their luggage had been swept away.

Tenzin entered the club she'd watched from the outside, immediately noting the sweeping glass windows beyond the front desk that opened out to the ocean. For the humans, the view was only darkness, but Tenzin could perceive the moon reflecting off the cold black water, the whipping wind that lifted the branches of Pacific cedar and eucalyptus.

They were shown through a thickly carpeted foyer and down a hall where Tenzin heard snatches of conversation coming from various rooms and corners. There was a large billiard room and a library on the left that seemed to have more computers than books. She heard electronic music thumping in the distance and the low, measured voices of men discussing Very Important Business.

Within five minutes, they were shown to their room and Tenzin was dropping her trench coat in a round leather chair with silk pillows. She removed her sunglasses and turned to Ben. "Dinner in the Icarus Bar? What are the chances Blythe-Bickman will be there?"

"In that particular bar? I have no idea. I think there are three bars in the club, and he could be in any one of them, but I'm fairly confident he's somewhere. It's Thursday night, and he usually meets friends here from Wednesday through the weekend. If you can drag it out, make yourself conspicuous, I have a feeling he'll find you."

"I can do that." She wasn't all that interested in steak, but she was told tourists liked eating them. "Did you bring toothpicks?"

Ben tilted her chin up. "Toothpicks?"

Tenzin bared her teeth. "I always get meat stuck in my fangs when I eat it. Especially beef."

His smile was precious. "Don't pick your teeth in public. I will make sure we have some toothpicks back in the room. That's exactly the kind of thing a spoiled heiress would be picky about, no pun intended."

"You act like I'm pretending, but this is likely how I would deal with humans regularly if you and Chloe didn't guilt me into being polite to modern human standards."

"Then I'm glad this con will let you get it out of your system. Come on." He reached down and slapped her butt. "Let's go trap an Englishman."

7

Ben watched from a table near Tenzin's as she ate her steak and ignored everyone in the bar, seemingly engrossed in her mobile phone. He watched Tenzin and watched others noticing her. Two men approached at different times; Tenzin— or Ming—was polite but coolly disinterested. She did manage to tell one man who she was and give a few details about her presence in San Francisco, just enough to pique his interest and get him whispering to his friends when he returned to the bar.

Ben watched as the information moved slowly but steadily through the club. Whispers and lingering looks at the new woman in their midst, not only beautiful but wildly wealthy and possibly very influential.

He saw people searching their phones and looking confused and intrigued in equal measure. Ben had chosen Tenzin's cover name wisely. Zhang was not only their sire's name but a common one in China, and many wealthy families in the tech industry carried it. Ming could be related to any of them.

Of course, Tenzin's aloof attitude carried the con. Never had Ben been happier that his partner intimidated humans. She was dismissive but not rude. Casual but not disinterested.

Ben heard Trevor Blythe-Bickman before he saw him. The young mogul entered the room exactly as Ben had expected, with a coterie of fawning acolytes surrounding him.

Blythe-Bickman's eyes immediately found Tenzin.

Bingo.

Interest was already piqued, but the man wasn't an idiot. He set up his group in a corner booth and immediately dismissed the louder members of the troop. Ben stood and buttoned his suit jacket before he made his way over to Tenzin and leaned down.

"Do you see him?" he asked in quiet Mandarin.

"He's impossible to miss. By design, of course."

"It won't be tonight, but he may make a first move."

"I'll draw it out."

"Play it cool. Maybe agree to a drink only."

"Tomorrow night."

"Agreed."

Ben stood and walked to the bar to order another soda water from the pretty redhead behind the bar. It seemed to be the rule at the club that the majority of the patrons were male but most of the staff was young, attractive, and female.

"How's it going?" the girl asked.

Ben shrugged. "Same as always." He leaned on the bar a little, keeping Tenzin in his sights but playing the part of the world-weary security guard. "How's it going with you? Is this the late shift for you or—?"

"Oh no. I just clocked in about an hour ago. This place is private, so it goes pretty much all night." She filled a fresh glass with ice and added soda water. "You sure you don't want anything stronger?"

Ben nodded toward Tenzin. "Working."

Her eyebrows went up, and she added a wedge of lime to his drink. "Oh wow. Okay. She's pretty important, huh?"

"Her family..." He pursed his lips. "They're protective. She doesn't go anywhere alone, if you know what I mean."

"Got it." She glanced at his arms, his lips. "So... are you based here in the city?"

"Shanghai." Ben sipped the soda. "I travel where she does."

"No kidding? I've never been to China."

"It's an interesting place. Lots of work for someone like me. Unfortunately, I don't have backup for this job."

"So no time off for you, huh?"

Ben let his eyes warm and offered her a flirtatious smile. It was always good to have an ally on staff. "I wish, but no."

The girl's eyes moved back to Tenzin. "Oh, I see TBB is already making a move."

Ben managed not to laugh as his eyes moved back to Tenzin. *TBB.* He was going to remember that. "Who is he?"

Trevor Blythe-Bickman was indeed making his move. He'd walked over to Tenzin's table and was making small talk. Despite the hushed atmosphere of the bar, it was all audible to Ben's vampire hearing.

"Have we met?"

Tenzin looked up. "I don't believe so."

"Are you sure?" The man put a hand disarmingly on his chest. "You look so familiar. Trevor Blythe-Bickman," he said. "I'm in finance here in the city."

And technology. And imports. And stolen antiquities and manuscripts.

"Is that so?"

This was the tricky part. Tenzin was going to have to walk the edge between being too aloof and putting the man off and being too eager to draw his interest. It was an operation that needed a scalpel when Tenzin was generally more of a sledgehammer.

Don't be rude. Don't be rude.

Tenzin cocked her head, and her shoulders relaxed a fraction. She put her phone facedown on the table. "Maybe you are familiar." She held out her hand. "Ming."

"Trevor."

"He's harmless really." The pretty bartender was speaking again. "I mean, he's rich and arrogant, but that's par for the course around here. Of the lot of them, he's pretty decent, all in all. Of course, he's a good tipper." She smiled and a dimple peeked out. "So I may be biased."

"Hey, you can tell a lot about a person by how they tip." Ben made a mental note to leave her a hundred. "So no security threat, huh?" He glanced over his shoulder, splitting his attention between the two women.

"Oh no. There's a lot of security here at the club you don't even see. You'd be surprised. We have important people here a lot, like for lectures and stuff. Nothing ever happens."

Tenzin and TBB were exchanging mild pleasantries. Tenzin looked polite but a little bored. She was stringing him along. She picked up her phone and checked the time.

TBB caught the hint.

"I think you've just arrived, haven't you?" His tone turned solicitous. "You must be exhausted. Maybe we could meet tomorrow for dinner."

"I have commitments for dinner tomorrow night." Tenzin pretended to consider him. "Maybe a drink after?"

"That would be fantastic. You're staying here at the club?"

"I am."

Ben made no attempt to hide his surveillance of the two, which was in keeping with his role as a bodyguard.

TBB offered to make reservations in the even more exclusive Chairman's Room for the following night at ten.

Perfect.

"I think I'd enjoy that," Tenzin said.

"—must be pretty tiring," the bartender said.

"My job?" Ben turned to the bartender and shrugged. "I've been doing personal security for the Zhang family for six years now. I was assigned to Ming when she left for university in the UK, so I'm pretty familiar with her routine. All in all, she's not too bad." He leaned on the bar and lowered his voice. "I have some friends who have clients... They're constantly posting from their hotel rooms, broadcasting where they are and what they're doing twenty-four seven, you know?"

The girl's eyebrows went up. "Oh yeah, that's probably a huge risk, right?"

"Ming, she's private. Not like that at all, so I can't complain."

"It looks like she and Trevor hit it off." The girl nodded at their table. "Maybe you'll get a night off."

Ben smiled. "I wish. Doesn't work that way." He saw Tenzin rise, and Trevor stood too. "That's my cue," Ben said. "I better go. Nice meeting you...?"

"Alexis." She smiled. "Nice to meet you too."

"Amir." He put his hand over his heart. "It's been a pleasure."

"How long is she here?"

"Four nights, unless something changes." He shrugged. "You never know."

"Hopefully I'll see you again."

"That would be great." He took out his wallet and she tried to stop him.

"Oh no, you don't have to pay. It's included—"

"It's not for the drink." He placed a hundred on the bar and winked. "Don't want to be a bad tipper."

The girl was all smiles. "You are too sweet. Thank you."

He saw Tenzin start walking out and hurried to catch up

with her, grabbing the door to the club before she could reach it. "Ming."

"Amir." She nodded slightly. "I think I'm ready to retire for the night."

"Of course." He followed her, walking just behind her right side. "Are there any plans I need to be aware of for tomorrow?"

"Drinks in the Chairman's Room."

"I'll make sure to adjust the schedule."

They didn't let go of their facades until they'd reached the door to Tenzin's room, locked it, and placed an additional electronic alarm at the base of the door.

Ben turned and hooked Tenzin around the waist. "Ming."

"Amir." She allowed him to pull her into his body while she floated up and out of her shoes. "Women's dress shoes are torture devices created by sadists."

Ben planted a hand on the ass he'd been staring at all night. "Clothes in general are highly overrated." He slid his fingers up her thigh, under her dress, and into a hidden pocket. Then he tossed one of her daggers onto the bed as he captured her mouth in a fierce kiss. "Good job tonight."

"I saw you flirting with that woman." She nipped his lip.

"Playing the game, Tiny." He nipped back, careful not to break the skin. "Just playing the game."

THEY ARRIVED at the Chairman's Room five minutes after Ming was scheduled to meet Trevor Blythe-Bickman. But while Ming was on the guest list, Amir was not.

"I am with Ms. Zhang," Ben said. "This is not negotiable."

The host for the Chairman's Room was not young, female, and sweet; he was an arrogant pain in the ass with a superiority complex and a patronizing smile.

"I am sorry, but only guests of the board are permitted in the Chairman's Room, and Ms. Zhang's name is the only one listed. I can't let you in."

"I'll be fine," Tenzin murmured in Mandarin.

Ben responded in kind. "Ming, you know the rules."

"I'm not in Shanghai, Amir."

"It's not permitted. Please don't force me to call your father."

Tenzin huffed out an impatient breath and turned to the host. "It is impossible for me to enter without my guard. If you could give Mr. Blythe-Bickman my apologies—"

"Ming?" The door opened and Trevor popped his head out of the lounge. "What's the problem, Joss?"

"Ms. Zhang's companion—"

"Guard," Ben said. "Amir Rios, Mr. Blythe-Bickman." He held his hand out, and the Englishman shook it. He kept his voice low and confiding. "I'm sure you understand that the Zhang family is protective of Ming. I cannot allow her to enter an unknown environment without me. Perhaps there is another location—"

"Don't be ridiculous." Trevor waved a hand. "Mr. Rios is also my guest, Joss. Please see that he has a table near ours." The Englishman crooked his arm for Ming. "Please, Ming, I'm so sorry about the oversight. I'll make sure it's not an issue in the future."

"Thank you." She glanced at Amir. "Keep your distance," she murmured in Mandarin. "You know *my* rules."

"Of course." Ben followed them into a round room with a large fireplace burning in the center of the room, wooden paneling on the walls, and giant plate glass windows that over-looked the lights of the city.

He didn't wait to be seated but positioned himself at a table halfway between Trevor's and the entrance, which gave him an excellent view of the whole room. If he was playing bodyguard, he'd play it to the hilt. Tenzin had this. The Englishman was completely into her.

Ben could tell good old TBB liked the idea of being with a woman valuable enough to have a full-time bodyguard. There was an element not only of exclusivity but of danger. The thrill buzzed around the man, who watched Tenzin with a greedy gaze.

A quiet server appeared at his elbow. "Welcome to the Chairman's Room, Mr. Rios. Can I offer you a drink this evening?"

"Soda water with a slice of lime," he said. "Is there food here?" He wanted to project the image of a weary employee, not a pampered guest.

"There is," the server said. "Let me get you a menu."

Ben unbuttoned his suit jacket and sat back, watching Tenzin and trying not to stare as the Englishman mentally undressed her.

Don't kill the mark. Don't kill the mark.

He was going to have to bite her soon. He needed her blood in him. He needed to claim her, needed to feel her amnis twisting with his. The urge to stalk over to her, yank her body-hugging dress up, and sink his teeth into her thigh was nearly overwhelming.

If Ben could get through another night of this, it was going to be a miracle.

8

She could feel his jealousy permeating the room, clawing at her skin and snarling for her attention. Tenzin couldn't let it distract her.

"I love history," she responded to the Englishman. "I studied in the UK, and I think my favorite place to wander was the British Museum. It was like... traveling the world all in one building."

"Yes, exactly," Trevor responded in his precise English accent. "All the hubbub you hear these days about taking things out of museums and sending them back God knows where. Why not keep them safe in a museum where they belong? A short trip to London and everyone can enjoy them."

Tenzin wanted to stab him. "Exactly." *You hypocrite.* She wasn't going to be satisfied with breaking into his house and taking the manuscript Ben wanted. She wanted his safe. "Someone was telling me you have a personal art collection that's quite remarkable."

The corner of his mouth turned up. "So you've been asking about me?"

Pig. "What can I say?" She lifted her chin. "I like to know exactly who I'm dealing with."

"I wish I could say the same about you, Ming. You're a very hard woman to read. And it's admirable how you've managed to keep your life so private."

"My family works very hard to make sure our privacy is respected." She sipped cognac from a cut crystal glass. "Your family has a much more public profile, I think."

He nodded deeply. "The Blythe-Bickman family prides itself on service to queen and country. Yes, my family has quite a history in the foreign service. In fact, my father was ambassador to Ethiopia when I was young."

"That must have been quite an experience."

"It was. An extraordinary way to grow up."

In reality, Tenzin knew that Blythe-Bickman had attended boarding school for most of his childhood and only visited Addis Ababa sporadically in his teen years.

"Do you ever loan pieces in your collection out?" Tenzin asked. "My father has an extensive jade collection he's amassed over many years."

"How fascinating." The man's eyes lit with greed.

"I've told him he should consider loaning it out, as you mentioned, so the public could enjoy it."

"I know I'd love to see it."

The corner of her mouth turned up. *Gotcha.* "As I'd love to see your collection. I wish I had more time in San Francisco."

Not one to let an opportunity pass, Blythe-Bickman's next question was predictable. "When are you leaving?"

"On Sunday evening." She sipped her drink. "This trip is short."

"That's plenty of time," he said. "It's only Friday. Come by tomorrow afternoon."

"The afternoon?" She shook her head. "I am so sorry. My

days are completely filled by family and business obligations. But thank you. It's a kind offer."

"How about your nights?" he fired off. Then he caught himself and smiled. "I'm sorry, was that forward?"

She kept her smile small and demure. "You're inviting me to visit your private residence tomorrow night?"

"To see my art collection," he said. "No ulterior motive, I promise you."

Tenzin made a show of looking at her bodyguard. "I suppose as long as Amir clears it, my family couldn't have an objection."

"Of course," he said. "I understand the security concerns, of course." He leaned closer. "Though... it's a large house. I'm hoping we might find a few minutes of privacy. If that's something you'd like."

Tenzin raised an eyebrow. "My employees understand boundaries."

"Excellent."

"Amir" was nearly ready to explode. She could feel his amnis licking at her neck. A faint breeze gusted through the room, causing everyone to turn.

"How strange..." Trevor looked around. "Is there a window open?"

Distract the human, Tenzin. "What time would work for you tomorrow? I'm busy until nearly nine." That covered her until sundown.

"That's perfect. I'm free at eight—why don't I meet you here with a car at nine and we'll head to the house. I'll have my housekeeper prepare dinner if you'd like."

"Something light," she said. "I'm sure I'll have eaten my weight in food by the end of the day. You know how business dinners are."

He raised his glass. "It's a date."

Tenzin smiled coyly. "I'm looking forward to it."

~

BEN ROUSED her the next night in the most pleasurable way possible. She'd been meditating in one bedroom while he slept in the other. The blackout shades provided by the club were surprisingly good at lightproofing the rooms, and he hadn't needed to hide in the closet.

She was contemplating the wood grain in the wall paneling and imagining the age of the tree when she felt him behind her. He slid a single finger down her spine, causing her to shiver and come back into her body.

Tenzin blinked. "Have you ever contemplated the immortality of trees?"

"Trees are not immortal." His lips touched her neck. "We are." His fangs scraped along her skin, teasing blood to the surface but not releasing it.

"How old must this tree have been when it was cut? Now it is preserved in this way, living but frozen. Like Mithra's bones."

His hands slid from stroking her back to cupping her breasts. "I don't want to talk about trees. Or bones."

She pressed back and felt his erection at her back. "Are you sure? What about that one?"

His chuckle was low and wicked. "But Ming, your father would not approve."

She twisted in his arms and pulled him over her. "I do not care. Ravish me, Amir."

"As you command, Ms. Zhang." He was already naked and aroused. "After all, you need to look like you've put in a very hard day's work." He rocked his hips between her thighs. "Let's see if I can make you look appropriately ruffled."

THEY LEFT the room through the window when it was dark outside, dressed in business suits, and flew several blocks until they could hire a car to take them back to the club. When they arrived, Trevor Blythe-Bickman was already in the lobby.

"Trevor." Tenzin gave him a small wave. "I am sorry we're late. If you give us a half an hour, we'll be ready."

"No problem."

Ben smiled, still scenting his amnis all over Tenzin's skin. "We'll freshen up and be right with you. Do you have a car waiting?"

"It's my personal vehicle if that's all right."

Ben took a moment to consider. "If you can let me look it over—"

"Amir, don't be silly." Tenzin attempted to look exasperated. "I'm sure it's fine."

"Protocol." He looked at Trevor. "You understand."

"Of course." The glint of excitement was back. Ming was dangerous. Desirable. "That's absolutely fine."

Ben and Tenzin went to change into more casual clothes. Tenzin brushed her hair into a smooth black curtain and applied a light perfume. Ben changed from a suit into simple black pants and a black button-down shirt. Over that, he wore a black trench coat with discreet pockets.

Within a half hour, they were walking to Blythe-Bickman's car where Ben performed a cursory check. This would be interesting. The car had more electronics than any vehicle he'd ever ridden in. If it managed to start with two vampires inside, it would be a miracle.

Ben patted the hood and looked up. "It's clear," he said to Tenzin and the Englishman.

It was clear, but it didn't start.

Trevor tried starting it a number of times. "I just don't understand."

Tenzin and Ben attempted their most innocent expressions.

"Technology," Ben said. "It's a mystery."

At the end of the day, they ended up calling a private car for themselves while Blythe-Bickman called a tow truck. Ben could tell he was embarrassed when they arrived at his house.

Good. He'd be even more motivated to impress Ming.

The massive Tudor mansion in Pacific Heights was on the corner of a block of similarly massive houses. A high wall surrounded the property, and a guard stood at the gate, waiting to open it when they pulled up. They rolled through the automatic gate and entered the immaculately lit yard. Potted plants bloomed in neat rows along the drive and softened the front of the dark brick house.

"What a lovely home," Tenzin said. "Has it been in your family a long time?"

"Not long. I bought it when I sold my first start-up." Trevor smiled, already back in his groove. "It's a good investment, and it has plenty of room for my collection."

Ben remained silent in the back of the car while Tenzin flirted mildly with the Englishman. Subtlety was the rule of the night with this man, and she was playing it perfectly. She was impressed, but not too impressed. Interested, but also checking her phone for messages.

They entered through carved wooden doors, and Ben took a station outside a small sitting room where Blythe-Bickman's cook served the couple a light dinner. The maid offered to take his coat, but he demurred and kept his attention fixed on Tenzin and her human admirer.

Who *really* liked to talk about himself.

Ben tried not to be annoyed; if the man had lived alone, the job would already be done. They could have used amnis to enthrall him and he'd have handed over the keys to his safe, the family silver, and his watch collection with a smile. Sadly, there appeared to be at least two servants in residence, and they didn't want to attempt to wipe three minds if they could avoid it.

Although...

As he watched the cook and the housekeeper bustle around the house, he realized that neither of them ever headed upstairs. Maybe that was the key. If Tenzin could get Blythe-Bickman upstairs, she'd have him under her command.

They finished their small meal, and Ben watched the Englishman start showing Tenzin around the house. They entered the room with the manuscripts that Ben had seen in the architectural magazine, and he followed them at a discreet distance, examining the pieces but finding nothing like the eighth-century illuminated devotional they were looking for. Ben was scanning the shelves for a distinctive type of chain stitching on the binding that his uncle told him would mark the manuscript as Ethiopian.

Nothing in the library matched the description that Giovanni had given him or the pictures he'd seen, though he did see a cross that he knew was Ethiopian sitting in a corner of the bookshelves, tossed in with other Orthodox crosses. It was carved wood and painted in rich colors, with the twelve distinct spikes at the top that denoted a typical Lalibela-style cross.

As the Englishman and Tenzin headed out of the library, he slipped the relic in his pocket. The man probably wouldn't even notice it was missing.

As they worked their way through the downstairs rooms, Ben noticed Blythe-Bickman's body language changing. He was more possessive, more personal. As they moved back toward the foyer, Ben knew exactly where the man was heading.

They turned toward him at the base of the stairs, and

Tenzin looked him in the eye. "Amir, Trevor is going to show me his private gallery upstairs. You'll wait here."

Ben put his arms behind his back and stood at attention. "Are there any outdoor exits?"

"No," Blythe-Bickman said. "There is a large balcony, but there aren't any exits from it. The only way in and out is this staircase, okay?" He was patronizing now. "So just... make yourself at home." He smirked. "Downstairs."

Ben met Tenzin's eyes and saw nothing but wolfish excitement in her gaze.

Oh, my adorable, greedy little magpie.

Ben nodded at her and turned to take up a position in the foyer while Tenzin followed the Englishman up the stairs. He heard low, excited whispers and knew that whatever Tenzin had planned for the Englishman, it was not at all what the human was expecting.

9

Human men were so predictable. Trevor was so excited to get Ming alone he nearly assaulted her on the upstairs landing. If Tenzin hadn't slipped away, she never would have drawn him farther into the house.

"Now Trevor, I really did want to see your art collection." She pressed a finger to his searching lips. "Don't worry. Amir knows what his directions are. We have plenty of time."

The man was flushed and his heartbeat was pounding. "Ming, you're so beautiful. Smart. Intriguing..."

She allowed her lips to hover over his. "Patience."

He shook his head. "You are so mysterious, darling."

And you are so obvious. She took his hand and led him farther along the corridor, turning left into what looked like a long gallery. She could see french doors leading out to the wide covered balcony she'd seen from the front entrance of the house.

She turned to Trevor, allowing her voice to become slightly breathless. "Are we alone up here? *Really* alone?"

"Yes." He put a hand on her waist and tried to draw her closer. "The staff doesn't come up to the second floor except on Tuesdays when they clean. It's my sanctuary."

"One must have... privacy." She allowed him to draw her close. "I envy you, Trevor. Your family doesn't control you. You are free."

His eyes were dark and greedy. "Let me make you free." He tried to kiss her, and she flooded his senses with amnis.

Unfortunately, Tenzin might have overshot the goal, because the man's eyes rolled back and his head landed with a thud on her shoulder. He slumped against her, pushing her into a wall.

"Oops." She pulled back some of her power as she guided him toward a chaise under a window in the gallery. "Let's just set you here for a moment." She looked at him sleeping soundly and then looked to the right toward the stairwell. "Benjamin is not going to like this."

She walked back toward the landing and whispered, just loud enough for Ben to hear. "He's out."

She heard his light footsteps floating up the stairs.

His eyes were guarded. "The servants—"

"Only come up here on Tuesday." She waved him into the gallery and stood in front of Trevor, her head cocked as she watched him sleep. "It's his 'sanctuary.'"

"Did you find out where his safe is?"

"Ah..." She pursed her lips. "The thing is—"

"You overdid it on the amnis, didn't you?"

"He was trying to *kiss* me." She wrinkled her nose. "I only let you do that, remember?"

"And I'm very glad, Tiny, but did you have to put him quite so far out?" Ben knelt and patted Trevor's cheek. "He's barely breathing."

"You know, I think he was really stressed." Tenzin put her fists on her hips. "He probably *needed* this."

"Well, we *need* to get his combination." Ben reached down

and hoisted the man over his shoulder. "Are we guessing the safe is in the bedroom?"

"He seems unimaginative, so yes."

Ben carried the Englishman down the gallery and back toward the hall where several rooms branched off. There were two empty bedrooms, but none of them looked like the main suite. They walked back through the gallery, and Tenzin paused in front of a particularly beautiful silver necklace hanging on the wall.

"I think it's Hmong," she said. "And several hundred years old. Can I—?"

"Safe first," Ben said. "Then you can browse."

That was definitely not a no. Ben was being surprisingly larcenous, and she planned to take full advantage. "Tell me why you don't mind stealing from this one," she said. "Is it because he wanted to have sex with me?"

Ben and Tenzin followed Blythe-Bickman's scent, which led them to a vast bedroom suite with a sitting area, small office, and shelves and shelves of books. He tossed the sleeping man on the massive four-poster bed in the middle of the room. Tenzin noticed the barely concealed hooks in the posts but didn't say anything.

Apparently Blythe-Bickman wasn't quite as predictable as she'd imagined.

"I don't mind stealing from this one" —Ben scanned the luxurious room hung with art from all over the world— "because do you have any doubt that his family ripped off ninety percent of these things under the aegis of the British Crown?" He walked over to a silk-matted painting. "This watercolor is from Jodhpur, I guarantee you. I'm guessing eighteenth century. He has at least five similar paintings in the house. You think he bought them legitimately or paid a fair price?"

Ben walked to another artifact. "This mask looks West

African, and I'd say from the paint condition, it's at least two or three hundred years old. Why does he even own this? It belongs in a museum."

He walked to a figure that looked Native American. "This is from the Pacific Northwest, so maybe he bought this on the legitimate market, but where do you think all his family's fucking money came from? Exploiting poor people." He curled his lip. "This guy is the walking, talking definition of aristocratic privilege. So yeah, you can rob the shit out of him. He'll survive."

Tenzin walked over and patted Ben's shoulder. "Well, he's not walking and talking right now. And we have no idea where his safe is."

Ben turned in circles in the center of the room. "You know what? I don't think this bastard would keep the manuscript locked up. He likes to show off too much, and according to the information we got, this book is beautiful."

"I didn't see it in that gallery."

"I bet he doesn't have a safe; I bet he has another gallery." Ben narrowed his eyes. "A *personal* one."

Tenzin took a breath and filtered through the myriad scents in the room. For Ben, whose senses were strong but unstudied, it probably just smelled musty. But for Tenzin...

"It would have to be in a case," she said. "San Francisco has too much sea air for the book to be unprotected." She walked out of the bedroom, following her nose through the whole second floor, but she found nothing that indicated a priceless manuscript was being stored anywhere. She wasn't sniffing for vellum or gum arabic, she was searching for the faint scent of mold.

She walked back to the bedroom, where Ben was staring at a sleeping Trevor Blythe-Bickman. "He'd need a dehumidifying case, and I don't see one anywhere."

"And it would be noticeable," Ben said. "There was nothing like that in the library downstairs."

"The house is air-conditioned," Tenzin said. "The conditions in the library are probably sufficient for the majority of his collection because there are no windows."

"So where does he keep...?" Ben floated to the middle of the bedroom, looking back and forth out the windows on either side of the bed. "I'm getting that weird sense again."

Tenzin floated toward him. "You're right, it's subtle, but you're right. It's nothing like the mansion in Hungary, but..."

They both said it at the same time. "It's bigger on the outside."

Ben walked to the window and looked to the right. "There's a hidden room up here."

Tenzin walked to a silk tapestry hanging just to the right of the bathroom door and pulled it aside. "I told you," she said. "Unimaginative."

Ben walked to the window and looked out. "There are windows on the outside. I think he might have enclosed a balcony somehow." He looked at the door. "Let's see if we can find a way in."

Tenzin pressed an electronic panel set into the wall, and a set of numbers started to glow.

"Don't forget gloves."

Ben tossed her a sleek pair of leather gloves, and Tenzin put them on, quickly wiping the panel she'd just pressed. The last thing they needed was their fingerprints on file in some computer database.

"Okay, here's where we need him to wake up," Tenzin said. "We need the combination."

"But he's so quiet and dumb-looking right now." Ben cocked his head, watching the sleeping Englishman. "Try his birthday."

Tenzin snorted. "He wouldn't."

Ben shrugged. "He might." He reached in the man's pocket and found a slim billfold. "March sixth, nineteen eighty-nine."

Tenzin tried it, but the panel glowed red. "No."

"Did you try American or European dates?"

"Oh." She'd been in the United States too long. She reversed the month and day and tried again.

The panel glowed green; then a section of the wall popped out and slid to the side, revealing a thoroughly modern private gallery that positively glittered.

"You have got to be kidding me." Tenzin was giddy.

She walked into the hidden room and marveled. There were precious stones sitting in one case and a treasury of Byzantine jewelry in another. There was a mosaic framed on one wall that was a dead ringer for some of the Pompeiian mosaics she'd seen in a museum in Naples.

And standing alone at the end of the room was a white-marble-and-glass case holding a small manuscript open on a silk-covered book rest. The devotional was under another thick glass case, and Tenzin could hear the quiet hum of the dehumidifier working in the windowless room. She walked over and looked at the priceless work of art that had been Desta of Aksum's last and most personal work.

"Is that it?" Ben was at her shoulder.

"Yes." Tenzin had seen some other pieces that Lucien held dear, and this book had the same sublime beauty. But despite its age, the pages were even more colorful and well preserved than Lucien's examples.

"She was the scribe?" Ben stared at the book.

"No, the gospel was commissioned; Desta did the artwork."

Desta, most beloved daughter of Saba and sister of Lucien Thrax, had not only been an earth vampire, an accomplished scholar, and a famed beauty. She'd also been an artist of immense talent. The vampire commissioned the devotional written in Ge'ez when she converted to Christianity in the late sixth century, and she'd spent nearly fifty years completing the illuminations in the traditional Aksumite style of her human ancestors. The devotional was intended to be a gift for her mother Saba, but the ancient rejected it, unimpressed with her daughter's new faith.

"Are we certain this is it?" Ben asked. "Makeda's father—"

"Is a scholar of immense reputation, backed up by Desta's only living brother. Dr. Abel showed the pictures to Lucien, and Lucien says it's genuine." She couldn't pull her eyes away from it. "In addition, look at the style. Look at the binding." She placed her hands on the sides of the glass. "I don't feel any sensors, do you?"

"No, I don't think it's alarmed." Ben looked around the room. "He depended on a birthday combination lock for all this."

"Idiot."

"Arrogant."

Oh well, easier for them. "Did you bring the glass cutter?"

Ben's eyes went wide. "You said you were bringing it."

"Oh right." Her grin was impish. "You looked so panicked. It's in my purse."

"I'll pay you back later for that one," he muttered and walked out of the room while Tenzin perused the other offerings in Trevor Blythe-Bickman's gallery.

There was another artifact from Jodhpur that she'd be relieving him of, an intricately jeweled dagger that would look perfect in her collection. The paintings on the wall were primarily from European masters and held little interest for her.

"Oil, pigment, and canvas," she muttered.

"What's that?" Ben asked, returning with the glass cutter and immediately getting to work on the manuscript case.

"Paintings are fundamentally worthless."

"The market determines the value, Tenzin. They have worth because of their rarity and the skill involved. How can you devalue paintings but value manuscripts?"

"Because manuscripts contain knowledge."

"So does an e-book."

"Fine. Manuscripts are prettier. And they have gold."

"And they have gold," he muttered. "So did the Florentine masters."

It was an old argument, but one that reared its head at least once or twice a year. "When you're done with Desta's book, I want that dagger."

Ben glanced at her and smiled. "I knew you had your eye on that one."

They could only take what would fit in their pockets. They didn't need extra scrutiny when they made their exit. Luckily, Ben had brought a big coat.

"Did you mess up the sheets?" Tenzin asked.

"Oh, I thought I'd leave that to your vivid imagination," Ben murmured. "Almost done here..." A wide circle of glass popped out of the side of the case. "Hello, gorgeous." Ben pulled an acid-free roll of paper from his inside coat pocket and quickly bent it to fit the dimensions of the manuscript. Then he removed his gloves and opened a sealed hand wipe Giovanni had given him. He thoroughly washed his hands and waved them in the air until they were dry.

"This is better than gloves?" Tenzin asked.

Ben rolled his eyes. "I'm listening to my uncle here. He says gloves can do more harm than good with pieces this old."

"Okay." Tenzin tried to be patient. *Book people...*

When his hands were thoroughly dry, Ben reached inside the case and gently closed the devotional. It was the first time Tenzin had seen the cover, which was leather and inset with gems and carved ivory.

"It's incredible."

"It really, really is. Where did Blythe-Bickman get it?"

"Dr. Abel said was stolen from a church in the Tigray region in the 1920s, along with three other manuscripts by a different scribe. One of the Blythe-Bickmans bought it from the original thief, and it was absorbed into the family collection."

"Why is it in San Francisco?"

"I believe they were looking at a possible sale at one point," Tenzin said, watching Ben carefully wrap the manuscript in the paper sleeve he'd created. "That's when Dr. Abel was consulted. He realized what it might be and called Lucien."

"Fuckers." Ben finished wrapping the book, then slipped it into a silk bag taken from Beatrice and Giovanni's library. "I'm trying not to get nervous. If I mess this thing up—"

"Several different vampires and at least one human scholar will hunt you down," Tenzin said. "Okay, you finish this and I'm going to go mess up Trevor's sheets so he knows we had a fabulous night of passion." She motioned to the rest of the glass cases. "Can you open the rest of these for me?"

Ben smiled. "Ready to go shopping, Tiny?"

She grinned. "You know me too well."

10

They were sitting in Giovanni and Beatrice's library, watching as Lucien Thrax examined the book his long-dead sister had decorated with her art.

His eyes were old and sad. "It's almost as if I can see Desta working on it. The way she held her brush. The bottles of pigments and seeds and flowers she kept on her work table..." He reached for his mate's hand and knit their fingers together.

Makeda leaned down to examine the book. "They still make paints the same way." She glanced at Ben. "Did you know that? The churches in Ethiopia still make paints from the same flowers, minerals, and other ingredients that they've used for centuries. The colors hold up."

Ben cleared his throat and tried to speak normally, which was difficult when you felt like you were in the presence of vampire royalty. "I didn't know that. It's incredibly well preserved. The illuminations look nearly brand-new. At least we can say that about the Blythe-Bickmans. They preserved the book well."

Lucien muttered, "The Garima Gospels have been stored in

a stone church for the same amount of time, and they look just as good."

Makeda squeezed his shoulder. "At least it was kept intact. So many of our treasures have been lost. It's inspiring to see this one has survived."

Makeda Abel was a geneticist and Lucien's mate. She had been born in Addis Ababa but raised in the Pacific Northwest. Lucien and Makeda had a wary but respectful relationship with Lucien's mother, but they didn't spend much time with her.

Ben had met Saba and was always struck by her "otherness." She was the most beautiful—and most inhuman—vampire he'd ever come in contact with. And that was actually saying something considering the cast of characters who passed through his life.

Giovanni, always the official one, stepped closer. "So you are confirming that this book is the work of your sister Desta?"

"It is." He gently touched the corner. "I thought everything had been destroyed after her death." Lucien looked at Ben. "Do you know my sister's story?"

Ben glanced at Tenzin, but he couldn't read her expression. "I don't. I only know that she was killed."

"By a king of Aksum," Lucien said. "The dynasty that ruled Ethiopia for centuries. This prince, he loved her and she loved him. But when he realized who she was—*what* she was—his love died. He captured her in her day sleep, though she trusted him, and threw her into the sun." Lucien's eyes looked like wells of sorrow. "She burned, betrayed by the prince she had trusted. And my mother... went a little crazy."

Makeda put her hand on Lucien's shoulder. "In Ethiopia, even now, there are stories about the warrior queen, Yodit, who destroyed the Aksumite dynasty and ruled over the country for ᵈecades. She razed palaces and burned churches—"

"I still believe that was Arosh," Lucien said. "But it could have been either of them. My mother blamed the priests for Desta's death. She imagined they were the ones who told the prince to kill her daughter because she was a demon." Lucien shook his head. "We have no idea if that was true or not, of course. My mother has made her peace with Christianity now, but she still holds to no human faith."

Makeda said, "After a period of time, Yodit abandoned the throne and the Zagwe dynasty rose, but not before Yodit had thoroughly plundered the Aksumite treasuries."

Lucien added, "My mother gained an enormous amount of wealth in that period. There were many regional lords paying her tribute."

Ben's ears perked up when he heard the word *tribute*.

"So it's possible that Saba did hold the bone scroll at some point?" He asked. "You agree with Tenzin?"

Lucien shook his head. "I don't agree with Tenzin, because I don't think it actually exists."

"My father says it does," Tenzin said. "My father does not lie."

"Your father could be mistaken," Lucien said.

"The Manichaean he met was clear. He'd been instructed to take the scroll to the emperors of Aksum to be kept safe and for translation. It was written in an unknown language, but even so, they knew it was an object of power. They wanted to store it with the Ark."

"The Ark of the Covenant?" Ben asked.

Tenzin rolled her eyes. "Obviously."

"So if it was taken to the emperor, it's possible Arosh does have it," Ben said. "Your father said he was in Aksum."

"I don't think the scroll stayed in Aksum," Tenzin said. "And neither did the Ark. Many people don't realize that the Ark moved around the country. It went south; it went north. It was hidden in many places before the church of Mary where it is today."

Beatrice spoke up. "I always thought the Ark of the Covenant was in a government warehouse." She looked at Giovanni. "Top. Men."

Ben and Giovanni smiled. "You're ridiculous," Giovanni said. "But Tenzin is right. There are several different junctures where the bone scroll could have been separated from the Ark."

"But you're going to try to find it?" Makeda asked. "Where are you going to start?"

"Addis," Ben said. "We have reason to believe that this manuscript isn't the only artifact from Desta that we can use to placate your mother." Ben exchanged a look with Tenzin, who gave him a small nod. "Tenzin and I have sent feelers out with several dealers and traders we work with. One came back with an intriguing prospect."

"Which is?"

"We think that Desta's crown has survived."

Lucien's eyebrows went up. "Really?"

"We're not positive, but if we could get it, do you think that Saba might be willing to let the bone scroll leave her territory without causing a major international vampire incident?"

Lucien looked at Tenzin, who had wiped her expression clean.

What is going on with you?

There was something between Lucien and Tenzin. Ben could see it. Something they weren't telling the rest of the group. "Tenzin?"

She turned to him. "Yes?"

Ben hardened his voice. "What is going on?"

"If the scroll exists, it's not Saba who is going to have a problem with your taking it," Lucien said. "It's Arosh. Both of them believe in the blood of Mithra theory, and Arosh thinks Mithra is his sire."

It was enough to distract Ben. "What's that?"

"Arosh," Lucien said again. "He never knew who his sire was, but since his children are sired to wind, he believes his sire must be Mithra." Lucien shrugged. "It's not preposterous. How many ancient wind vampires were roaming around Central Asia when Arosh was turned? Probably not that many."

Tenzin muttered, "Maybe more than you think."

"Either way," Lucien said, "it's Arosh who will be the problem, not Saba. This manuscript alone will be enough for her. Desta's crown? As the Americans say, it would be icing on the cake."

LUCIEN AND MAKEDA had returned to their lodging for the day while Giovanni, Beatrice, and Ben cleaned up in the library. Tenzin sipped a glass of blood-wine and watched them, thinking about what Lucien had whispered to her before he left.

"You must tell him. You must tell them all. Otherwise, you're sending them into what could be a fight with a blindfold over their eyes."

It was true, and Tenzin felt the weight of knowledge like a rock in her stomach. She looked at Ben, then at Beatrice. They would be angry. To what extent, she didn't know.

But she knew Lucien was right.

"Benjamin." She didn't have to call his name loudly to get his attention.

"What is it?" He walked over, and she saw the knowledge of secrets in his eyes. "Are you finally going to let me in on what you and Lucien weren't telling the rest of us?"

She looked at Giovanni and Beatrice, who were watching

them. Then she turned back to Ben. "This has to do with the night you died. Do you want to talk here?"

Giovanni and Beatrice were at Ben's side in a blink.

"This has to do with Johari," Giovanni said. "Saba's daughter who—"

"She's one of Saba's army," Tenzin said. "She's not a true daughter."

Saba had an army of "children" now—those she had healed from Elixir poisoning—who were grateful for her healing and ready to do her bidding, but none of them had Saba's true amnis as Lucien did. They held mere shadows of her power, but she had their unwavering loyalty.

"Johari stabbed me," Ben said coldly. "She wanted Zhang's sword for herself."

It was as if she was living the night again, seeing Ben's blood seep from a sword through his spine. His face, pale as death...

Pale as the vampire he had become.

I didn't want to die yet.

He had been so angry with her; he would be angry again. But Lucien was right; Ben needed to know.

"After I took you to Zhang..." Tenzin forced the words out. "After he took you back to Penglai, I hunted Johari down within a few nights," Tenzin's mind drifted back to a storm over the Philippine Islands and a boat bobbing in the churning sea. "There were others on the boat, earth vampires. They tried to kill me, but they died quickly. Then I found Johari." She looked up. "I told you I didn't kill her."

"You said I asked you not to," Ben said. "When I was dying."

"But you didn't die," Tenzin said. "And when I found that vampire, she said that wasn't her intention."

Ben crossed his arms over his chest, his face set in stone. "I'm sure I was only collateral—"

"She was following orders," Tenzin said. "Orders from her sire. From Saba. She told Johari to wound you enough that you would have to turn."

Beatrice's hand came to Ben's shoulder. "What?" An expression of betrayal wrecked Beatrice's face. "But Saba healed Giovanni."

"She's not *good*, Beatrice." Tenzin shook her head. "She never has been. Saba's daughter was sent to steal the sword but also to make sure that Ben became a vampire," Tenzin said. "She even told Johari that I had to be the one to make the request."

Ben's fangs grew long. "Did you—?"

"Never. I would *never* ask Saba for anything, and especially not for that." Tenzin felt her lip curl up at the same time the spear of pain pierced her heart. It wasn't Ben's fault that he doubted her. The night sky knew she'd gone behind his back enough times to make him doubt. "Do you believe me?"

Ben hesitated, but Giovanni spoke. "Of course we believe you, Tenzin. You and Saba have never been friends. That story sounds like it was dreamed up to make a reluctant soldier think she was doing the right thing."

Beatrice still looked stunned. "But Saba—"

"Saba does not see right or wrong as we do." Giovanni sounded tired. "She has little value for personal autonomy or individual rights. To her, those are all very modern concepts."

Ben's voice was bitter. "So making sure I was a vampire serves her purposes somehow."

"Yes," Tenzin said. "That is the only thing I can think of."

Tenzin watched Ben. He still wasn't looking at her. It didn't matter what Giovanni or Beatrice thought. Not really. It only mattered—

"Why didn't you tell me before?" His voice was dark and

cold when he finally looked at her. "It's been three years since I was turned and not once—"

"What would it have benefited you to have an enemy you could do nothing about?" Tenzin said. "You will never be stronger than her, my Benjamin. If you had flown off—"

"You think I'm that big an idiot?" he shouted. "I know she's more powerful than me." The air in the library whipped around, confused by his anger. "I deserved to know."

"I'm telling you now," Tenzin said. "Because it could be important now."

"But not before," he said. "I didn't have a right to know before?"

She tasted her own blood in her mouth. "You had the right."

"Then why the *fuck* did you wait until now?"

Ben turned and stormed out of the library, leaving Beatrice and Giovanni alone with Tenzin as she ached in the wake of his fury.

"I knew it would hurt," Tenzin said softly. "And he was already hurting so much." Her eyes rose to Beatrice. "I would do anything to protect him. *Anything.*"

Beatrice looked away, and Tenzin saw her blinking her eyes hard.

"When you love someone," Giovanni said, "it's impossible to shield them from everything, Tenzin. And sometimes shielding them only makes the hurt worse."

Tenzin looked at the door where he'd stormed out and wondered how dusty her warehouse in Pasadena had become. Ben needed space, and he wouldn't want to see her. She'd retreat there for the night.

She reached for the shoes she'd dropped under the table, then stood. "You know, I blame you for all this, Giovanni Vecchio. I was happy only caring about three people in the world. Then you had to go and make a *family*." Tenzin's voice was bitter to her own ears. "It's your fault."

"I know."

"But you're not sorry, are you?"

His eyes were a little sad, but he smiled. "Not even a little bit."

She walked out of the library, out the front door, and took off into the night.

11

B eatrice found him in his old room, staring at the pictures he'd tucked into the mirror above the dressing table. They were mostly from high school and college. Snapshots of him and Chloe at the prom. Fabia kissing his cheek as he grinned at the camera. A drunken night out with Ronan in Campo di Fiori when they'd both been human.

"Hey," she said. "Do you need anything?"

Saba's blood flowing over my hands.

The violence of the instinct shocked him out of silence. "No. I already fed tonight."

Beatrice came and sat next to him on the bed. "I understand why you're angry. You have every right to be angry that she didn't tell you."

What would it have benefited you to have an enemy you could do nothing about?

The audacity. The fucking audacity.

This was typical Tenzin. Going behind his back, keeping things to herself, pretending like she always knew better.

"I also know exactly why she didn't tell you," Beatrice said. "And I don't know if I would have, if it had been up to me."

Ben turned to his aunt. "What the fuck?"

"Put yourself in her shoes." Beatrice closed her eyes and squeezed tight. "God knows I haven't been very good at doing that the past few years."

Ben was silent; he didn't know where Beatrice was going with this.

"I wanted to be the one to change you." Her voice was quiet. "Is that stupid? I'm young; nowhere near as powerful as your sire. You'd be a water vampire, and that doesn't suit your personality at all, but I wanted to be the one. Gio adopted you, and I came along later. I know I'm not your mom, but—"

"The best thing my mother ever did for me was to surrender custody of me to a vampire, Beatrice." He stared at the ground. "You were way better than my mom, okay?"

"Still, I was being selfish. You were grieving your human life, and I took it out on Tenzin."

"She's not a saint."

"She's not the enemy either." Beatrice took a deep breath. "I was really angry with her, but I don't know how much was really for you and how much was my own messed-up feelings."

"Well..." Ben fell back on a simple truth that had been the only explanation he'd had for so many puzzles in his life. "Vampire families are really fucking complicated."

Beatrice shook her head. "Isn't that the truth?"

They sat in silence for a few more minutes.

"What are you going to do?" Beatrice asked.

"I don't know."

"I know you still have issues—every relationship has issues—but clearly the two of you have made peace with each other. I don't want to interfere with that, because the bond the two of you have isn't like anything I've ever seen before." She finally looked at him. "It was only ever her for you. I know you had your girlfriends and your flirtations, but in your heart, it was only ever her. And the love she has for you—"

"She's never said it." His smile hurt. "I don't think she ever will."

Beatrice took his hand and knit their fingers together, palms facing each other. "I love you so much. I love Tenzin, and she loves me. And she loves Giovanni and Sadia. She loves Chloe. What she feels for you... it's so much more than *that*." She squeezed his fingers hard. "Knowing Tenzin, the words we use to describe our feelings probably seem cheap to her. Do you know what I mean?"

ENGLISH NEEDS BETTER WORDS.

Then find another language to tell me how you feel. You find the right words to tell me, and I will learn the language.

Ben closed his eyes. "I know what you mean."

"As for what happened with Saba? How many times have you hidden something from Chloe because the truth would only hurt her? How many times have you left out a part of a story so you didn't provoke a fight among your friends? We all do that, Ben. It's a way of protecting the people we love. She didn't hide it from you to hurt you."

"But she obviously thought that I'd go off, half-cocked, and try to hunt Saba down or something."

"Would you have?"

"Maybe," he muttered. "I was pretty stupid a couple of years ago, and I wasn't very careful with personal safety."

"Yeah. So she was probably right."

Fuck.

Ben sighed. "Yeah. She probably was."

"Remember when I told you last year that a five-thousand-year-old vampire wasn't going to change?" Beatrice bumped his shoulder with hers. "I was wrong. She has changed. Not who she is, but how much she's allowing herself to feel. There was a wall around her for as long as I've known her. As long as Giovanni has too."

"She still has a *lot* of walls, B. Trust me on this."

"Maybe, but she's given you the key." She stood and touched his chin, tilting his face up until he met her eyes. "She trusts you, Ben. And that changes everything."

THE FIRE CAME CREEPING into his sleep, slipping under the door of his old bedroom and teasing his nose with the smell of smoke and incense. He rolled over in his bed, his arm falling to the ground, and felt the heat teasing his fingertips.

His eyes flickered open, and he lifted his arm to see his right hand engulfed in flames, but his skin wasn't blistered or black.

A man in black robes with fearsome tattoos marking his cheeks stood at the foot of his bed, smiling silently.

"You think to take what is mine?" The man reached toward the door and with a flick of his finger, it swung open, revealing a blazing inferno across the threshold where his childhood home had been engulfed in flames. *"I will burn everything you hold dear."*

Screams rose as smoke choked the breath from Ben's lungs and tears streamed down his face. But even as the fire choked him, he was not consumed.

TENZIN DIDN'T COME BACK to the San Marino house the next night, but she found a note at her warehouse that simply read: *Going home.*

Since he'd be seeing Beatrice, Giovanni, and Sadia in a couple of weeks, he flew himself back to New York, following the path that Tenzin had taught him, which took a little over three nights. He flew over the desert, stopping at a refuge near Santa Fe. Then he headed northeast, stopping at a hideaway near a waterfall in the Ozarks. From there, he made the Chesapeake Bay just before sunrise, and from that it was only a short flight north to get home.

Ben was crossing high over the Brooklyn Bridge when he sensed her. The air over Manhattan was misty and humid, and the wind felt thick with a coming storm, but he sensed her anyway. When he landed on the rooftop, he saw her through misted glass panes, sitting in the greenhouse in their roof garden.

Ben was silent when he entered, watching Tenzin gently hold Layah, her female lovebird, on her outstretched pinky. Layah was fluffing her yellow and orange feathers as Harun, her mate, watched from a nearby palm frond.

"Are you still mad at me?" Tenzin asked, keeping her voice steady. "Please don't upset the birds. They've just become accustomed to me again."

Ben sat at the small bistro table. "I'm not mad."

"Then I'm sorry." She frowned a little bit. "I feel like I spend much of my life apologizing now. As if I am always doing the wrong thing."

It was such a Tenzin response; he had to take a moment before he responded. "If I was still angry with you, would you have apologized?"

"No. Because I don't think I was wrong. I am sorry you were hurt, not that I didn't tell you."

Yes, that sounded about right. "Why didn't you tell me about Saba sooner?"

She gently set Layah next to Harun, who began to furiously

groom her, displeased with being separated from his partner for even a few moments.

"What good would it have done?" Tenzin pulled up her knees in the ridiculously flexible squatting position she favored when she was relaxing. "I told you I found Johari, and I didn't kill her. You asked me not to kill anyone, and I didn't."

"What did you do to her?"

She didn't speak at first.

"Tenzin?"

"I cut off her hand and threw it into the ocean. Then I flew to Nairobi, found the vampire she loved, and told him that Johari had killed an innocent student and mortally wounded someone who considered her a friend." Tenzin shrugged. "It was all true. Her hand will grow back, but he will never see her in the same light as he once did, and she deserves that."

Ben almost found himself feeling sorry for Johari. "She was foolish to make an enemy of you."

"I don't consider her an enemy." Tenzin held her pinky finger out to Harun, but he ignored her. "She is nothing to me. A pawn, just like so many others who belong to Saba. Johari was following orders," Tenzin said. "As she must. Saba's children are not rebellious. Even Lucien—as old and independent as he is— he will not defy his sire."

"I wouldn't ask him to."

"Good," she said. "Because he would not."

Ben rose and walked to the small refrigerator that they kept in the glass house. He pulled out a small bottle of blood-wine and cracked it open on the edge of the table. Then he took a long pull and felt the edge of his hunger fading away.

"I need to feed," Ben said.

"Gavin's pubs are open until dawn."

"I know. I just don't want to see anyone quite yet." He focused on her feeding sunflower seeds to the birds. "I was panicking a bit when I went to the warehouse. Thank you for leaving a note."

She shrugged. "I guessed that you would need some time to brood."

He took another long drink and blurted out, "I keep waiting for you to get bored with me and leave."

Tenzin froze, and Ben sat in silence, his heart exposed and beating furiously between them.

She looked at him, but she didn't offer any platitudes. Which was good, as he wouldn't have believed them.

"I cannot promise that will never happen. Not bored with you exactly. Just... bored."

That he would believe. "Can you promise me that you'll come back?"

Tenzin considered it. "Yes. I can promise that."

And he could live with it. "Give me a little warning if you feel it coming."

She nodded again. "I can do that."

His dream from the night before haunted him.

I will burn everything you hold dear.

It didn't take a genius to figure out Ben was scared of going up against an ancient fire vampire even more powerful than the extremely dangerous fire vampire who had raised him.

"Why do you really want to do this job, Tenzin? Lucien thinks the bone scroll is a myth, and if it exists, there's no guarantee that Saba or Arosh would even be able to use it. It's dangerous, difficult, and could easily land us in a lot of trouble with people we don't want to fight with. Normally I'm with you on this kind of job—"

"No, you're not. You're notoriously cautious, Benjamin."

"I have to be cautious because you're not!"

"It's an important artifact," she said. "And even the chance that they may use it to control all four elements is too much power concentrated in one place."

"There are lots of dangerous and important artifacts out there."

"And I don't like the idea of Saba and Arosh having more influence. Even the rumor that they hold that bone scroll shifts the center of power back toward the West. That is why my father came to inform me of it."

"So we can find it and use it for the council in Penglai?"

"Absolutely not." She looked up. "I would never agree to that, and Zhang knows it. Besides that, the whole of Penglai is about *balancing* power," Tenzin said. "From the eight immortals to the very architecture of the island. The bone scroll is the antithesis of balance."

"Again, who is to say that Arosh or Saba would even be able to use the thing? If the blood of Mithra legend is correct—"

"Saba told Johari that I wanted you hurt." Tenzin looked away. She stared into the distance, and he saw her jaw clench. "She told her daughter that I wanted to force your turning."

"But you didn't tell her any of those things." Fuck. Had she been lying about that too? "Right?"

"Of course I didn't tell her that."

"So why do you want—?"

"What if she wasn't lying?" Tenzin stared at the ground. "What if part of me did want that? What if Saba thought she was doing me a favor?" Her lip curled up. "It makes me want to kill her."

"You can't kill Saba, Tenzin." He didn't even know if that was possible. Saba was a power unlike anything Ben had known. There was no fighting with her; there was only negotiation.

"I know I can't kill Saba." She glared at the wall of the glass house.

"Okay, now repeat that until you start to believe it." Ben walked over and sat on the floor next to Tenzin. "We're not going into Ethiopia to start a war. That's the whole point of bringing her Desta's manuscript and her crown. To remind Saba of what happens when she loses her temper and to trade for the scroll and safeguard it. Convince her that its best place is with us."

Tenzin was silent.

"Right?" He prodded her with his knee. "No war. No wanton destruction of valuable global heritage sites."

"No war," she finally muttered. "No damaging world heritage sites."

Ben sat down next to her. "Besides, you and I both know that you had no plans to force turning on me because you were arrogantly sure that you'd eventually have been able to persuade me to choose it for myself, right?"

Tenzin nodded. "That is true. But I do not consider that arrogance; it is simply confidence."

Ben put his arm around her and kissed the top of her head. "See? So Saba wasn't right. She wasn't reading your mind or your motivations at all. She was just... taking advantage of a situation and trying to steal your father's treasure."

Tenzin rested her head on Ben's shoulder. "I am glad you are home, my Benjamin."

"Me too." He played with the ends of her hair. "Want to go get some blood for me, then come back and have wild sex?"

"Yes." She nodded. "That is exactly what I would like to do."

12

Tenzin had reluctantly agreed to fly across the Atlantic in Giovanni's converted cargo plane, but only because it saved a considerable amount of time. Plus she disliked being cold and wet, and the shortest route to the Horn of Africa was inconveniently close to the North Pole.

So she bundled herself into the plane with the abnormal amount of luggage Chloe had insisted on packing for her, her amnis-proof tablet loaded with computer games, and the promise of a private compartment when she got sick of the other people on the plane.

It wasn't just her, Ben, and Chloe traveling on this trip. Giovanni, Beatrice, and Sadia were coming with their entourage, which included Dema, Sadia's nanny; Zain, their driver who was far more than a driver; and Doug.

She had never met Doug, but he was middle aged for a human, on the shorter side, was grey at the temples, and had a bit of a belly. He was not at all what Giovanni usually chose for security, which meant he must have had other skills that were secret.

Tenzin needed to keep an eye on Doug.

In the meantime, Ben and Giovanni were engaged in a lively exchange about the crew they would need in Ethiopia, while Chloe, Dema, and Sadia watched a movie and Tenzin played a game where you accumulated flowers and made gardens explode. It was both pretty and destructive. Satisfying.

Except for those damn annoying computer bees.

"I guarantee you," Ben said, "from looking at the terrain and the sites we're going to be searching, we need an earth vampire. Not for the British compound, but for the north? Absolutely. Tenzin and I can fly there, but we need someone like Carwyn—"

"Carwyn is busy right now; I told you. He and Brigid have another job, and honestly, they're not looking to make waves in that part of the world, especially outside the aegis of the Roman Church. They have very little sway in the Horn."

"Not Carwyn, I mean someone *like* him. A local would be best," Ben said. "Let's face it, not all earth vampires are going to understand the delicacy of the operation, and the first thing that will kill this mission is going in heavy-handed. The whole point is restoring cultural treasures, not destroying them."

Zain spoke to Doug, who was sitting in the booth across from him. "We're going to have four-wheel drives, right?"

Doug nodded. "You're not getting anywhere in the north without them. Unless you can fly."

Zain laughed a little. "Not this one; and no, thank you."

"A local?" Giovanni shook his head. "You're looking for an earth vampire in Ethiopia or even East Africa who doesn't owe allegiance to Saba? It's not going to happen. Even those who aren't directly in her line are going to have allegiance to her in some way."

Tenzin kept her attention on the exploding flowers. Giovanni was right; Ben was asking for the impossible.

Beatrice chimed in. "Ben, what are you looking for specifically? Someone with local knowledge? Or someone who just understands delicate excavations?"

He sighed. "I mean, preferably both."

Giovanni said, "And that's what I'm telling you. You're not getting both. Now Doug—"

"You already explained about Doug—"

Tenzin's ears perked up. *What about Doug?*

"—so I guess someone with some kind of archaeological or anthropological experience would be best. I know you know some vampire archaeologists, Beatrice—"

"No." She was looking at her phone. "I'm actually not thinking of an archaeologist at all." She pointed her phone screen at Ben. "What do you think?"

Ben leaned forward to look at the screen, then sat back in his seat with a frown. "He's an adrenaline junkie."

"I wouldn't say that." She showed the phone to Giovanni. "This was from last year. He was just there. I mean, he may get a little overenthusiastic at times—"

"Hardly unusual for someone in Carwyn's clan," Giovanni muttered.

Tenzin looked up from her game. "If you're thinking about inviting Rene DuPont into this group, I will be leaving it. I do not have the patience for that man right now."

Ben's lip curled. "Really? You think I'd stoop that low?"

Giovanni cocked his head. "Actually, that's not a bad idea. Rene's a treasure hunter, but—"

"No." Ben was firm. "Absolutely not. I'll get on board with Beatrice's suggestion if it's between the two."

The smile that Giovanni managed to hide told Tenzin that was exactly the reaction the vampire had intended to provoke.

Sneaky Italian.

The conversation became intriguing enough that Tenzin finally stopped playing the exploding-flowers game. She walked over and motioned to Beatrice, asking for her phone. She looked at the social media account the immortal published, though he wisely avoided more than a hint of his face in the pictures. She scrolled through his pictures of cheese wheels and saw an album full of mountains.

The Andes. The Himalayas. The Scottish Highlands.

And the Simian Mountains in Northern Ethiopia.

Daniel Rathmore was her friend Carwyn's youngest son, a farmer of some kind and an adventurer. Tenzin barely knew him, but she knew Giovanni and Beatrice had spent time with him in Cochamó and Ben knew him through family connections.

"He's been in these mountains?" she asked.

"He's been mountain climbing there," Ben said. "I don't know if that means anything other than he came here as a tourist."

"Still." She shrugged. "He's the priest's son, so he may have the personality of an overgrown puppy, but he'll respect the sacred sites. I agree with Beatrice; he's a good choice."

Giovanni turned to Doug. "Doug?"

The human nodded. "I've run across him over the years. He's not the worst choice. Not the best one, but I agree with you —finding someone without loyalty to Saba is the sticking point. Call him up. The adventure aspect will probably tempt him more than the money, which isn't a bad thing."

Tenzin narrowed her eyes at Doug. Giovanni was checking with Doug after she'd already given her approval?

Yes, she definitely needed to keep an eye on this human.

BEN HAD NEVER SPENT an extended period of time in Addis Ababa, but even so, the pace of transformation in the capital city of Ethiopia—the rapid construction, dense traffic, and constant roadwork—were things he always blanked out. The city was constantly evolving, with skyscrapers and new apartment buildings springing up like reeds as city-beautification projects refaced the sprawling capital that hosted hundreds of embassies, charities, and the headquarters of the African Union.

Addis was a city in constant flux, and the pulse of activity was evident everywhere, even at the airport in the middle of the night.

They arrived at the private terminal of Bole International Airport and were swiftly led through immigration and customs by none other than Doug, who proved to speak fluent Amharic. He greeted the officials they met like old friends, shaking hands and bumping shoulders as they made their way through the terminal.

Sadia was sleeping on Ben's shoulder, and Tenzin kept a close eye on the crowds, which were substantial even at midnight.

They walked out into a cool, misty night and saw the lights of the Bole District rising in the darkness. It was the start of the rainy season, and Ben walked carefully as they descended the long damp walkway, led by nimble porters carrying their luggage. Ben spotted two black Toyota Land Cruisers sitting on the curb.

"They're older," Doug said, "but well-maintained. I had to call around to find any without too many electronics that would still be comfortable."

"These are great." Giovanni turned and reached for Sadia, who woke briefly as they buckled her into her booster seat. "Did you already call the house?"

"The compound is ready," Doug said. "This time of night? It'll only take about fifteen minutes to get there."

Ben saw Tenzin staring at the vehicles. Spacious cargo planes were one thing, but cars...

He put a hand at the small of her back. "We don't know where we're going." He looked at the crowd of people in front of the airport, all clearly waiting for arrivals but staring at the foreigners who had arrived—a varied crew of Americans, an Italian, and one lone Asian woman. Probably not the strangest sight residents had seen but still something they'd remember.

"If we walk into the darkness," Ben said, "they will definitely be watching us. And we will not be able to fly off without anyone seeing. We are not going to blend in here, Tiny."

She glared at the vehicles. "What if I sit on top?"

"Also something that would stand out," Ben said. "Just remember, it's only for fifteen minutes."

After the luggage was loaded on top of the Land Cruisers, Doug got in the driver's seat of the lead vehicle and Zain took the rear truck. Sadia, Giovanni, Beatrice, and Dema squeezed in with Doug, which left Tenzin, Chloe, and Ben with Zain.

Ben hopped in the passenger seat in front. "You have any idea where we're going?"

"I have a rough map," Zain said. "But mostly I'm following Doug."

The question finally burst out of Tenzin. "*Who is Doug?*"

Ben smiled. It must have been eating at her the entire flight. "Doug is our local fixer, Tenzin. He's worked and lived here for about thirty years, and his wife is Ethiopian."

"So why isn't his wife guiding us?" Tenzin asked.

"Probably because she's a civil engineer and not a spy," Zain said, craning his neck to look for Doug, who'd entered a traffic circle. "Don't worry. Doug knows his way around."

Chloe appeared to be wide awake even though she'd hardly slept on the plane, according to Dema. "I'm just so excited to be here. It's my first time in Africa."

Zain glanced in the rearview mirror. "Oh yeah? How is that possible? You've been to Europe a lot, right? It's not that much farther."

"Yeah." She looked slightly uncomfortable. "I heard from a couple of people that Africans aren't exactly friendly with Black Americans. I think that made me worry a little bit."

Zain shook his head. "I think that's a misconception. Or maybe it depends on the country, I don't know. I doubt you'll run into that in Addis. Honestly?" He looked at her again as he exited the circle and continued following Doug off a main road and onto narrower, cobbled surface streets. "You're probably more likely to get people who assume you're Ethiopian and raised in the US. Prepare to learn some basic Amharic, my friend, because everyone is going to want to talk to you."

"What about you?" Chloe asked.

Tenzin said, "Zain looks West African."

"Bingo." He nodded as he maneuvered through mind-bending traffic that did not seem to respect any signal or rule. "My mom took one of those DNA things under an assumed name—my dad is paranoid about privacy—and we come mainly from Senegal and Ghana."

"Interesting." Ben looked at Chloe, then Zain. "I'm a mix of everything, I think. Puerto Rican on one side—"

"Which is literally like three or four in one," Chloe said.

"Yeah. And Lebanese on the other side." Ben shrugged. "So I'm a man of the world. I envy you two though. I think you're gonna fit in a lot better with the locals than we are."

Zain laughed. "I can't argue with you there, my friend."

Tenzin said, "I don't know what my DNA would show."

"Old as dirt?" Zain said.

Tenzin smiled a little. "From a scientific perspective, I am actually far older than dirt."

Chloe kicked the back of Zain's seat. "I was going to guess Mongolian."

Ben turned and looked at her. "I don't know what the scientists would do with your DNA, Tiny. But we're in the birthplace of humanity here. You're probably a lot closer to home than any of the rest of us."

Tenzin looked out the window and watched the crowds that still flooded the streets downtown. "You're not wrong. Look past skin color, and you see every kind of face here. African, European, Middle Eastern, Asian, even Indigenous American. This place? It's very, very old."

And Saba had come before it all. Ben thought about the task they had set out for themselves. Were they being utter fools? Could an object as powerful as the bone scroll really exist in a place controlled by the most powerful immortal on the planet without her knowledge?

And if it existed, was there any way they'd manage to wrest it from her control?

13

From the night sky, the city looked like a tangled web of highways, cobblestone roads, and narrow alleys flung across a series of hills. Dominated by vast government compounds and towering buildings downtown, the city spread out along the edges, where new houses and roads were lit by electric lights and rumbling trucks sped from the capital to the arteries going to every region of the country.

The capital city had been designed in the 1800s by the Emperor Menelik and was situated in the very center of the country, intended to be a capital city for all people of the empire. As the national capital of the only country on the African continent free from European colonialism, it was host to the headquarters of the African Union, a massive United Nations compound, and countless missions, international organizations, and research institutes.

Ben hovered over the maze, transfixed by the traffic churning in the streets. At night, cool traffic lamps illuminated the major streets while lights flashed on skyscrapers, music pumped from dance clubs and restaurants, and shops stayed open to catch those customers heading home from work.

Tenzin found him among the drifting clouds; there was a storm creeping in from the east.

"It reminds me of New York," he said.

"Not at all. New York is on a grid. Addis has no grid."

"Not that." Ben shook his head. If he managed to find his way back to the large compound Giovanni and Beatrice were renting, it would be a miracle. "No, just the busyness. It's a twenty-four-hour city like New York."

"Perhaps that's true. I enjoy that the occasional sheep or donkey still wanders into town though. You don't often see that in New York."

Ben smiled. "No. And the city's poorer for it, don't you think?"

"Agreed." She hovered in front of him and waited for him to enclose her in his arms. Ben loved floating with Tenzin like this, wrapped in her amnis and her arms, surrounded by their element and drifting with no particular purpose.

"Why are you brooding, my Benjamin?"

"I'm not brooding." He tucked a flyaway strand of her hair behind her ear. "I'm thinking."

"You often think with a frown on your face. I consider that brooding."

"I just..." Ben turned and pointed his face to the north. "Look at that."

"Look at what?"

The northern stretch of mountains above Addis Ababa got higher and more inaccessible. In the distance, Ben saw no lights. No signs of urban modernity. What lay to the north were the bones of an ancient and secretive kingdom with stories, myths, and lore stretching back for thousands of years.

"Giovanni, Beatrice, and I are meeting with Saba's representative tomorrow night," he said. "Gio has to give her a timeline, and he's already told me he's going to tell her three weeks. He's going to be doing some research; it's a family vacation. All that stuff. He's making excuses for us, but we have limited time. Three weeks and what?" He gestured to the north. "Two thousand mountains?"

"I think we can do it. And we're not going to look at two thousand mountaintops. Not all of them fit the parameters of Aksumite treasuries."

"Do you know how many old monasteries are in this country, Tenzin?"

"I believe there are currently close to eight hundred."

"Eight hundred." Ben shook his head. "Think about that number."

"I'm not saying we won't have to use our time wisely," Tenzin said. "And we may need to stay slightly longer than three weeks." She laid her head on his shoulder. "I have places we can hide."

"Tenzin, don't ask me to make a liar out of my uncle."

She sighed. "Fine. I'm sure there's a way we can narrow things down. After all, your aunt and uncle are research professionals."

"I mean, we've already marked the obvious places," Ben said. "We'll search those first."

"But if they're obvious to us, they're likely obvious to others," Tenzin said. "So there is that."

"You have to admit, we'll have an easier time accessing the majority of them."

Tenzin squeezed him around the waist. "I do love a mountainous and inaccessible country."

"I'm amazed you don't have a house here."

"There are a few caves I'm particularly fond of in the Simian Mountains, but I don't see Saba being happy with me putting down roots here." She looked up. "Her alliance with my father has always been wary at best."

"Still..." Ben began to float toward the ground in the general direction—he was guessing—of their compound. "You and your father haven't been joined at the hip. Historically speaking."

"Saba does not understand family estrangement." She gently steered him away from the football stadium. "None of Saba's children were ever estranged from her. She didn't permit it."

Ben frowned. "You can't... I mean, sometimes it just happens, right? Children want to go their own way, there are disagreements—didn't Lucien say that Desta and Saba disagreed when his sister converted to Christianity?"

"Oh yes, they were at odds," Tenzin said. "But they weren't estranged. If Saba had asked Desta to join her for any reason, she would have done it."

"Really?" Ben shook his head. "That's... interesting."

"That's who she is." Tenzin paused, looked up, and tapped his chin. "Don't ever forget she's like a magnet for our kind. We all feel a pull toward her. That's part of why her cure works so well for any poisoned vampire."

"Saba's Cure" was still the only antidote known to cure Elixir poisoning, a debilitating vampire virus that broke the amnis, rendering a vampire nothing more than a shell of their former self. But by taking the cure, you were aligning yourself with Saba forever. All former relationships, all elemental ability, would be lost to the earth and to her clan.

"It's no wonder she's getting arrogant," Tenzin said. "Her army must be in the hundreds now."

For a vampire army, that was a lot.

A *lot*.

Ben looked down. "Where are we going?"

"There's a park I want to show you," she said. "It's brand-new and there are fountains."

"Fine." He rolled his eyes. "But then we're going back to the house, right?"

"If you want to." The last two hundred feet, they dropped rapidly, landing on soft grass that sloped down a gentle hill that overlooked a river. Tenzin had kept them in the shadows, and they both stayed frozen as they checked their surroundings.

Nothing stirred, so they stepped forward and into the moonlight.

Tenzin nearly skipped down the hill. "We have to bring Sadia here!"

Ben swept his eyes over the buildings that looked to house different exhibits and the stages that appeared prepared for music or dancing. "It might be more fun for her during the day."

Tenzin waved a careless hand. "Oh, we can do both. Rather, we can take the night and Dema and Zain can take the day. It's good for her to be well-rounded."

Sadia sat on his lap back at the compound and put both hands on his cheeks. Whatever important news she was sharing, she needed Ben's full attention.

"Ethiopians eat with their hands," she said. "For everything. Not just hamburgers or sandwiches."

Ben smiled. "Do you like it?"

"Do I like it?" She rolled her eyes in rapture. "It's just the *best*! And they eat bread with everything because that's like their spoon. They pick up the food with the bread and it's called injera and at first I wasn't sure I was going to like it because it's kind of sour, but then Mika said that she could make a less sour one for me if I wanted and she did and I liked that very much."

"Less sour injera?"

"It's still sour." She raised a small finger. "But not *as* sour."

"I see." He hugged her and tickled her sides until she squirmed away. "What did you and Dema do today?"

She pulled him across the compound toward the massive mango tree that dominated the center. There were three houses within the walls, the main house, which rose four stories and was fronted with wide balconies. Giovanni, Beatrice, Sadia, and Dema shared that house, along with Doug.

In addition to the mansion, there were servants' quarters in back that housed a security guard and a cook, and two guest-houses, one of which was a *tukul*, a traditional round house with thatched roofing. Of course, this *tukul* was more luxurious than those in the country and was fitted with all the modern luxuries. Chloe had one of the bedrooms there, and Zain had the other.

Ben and Tenzin had a long, rectangular house at the back of the compound with a wide front porch and two light-safe rooms. Ben had a feeling it was the original house in the compound because the gardens around it were lush and the red stones that fronted it had a beautiful patina of age.

All around the edges of the compound were thick walls with security wire on top, and within the walls was a dense hedge of ficus plants that soared over the wall and created the feeling of an oasis. Hibiscus flowers, plumeria, and lilies burst with color during the day and at night. Creeping plants and fragrant herbs lined the cobblestone paths that linked the houses to the large central courtyard dominated by the old mango dripping with fruit.

"Where are you taking me?" Ben smiled as his little sister pulled him along.

"To meet Mika."

"Didn't I meet Mika last night?"

"No, that was her mom, Mazaa, and she's gone now, but she still runs the house, but she's not here all the time."

Since the house was owned by an old friend of Giovanni's

who was most definitely a vampire, Ben guessed that both Mazaa and her daughter were accomplished day-people.

That was confirmed when Ben saw Zain lounging under the mango at a table with a beautiful woman with her hair in braids who was pouring wine into two glasses. From Zain's posture, Ben could tell the man was comfortable, which meant he was with a colleague.

"Mika!" Sadia ran to the young woman.

The woman's face brightened with a smile. "Miss Mango!"

Sadia had been eating mangos all day, as evidenced by the sticky-sweet smears on her shirt and her cheeks. She giggled at the nickname. "This is my brother I was telling you about. He is a vampire and he can fly but his fangs are just normal and not curvy like Tenzin's teeth."

"I see." Mika's expression was one of charmed delight. She clearly enjoyed having a child running around the place. The woman stood and looked at Ben. "Just normal fangs then?"

"I'm so sorry to disappoint." He offered his hand to shake; a necessary gesture since older vampires generally avoided direct contact. "Ben Vecchio. It's very nice to meet you."

She took his hand with a smile. "Welcome to Addis. I hope you rested well."

"We were very comfortable, thank you."

She gestured to an empty chair at the table. "Would you like to join us for a glass of wine? I also have blood-wine if you'd like. It's Portuguese."

"That sounds great." Ben sat and Sadia dragged a small wooden stool over to sit next to them.

Blood-wine production, while still centered in Spain and France, was branching out, with the drink becoming ever more popular as the secret of its production had leaked to the broader vampire world.

It wasn't as nutritious or as filling as fresh blood, but if you hadn't fed that night and you were young, like Ben, it was enough to hold you over until you could hunt. "Zain, I was going to ask you and Doug about donor bars in the city." He needed to feed that night, and Tenzin would need some blood soon.

Zain nodded at their hostess. "Mika was just telling me there are several in Bole. That's the neighborhood where the airport is."

"There's one in Old Airport too," Mika said. "But it's more like a private club, and I don't know if you want to bother."

Ben cocked his head. "Are all the fancy neighborhoods in Addis around airports?"

She smiled brilliantly. "We do seem to like them, don't we? Old Airport is a beautiful neighborhood. Definitely one of the more walkable ones in the city. Lots of shops and restaurants that will stay open after dark. So if you want to explore, it's a popular place."

"Do we need to worry about anyone getting too curious? My partner is Asian, so we don't exactly blend in."

Mika said, "If you stick to the international neighborhoods— Bole, Old Airport, Sarbet, and a few others—you'll be fine. People are used to Asian businesspeople here. There are so many. And more and more tourists all the time. In most places, Addis is very safe. Especially for foreigners."

Sadia leaned on Zain's shoulder, brushing his long locs to the side. "We went to the museum today in the morning time. Then we had a nap. Right, Zain?"

"Yep. Sadia, Dema, Chloe, and I saw... What was her name?"

"Lucy!" Sadia said. "She was the first... Um..."

"Do you remember?" Zain asked. "She was the first one who..." He leaned over and whispered to Sadia.

The little girl started bouncing. "She was the first human ancestor to walk on two feet."

"I see." Ben nodded. "That is very impressive."

"And we saw her with our own eyes." Zain winked at Ben. "Even though I'm pretty sure the actual skeleton is at Addis Ababa University with all the archaeologists."

Mika smiled. "I am very sure you are correct."

"Chloe met one of them, in fact." Zain sipped his wine. "It was just like you predicted, Ben. This woman was working at the museum and says something to Chloe in Amharic, and they ended up striking up a conversation. I think she did her doctoral work or something at UCLA."

"Really?" Ben's brain started churning. "She was an archaeologist?"

"Yeah, teaching at the university, I think? I'm not really sure. Chloe got her number though. They were going to get coffee or something."

Mika said, "That's so nice. People are so friendly here. I'm glad she's already made a friend."

"And the skeleton," Sadia said. "Lucy! She was, like, shorter than me, Ben. It was so funny."

"Wow. That sounds amazing." Ben wasn't really listening about Lucy anymore. Something Zain said turned on a light bulb in his mind.

The real skeleton would be at Addis Ababa University.

With the archaeologists.

Of course. *Of course.*

"Zain, did you say Chloe got this girl's number?"

14

The meeting with Hirut, earth vampire of Saba's line and current administrator of the immortal community in Addis Ababa, happened at midnight in the gardens of Zoma, a contemporary art museum in the Mekanisa neighborhood. Ben flew to the site and waited just inside the green metal gates for Giovanni and Beatrice to arrive. The neighborhood was asleep, and only a few streetlamps were visible burning on the narrow track to the main road.

He nodded to the guard, who gave Ben a small salute but otherwise didn't react to seeing a foreigner flying into the garden like a bird. Clearly he was in Hirut's hire.

Distant headlights flashed, and a few minutes later, the black Land Cruiser stopped in the small cobblestone parking lot. Giovanni and Beatrice got out of the truck, looking like the sleek and sophisticated vampire power couple they were.

Would Ben and Tenzin ever look that cool? Probably not.

They strode toward the gates and waited for the guard to open them; then they proceeded down a path to the left that led them beside intricately handmade mud-and-straw-constructed buildings molded into various shapes. Waves and chains, birds' nests and flowers. It was nothing like anything Ben had ever seen before.

"This museum is extraordinary," Beatrice said. "I can't imagine how long it must have taken to make all this."

"And the gardens are beautiful," Giovanni said. "Also, I think they're entirely edible. I believe this is an experimental project in urban agriculture and building."

Ben nodded at a sign in the distance, visible in the moonlight. "There's a school here too."

A school with guards. Lots of guards. Ben felt them all around him, vampires waiting in the shadows, wandering the grounds, and at least one overhead. Hirut might have been meeting them in a friendly location, but she was taking nothing for granted.

"Fascinating." Giovanni paused at the end of the path; then he waved them toward the left. "This way. I can already smell the coffee roasting."

They followed twisting paths through towering alleys of false banana trees and found themselves at the top of a large, rectangular green. In the distance, a flame tree bursting with red-orange flowers was blooming, and beneath it, a woman in a pure white dress was sitting under the tree on a low stool, roasting coffee over a charcoal fire.

Another woman in white sat a little in the distance at a table sprinkled with flowers. Four wine goblets were in front of her along with a pitcher full of fresh blood. She wore a traditional Ethiopian dress with intricate embroidery at the collar and a *shema* shawl over her head and crossed on her shoulders. Her jewelry was pure gold and—Ben was guessing—quite old; an amulet rested on her forehead with a large red ruby at the center, and gold chains draped along her temples, holding it in place.

Giovanni paused at the foot of the table. "Hirut Gedeyon,

thank you for your welcome. I am Giovanni Vecchio, son of Andreas, water vampire sired to fire. And this is my mate."

Beatrice stepped next to Giovanni. "Thank you, Hirut. I am Beatrice, daughter of Stephen, water vampire sired to water. And this is our son, Benjamin."

Ben was getting to be a professional at protocol, and he caught the nuances of how Beatrice and Giovanni had introduced themselves, which was formal but familiar, emphasizing family connections and not professional associations.

"Thank you, Hirut." Ben bowed a little, as befitting a child of Zhang. "I am Benjamin, son of Zhang, wind vampire sired to wind. Thank you for hosting us in this beautiful garden and in your city."

Your very secure city. Ben felt at least three more vampires creep closer.

He could smell the coffee roasting, along with the scent of frankincense wafting from under the flame tree. The woman roasting coffee had her head covered, focused on her task.

"Welcome to Addis Ababa." Hirut rose and gestured to the empty chairs. "I have prepared a pitcher of fresh blood for us tonight."

"That's so thoughtful," Beatrice said. "I'm sure you've heard that our son is young."

"Young." Hirut sat again and crossed her hands in her lap. "But very powerful."

Well, that would explain the guards. Clearly Hirut knew who he was—unfortunately, most vampires did—and was suspicious. Fair. Irritating but fair.

"Has your partner accompanied you on your journey?" Hirut poured blood into each goblet and passed them to each guest. Then she deliberately drank first.

Ben took a drink and enjoyed the sweet rush of fresh human blood against the back of his throat. He was young enough that it was a challenge to focus and not gulp down the whole glass. "If you mean Tenzin, yes, she has. She sends her greetings; she is currently at our compound with my little sister, who's only seven."

Leaving one immortal in the party to guard the human members was a perfectly acceptable gesture, especially when a child was involved. At Ben's suggestion, they'd chosen Tenzin, which left the compound very well guarded.

Also, it kept Tenzin from sticking her foot in her mouth and causing an international incident. Ben liked to think ahead.

Hirut's attention seemed to be focused on Ben. "I understand that you work with your uncle, but in a more... acquisitive capacity."

Ben answered very carefully. "We find lost items, mostly for immortal clients who have misplaced them or had them stolen over the years." Ben glanced at Giovanni, who only gave him an encouraging nod. "We recently retrieved a lost icon for a leader of the Poshani people in Eastern Europe, a valuable cultural item which had gone missing because of a human theft."

"An honorable deed then," Hirut said. "To return such a treasure to her people."

"We were happy that it found its rightful home again."

Giovanni said, "Hirut, you have known my work for years. I retrieved a manuscript from Berlin that is now in the Ethnographic Museum at the university."

"Indeed." Hirut nodded. "That service to my father is why you have been welcomed here despite being in the company of those who have... murkier reputations."

Ben tried to pretend it didn't sting, but it did. "Hirut, I hope you know that Tenzin and I—"

He stopped speaking when she raised her hand. "Giovanni, you know the history of this place. For centuries, humans and vampires have come from outside our historical borders and taken cultural heritage from Saba's people, human and vampire alike. We have reason to be wary."

Giovanni placed a gentle but firm hand on Ben's shoulder before he could respond. "Knowing that I know that," he said, "you have *my word* that there will be no manuscript, no artifact, not even a paperback book taken out of Ethiopia without your queen's permission."

Ben kept his eyes steady on Hirut. In the distance, the scent of coffee came closer. The woman roasting the beans was passing around the freshly roasted coffee on an intricately carved wooden tray, wafting the smoke from a small brazier over each guest with a dark, graceful hand.

For a moment, Ben looked up and gazed at the woman, who locked eyes with him.

Large eyes, so dark brown they were nearly black, were rimmed with black kohl and thick lashes.

Old memories flashed in his mind.

The smell of green earth and growing things.

Power, the air redolent with it.

Boy, you are faithful... Your time is not now.

The smoke cleared, the woman walked away, and Ben was left with tears in the corner of his eyes. From the smoke? Was he imagining things?

The woman in white seemed to go unnoticed by everyone but him, just another human woman preparing coffee for guests. The shema she wore covered her face as she sat in the shadow of the flame tree; Hirut and Giovanni were still discussing the terms of their visit.

"...to go north," Giovanni was saying. "The historical sites in Gondar are something I'd love to share with Beatrice, along with the island monasteries on Lake Tana."

"And Lalibela," Hirut said. "Your family should not miss that."

Giovanni bowed a little, and Ben internally rejoiced. Lalibela was far closer to their search area than Gondar was, but they hadn't wanted to appear too eager to visit that historic city.

Hirut said, "While you are there, you might offer us the benefit of your expertise. There is a priest in Lalibela who has been studying a newly found manuscript of the Gadla Lalibela."

"The hagiography of King Lalibela?" Giovanni asked.

"Yes, exactly. He might benefit from your expertise in some regards," Hirut said. "Since we have an expert on ancient manuscripts visiting, it would be delinquent of me not to ask on his behalf."

"I would be honored to help in any way I can."

"And Beatrice?" Hirut turned to Beatrice. "I know your reputation as a scribe. If there are manuscripts you would like to study while you are here, I can try to arrange it."

"Obviously, the Garima Gospels are compelling, but I understand the difficulty at the moment."

"You are correct." Hirut nodded. "It is not currently possible, but at another time this can be arranged."

Giovanni continued. "The trip to the north is the primary reason for our visit. Beatrice hasn't seen the historical sites, and our daughter is old enough now that she can appreciate them as well."

Hirut turned to Ben. "And you? What is your aim? Do you and your partner have a client?"

The plan had been for Ben to avoid answering anything close to Hirut's question directly, but he glanced at the woman under the tree, then back to Hirut. "I do."

Giovanni and Beatrice froze.

Ben looked Hirut directly in the eye. "I cannot tell you her identity, but I can confirm everything my uncle promised: There will be no artifact taken from your country by my partner or me without Saba's permission. We are not here to steal; we are here to restore."

A hint of a smile touched Hirut's lips. "Your honesty and directness do you credit, son of Zhang. I am glad you were truthful with me; I would not have believed you otherwise."

The woman under the tree returned with small cups of strong coffee, but again she was obscured by the brazier of charcoal she put in the center of the table. The scent of frankincense overwhelmed him as Hirut offered sugar and honey around the table to sweeten the coffee.

Was he imagining things? Was his memory tricking him? What was going on? Still, no one other than Ben seemed to even notice the woman, and there was no hint of amnis coming from her. She moved like a ghost in the night.

His memories of Saba from when he was human were of a being of immense power. Even as a teenager, he'd been able to feel how completely inhuman she was. Was his mind playing tricks on him? Or was Saba hiding in plain sight and somehow fooling his aunt and uncle?

"Ben?" His uncle's voice brought him out of his reverie.

"Yes?" Ben looked up. Everyone was looking at him.

Hirut appeared amused. "Do you not like the coffee? It's very strong. Some young vampires don't care for it. I can get you some warm water if you'd like."

"No." Ben sipped the traditional Ethiopian buna, double boiled in a clay pot until the taste reminded him of dark chocolate. "I love it actually. Much smoother than espresso."

"Thank you." Hirut finished the coffee in her tiny cup and set it down. "Before we go, is there anything I can tell you about immortal resources in the city that you don't already know?"

～

BEN WANTED to return to the compound immediately after the meeting with Hirut broke up, though Giovanni and Beatrice accepted the woman's offer for a tour of the garden. As he was walking back to a shadowy corner of the garden to take to the air, he scanned the area, looking for the woman in white, but he saw nothing.

Questions swirled in his mind. Had that been Saba? How had she seemed so human? If she was in Addis, why wasn't she meeting with visitors herself? And if that had been Saba and she'd cloaked her power so effectively from Giovanni and Beatrice, why had she revealed a whisper of it to Ben?

The last thing he'd expected to run into as he was descending into the compound was Tenzin and Sadia flying up through the trees.

Both of them froze when they saw Ben, staring at him with wide eyes.

Sadia was not supposed to be flying. Tenzin had done it when she was a toddler, and it had been quickly outlawed. Not that anyone really thought Tenzin would drop Sadia, but the sensation of flying made the baby puke more often than not.

Also, it just freaked Beatrice out.

Sadia stared right at Ben. "I asked her."

Ben looked at Tenzin.

"I said yes." Tenzin was wide-eyed but clearly unapologetic.

He was not getting in the middle of their terrifying girl gang. "Okay, you probably have about thirty minutes before Giovanni and Beatrice are back. I don't want to know."

He floated down to the courtyard and sat under the mango tree where Dema was lounging with her feet on a footstool and her hands around a large cup of tea.

Ben glanced up at the sky, then to Dema. "So you're not worried about—?"

"Do you actually think anything would happen to Sadia when she's with Tenzin?"

Ben considered it. "Intentionally? No."

Dema shrugged a little. "It's not my job to protect her from accidental bumps, bruises, or a scratch from a random tree branch that Tenzin gets a little too close to. If anyone came after that girl, that vampire would flay the skin off their bodies without a second thought."

Ben nodded. "You're not wrong."

"How did the meeting go?"

He decided to keep his suspicions about the strange woman under the tree to himself. Until he could speak to Tenzin. "It went well. Her main concern was me and Tenzin stealing stuff, and I think I reassured her well enough."

"If anything, you're putting things back, right?"

Except a superdangerous object of immortal power. "Yep. That's absolutely what we're doing."

Dema stared at him as she sipped her tea. "The number of words you took to answer that tells me you're definitely stealing some stuff too."

Yeah, he couldn't lie. Even after he'd become a vampire, Dema was scary.

15

Ben lounged in a pair of loose shorts, enjoying the promise of rain in the air. Tenzin hated the rain, but he was enough of a Californian that he loved it. He loved the smell of it in the air and the heaviness of the clouds. He loved it when the clouds broke open and the sky poured down.

He watched Tenzin change from a pair of leggings and a loose tunic into a clean shift that drifted to the middle of her thighs. Before the shift fell, he noted the delicate line of tattoos that arced across her hip bones and the dots down the back of her legs.

Those were secret things that no one saw but him. Precious insight to her habits and eccentricities.

She was meticulously clean, never letting the clothes she wore out in the world even touch the bed they shared. Unless they were stuck in a cave somewhere, she had never deviated from that.

She didn't sleep, but she always lay with him until he did. She pressed herself to his body from breast to foot, twining herself around him like a vine. She said far more with her body than she ever did with her mouth.

"You're staring at me."

"I like to look at you." He'd missed looking at her for two years. There was a knowledge between them now, a realization of what they had lost and what they had gained. Beyond the newness of their sexual relationship and their deepening intimacy, there was a realization they had both learned in the most painful way.

They did not want to live without each other.

But for how long?

Despite her age, nothing about Tenzin felt permanent. She was like the wind slipping around him as he flew. Grasping onto her would be a lesson in futility, and Ben couldn't shake the feeling that Tenzin was still hiding things. A large part of him didn't want to know.

She will always have secrets.

Tenzin walked to him and climbed into bed. "Did you take a shower?"

"Of course. Lots of bugs here."

Her eyebrows went up. "Yes. But you know that means there are also many birds."

"I like the birds." He felt the sunrise start to tug on him. "Not the bugs as much."

"But you don't get one without the other." She lay next to him and stretched out along his body, pressing her face into his chest to smell his skin. She stared at the slight stubble growing along his jaw and rubbed her fingers across it. These explorations were typical for her. She had no qualms about any curiosity or interest in his body.

"You fed tonight?"

"I did. Hirut had fresh blood for us at the meeting."

"You made sure she drank first?"

"I'm not an amateur anymore, Tiny." Ben ran a hand down

her silken hair. He loved the weight of it sliding between his fingers. "Have you found a sword or two yet?"

She smiled and her eyes lit up. "Maybe."

"I've seen pictures of the traditional Ethiopian shotel. I don't think you have one of those in your collection back home."

"I have a Persian sword that's very close, but you are correct. I'll be procuring one on this trip, but I suppose since Giovanni is with us, I'll have to actually *buy* it."

He could hear the annoyance in her voice, and it made him smile. "I suppose you will."

Her head popped up. "Did you know Ethiopians used hippopotamus skin to cover their shields?"

"That makes sense. I certainly wouldn't want to stab a hippo. They are pretty horrifying."

"They call them water horses, but their blood is disgusting. Nothing at all like actual horse blood."

Ben closed his eyes. "I'm trying to imagine... Nope. Don't want to."

She lay on his chest again. "Horse blood was a regular part of my diet when I was young. The horses were part of the clan. We didn't kill them; we cared for them and we drank their milk and their blood when we couldn't find humans."

Not unlike some African ethnic groups that still drank the blood and milk from cows. It made sense. He often had to remind himself that Tenzin was forged in a far hotter furnace than anything his soft, twenty-first-century ass had experienced.

He still didn't want to know about the hippos though.

"I think Saba was at the meeting tonight." His eyes were getting heavy.

His words made Tenzin sit up. "Ben, don't fall asleep. Explain."

"I don't know for sure... Didn't make sense. She was roasting coffee."

"Roasting coffee? Did Giovanni and Beatrice see her?"

"No. I mean yes, but it was like they didn't even notice her. Like she was just a human."

"If she cloaked her power—which she is definitely capable of doing—to fool them, how did you sense her?"

"I don't know." He blinked rapidly. "Maybe she wanted..."

"What? Wanted what?"

"To say hi." He shrugged. "Or something. Maybe I'm imagining things."

"Do you really think that?"

He shook his head. "It was her."

Rain spattered on the metal roof over them, then poured down, the sound further lulling him into his dawn sleep.

"What game is she playing?" Tenzin looked around the room as if the small chamber might offer some answers. "Is she with Arosh? Is he searching on his own? Does he have it already? Lucien said... But would Lucien really know? Would he tell me if he did?"

Ben had nothing more to offer. He was too sleepy, and he knew the sun was rising. "Tenzin." He reached for her, and she lay down beside him.

"Benjamin." She wrapped herself around him again. "My Benjamin."

"Stay with me."

"I will." Her voice wasn't sweet then, it was determined. And Ben knew she was saying nothing but the truth. She would stay with him all day. And if anything tried to hurt him?

She would slay any danger that came.

THE FIRE WAS HEADING STRAIGHT toward him, barreling down a narrow stone passageway. He could already feel the heat teasing his skin. Behind the flames, someone was laughing, his voice rising in the night like a terrible bell tolling an alarm.

"Mother."

Ben turned to see a figure walking away from him, disappearing into the earth as the fire overtook him and his skin started to blacken and curl from his body.

"Mother?"

He turned toward the fire and saw his family in the middle of it. Giovanni, Beatrice, Sadia, and Chloe were trapped in the middle of the flames, screaming but unconsumed.

He heard something drop to the ground next to him, and his head spun again.

She was on the ground, her hair smoking and flames licking along her skin. Her body was splayed out, crumpled on the rock floor like a fallen bird.

Her eyes were open but lifeless, and as he watched, her body began to dissolve.

"No, Tenzin! No!"

BEN WOKE at dusk to Tenzin's back against his chest, his sickening dream twisting in his belly like spoiled blood. He'd rolled to his side during the night, and she'd found a space within his arms. His eyes fluttered open as he woke, and he saw the nape of her neck, inches from his mouth.

Bite.

Hunger roared through him, and he felt wild. His instincts told him to take; his arms tightened around her.

A simple pinch to his ear calmed him a little.

"You're hungry," she said. "You need to be drinking more."

He laved his tongue against her neck. "I took blood-wine last night. And fresh blood."

"Less blood-wine and more blood." She turned to look at him over her shoulder. "Your fangs aren't the only things that woke up hungry." She wiggled her hips.

"Tease," he growled.

"Far from it." She tried to turn in his arms, but Ben held her tight. "So what is your plan, my Benjamin?"

He couldn't bite her without an invitation, but he could make her want his bite. He knew she felt pleasure from it. He moved his hands down her body, caressing her breasts and sliding his hands under her shift. The curves of her form were subtle but deliciously feminine. He felt softness on her belly, the rise of her hips. She arched her back and pressed her bottom into him; he was hard as iron.

He seduced her, taking his time to explore every inch of her body until she was twisting in his arms, trying to take control. But as soon as she did, he let his fingers dip between her thighs and she let out a soft moan.

"Tilt back," he whispered in her ear, scraping his fangs where he felt a single pulse in her neck.

Tenzin arched back and Ben entered her from behind, keeping his hands moving over her body and between her legs, stoking the fire that was building.

When she came, she tightened around him and Ben nearly lost control. His hips sped up and he flipped her onto her belly, hiking her hips up so he could move faster.

"Yes." She gasped. "Yes."

Her neck was right there.

Right there.

But she didn't tell him to bite. His fangs drew blood in his own mouth when he came, and he collapsed over her, pressing his face into her shoulder and kissing along her spine.

We have to talk about the mating thing.

But he knew it would probably provoke a fight.

But we have to talk about the mating thing.

Her body was loose and languid in his arms. "You're thinking very loud."

"Am I?" He didn't get tired when he had sex now. It was odd, but there was something he liked about the exertion necessary to make love when he'd been human. He missed that a little bit. Then again, he didn't miss needing recovery time.

"Do you want me to ask what you're thinking about?"

It was such a Tenzin question, he had to smile. "Do you actually want to know what I'm thinking about?"

"I don't know. It could be something banal regarding sex, and that doesn't interest me. Or it could be something about hunger. Or something about seeing Saba last night at the meeting with Hirut."

Aha. So that's where her mind was. Well, one could never say that she didn't have focus. "I was thinking about banal sex things."

She turned in his arms and faced him. She had a small frown on her forehead. "I want to be clear that sex with you is not banal. I was merely saying that often thoughts *after* sex are quite boring. And have nothing to do with the sex we had."

"What do you think after we have sex?" He was going to regret asking that, wasn't he?

"Just now, I was thinking that I like that position very much because it allows you to stimulate much of my body while we are having intercourse."

Okay, that wasn't too bad. "Noted. I like that position too."

"And then immediately after, I was thinking about you seeing Saba at the meeting with Hirut."

"You've been obsessing about that all day, haven't you?"

She sat up. "Why would she do it? It makes no sense!"

He shook his head and reached for her hand. "Tenzin, Saba has always been this mythical figure to me. I mean, when you first told me her role in my turning, I couldn't even say I was surprised." He took a breath and tasted the lingering scent of rain and the flowering plumeria bushes outside their door. "What am I to her? Honestly? I'm a nobody. Sure, I'm a powerful nobody because I'm Zhang's son now, but really..." He hated to say it because he already felt like Tenzin was carrying guilt—or whatever feeling that passed for guilt with her—about his turning. "I think that her role—with the Night's Reckoning, with Johari stabbing me—I don't really think that was about me. I think that was about you and your dad somehow. I was just... there. Maybe she saw me as a weakness for you."

She nodded. "You *were* a weakness for me."

"Thanks?"

Tenzin shrugged. "I cared about your life. Anyone I care about is a weakness; that was why I insisted that Nima be isolated on Penglai if I was traveling."

There were so many times over the years that Ben wished he could have a conversation with Nima. This was definitely one of those times. "Well, thanks for not locking me up, I guess."

"I'm just saying you would have been safer."

Ben sat up. "This conversation has veered way off track. Saba was there. Probably. And she revealed herself to me probably for this exact reason, to get us confused and questioning."

Tenzin nodded. "We have a plan."

"We have a good plan." He counted on his hand. "Steal Desta's devotional, check. Find Desta's crown—we're getting there. Then find the bone scroll—"

"Which has only been lost for a little over a thousand years."

Ben stared at her. "You're not helping."

"I'm only saying we've found older things."

"Exactly." He rubbed her back. "So we find the bone scroll, trade all of Desta's treasures to Saba for it—"

"Then escape from Arosh, who is going to be very pissed off."

"But we can fly, and he can't."

"How convenient." She smiled, and seeing her fangs just made him hungry again.

"Okay, I really need to eat."

16

"Why do you want to meet Liya again?" Chloe leaned back in her seat and scanned the outdoor restaurant that smelled of frying lamb and berbere spice. "She was happy to meet me, but I now I feel weird."

"Why do you feel weird?" Ben looked around the spacious garden where every table was full and the patrons all looked local. "Zain was right; you definitely blend in here."

Chloe laughed a little. "I've never been around so many Black people in my life. I just wish I could talk to more of them."

"I know what you mean." He sat across from her, enjoying the clamor of human life around him and the pumping music coming from inside the restaurant. The setup was more like a beer garden than a single restaurant, with two small places serving meat and vegetarian dishes to tables scattered around a large garden shaded by cedar trees while servers in black-and-white uniforms carried bottles of beer and large drafts across the patio.

Initially he'd wanted to sit inside—better to control the environment—but the noise had become far too loud for his sensitive ears. He could barely concentrate, so they'd moved outside.

"But really" —Chloe wasn't letting up— "why do you want to meet Liya?"

"I'm meeting a fellow Angeleno in Addis." Ben sipped the chilled beer the waitress had poured into a clear glass. "What's weird about that?"

Chloe narrowed her eyes. "Because you and Tenzin are here on a job, and this nice woman I met who just happens to be an archaeologist is suddenly very interesting to you."

"She's an archaeologist. Everyone is interested in archaeologists. They're cool."

"Ben! I didn't meet Liya with ulterior motives in mind! I thought I was just making a friend."

"You did." He took another long drink of beer. "And I want to meet her too."

Chloe closed her eyes and rubbed her temple. "Remind me to only meet boring people from now on."

"Impossible."

"Chloe?" a cheerful female voice called from the entrance to the garden.

Ben turned and saw a smiling woman with a cloud of dark brown curls waving from across the lawn. She walked around, stopping once to say hello to a friend at another table before she continued toward them.

"You must be Ben." Liya, a pretty human whom Ben guessed was in her late twenties, held out her hand. "Heyyyy, it's so nice to meet you. Chloe talks about you a lot."

Ben had already risen when she approached the table. He shook her hand and smiled. "Great to meet you too. I hear you're from our neck of the woods."

"Well, not lately. Chloe says you live in New York now." Liya sat and waved for a waitress. "I'm so glad to be done with traffic today. It was brutal."

"I hear you." Ben sat across from her and examined Dr.

Liya. She was beautiful, like so many Ethiopian women were, with a heart-shaped face and medium brown skin. Her mouth was bow-shaped and quick to smile. "We're in New York now," he continued, "but we both went to high school in Los Angeles. Most of my family is still there."

"Mine too," Chloe said. "Though we're still not really speaking."

"Oh my God, and my family calls me every day." Liya laughed. "My parents were both born here in Addis, so they're happy I'm working here now—and I love it, obviously—but they call every day."

Ben smiled. She had an infectious smile and an easy personality. It didn't surprise Ben at all that Chloe and she had hit it off.

"I tell them," she said, "if you're missing Ethiopia so much, then come for a visit. It's a long way, but they're both retired now." She threw up her hands. "What can I say? They're stubborn."

"Can I ask why they moved to the States?" Ben asked.

"For work. My mother is a doctor and was invited to work in the US. My father was a commercial pilot, so he was able to work anywhere. They moved when my oldest sister was about three years old."

"They must be proud that you're back here, huh?" Ben waited for the waitress to set down a beer for Liya. "Chloe said you're an archaeologist."

Liya nodded. "I am. I grew up hearing all the stories about Ethiopian history and being in love with Indiana Jones, so I don't think anyone was surprised."

Chloe said, "But who wasn't in love with Indiana Jones?"

"Exactly!" Liya laughed. "Don't get jealous, Ben."

"Why?" Ben looked at Chloe, who was sitting on the same

side of the table as he was, and wondered if Liya might have gotten the wrong impression. "Oh, we're not together."

Liya's eyebrows went up. "Oh, I'm sorry. I assumed—"

"We dated in high school," Chloe said. "But my boyfriend is Scottish and much cuter than Ben." Chloe winked at him.

"Thanks." He pretended to scowl. "My..." Fuck, what was he supposed to call Tenzin? "...partner is here in Addis, but she'd already made plans tonight." To play Minecraft with Sadia. "Chloe's boyfriend may end up flying over though, right?"

As in actually flying since Gavin Wallace was a wind vampire like Ben.

"We thought he might, but his business stuff is taking longer than he originally thought," Chloe said. "He does nightclub development, so he's overseeing the final details on a new place his company is opening in Lagos right now."

"I've never been to Lagos," Liya said. "I know it's huge, right? Like three times the size of Addis?"

"Something like that," Chloe said. "I just know Gavin is kind of over it. Right now it's just another place that needs a lot of work. Hopefully we can visit again when everything is done and have a little more fun."

"I can definitely understand that." Liya looked between Chloe and Ben. "But speaking of fun, what are your plans in Ethiopia? What are you going to see?"

"Lalibela for sure," Ben said. "We're flying up there next week."

Liya kissed her fingertips. "You have to. The churches are amazing."

"I've seen the pictures," Chloe said. "I'm really excited to go."

Which was *not* an exaggeration. Chloe had been talking about it for weeks.

"And I'd like to go farther north," Ben said. "But it'll depend on how much time we have."

Liya was nodding. "Gondar is amazing. And I'm sure you'll fly through Bahir Dar, and that has the island monasteries that are so fascinating and beautiful. Lot of mosquitos by Lake Tana though, so I hope you brought bug spray. It's hard to find here; ask me how I know." She grimaced.

"You must know a lot about the north," Ben said. "Being an archaeologist and everything."

"I know quite a bit." Her smile was a little crooked. "To be honest, most of the funded expeditions in Ethiopia are in that area, so it's well known. Of course, most of that funding goes to foreign teams and not local ones."

Ben's eyes went wide. "Really?" Opportunity was sounding an alarm in his head. "That seems backward. What about you? Are you considered foreign or local here?"

"I mean, I'm not strictly Ethiopian; I'm diaspora, but having a doctorate from UCLA definitely helps when it comes to getting funding because a lot of it comes from Europe or America. But I want to bring an Ethiopian perspective to Ethiopian archaeology, you know? It's been dominated by people outside the country for a century." Liya's smile was rueful. "In the current climate, if I wanted to excavate up in the north at one of the traditional sites, I could probably get funding"—she snapped her fingers—"like that."

Chloe asked, "But that's not your area of interest?"

"Nope." She spread her hands. "What can I say? I know people like the flashy stuff like gold artifacts and manuscripts, but I want to go dig around in mud." She laughed. "I'm trying to get funding together for an excavation at an early human site along the Blue Nile, but it's not looking too good."

"Really?" Ben asked. "I'm surprised."

"It's like I said, the flashy stuff gets the attention. Finding out how early humans lived isn't quite as exciting as gold artifacts. But I'll make it!" she said. "It might just take a little longer. I have a grant application in with the cultural preservation agency right now, so I'm hopeful."

Ben raised a glass, ecstatic that he'd found his way in. "Hear, hear. To Liya and to the mud along the Nile."

Chloe joined him. "May you find lots of interesting things and maybe even your very own Indiana Jones partner."

Liya raised her glass. "I will toast to that."

BEN AND CHLOE took a cab back to the compound, only to find an unexpected altercation happening just inside the gate when they arrived.

Daniel Rathmore was pushed up against the stone wall, and Dema had a knife slightly smaller than a machete against his neck. Far from looking angry, the lanky Englishman looked delighted.

"Why didn't you tell me you were working in California?" He turned his head to the sound of the gate opening. "Ben! Good to see you."

Chloe turned and saw the pair. She let out a slight "Eep!" and put a hand over her mouth.

Ben didn't make a move to help Daniel. He had no idea what the Englishman had done, but he probably deserved Dema's knife. "Dan, how's it going?"

"Really great. Fantastic actually. Absolutely thrilled to be working on this project with you. Why didn't you tell me Dema was working for Giovanni?"

Chloe was hitting his shoulder as if he ought to be doing something, probably because of the machete.

Ben ignored the hand hitting him. "You know, it didn't even occur to me that you'd know my sister's nanny."

"Nanny?" Daniel grinned even wider.

"Give me one excuse to kill you," Dema said quietly. "Just one is all I need. You know I will not have a problem getting rid of your body."

"Darling, you were always incredible with children; it's a brilliant idea. I hope she's a little firecracker; that will keep you on your toes."

Chloe tugged his arm. "Ben—"

"I have no idea." He put his arm around Chloe and led her away from the pair. "And it's probably none of our business. If she was really going to kill him, she'd have done it already. You know Dema."

"I mean" —Chloe looked over her shoulder— "I thought I did."

He patted her shoulder. "We all have that one embarrassing relationship we don't want to talk about, okay?"

They walked back to the table under the mango tree where Zain was enjoying wine with Mika.

Zain raised a glass. "Hey, you guys. Did you see that Daniel got here?"

"I did." Ben sat down with a nod. "He's earlier than I expected, but it sounds like he's excited about the project."

"That's good." Zain swirled red wine around his glass. "Ben, you should try this one. You'd like it."

"Thanks." He reached for the wine bottle. "Good meeting tonight with Chloe's new friend. I think I have an idea for an opening there."

Chloe flopped into her seat and stared at Ben. "Are we really not going to talk about Dema trying to murder Daniel?"

Zain shrugged. "I mean, I don't think she'll actually hurt him."

Mika frowned. "What's going on?"

Chloe said, "Daniel Rathmore, Giovanni's friend who's here to help with the project—"

"Earth vampire from England," Ben broke in.

"Liiiiittle bit of a player," Zain muttered.

Chloe gave them both dirty looks. "He's at the front gate, and Dema has a knife against his throat."

Mika's large brown eyes went wide. "And he's an *ally*?"

Ben looked around. "Is Sadia in bed already?"

"She went down an hour ago," Zain said. "Giovanni and Beatrice are with Doug."

"Oh good."

Mika was still clearly alarmed. "What should we do about—?"

"Nothing." Ben and Zain spoke at the same time.

"Dema doesn't pull a knife on people unless they've earned it," Zain said. "I don't know what's going on, but I'm sure they'll sort it out."

"She's pulled a gun on me countless times," Ben said, "and I'm clearly still alive."

"Gunshots won't kill a vampire," Chloe said.

Mika pursed her lips. "Well..."

"They will if it's directly aimed at the base of the neck." Zain glanced at Ben. "Not that we've trained for that or anything."

"Hey, as long as I'm not the one in your sights, I'm not worried." Ben sipped the wine. Zain was right; it was delicious.

No less than a minute later, Dema joined them at the table in silence. Reaching for her ever-present thermos of tea, she poured a large helping into an empty wineglass.

Chloe was the only one brave enough to break the silence. "Is Daniel still alive?"

"Obviously." She sipped her tea. "Mika, I showed him

where he's staying. The second room in the garden house, right?"

Mika nodded.

"Good."

Chloe opened her mouth again, closed it, then reached for the bottle of wine. "Vampires are weird."

Dema nodded but didn't say anything.

Zain asked, "So Gavin's coming by the end of this week, huh?"

"Sadly no. Change of plans." Chloe stared, wide-eyed, at Dema. "If plans change again though, I'll make sure to let all of you know."

"Good." Dema nodded. "I don't like surprises."

17

The meeting with Doug happened the following night just after ten o'clock. Most of the humans were sleeping, but Doug and Zain—being the team drivers—had joined Ben, Tenzin, Beatrice, Giovanni, and Daniel in the compound's lavish library.

The house had once belonged to a French diplomat, and the furnishings showed it. The room was decorated in ostentatious European pieces, and oil paintings hung on the walls. The narrow windows had been converted to be light safe with heavy shutters painted in similar classical themes.

Doug had found the largest computer monitor in the house and had put up a computer-generated diagram of the British embassy on the screen.

"It's a huge compound, as you can see, but we're ignoring pretty much all the public buildings." He motioned to the left side of the diagram. "This is where all the security is run, but I've taken a look and..." He shrugged. "I'm not impressed. They're really depending on reputation here." He nodded at Ben and Tenzin. "For you two, getting in is going to be simple." He gave an overview of the public buildings. "There are artifacts and manuscripts scattered over the entire embassy compound—most notably there are quite a few books and more than a few historic maps in the officers' club here." He pointed to a round building. "It's a traditional *tukul* structure—those are the old-fashioned round houses with the grass roofs—but don't be mistaken, it still has modern security. Cameras mainly."

Ben asked, "Where do the video feeds go?"

"Here." Doug motioned to a building right on the front row that faced the road. "All the security is run through here, and there is an embassy-wide alarm. If the guards see anything suspicious on the video feeds, they're supposed to hit that alarm, which would alert basically everyone living in the compound. It is loud. It is effective. You do not want to be seen."

"But you don't know where all the cameras are?"

"No. That's where your electronic sense and simple observation is going to have to come in."

Ben had been working harder every year on detecting electronic waves and signals. He was nearing perfect accuracy with most regular-frequency electronic equipment.

Tenzin asked, "Who lives in the compound? Are there soldiers?"

"No, but the ambassador and his family do live there, and he does have security at the main house." Doug pointed to a large European-style home near the back of the compound. "In addition to the ambassador's house, there are twelve other residences within the compound, including a couple of the *tukuls* which are still in use for guest housing. There are several kilometers between the front gate and the ambassador's house though. It would take time for more than basic security to reach you if the alarm was tripped."

"Sheesh." Ben leaned forward. "There's like a small city in there."

"Like I said" —Doug gestured to the screen— "it's a huge

place and very spread out. Pool, houses, stables, and playing fields. There's even a golf course and a private medical center."

Giovanni tapped his chin. "But despite that, they mainly depend on perimeter security?"

"Yes, and it's not good." Doug flipped to a series of pictures. "The embassy is set on a hill above the city, and the mountain behind it is covered in forest. There's a gravel path beyond the back wall that local people use to cross the hill between this creek" —he flipped to another picture— "and the road. I don't think it's pertinent to you two" —Doug looked at Ben and Tenzin— "but at night there's a pack of hyenas that hunt all along this trail. That's going to keep most humans away."

Tenzin perked up. "They hunt people?"

Doug grimaced. "Hyenas will take dogs and children if they're hungry, but they're mainly scavengers. If these guys don't get enough garbage from the human population in the forest, they might go after serval cats in the forest. Monkeys. That sort of thing." He flipped to another picture. "The forest at the back of the embassy and then extending beyond the wall is pretty dense. Mainly eucalyptus trees. Some cedar. Now, there are reports of a couple of leopards in that area, but again, I don't think that will be an issue for you two."

Daniel raised his hand. "Can I be part of this break-in? Please?"

Giovanni glanced at Daniel. "Isn't this your embassy?"

Daniel waved a hand. "Listen, we all know the sins of my fathers. You'll get no excuses for England from me. I just really want to see the leopard. And the servals." He tapped a busy foot. "Maybe the monkeys. I like monkeys."

"Go on safari," Ben said. "You're staying put for this. We have to come from the air if we're going in without being spotted, and we don't need extra baggage." Ben nodded. "The trees in back. That's the best entry. We can drop in and no one will see us."

"I agree with Ben." Doug flipped back to the embassy diagram. "If you wait for a nice stormy night with some fog up there on the hills, you'll be well camouflaged from the air. And don't worry about sensors or lasers or anything like that. Security is not that advanced." He raised a finger. "Now, you may have to deal with electronic alarms on the ambassador's house, which is where we believe the private safe is mostly likely to be, but you'll be able to deal with that..." Doug shrugged. "...in whatever way you two normally deal with those things; I don't ask questions."

"And what are you looking for again?" Daniel asked. "Sorry, the information I received before I took off was vague at best."

The lights in the house suddenly switched off.

"Power outage?" Giovanni asked.

"The generator will switch on in a minute," Doug said. "It's pretty common, especially during the rainy season."

Ben turned to Daniel. "We're searching for a fourth-century Aksumite gold crown that we've been told is held in the private safe here in the embassy. Apparently it was acquired on the black market several years ago."

"Naughty, naughty Nigel," Daniel muttered. "Or whatever the current ambassador's name is. Why haven't you turned that one in to the proper authorities, hmm?"

Doug said, "We suspect that most of the European governments keep stashes of Ethiopian antiquities they've received as bribes or taken as spoils during conflict. They turn them over to the Ethiopian antiquities authority whenever they need a good splash of PR or are trying to cover up an embarrassing story."

The lights in the room suddenly switched on again, and Doug set about rebooting the computer, which had blinked off.

"The British aren't even that coy about it," Ben said. "I've seen pictures of the officers' club and the chancery. They have their goods on display."

"But not the really valuable stuff." Doug had the computer on again and turned to a new slide. "That's in the residence." He pointed to a diagram of a large rectangular house with two distinct branches. "Okay, the house is built around two court-yards that extend from the main hall and the formal dining room that's used for parties and that sort of thing. The west side is the residence, and the east side used to be offices, but it was converted to entertaining space after the chancery building was finished. Library, meeting rooms, billiard room, things like that."

Tenzin leaned closer to the screen. "It's only one story?"

"At various points it's actually four, but you're going to focus on the ground floor and the basements, which are where the private treasury is."

Ben crossed his arms over his chest. "And we know for certain—"

Doug cut Ben off. "We don't know anything for certain, but let's just say I am fairly sure that these rooms" —he pointed to two rooms on the east side— "are where you're going to find your safe."

Daniel raised his hand again. "And once you get this crown, you're going to give it back?"

Tenzin pursed her lips. "Eventually. That is the long-term plan, yes."

Daniel scratched his chin and frowned. "So... you're going to do what these blokes have been doing? Trade valuable cultural antiquities for good public relations with the vampire in charge of Addis?"

Tenzin turned to Ben. "He was the only option?"

He reached over and took her hand. "He was the best one, yes."

Tenzin stared at Daniel until the earth vampire began to squirm.

"Fuck, my father was not exaggerating about that stare," he muttered. "I'm just saying..." He cleared his throat. "It's clearly an effective strategy and an excellent plan. Well done, you."

Giovanni smiled. "At the end of all this, Daniel, a mother will have her daughter's crown returned to her, along with her personal devotional book, and we will have safeguarded an incredibly dangerous immortal artifact that is in no way native to this country."

"Good." Daniel's voice was back to chirpy. "Excellent." He glanced at Tenzin. "That all sounds... very good."

BEN AND TENZIN watched the ambassador's house through the trees. They were perched in a stand of eucalyptus, staring at four canines barking at them from the ground.

"Dogs." Ben grimaced. "He didn't think to check for dogs?"

"An ancient and still-effective alarm," Tenzin said. "It's good we came; let's see how they react."

A voice in Amharic called from the back of the ambassador's residence. The dogs didn't listen at first, but there was a sharp whistle, and they retreated.

"See?" Tenzin smiled. "They don't pay attention to the dogs. I suspected as much. The dogs are probably constantly barking at the hyenas beyond the gate."

"And it looks like they're going into a kennel." Ben craned his neck and peered through the misty night. A light rain was falling, and the clouds hovered close to the ground. "So they're not in the house at all."

"I see one perimeter guard," Tenzin said. "And he only walks around once an hour."

"This is going to be very easy," Ben said. "Which makes me think there's something we're not seeing."

"I've checked the roof for wildlife and I don't see any."

"Wildlife?" Ben glanced at her, then scanned the roof. "What would live on the roof?"

"I mean... if we were in Asia, sloths maybe."

"Guard sloths?"

"I'm just saying they're more effective than you might think." She adjusted her position on the cedar branch. "I love the smell here."

"So do I." The rain falling in the grove of eucalyptus and cedar reminded him of nights in San Francisco. "When we're done with this, what do you want to do?"

"Honestly?" She turned to him. "I need some time away from cities." She nodded toward the twinkling lights of Addis in the distance. "New York. Addis. Los Angeles."

"You need quiet." Ben tried to imagine life without Tenzin, even for a short time. "I get that; I do."

They'd spent two years apart, and it had been the longest two years of his life. They'd been back together less than a year, and he was still trying to figure out what he meant to her and what she was to him.

Was he her mate? He only knew vampire mating from Giovanni and Beatrice, who were also married in the Catholic Church. He knew Tenzin would never go for marriage, and he didn't want to ask her.

But as her mate? She'd had a mate before, and he'd died. Was it fair to ask her for that again? Ben knew that Tenzin was possessive of him—that he was *hers*—but he was still trying to wrap human ideas of a relationship around her. He didn't know how else to define what he felt for her.

He loved her. He wanted her to belong to him. In his human life that would mean marriage and commitment, but he didn't know what that meant for a five-thousand-year-old vampire, and he didn't know how to bring it up.

He felt his anger starting to rise.

Tenzin kept her eyes on the dark house. A few windows were glowing on the west side, and she watched them intently for movement.

It wasn't fair. Ben had been human only a few short years ago, and he thought he was doing pretty damn well at adapting to immortality, but if Tenzin thought they could have a partnership—romantic or personal—where she just took off and disappeared for who-knows-how-long and he had to wait and see—

"You could come with me when I go." She turned to him. "If you'd like. I'd like to show you the valley in Tibet where I go to rest."

Ben blinked. "Oh."

"You thought I wanted to go alone." The corner of her mouth turned up. "I could feel you getting angry."

He didn't apologize for it. "You do that sometimes."

"And if I need time alone, I will tell you." She reached for his hand and pressed their palms together. "But I don't need time away from you. I just need time away."

His fingers squeezed hers once, then held them loosely as he and Tenzin watched the house. "I'd love to see Tibet."

She smiled. "Good."

18

Tenzin sipped her third cup of Ethiopian coffee that night. Ben watched her with narrowed eyes. "Are you sure caffeine has no effect on immortal systems?"

They were sitting in a restaurant near a busy intersection. Fruit vendors hawked their wares on the street outside, trying to empty their carts as people sped home from work.

She looked at him and raised her empty cup. "What do you think this coffee is going to do? Keep me awake all day?"

Tenzin still hadn't told Ben she'd been sleeping a little bit. It was one of the secrets she had a hard time admitting because sleeping made her feel vulnerable. It was also one of the reasons she refrained from taking Ben's blood, especially when they were in Saba's territory.

Ben would only think about taking her blood if she took his, and she resisted anything that might make her more vulnerable, especially here. Even the drifting sleep she experienced from the blood she'd already taken was more sleep than she'd had in thousands of years.

"Tenzin?" Ben snapped his fingers in front of her nose. "Come back."

"I don't remember when I stopped sleeping." She met his eyes that saw too much. Perhaps she could bare this part of herself without becoming too vulnerable. "I think I stopped because bad things happened when I slept."

Ben reached for her hand but said nothing.

"When I was young, I could not control it. You understand that." She looked away and set down her empty cup. "But over time I was able to stay awake longer and longer. Eventually I didn't sleep at all, so I learned to meditate to rest my mind."

"And you still meditate."

She nodded. "For hours." That was still true. Most of her days were spent in meditation, the only way her mind could rest since her body did not.

"So that's good." He squeezed her hand. "Maybe in time—when you feel safe—your body will learn how to sleep again."

Was that why? Tenzin blinked. She had not considered that Ben's amnis—that his bond with her—had made her feel... safe.

She leaned toward him and touched his jaw, feeling the strong bone beneath the skin. Her fingers trailed down to the delicate skin covering his neck. "You are beautiful and strong, my Benjamin. But if I never sleep—"

"I'll try not to take it personally." He leaned over and brushed a kiss against her mouth. "I know."

"I am a very old woman, after all." There was a human saying about old dogs and new tricks, but it was actually a very bad saying because old dogs were just as intelligent as puppies and could respond to human training with the proper motivation.

So perhaps... her body could learn to respond to new instincts as well.

Ben smiled and brushed a thumb along Tenzin's cheek. "Chloe's friend is coming."

"I see." Tenzin sat up and looked around the restaurant where they had eaten a small meal.

Well, as small a meal as was possible to get in Ethiopia, which seemed to specialize in filling entire tables with colorful dishes. It was delightful to have so much variety, but she hoped someone was eating the food left over.

The restaurant was a popular one with open-air seating, short tables and chairs, and loud traditional music. The crowd was mostly local, but a large tour group in matching blue shirts filled one corner, and a few other foreigners—*faranji* as the locals called them—filled other tables, sometimes with Ethiopian companions and sometimes on their own.

"I have not seen any other East Asian women in this country," Tenzin said. "All the Chinese businesspeople are male."

"I noticed that." Ben waved at a woman walking down the stairs into the dining room. "I've seen a few Indian women though."

"Yes. I did notice that. This is Chloe's friend?" Tenzin found herself feeling possessive and attracted at the same time. The woman walking toward them was absolutely beautiful. Tenzin scooted slightly closer to Ben as the human approached.

Her cheeks were full, and two dimples showed when she smiled. Her hair curled in spirals around her head, and her eyes reminded Tenzin of the iconic art she'd seen in churches and museums. Dark brown and thickly lashed, the woman's eyes dominated a heart-shaped face decorated by a bowed mouth.

Tenzin spoke in Mandarin. "Are all the women in this country so beautiful?"

The corner of Ben's mouth turned up. "You're asking me?" He lowered his mouth to her ear and whispered, "They are beautiful, so why can't I keep my eyes off you?"

She wasn't able to respond before the gorgeous woman sat.

"Hello." She reached her hand across to shake Tenzin's as

she put her purse on a spare chair. "You must be Tenzin. I'm Liya, and it's *so* nice to meet you."

"It's very nice to meet you as well. Your country is a fascinating place."

"Thank you!" She was still smiling. "Ben and Chloe told me that you're a dealer in Asian art, is that correct? You must travel a great deal."

They had decided that Tenzin being an Asian antiquities dealer was less suspicious than calling her a treasure hunter and admitting she liked all shiny, valuable things from anywhere in the world.

"Yes. Most of my experience is in Asia, though Ben and I currently work in New York." That was all true. New Year's resolutions intact. "And you are an archaeologist, is that correct?"

"It is." Liya eyed a platter of food that passed.

"Are you hungry?" Ben asked. "I can't thank you enough for recommending this place. It's fantastic. We already ate, but if you're hungry—"

"If you don't mind." Liya said, "I'm going to order some shiro. I was supposed to get dinner with a colleague, and then I was delayed, so we had to cancel."

"Please," Tenzin said. "Order food. We will be happy to watch you eat."

Ben covered his laugh with a cough. "Tenzin and I are still trying to get the hang of how Ethiopians manage to eat without making a mess with the injera."

Liya waved a server to the table. "Practice, you know? You'll get the hang of it." The woman ordered in Amharic and asked Ben and Tenzin if they wanted anything else to drink. Ben decided to order a beer, and Tenzin ordered a bottle of the local sparkling water.

"Chloe mentioned that you might have a customer who was

interested in funding my Nile River dig?" Liya said. "I have to admit I'm surprised and a little skeptical, but even if you wanted to pass along a phone number, I'd appreciate it."

"They are very interested," Tenzin said. "And I can say that with certainty because the client is actually me."

Ben and Liya were both silent, which didn't surprise Tenzin. This conversation was not going as she and Ben had rehearsed, but Tenzin'd had a sudden instinct that Dr. Liya Tegegne would respond better to directness.

And she did not appear to be overly charmed by Ben, which was to his disadvantage. He would probably try to flirt with Liya during negotiations, and that wasn't going to work.

Tenzin leaned across the small table. "Let me be very clear: I am opposed to the theft of indigenous art and antiquities that rob a country of its culture even in the name of so-called preservation. I think most of those arguments are poorly thought out and selfishly motivated."

Liya was still blinking. "Okay. Cool. On the same page there."

"But Ben and I have very good reason to believe that a Near Eastern scroll is located in this country and was brought during the Aksumite period. It is not an Ethiopian artifact, and we are trying to find it. It is very important that we do, because others are looking for it too, and they would likely not be as respectful or ethical as we are."

Okay, that might not have been fair to Arosh, but the vampire was really kind of an asshole, and she'd thought so for years.

Liya sat back in her seat. "Okay. Um... Wow. I don't really know what to say."

"What we are proposing is access to information you likely have regarding the location of possible Aksumite sites that have not been well explored. We would use as soft an approach as possible in exploring those sites and would guarantee no removal of any artifacts that are Ethiopian or Aksumite in origin."

Lila held up her hands. "Wait. What? What are you saying? You're telling me—"

"That there is an artifact of Persian origin that multiple parties will be looking for, and we're trying to find it first. That's why we are offering to help. We *will* be exploring sites, but we could look more intelligently and more carefully if you helped us with information."

Liya looked skeptical. Tenzin could hardly blame her.

"And in exchange for this... information," she said, "you'd fund my excavation on the Blue Nile."

"I would be willing to fully fund you for five years no matter the outcome of our search. Not only do I want the information from you about this scroll, but I also admire the work you are trying to do. Early humans had complex lives and communities, and I think it's important for modern humans to understand them."

Ben put his arm around Tenzin and cleared his throat. "I, for one, am often confused by the motivations of early humans. I find some of their choices... baffling."

Liya frowned. "I don't know what to say. I mean... yes, I know some sites that could be Aksumite in origin, but what you're proposing—"

"Is far less invasive than what others might do searching for this item." Tenzin waved her hand. "Which again, I want to emphasize is not Ethiopian. Or Aksumite. Or Sabaean."

The archaeologist huffed out a breath. "Can you tell me anything about it?"

"It was created in Persia sometime in the early second century and was written in an unknown language. At some point—I'm not sure when—it passed into the hands of a

Manichaean sect that specialized in collecting manuscripts and other religious wisdom. It was taken to Kucha, a city in Central Asia along the northern Silk Road, because the Manichaean priests in that city were renowned for their language and translation skills."

"So they were able to translate this unknown language? What was it?"

"They never found out." Tenzin could tell the woman's natural curiosity had taken over. "But prior to World War I, there was a German expedition to Kucha and over five thousand manuscripts including letters were found, one of which speaks of an unusual scroll from the West with unknown writing. They thought it might be an early form of Akkadian, and the best scholars of the time—"

"When was it dated?"

"Eighth century," Ben said. "Though the scroll itself is much older."

Tenzin continued, "They sent it to the Aksumite court because they believed the scholars there would be able to translate it."

"And after that?" Liya was clearly into the story now. "There's no further record of it?"

"Nothing. The last mention we have is from Kucha."

"And we know the scroll was in Kucha for some time before they sent it to Aksum," Ben said. "They must have been really stumped."

"It's possible..." Liya was considering. "I mean, Akkadian was an Eastern Semitic language and Ge'ez is a Southern Semitic language, but it's possible that there were Aksumite scholars at the time who might have had some kind of knowledge of this earlier language that we've lost."

"I'm sure that's what the Manichaeans were counting on," Tenzin said. "The question is: Can you help us?"

Liya had moved from uncertainty to suspicion. "What do you want this scroll for?"

"We believe it belongs in a research library." Ben took over. "There's one in Italy that specializes in Near Eastern manuscripts. We're not locking it away in some private collection or selling it." He handed Liya a card. "I promise. You can check them out. Research the library. It's private but open to scholars from around the world, and their focus is the Ancient Mediterranean, Near East, and Levant."

Liya sat back in her seat, the food the server had brought to the table seemingly forgotten. "I'm going to check this out."

"That's all we're asking."

"And if they're legitimately a research library, then... yes, I will help you. But only because you've said that other people are looking for this."

"We have no interest in taking anything from the country that is part of Ethiopian heritage," Tenzin said. "This is something entirely different, and it needs to be analyzed under very special conditions."

Liya nodded. "I appreciate your honesty." She started eating. "You know, if you'd just tried to bribe me with the dig money, I probably would have reported you."

Tenzin looked at Ben. Was her expression smug? Maybe a little.

The woman looked up. "Do you guys want to order coffee or anything? We still have a lot to talk about, and coffee is usually a good idea."

Tenzin nodded. She was really starting to love this country.

19

Tenzin squirmed like an unruly child. "I do not like wearing a pack on my back. I feel like a donkey."

Ben glanced over his shoulder. "You don't look like one, and it's practical. Stop complaining."

They were sitting on the same perch they'd chosen the night before that overlooked the back of the ambassador's house at the British embassy. They were trying to provoke the dogs, but so far they weren't having any luck.

"I'm starting to feel like it was a bad idea to leave Daniel at home," Ben said. "If anyone could provoke a couple of canines, it would be him."

They wanted the dogs to start barking so the guard would get annoyed with them and lock them in the kennel. So far, the dogs had been reluctant to leave the covered veranda that sheltered them from the rain.

"Are you sure Daniel didn't follow us?" She looked over her shoulder to the woods beyond the embassy walls. "He was very intent on seeing that leopard."

"I hear movement behind the wall, but I have no idea if it's a vampire or hyenas." He shook his head. "This storm is messing with my senses."

"Electrical storms will do that." Tenzin floated up and returned with something clutched in her hand. "Let's see if this helps." She showed him a handful of the small pods off the eucalyptus tree.

"Good thinking."

Tenzin searched for a target and found a handy one on a metal trash can near the rear kitchen entrance. She flew over and aimed a pod at the cans.

Ping!

It wouldn't have been loud enough for a human to hear, but the dogs perked up immediately. Tenzin pitched another one at the cans, and the dogs went crazy.

The two German shepherds flew off the verandah and across the muddy yard, barking their heads off in the direction of the trash cans. They barked until the guard came running and shushed them. He ordered them back to the verandah but didn't lock them up.

Tenzin flew back to their tree. "They're still loose?"

"I think this guard is a little more patient than the last one." He held his hand out. "Let me try."

Barking at trash cans was one thing, but waking up the house was another. Ben aimed the pod at a window that had been the last one in the house to go dark.

Ping!

The dogs lost their heads again, running around and jumping into the flower beds underneath the window, barking at the suspicious noise.

This time the guard railed at them, yelling at them until, cowed, they went back to the verandah. He herded them into the covered kennel, muttering at them and shaking his head. The rifle he carried was slung casually on one shoulder, and though he glanced into the woods, he didn't walk out to examine the trees.

"Excellent." Ben nodded. "Now we wait for the dogs to sleep and the guard to do one more round. Then we go in."

"I found where the electricity cutoff switch is."

Ben had decided that the number of times the power went out in Addis—particularly when it was storming—made a simple power outage the easiest way of breaching the house alarms. He figured at night, when everyone was sleeping, they'd have at least a half an hour before the guard noticed that anything was amiss.

Ben and Tenzin remained in the shelter of the trees, getting progressively more soaked as they waited for the house to go completely quiet. Ben could hear the dogs snoring, all the lights were out in the ambassador's house, and the guard was nodding off near the front entrance when they finally decided to go in.

THEY FLEW DOWN from their perch and shook off the damp as best they could under the verandah. Tenzin flew to the breaker box on the side of the house, and Ben could feel the nearly imperceptible shift in energy when the electricity went completely dead.

Using a set of lockpicks, he quickly opened the french doors leading to the dining room; then he waited for Tenzin to catch up. When she finally appeared, she looked like a cat that had fallen in a lake.

"I hate being wet."

He smiled and tucked a wet chunk of hair behind her ear. "You look adorable though."

"I want a warm bath when we get home. Maybe a steam bath."

"I'll see what I can do." He nodded toward the darkened house. "Can we go steal some stuff now?"

She perked up. "Yes, please."

They split up and went to work, checking each room for hidden safes, doors, or wardrobes. The dining room was a bust, as was the meeting room, library, and one room that looked wholly devoted to maps. There was also a room full of athletic equipment and a salon that held a grand piano and pretty much nothing else.

Ben was starting to fear they'd have to intrude on the residence side, which he had wanted to avoid, when Tenzin hit pay dirt in the billiard room.

There was a tall locked cabinet that seemed like it would be the perfect place to store cue sticks, but why would it be locked? Ben quickly picked the small lock and opened the cabinet to reveal exactly what he'd expected, cue sticks, frames, and various sets of billiard balls.

"Wait." Tenzin moved him to the side and worked a single fingernail into the velvet edge of the frame holding the sticks. "It's too deep for only this. There's something behind it."

"A false bottom?"

"Or back." She couldn't budge the velvet backing. "There has to be a trigger."

Ben searched the rack for anything that looked out of place and found a single bracket where the velvet seams ran around the base of the bracket instead of being smooth. The base was worn in a way that the other brackets weren't. He gently pushed in and was rewarded when the bracket sank into the wall and triggered a soft click.

The front of the cabinet swung open to reveal a simple wooden door, which was also locked, but this time it was a combination.

"Let me." Tenzin nudged Ben to the side and put her ear

next to the lock. While humans needed extra equipment to hear the delicate clicks of an old-fashioned combination lock, vampire ears were better. Within minutes, Tenzin had the lock open and a door leading to a set of stairs finally revealed itself.

"Interesting." He left the door open—God knew if there was a way out from the inside—and he and Tenzin descended the stairs.

The feeling of confinement made his amnis twitch. He was a creature of air now, and the longer he spent in his element, the more confinement uneased him. He wasn't claustrophobic, but he definitely preferred having space.

They reached the bottom of the stairs, and Ben was pleasantly surprised. It didn't smell like a normal basement—there was no earthen smell or dampness. The walls were lined in cedar and the floor was polished stone. It was cold and windowless, but other than that, it felt exactly like the rooms in the main house, even down to the wingback chairs and reading nook in one corner.

Ben turned in a circle. "Where is it? It has to be down here somewhere."

Tenzin walked over to a tapestry hanging on one wall. "Here." She pulled back a corner and Ben saw the vault door.

He held up the tapestry and asked her, "Can you get in?"

She cocked her head, then crouched down to examine the large wheel that blocked the door. "It's really just a combination lock with fancier clothes. I can get in, but it'll take a little longer."

Ben was mentally calculating how much time they'd already spent in the house. They were nearing twenty minutes at least. "Get to it," he said. "This is what we came for."

Tenzin put her ear to the large metal door while Ben held the tapestry up. She fiddled with the lock, turning it right, then left, making mental notes when she hit a catch in the combination.

Ben kept his ear aimed at the stairwell and was shocked when he heard a small tapping coming near the door.

"Shit," he whispered.

"What? I'm almost done."

"Someone's coming."

Tenzin's head popped up. "What? I don't hear... It's a dog."

"A dog?" He shook his head. "The dogs don't go in the house."

The corner of her mouth turned up. "This one does."

The clicking of nails on the stairs was unmistakable. Just as Tenzin unlocked the combination and wheeled the door open, a tiny ball of fluff trotted from the base of the stairs over to them and looked up. The animal's fur was grey with a bright white vee marking his forehead. His ears were floppy grey puffs, and his tail was a pom-pom curled over his back.

"What is that?" Ben asked.

Tenzin laughed a little. "I believe that's a shih tzu. Or a Tibetan lion dog."

"Lion dog?"

The small canine squinted up at them, and a low growl came from his tiny squashed face.

"Yes," Tenzin said. "They were prized by Chinese royalty. Known for their playful personalities and..."

The dog opened its small underbitten mouth and let out a loud string of yaps that threatened to pierce Ben's eardrums.

"Shit!" He reached to pick the dog up before it could make any more noise. He put a hand over the dog's muzzle, but the creature continued to growl and bark.

"Yap yap yap yap!"

"Loyalty," Tenzin said. "They're known for their loyalty."

"How do we make it stop barking?"

"Yap yap yap!"

Ben was certain that lights were being tried all over the residence, and even though they were in the basement, the dog's piercing barks were echoing everywhere.

"Tenzin, do something!"

"They're usually quite sweet." She batted Ben's hands away. "Don't smother the little thing. He's only doing his job."

"You take it then!" Ben held the animal out to Tenzin just as it opened its jaw and snapped Ben's finger, drawing blood. "Oh, you little—"

"Come here." Tenzin lifted the dog up to her face and answered its growl with a curled lip and growl of her own.

The little thing let out a small whine and quieted down. Then Tenzin took something from her pocket and gave it to the dog.

"What is that?"

"A piece of bread." She ruffled the fuzzy head and lifted the collar. "Bowie. Bowie likes bread."

And Tenzin apparently. After her growl and offering of food, the little ball of fluff had settled into the crook of her arm and snuggled down. Every time Ben got too close though, it growled. Just a little.

Ben snuck back out of the basement and waited at the door to hear if any humans were stirring in the house. He heard a few loud snores, then a murmured admonition and the snoring died down. Five full minutes later, he returned to the basement to see Tenzin standing next to the safe door, the dog nestled happily in her arm.

"Enough dogs," he muttered. "Let's see what's in here."

He pulled the door wide and walked inside, lifting the electric lantern he'd brought and swinging it around the room.

"Damn, Nigel." Ben shook his head. "You have been a greedy boy."

The walls of the room were hung with gold-framed paintings and various crosses that looked to be solid gold. At the end of the room in a glass case was a velvet, gold, and pearl crown sitting on a blue velvet rest. There were carved masks and bronze artwork. Ben spotted the carved wooden box on his second pass.

"Here." He set the lantern down and reached for the box. "Look at the carvings. They're typical of Lalibela artwork."

"Lalibela?" Tenzin frowned. "That was the Zagwe capital."

"So maybe it was found there," Ben said. He lifted the hinged lid of the box to reveal a delicate gold, pearl, and diamond diadem. "Oh my God. Here it is."

"Desta's crown," Tenzin said. "It looks just like Lucien's sketch."

The delicate circle of gold was rich with pearls and bright blue stones that sat in a diamond-cushioned setting. The motif was lively, with paper-thin gold leaves circling the diadem. Pearls hung from the bottom of the crown with one giant gem in the center that would hang on the wearer's forehead.

"It's stunning," Tenzin said. "Truly fit for a queen."

"Or the true love of an emperor at least." He nodded toward the other crown. "Any ideas about that one?"

"Later era," Tenzin said. "But still well over two hundred years old. Solid gold and velvet. The stones alone are worth a fortune. I don't think that belongs to the British government, do you?"

"Definitely not." Ben closed the box that held Desta's crown and turned to the crown. "I have an idea." He looked around the room. "One that might gain us some goodwill here in Addis."

Tenzin rubbed Bowie's furry head; the dog was completely under her spell now. "I have a feeling I might know what you're thinking."

"Crowns, crosses, and I see at least one manuscript that

looks like a contemporary of the Garima Gospels." He shook his head. "All of this should be in museums."

Tenzin looked a little crestfallen. "You mean we're returning *all* of it?"

"All of it, Tenzin." He picked up the box. "Except for this one. This is for Saba and Saba alone."

Bowie whined a little when Tenzin stopped petting him.

"I know, Bowie." Tenzin sighed. "I feel exactly the same way."

20

Giovanni watched with wide eyes as Ben and Tenzin unloaded everything they'd managed to stuff in their backpacks, along with the wooden box that Ben carried and the small dog Tenzin hadn't yet returned.

What could she say? Every time she put it down, it started barking.

Giovanni shook his head. "You cannot keep the ambassador's dog, Tenzin."

"You tell her," Ben muttered. "I couldn't get her to leave it there."

"He threatened to wake the house every time I put him down," she said. "What was I supposed to do? Let us get caught because Ben doesn't like the dog?"

"He bit me!"

"You did not make any effort to establish dominance," Tenzin said. "Lion dogs are small but very proud." She didn't understand why it was a hard concept for him. He was certainly not shy about establishing dominance with human or vampire males.

Sadia had followed them in the library, and she was jumping up and down. "Can we keep him? He's so cute!"

"No, Sadia. He belongs to another family." Giovanni unwrapped a particularly beautiful cross with a Star of David worked into the gold. "And you have a dog at home. My God, they had all this in their safe?"

"And more," Ben said. "We couldn't carry half of it. We just took the most valuable pieces from what I could tell."

Sadia was petting Bowie's head. "He's so fluffy!"

Tenzin handed the dog to her. The little lion dog was panting and wagging his tail so furiously Tenzin thought his butt might just fall off. "Take him out to the garden. He probably has to urinate."

"Okay." Sadia bounced out of the library with Bowie in her arms.

Ben pointed at the door. "You're taking it back."

"Tomorrow night." She shrugged. "Let Sadia play with him tonight. I don't think he gets enough attention at that house."

"That dog looks pampered within an inch of its life," Ben said. "Can we talk about these crosses please?"

There were over a dozen crosses that appeared to be solid gold in every configuration imaginable. Lalibela-style, Gondar-style, Coptic-style crosses, and those with Judaic iconography.

Giovanni touched them gently. "These all must have been taken from churches, but I have no idea how to get them back to their rightful places."

"We give them to Hirut," Ben said. "We're flying to Lalibela tomorrow night, right?"

"Yes. Doug and Zain have already left with the Land Cruisers. Mika has arranged other transport for us to the airport."

"Call Hirut tonight," Ben said. "Tell her we'd like a meeting tomorrow before we leave. If we return these crosses to her along with the crown and the manuscripts, she'll know where to send them, right?"

Giovanni nodded. "I would think so."

Tenzin said, "And we'll also garner more than a little goodwill."

"Yes, I imagine you're right." Giovanni looked at Ben. "And no one at the embassy is going to raise the alarm?"

"What are they supposed to say?" Ben pointed to the crown. "Oh, by the way, someone stole a bunch of antiquities that were looted a hundred years ago from our secret vault of stuff we're holding on to. Can the police investigate that for us or no?" Ben shook his head. "They didn't want anyone to know they had this stuff; they're not going to report it."

Daniel barreled into the library with a muddy face and clothes that definitely needed to visit a washtub. "Glorious. Absolutely glorious forest. The leopards were stunning." He pointed over his shoulder. "Is that the ambassador's dog Sadia has in the garden?"

"I told you he followed us," Tenzin said. "Yes. I'll return him tomorrow night. I'm a thief, not a dognapper."

"You're a dog *borrower*," Ben said. "Totally different."

"It is different because I'm giving the little animal an adventure. He's descended from wolves, you know." Not that you'd be able to tell from the soft fur, silly underbite, and elaborate tail. "If we give these to Hirut, she's going to know we have ulterior motives, but she might not care."

"Nevertheless," Giovanni said. "We told her that nothing of Ethiopian origin would leave Ethiopia without Saba's permission, and we're holding to that."

~

THE FOLLOWING NIGHT, as Giovanni and Beatrice prepared to move the household north to Lalibela, Ben and Tenzin met Hirut at the top of Entoto Hill, which overlooked Addis. Hirut strolled through the restored grounds of Emperor Menelik's palaces and throne rooms, which were open to the public during the day and used for the occasional state banquet in the evening.

"It's beautiful to see these things restored," she said. "I remember when they were built."

The cobblestone path was lined by towering cedars and flowering jacaranda trees. The gardens were a riot of color, and the fountains in the distance trickled a playful melody in the night. The stars were more visible on the hills above the city, and the night sky was a deep blue washed with drifting clouds.

"The complex is beautiful," Tenzin said, looking around the colorful buildings and lush gardens. "And very human."

"Thank you." Hirut gestured toward the banquet hall, which was painted with bright colors in front. "Saba approved of the buildings the human emperor built. They were royal without being ostentatious like European structures."

"Very natural. Their balance and proportions remind me of Penglai."

Hirut smiled. "I accept that as a compliment, though Saba's empire is, of course, far older than the Eastern court."

Tenzin held her tongue. Hirut was proud, as most vampires were, and doubly so being a direct descendant of Saba's line.

"Hirut, thank you for meeting us," Ben said. "We have enjoyed our time in Addis. The city and the people are very welcoming. It's a fascinating place, and I look forward to returning. I believe Giovanni told you we'll be heading north tonight."

The vampire nodded. "The churches of Lalibela are truly a grand sight and very holy places, a destination of human and immortal pilgrimage. I hope your family enjoys their time there." Her eyes shifted to the large duffel bag Ben had with him. "Is there something else you wish to share, son of Zhang?"

Ben paused and reached into the bag where they'd stored the treasures they'd taken from the British vault. "In the course of investigations for our client, we happened to enter a vault where there were many treasures from Ethiopia. This was... not a museum or any place that should have these items. Do you understand?"

What Ben was really saying was: we stole these, but it was for a good cause.

Hirut was listening. "Much of our cultural heritage was acquired by others in less than ethical ways. If you have happened to come across heritage items that you believe are the rightful property of the Ethiopian people, I am happy to accept them on their behalf."

What Hirut was really saying was: if you're stealing other people's stuff but giving us our treasure back, I'm not going to ask any questions.

"The most precious item we found was this." Ben carefully unwrapped the gold and velvet crown.

Tenzin said, "I dated it to the seventeenth century, but you may be able to identify it more precisely."

Hirut took the crown in both hands with a soft look on her face. "I remember the empress who wore this crown, a humble and devoted queen. Thank you for returning it. I will see that it goes back to the correct institution."

"Likewise, we found a collection of crosses that must have been looted from churches," Ben said. "Along with a number of scriptures in Ge'ez."

Hirut wasn't an easy vampire to read, but Tenzin knew the woman was surprised and delighted. "You said you were on a mission of restoration, and I confess, I doubted your intentions. I would like to apologize for my cynicism."

Tenzin gave her a slight bow. "It is cynicism born from bitter experience, daughter of Saba. I understand, as I understand duty."

"Do you?" Hirut met Tenzin's gaze, and the piercing look she directed toward Ben, then back to Tenzin, told her everything she needed to know.

Hirut knew what Saba had done to Benjamin. She knew about Johari and the Night's Reckoning. But like Lucien in California, Hirut was a servant of her sire. She would not cross Saba.

"I heard you have a new sister," Tenzin said. "From Zanzibar."

Ben turned to face them but didn't say a word.

"My mother has cured many," Hirut said. "I admit it has created... a complex family situation."

Because there were vampires who had taken Saba's cure, and then there were Saba's true children who had taken her own blood and shared her amnis. The cure was made from Saba's blood, but it didn't carry Saba's amnis the way that a naturally sired child would. In effect, Saba had two families now, an army of vampires loyal from her cure, and her true children.

Immortals sired directly from Saba's blood would have greater status and fulfill greater roles in her clan. Vampires like Johari, on the other hand, were more disposable. It was a recipe for rivalry and conflict.

"Your sister from Zanzibar..." Tenzin never let her gaze waver from Hirut's. "I understand she was injured when she was in Asia."

"She suffered to send a message to my mother," Hirut said. "That message was received."

"There are many kinds of thieves," Tenzin said. "And many kinds of treasure."

"I cannot disagree with you, daughter of Zhang. But know that my mother values all kinds of treasure, and gold is... not high on the list."

"Tenzin, why don't we finish giving these items to Hirut?" He pasted on a smile, but it was fake. Hirut probably couldn't tell. "We still have a lot to take care of tonight, and I'm sure she's busy too." He passed her the black duffel bag. "All the items are packed as carefully as we could manage. The manuscripts, in particular, should not stay in the paper sleeves for too long. I'm sure you have librarians or archivists who specialize in all that."

"We do." Hirut took the bag and held the gold crown in her other hand. "My thanks on behalf of the people of Ethiopia. You have done us a service tonight. These items will find their rightful place, I assure you."

Tenzin bowed more deeply. "We were happy to perform a service for our host. I pray it will not be forgotten."

"I promise you it won't."

THEY WERE PACKING the last of their backpacks when Mika tapped on their doors. "Ben? There's a Dr. Liya Tegegne here to see you?"

Tenzin saw Ben fist pump. He actually pumped his fist up and down several times.

"Yes!"

"Mika only said she was here," Tenzin said. "Not that she was here to help. Don't count your ducks in a row."

Ben frowned. "What?"

"Don't count your ducks in a row." She waved a hand. "You know, do not count on things that have not happened yet."

"Chickens before they hatch." Ben smiled. "Don't count your chickens before they hatch."

"Oh, that makes much more sense." Tenzin set down her backpack. "I told Sadia she was mistaken, but she told me she was very sure it was ducks."

Ben put a hand on the small of her back and nudged her toward the door. "Okay, let's go see what Liya has to say."

"I admit," she said, "if she can help us, I will be relieved. The search area is massive."

"I know."

Liya was sitting under the mango tree, sharing a glass of wine with Mika. When she saw Ben and Tenzin, the archaeologist broke into a huge smile. "Why weren't we meeting at your compound all along? This place is beautiful!"

"Thanks." Ben looked at Tenzin. "We're actually heading to Lalibela tonight, so we were curious—?"

"Tonight?" Liya shook her head. "Rich people. You must have a private plane or something."

"Something like that," Tenzin said. "Have you thought any more about my offer?"

"I have, and I checked out the library you mentioned. It wasn't easy to find outside sources, but I talked to the librarian in Puglia, along with a couple of friends of mine at UCLA, and it sounds like it's all legitimate." She reached into her bag and took out a manila folder. "Even with all the special circumstances, I still feel strange handing these over to you." She pressed the envelope to her chest. "You have to promise me that you'll be careful."

"We will use as light a touch as you have ever seen," Ben said. "The team we have with us is second to none. I promise."

She still looked doubtful, but she handed the folder over. "I've listed nine sites on there, but I believe the top four are the most likely locations based on the criteria you described to me. They're all former treasuries from the Aksumite dynasty. Two of them are active church or monastery sites, so please respect the wishes of the priests in those places. If they tell you you cannot dig, you must promise to listen to them. They have their reasons."

Ben flipped through the folder, and Tenzin said, "We understand."

She understood, but she promised nothing.

"Okay." Liya took a deep breath. "Okay, I'm trusting you." She nodded at Tenzin. "And I'm expecting you to follow through too; I really need that funding for the Nile dig."

"And you will have it." Tenzin held out her hand. "I'm looking forward to working with you, Doctor."

21

B en and Tenzin flew out of Addis near midnight, when the traffic in the streets had finally died down, working people had returned to their beds for the night, and the only activity was the street dogs trotting down the avenues and the clubs in the Bole district still pumping music into the air.

As they rose over the city, Ben surveyed the fascinating place. It was a place of diplomacy, commerce, and all the strange ways in which they overlapped. It was a place of religious devotion where churches and mosques were often only divided by a road or an alleyway. It was a young city but a growing one, bristling with concrete towers that rose higher every year.

Tenzin glanced down. "I will not miss that city."

"You don't miss any city, Tiny."

She tucked herself under his arm in a position she often took when they flew together. "I know. I am craving quiet."

They headed north to Lalibela, a small town in the mountains of the Amhara region with a population of less than twenty thousand people. Lalibela had been a previous capital of the empire during the Zagwe dynasty, which had followed the

Aksumites, and it was known as a place of pilgrimage because of the eleven monolithic churches carved from rock.

Ben had only seen pictures of the place, but he knew the churches were spectacular. Also spectacular? Its location as a launching area for their explorations in the north. Lalibela was within three hundred miles of most of the sites they planned to explore, and all the major ones, which meant they could get there easily within a night. They'd have to camp out to give themselves time to search, but according to Daniel, there were plentiful caves and natural light safes in the region.

They flew directly north, following the path of a river they could see from the sky, climbing higher and higher as they followed the valley. They flew over sleeping villages and small towns where only a few lights were burning. The air lost the scent of car exhaust, trash, and humanity. Clear, crisp breezes twisted around them, welcoming them to clear, cold skies.

They took shelter for an hour in a cave high on a forested peak when a sudden storm swept through the valley. Ben spread a camping roll along the stone floor and a blanket from his backpack. Waiting at the mouth of the cave, Tenzin stared into the curtain of rain.

"There is a wildness here that reminds me of Tibet."

Ben patted the seat next to him, and Tenzin joined him on the cushioned floor.

"Tibet?"

"Even though people have lived in those mountains for thousands of years, the hills have not changed. The people change themselves to the environment, not the other way round."

"That's a beautiful thought." He rested his chin on the top of her head. "Tell me about Tibet."

"There is a valley, narrower than this one, and the mountains are very steep. There are wild sheep on the ridges, and people climb very narrow paths to hang flags along the top so they will flap in the wind. They believe that every time the wind moves the mantras written on them, a prayer is offered up."

"The rainbow flags you see in pictures?"

"Yes." She smiled a little. "They are very colorful. And there is a cave high on the cliff there where the local people give me offerings."

"A cave with offerings?"

"More like a shrine, I suppose."

Ben blinked. "They think you're a god?"

She shrugged. "Or some kind of holy person. I was there for hundreds of years and I didn't age, so I imagine it makes sense to them."

Ben murmured. "They literally treat you as a goddess."

"Yes."

"This explains so much." He squeezed her shoulder. "So much."

"And in the valley below the cliffs there is a river. It's very cold, and on the banks there are birch groves. I love to fly over them. The leaves are beautiful when the wind moves."

Ben frowned. "I think I remember something like that. Maybe you've told me that before."

"Perhaps." She rested her head on his shoulder. "I can rest there, my Benjamin."

"Good. I want to see the place that gives you so much peace."

"You will."

They watched the rain pour over the eucalyptus trees outside the mouth of the cave, and the fresh, astringent scent filled the air around them.

"I love that smell," Ben said. "It reminds me of flying along the coast in California."

Tenzin turned to him and captured his mouth with hers. "I want to show you everything." She kissed along his jaw. "When I see things with you, it's like they are new again."

Ben slid his arm around the small of her back and lowered her onto the blanket. He slowly kissed from her forehead, down her temple, and along the rise of her cheekbone. He nudged her chin up and peppered her neck with soft kisses, resisting the compulsion to sink his teeth into her neck.

His fangs ached in his jaw, but he focused his entire energy on Tenzin. He listened to her breath and the gentle cues when she experienced pleasure. She was a quiet lover, and he'd had to become an expert in reading the subtle signs she gave him. It was another language he hadn't spoken before he loved her.

The sudden exhale when he kissed the side of her breast. The shiver in her thigh when he scraped his teeth along the inside of her knee. The way her body twisted under him when she approached climax and the satisfied sigh when he entered her.

Her skin was damp from the mist and his kisses. Ben lay over her, their bodies locked together, and he pressed his cheek to hers.

"I love you," he murmured. The enormity of his emotion nearly overwhelmed him. What he felt for her was so much bigger than anything he'd felt before. He could feel his amnis kissing her body, whispering in her blood. His body felt like it could explode, not with pleasure but with the pain of feeling so damn much.

"I love you," he said again. He braced his arms up and rocked their bodies slowly in the darkness. "I want you to be my mate."

The grey of her eyes seemed to darken and change. "Ben—"

"Just think about it." It was the only thing that seemed to capture the enormity of his feelings. He needed some tie to her, something permanent. He wanted to claim her in a fundamental way. "I love you."

He lowered his mouth to hers and stole her breath before she could speak again. Then he reached down and hitched her knee up, going deeper as they made love.

There it was, the language her body used to speak to him. The way her eyes grew darker and her skin prickled beneath his fingers. The subtle vibration of her blood and the fangs she bared when pleasure overtook her.

Tenzin came with a small cry and an arched back. He held her in her pleasure, watching her face as she lost control. For a few seconds, she let go and it was glorious.

Then her eyes became fierce and she locked her legs around his hips, driving him deeper as she wrung the climax from his body.

Ben groaned his release, bracing himself over her so that he didn't collapse, but Tenzin pulled him down until his chest was nearly crushing her. She wrapped her arms around his shoulders and held him.

"Stay," she said. "You're not going to break me."

No, but she might break him. Ben buried his face in her neck and inhaled her scent. He ached for her blood. He wanted it so much his mouth opened without thought and his fangs scraped along her skin.

"No." She pinched his neck. "Not tonight."

He quickly closed his mouth. "Sorry."

"I understand," she said. "I want it too. But there are things... We should talk about what it means."

"I know what it means." Ben rolled off her and felt the cold stone of the cave against his back. "I was raised by a mated vampire pair, Tenzin. I know what it means."

"You know, but you cannot know truly until you have experienced it, Benjamin."

A bitter taste came to his mouth, and he spoke without thinking. "Like you and Stephen?"

Tenzin said nothing, but she slowly stood and walked to the back of the cave where her backpack was tucked in a corner.

Shit. He was an ass. "Tenzin—"

"I don't want to talk about Stephen." She rubbed a small towel over her body and cleaned up before she clothed herself in a tunic and leggings again. "The rain has let up. We should go so we're not caught before dawn."

"I'm sorry."

Her eyes were blank. "Don't be sorry. We have to talk about it. I just don't want to talk tonight."

She made mating sound like some kind of chore or task, not the romantic bond he'd always imagined it to be.

Ben caught her hand as she walked past. "Remember, I'm still a little impulsive and I say shit I don't mean to because of it. But I love you."

She cupped his cheek in her hand and rubbed her thumb across his lips. *"Baina min khar."*

"Are you ever going to tell me what that means?"

She shrugged. "It doesn't really translate into English."

THEY LEFT the river valley and flew northeast, cutting across wider valleys and high plains. They were nearing Lalibela, crossing a plain between two rivers when Tenzin stopped.

Ben turned and flew back. "What is it?"

She frowned. "There's something strange."

He turned and sent his senses out. "I don't feel anything."

"Wait for a minute." Her gaze was fixed on the dark horizon. "They are coming."

He saw it seconds after, a dark whirlwind in the distance, sweeping across the plain and twisting high in the clouds.

"Ziri." Tenzin narrowed her eyes. "He likes to make a show."

"Tenzin, there're more." He rose in the sky and watched through the clouds. The stars were obscured over a far greater area than just a single whirlwind. It was as if a cloud was gathering as a wall across the high plain. "Holy shit."

Tenzin flew higher, joining him in the clouds. She made a face. "It's Inaya. Ziri's little girlfriend also likes to make an entrance."

"Where are they going?" He asked. "And who do you think—"

"Saba would have asked Ziri to travel with her to be faster," Tenzin said. "Remember, she's an earth vampire. She's just as slow as Giovanni and Beatrice without flight."

"And why would Inaya—? Oh. Arosh."

"Yes, he'll need an escort too, though I'm surprised he didn't simply recruit one of his children since all of them are sired to wind." Tenzin watched the wall of wind and dust move across the valley. "Saba must have called in a favor, because Inaya is no one's errand girl. They must be paying her well or promising something in return for her cooperation."

"They're headed north too." Ben saw them sweep across from the west and head in the same direction Ben and Tenzin were going; only they were heading there much faster. "Do you think Hirut told them who we were talking to in Addis?"

"I have no way of knowing," Tenzin said. "It's possible Liya could have talked to Hirut and she would have no idea. Hirut could have wiped her memory. She could have sent someone to spy at the university." Tenzin looked at him. "I told you, this is her territory. Every vampire holds allegiance to Saba."

Ben's heart began to sink. After their success in Addis, after breaking into the embassy, finding Desta's crown, and narrowing the search area in the north, Ben had actually felt like this long-shot quest wasn't quite as improbable as he'd thought.

Tenzin's words poked a hole in his hope balloon.

"Come on," Tenzin said. "Let's keep going. Seeing them like this? When you think about it, it's good news."

"Oh?"

"Yes." She smiled at him. "That means my father was wrong, at least in part. Arosh doesn't have the bone scroll. He and Saba are looking for it too."

22

The compound in Lalibela was situated on the top of a hill that overlooked the old town and the steep valleys below. Everything in Lalibela seemed to be built on an angle. The roads wound around steep slopes, and fresh vegetation, newly sprung from the season's rain, clung to the mountains like the stubborn goats that grazed on it.

Human residents walked up and down the narrow roads, dodging bright blue tuk-tuks that beeped as they ferried residents through the mountainous village and over bumpy cobblestones.

But the sky was brilliantly clear and the stars shone brightly when Ben and Tenzin finally landed on the dark road that led to the compound. Ben raised his fist and pounded on the metal door, which opened with a great, rasping groan.

Dema was waiting for them. "You could have just flown in."

"And risk your machete for surprising you?" Ben shook his head as Tenzin ducked under his arm and into the compound. "No, thank you. Is there water?"

"Plenty." Dema nodded to the stone house where Tenzin was already headed. "Come on inside. You'll like this place."

Like everything else in Lalibela, the house was built up, a three-storied structure built of dressed-stone blocks, angular in form and beauty. Balconies stretched across the second floor, and the house wrapped around an inner courtyard tiled in red with a trickling fountain in the center.

"This place used to belong to some politician in Addis, but he was arrested for corruption," Dema said. "Now it belongs to Hirut."

"Saba's daughter owns this house?" Ben asked.

Dema shrugged. "Seems like every vampire we meet in this place is Saba's relative or in her line. It's impossible to avoid the connection."

"Yeah, I'm getting that."

"There are plenty of light-safe rooms on the second floor and even one on the third. There's also a new basement dug into the bedrock. It's pretty cool."

"Sounds like it." Ben couldn't muster up any excitement though.

Ever since they'd seen the dust storm south of Lalibela, he'd felt a sense of dread settle over him. Now that they had all the leverage they could find, Desta's crown and her devotional, the enormity of what they were attempting was beginning to weigh on him.

A scroll that purported to show vampires the secret of controlling every single element at once. He couldn't even fathom it. He'd seen the havoc one single ancient could create if they lost their temper. Arosh, the fire vampire purportedly searching for the bone scroll, had leveled cities and wiped out civilizations according to his uncle.

There was no way on earth that vampire needed to be able to control the wind, the earth, and water too.

Why would she want him to? The whispering voice stopped Ben in his tracks. Saba was the biggest, baddest vampire in charge. Why would she want Arosh to find a scroll that could make him more powerful than she was?

He doesn't have it yet.

Tangled thoughts crowded his mind as he entered the house. He was immediately greeted by Zain, who handed him a glass of water and a bottle of blood-wine.

"Figured you'd be parched by the time you got here." He slapped Ben on the shoulder. "It's a lot dryer here than in Addis."

"I can feel it." His skin felt tight and his throat burned. "Tenzin?"

"Already exploring your digs on the second floor." Zain nodded toward the stairs. "The rest of the humans and vampires are settling in. Dema and I just waited up for you two. Figured you wouldn't want to land in an empty house."

"Appreciate it." He lifted the bottle of blood-wine. "I'll take this up. You two get some rest."

Zain yawned. "If the churches don't wake us up. The priests start praying early here."

And broadcast it on loudspeakers through the town. Ben had discovered that little trivia fact in Addis. Luckily, vampire sleep wasn't disturbed by much, so the subtle sounds of early morning chants had been his brief but peaceful companion every time he drifted to sleep for the past week.

Ben walked up the stairs, feeling the comfortable hum of amnis from his aunt and uncle below his feet. Dema was speaking softly, heading toward the wing of the house where Sadia must be resting, and Ben felt Daniel's vibrant energy coming from upstairs.

He found the man on the second floor, sitting on the ground and looking out over a narrow valley.

"This is beautiful," Daniel said. "Places like this? They're so beautiful."

"All the wild?" Ben looked out over the dark valley, and it felt untamed to him. The wind whipped around the rocks and licked over the rivers in the distance, bringing the scent of green growing things, dust, and humanity.

"It's not the wild." Daniel shook his head. "It's the harmony." He put both his hands down, placing them on the raw stone that made the house. "People have lived here for so many centuries. They carved holy places into these rocks, used the rock to build shelter and make roads. It's all connected, you see?"

Ben couldn't see, but then, he wasn't an earth vampire. "I guess it's a little like the Native people in the southwest, right? They made their homes out of mud brick and rock, right? That's why Santa Fe is so unique."

"It's a little bit like that, but there's something here that's so deeply..." Daniel sighed with a smile on his face. "...loved. The earth here is loved deeply. It's an extraordinary feeling."

Ben smiled, and for the first time, he really saw Carwyn in Daniel. The earth vampire had helped raise him and had one of the biggest hearts Ben had ever known. But Daniel, on first impression, came across as whimsical and flighty.

"I'm glad you're with us." Ben patted his shoulder. "You clearly love people, and you love the earth. That means you'll take care of both."

A shadow crossed Daniel's eyes. "I haven't always taken care of people," he said. "Not the way I should have."

Ben looked at him and remembered Dema's knife against his neck.

Dema doesn't pull a knife on people unless they've earned it...

"So change." Ben leaned against a stone pillar and looked at the man. "Be a better person. A new person if you need to. God knows I never wanted this life, but I'm managing."

Daniel turned to him. "You've taken to it well."

"That's what you do when there are people in your life who love you," Ben said. "You manage, you adapt, even if it's not what you planned."

"You're a good vampire, Ben Vecchio." Daniel smiled. "Quite an excellent one, in fact."

"If I am, it's because of Beatrice and Giovanni."

"And Tenzin."

Ben smiled. "Always Tenzin."

He could feel her in the distance, floating in the air and rolling with the breezes that licked up from the valley floor. "I need to go," he said. "Don't get careless." He nodded at the brightening horizon. "We're going to need you soon."

Daniel grinned. "So are you going to carry me, or will it be the little one?"

"Uh..." Ben laughed a little. "You don't want her to carry you," he said. "Trust me. She will bitch about how much you weigh the entire flight." He walked up the stairs, letting her amnis pull him.

Ben could see her in the distance, just as he'd pictured, floating in the night wind and staring up at the stars overhead. He joined her, drifting toward her in the darkness, knowing she could feel his approach.

She reached out and tangled her fingers with his. "The stars."

"The quiet."

Tenzin let out a long breath and closed her eyes. "I love this place."

It seemed that everyone did. "Is it the elevation?"

"Yes. And the wind. The air currents. The stars. The silence. The air smells like pepper trees. Did you catch it?"

"I do now that you mention it."

"This is peaceful."

"I'm glad." He let his body float toward her, turning his head when he got close.

She turned her deep grey eyes to him. "Hello, *min khar*."

"Hello. Did you find our room already?"

"Yes, it's light safe and has a very nice bed."

He winced a little. "So it's as stiff as a wooden board."

"Like I said, it's very nice."

Tenzin's love of very firm mattresses always amazed him. It wasn't that he couldn't sleep on hard mattresses. He was a vampire; he could sleep on rock if that's where he landed. But Tenzin didn't sleep. She actually chose to spend her hours of waking meditation on surfaces that could be used as a building foundation.

He twisted a lock of her hair around his finger. "Are we starting tomorrow night?"

"No." She pursed her lips. "I promised Chloe and Sadia we would spend our first night here. We'll start searching the following night."

"Okay." It wasn't a bad idea; it was just that Ben was feeling the pressure. Arosh, Saba, and their cadre weren't taking time off to socialize and see the sites. "Do you think if Arosh finds the bone scroll we'll get any warning, or will we just get wiped off the planet in a wave of elemental power?"

She turned her head and brushed a kiss across his lips. "So doubtful, Benjamin. The elders of Alitea are just as fallible as the elders of Penglai. Trust me; they only act all-knowing to keep young ones in awe."

"Young ones like me?"

"Like you. And Beatrice and Giovanni." She patted his cheek. "Trust me, after you pass your first thousand years, your perspective on authority really changes."

Ben bit his lip to keep from smiling. "I guess I'll have to take your word on that."

"You should."

~

THE FOLLOWING NIGHT, they were regaled by tales of the fascinating city, told by Sadia and, to a lesser degree, Zain. Ben was surprised his little sister was so intrigued by the place. But then, she wasn't exactly an ordinary six-year-old.

"And there were kids—like my age, Ben—and they were walking all by themselves. And some of the boys have their own carts." She leaned closer, shoving what looked like a chicken nugget in her mouth. "And they have donkeys. Donkeys that pull the carts! And they stand on the back and the donkey goes like this." She hopped down and pantomimed a trotting donkey. "And the boys are just standing on the back of the carts like this." She mimicked holding reins. At least that's what he was imagining. "And so they have, like, their own cars practically."

"But they're donkeys with carts," he said. "Not engines."

"Ben." Sadia rolled her eyes and got back in her seat. "Donkeys are much better than cars. Donkeys are smart. And they carry stuff, and Dema today said that all the donkeys wandering around the town? They all know how to get back to their houses, all on their own."

Ben took a long drink of water. "Clearly I have not given donkeys enough consideration."

"They're like, the best things," Sadia said. "Way better than cars."

"You already sound like your father," Tenzin muttered.

Giovanni was well known for appreciating a solid equine mount instead of modern vehicles. He was a fan of original horsepower, not the technological variety.

"And Ben." She tugged on his shirt. "There's a whole church with secret rooms."

"I've heard about that." Ben had heard that some of the churches only allowed women in parts of the church and that the holy of holies in each church, where they kept a replica of the Ark of the Covenant, was only accessed by the head priests. "But you still got to see a lot."

"Yes. And there was an angel church—that was my favorite —because it was really high up and I thought, Yeah! Because it's the church for the angels and they can fly."

He nodded and drank his blood-wine. "That's good thinking."

"Ben, do you think angels were really just wind vampires like you and Tenzin?"

Ben nearly spit out his blood-wine. "What? No."

"Yes," Tenzin said. "That's the most probable explanation."

"Tenzin, angels appear in Christianity, Judaism, Islam, and multiple other religions. Can we not discount the spiritual beliefs of millions because—"

"'Cause I was thinking if people back a long, long time ago," Sadia continued. "If they didn't know what wind vampires were, they could think they were, like, creatures sent by God. Like angels."

Tenzin nodded. "That's entirely plausible."

Great. Giovanni and Beatrice were going to blame him when Sadia gleefully told her very Catholic great-grandmother that angels were really just wind vampires.

"Hey, Sadia." Ben could only think about one thing that would distract her from the *angels were vampires* train she'd been caught on. "Why don't you tell me more about the donkey carts?"

23

"I can carry him," Tenzin insisted.

"Tiny, you don't want to carry him. You hate carrying people around."

She shrugged. "Fine. If you insist, you carry the earth vampire."

If he insisted. Ben barely controlled his eye roll. He shifted the backpack on his shoulders and held his arms out to Daniel. "The night's not getting any younger," he said. "We better go."

Daniel stepped up to Ben and held out his arms. "Which way do you want me to face? Are we hugging it out?"

Ben smothered the laugh. "Please don't make me stare at you for two hours, Dan."

"Fine." The man sighed and turned his back to Ben, who put his arms around the man's chest and pulled him tight. "I do feel very secure." He patted Ben's arms. "Thank you, Ben."

He turned to Tenzin. "Are you sure we need an earth vampire?"

"How much digging do you want to do?"

"Fine." Ben took to the sky, barely feeling the weight of the man in front of him. He did what Tenzin suggested and created a bubble of air around them, cutting down the drag from Daniel's gangly frame and their heavy packs.

"We're going north, right?" Daniel yelled.

"You don't have to yell," Ben said. "You don't feel the wind, do you?"

"Oh." Daniel turned a little. "No, I don't. That's very odd."

"Trust me, you're going to appreciate that when we get to Hawulti and your teeth aren't filled with bugs."

"All these insights into wind-vampire transportation," Daniel said. "Fascinating."

They flew north-northeast for about two hours, Tenzin leading the way. She began to descend as they crossed over a round, green-blue lake that looked like an old volcanic crater. The land rose and fell beneath them, a series of hills and valleys marked by small towns and isolated electric lights.

Ben finally saw where Tenzin was heading when she circled around, approaching the hill from the north. Sitting on top of a hill was an island of forest among cultivated land with a round church in the center.

"I've read about these!" Daniel said. "The church forests of Ethiopia. They keep the land around the church wild as a representation of Eden."

"Really?" That was cool. "I don't think the site is actually in the church, but it makes a sheltered place to land."

"Oh right. That makes sense."

Daniel had been a relatively easy passenger considering he really was all arms and legs. He hadn't wriggled or shifted too much in Ben's arms.

Ben followed Tenzin as she descended to a dark corner of the forest, well away from any electric lights. If there was any wildlife or human life awake, Ben couldn't sense it. There was only the wind, the trees, and the stretch of rocky plain that stretched beyond the trees.

They landed in the forest, and Ben could immediately feel the sense of calm the church fathers no doubt wanted to evoke. The night birds had fallen silent at their approach, but insects sang and the wind soughed through the branches overhead.

The forest floor was soft and damp from a recent shower, verdant with new and growing things; tiny pale flowers were popping up along the base of the trees. Small saplings grew in clearings, and a stacked rock wall surrounded everything.

He heard scattering footsteps in the distance and knew small creatures were running from the scent of large predators.

"This is magical." Daniel wandered through the dense woodland, so different from the surrounding landscape. "Imagine, the hills were once covered in this kind of forest."

Ben looked around. "Beautiful."

"But over time..."

Tenzin kicked at a pile of sheep droppings. "People graze animals. They have to eat."

The more people, the less wild. That's what Ben was learning the longer he lived. "At least this piece has been preserved," he said. "Tenzin, where did Liya indicate the possible site was?"

Tenzin was already looking at the map. "This way." She pointed past the wall. "This is one of the active sites she mentioned, so let's take care not to wake up any priests."

"Sounds like a plan to me." Daniel followed Tenzin, hopping over the stone wall and leaving the dark safety of the forest. "And let's not tell my father we're digging for treasure on holy ground, shall we?"

"It won't be the first time," Ben muttered.

Daniel shot him a dirty look.

"What?" Ben looked around at the terrain as they left the shelter of the church forest.

There were no houses nearby, and only the hint of cultivated land that started on the terraced hillsides. Still, his senses were on alert.

"Are you getting any old vampire signatures?" Daniel asked Tenzin.

"Nothing." She shook her head. "None of our kind have been here in a long time."

"I'm sensing the same thing," Daniel said. "Lots of human activity, but no immortal."

"That's good." Ben watched Daniel. "Are you getting anything from the ground yet?"

"Not yet." He looked at them, then looked at the ground. "Just to warn you, I need to get significantly more naked to do this properly."

"That's what she said," Tenzin muttered.

Ben looked up. "Tiny!"

Tenzin looked surprised. "What?"

"That joke actually worked." Ben was astonished. Tenzin's attempts at anything approaching a joke about sex usually fell very flat. "Good job."

"Thank you," she said. "I've been out of isolation for fifteen years now, and I can finally tell a joke that makes sense."

He looked at her while Daniel was stripping to his skin. "You know what? Don't minimize that accomplishment. You should be proud."

"I know who should be proud, and it's Daniel for his very well-developed—"

"You know what?" He put his arm around her shoulders and casually pinched her lips together. "Don't spoil your moment of triumph. Let's let the earth vampire work."

"Mm shh gnnng naa ahshhh."

"Shhhhh." He kissed the top of her head. "We should be quiet."

She reached up, grabbed his hand, and sank her fangs into his wrist.

"Ow." Ben winced but didn't say more. It hurt... but it also felt good.

Behold, the twisted nature of vampire relationships.

Daniel was lying on the ground; he was, in fact, stark naked. Ben and Tenzin watched as the ground slowly opened up and closed around him. He could feel Tenzin shudder under his arm. She dreaded being underground and sometimes lost hold of reality when that happened. He knew from firsthand experience that anything causing her to taste dirt was reason for concern.

Ben didn't know if it was his imagination or not, but he could almost feel Daniel moving around below them.

"Tenzin, is there any way we could be—"

"You control air, Benjamin." She looked up at him. "There is air everywhere. In the earth. In water. Even fire feeds on what we offer it."

A light went on inside him. "Fire feeds on air."

She nodded slowly.

"So if we needed to quench fire—"

"It takes very fine control," she said. "But I know you've been thinking about Arosh."

"But it's possible? Nothing is a vacuum, so how would you—"

"How do you fly without eating bugs?" She cocked her head. "Think."

"I create a bubble of air."

She shrugged. "So create a bubble without air." Tenzin walked off, tracking a subtle rise in the hillside that was overgrown with brush and a few wild flowers that hadn't been eaten by the goats yet. She pushed her arms out, palms facing down. "Here."

As if on cue, the ground beneath her started swelling. A few moments later, a filthy Daniel popped his head out of the ground like an overgrown meerkat. "I definitely found something."

Ben crouched down. "Can you clear it?"

"It'll take a while. The ruin isn't intact. It's all fallen in on itself."

Ben knew that even unearthing a site without painstaking documentation was anathema to professional archaeology, but they simply didn't have time. "Gently please," he said. "Expose the site as carefully as you can."

Daniel crawled out of the ground like a kid climbing out of a pool. He knelt on the ground and dug both hands into the earth. He was covered in dirt from head to toe, but Ben had to admit that watching him work was oddly entrancing.

The ground was re-forming before his eyes, a shaking, trembling shift that sent vibrations into the air and dust into the sky. Tenzin quickly wafted away the debris as centuries of topsoil, dust, animal bones, and rock were shunted away from the site in a smooth torus of earth.

Hours after he had begun, Daniel sat back and breathed out in relief while Ben and Tenzin stared at the ruins that now lay exposed to the night sky.

Daniel had exposed four walls and the collapsed structures within them. There were toppled benches and even a few pieces of dry wood that had been preserved beneath the ground.

"Amazing." Tenzin rose and floated herself into the pit. "You have proven your worth, son of Carwyn."

"Thanks." Daniel looked exhausted. "I need to hunt."

Tenzin waved him away. "There are plentiful cattle in a small pen halfway down the hill in that direction." She pointed over her shoulder. "Let us work."

Ben gingerly floated over the walls and joined Tenzin. "Where do we start?"

She pointed to some of the stones lying on the ground. "Here, do you see it?"

Ben crouched down. "It's stained. Like... It's dark, so maybe—"

"Fire." Tenzin touched the toppled stone with the tip of her shoe. "What you're seeing are scorch marks."

"Which means?"

"Which means that Arosh and Saba were probably already here." She stood in front of the last standing wall, which had flecks of paint still clinging to it. "This is a picture of a king, not a saint."

"So this wasn't a church."

She frowned. "Depends on the king. There were numerous Ethiopian emperors—like Lalibela—who were priests as well as kings. Some are venerated as saints now." She held her hand in front of the wall. "But no, I don't think this was a church." She looked around. "It's not built correctly for that. You've seen Ethiopian Orthodox churches now. What's missing?"

"I've seen newer churches, Tenzin. I don't know if anything I've seen about them—"

"The fundamentals of the church structure have not changed in centuries." She walked over and stood in front of him. "Look. Tell me what you notice."

Ben turned in place and immediately saw what she was saying. "Where is the *maqdas?*"

The *maqdas*, or "holy of holies," was a feature pointed out in every single Ethiopian Orthodox Church they'd visited. There was nothing in the ruin that suggested such a structure. It was a simple square stone building, though obviously fitted with niches, shelves, and concealed pockets.

"Exactly. There's no *maqdas* here, so this is not a church."

Now that she'd pointed them out, the scorch marks were obvious and everywhere. Ben kept his fingers off the stones, conscious of not spoiling the site any more than they already had. "So this was a treasury."

"A dressed-stone structure" —she pointed at the painted wall— "richly decorated once. Located on the top of a mountain, burned by Yodit," Tenzin said. "Rather by Saba and Arosh during their rage. Yes, I believe this was a treasury."

"I understand Saba's anger," Ben said. "But why was Arosh with her? Did he have a connection to Desta?"

"He once loved her too," Tenzin said. "That is what I have heard, though I don't know if it was as a lover or as a daughter. Likely they were lovers at some point."

Ben muttered, "Vampire families are so fucked up."

"He wasn't her *sire*," Tenzin said. "She was Saba's daughter."

"And Arosh was Saba's... consort? Lover? I don't know. I know Giovanni said they shared a lot of blood, so they were mated."

Unlike us.

"Saba shared blood with all of them," Tenzin said. "So if that is all it takes to be mated, she was mated to Kato and Ziri as well."

Ben tried not to let bitterness color his voice. "I'm just saying I don't understand how Saba would be okay with her lover also being involved with her daughter."

Tenzin spread her hands. "They are thousands and thousands of years old."

"And that makes a difference why?"

"Because relationships change, Benjamin. Young vampires like your uncle or even Carwyn may not understand this, but what does a *lifelong* commitment mean to a being like Saba?"

"Or you?"

Fuck. He said that out loud. Ben felt the amnis coursing through his body like a pulse. The air around him whipped up, swirling dust devils along the surface of the ridge.

Tenzin rose in the air, her eyes fixed on Ben. "I am very happy with what we have become, Benjamin."

"For now." He nodded and swallowed the burning lump that had formed at the back of his throat. "For now you're happy. Not bored. But not willing to be my mate. Even though you were willing to mate with Stephen and you claim that what we have is more."

Tenzin's face remained blank. "What do you want from me?"

"I want you to be my mate!"

They had risen well above the earth now, surrounded by the wind and the darkness. The stars were brilliant and clear in the sky—not a cloud obscured them—and the ruins of the old treasury were forgotten in the dust below.

She said nothing, and Ben felt like his heart had been ripped out of his chest and lay splattered on the side of a mountain.

Why stop now?

"I want forever, okay? And I know I don't realize what that means the way you do. I know that I am an idiotic baby compared to you. I know that. And I don't care. I never wanted this life, but I told you I'm learning to love it like I promised. And I *never* wanted forever unless that meant I could have you."

Her eyes weren't angry. They were sad. "You don't know what forever means."

"I fucking know that, okay!" The air whipped around them. "I know! And maybe in five hundred years I'm going to regret it, but damn it, Tenzin, why the hell can't you give me this? After everything we've been through, why won't you be my mate?"

24

Tenzin stared at him, stared at the hurt on his face and his obvious passion. His love and his vulnerability would always be her greatest weakness.

You do not even know who you are.

He was so young, so blissfully unaware of the passage of time. To Ben, forever was romantic. To Ben, commitment meant things she couldn't even fathom.

Don't force me into a promise we both might regret.

But for now...

For now, she could give him an answer that might assuage him, even if it wasn't the whole of the truth. It was part of it, and she could give him that.

Tenzin turned in the air, searching for any sense of others around—even a hint of another creature would be too much exposure to allow her confession.

She turned back to Ben and finally met his eyes. "Benjamin, sharing your blood is..."

Addicting.

Beyond pleasurable.

Thrilling.

Right.

She flew closer, reluctant to touch him. Their physical connection could be so distracting at times. "I would take your blood every night if I could. I would have your fangs in my own body every hour for nights on end."

A red flush swelled his lips and drew her eyes.

Take him.

No. He is your weakness.

He is my strength.

"So take it," he said. "That's what I want. I'm telling you—"

"It's complicated." She touched a single finger to his mouth. "The first time I took your blood, on Penglai, the night you woke..." She leaned close and whispered in his ear. "That day was the first time I slept even a few moments in thousands of years."

She felt his body seize and knew he understood the significance of the secret she had told him.

"You slept?"

"I slept." She allowed the mix of emotions to color her voice. "I dreamed, my Benjamin. I didn't know what to think at first. I didn't understand."

"You slept." Ben sounded like he wanted to celebrate. He sounded happy. Relieved even. He slipped an arm around her waist and drew her close, pressing his cheek to hers. "You told me you miss sleep, so why don't you want to—"

"The more I drink, the more I sleep. Right now we are in the heart of Saba's territory. I don't—"

"You think it makes you vulnerable." Understanding dawned in his voice.

Or some version of it.

Tenzin said, "I know it makes me vulnerable. Trust me, there have been assassins sent to kill me in my day rest. Saba has many allies who would do her bidding, immortal and human."

"So you don't want to take my blood while we're here because it will make you sleep more."

And you don't truly understand what forever means.

"Yes," she said. "It's just not wise right now. There is too much at stake. Your family is here, and I must not do anything to endanger—"

"Shhhh." Now he put his own finger on her lips. "Tenzin, I understand." He replaced his finger with his lips, and she liked that much better.

She wrapped her arms around his neck and drew him closer, twisting into the night sky as his amnis cooled and settled. She could feel it in her own blood. He was there now. Though it had been weeks since she'd taken a sip of his blood, his amnis wasn't leaving.

You are the liar.

She hushed the voices in her mind and concentrated on his lips. His hands holding her. His blood inside her.

Liar, liar, liar.

He was already a part of her. He always would be. There were those she had cared for who had left her, those whose presence in her life was sweet but fleeting.

Ben was not that.

Liar, liar, liar. You don't know who you are.

Quiet.

Ben took her cheeks between his hands, and his smile broke her heart. "Tenzin, you *slept*."

"And I dreamed."

"Is this why you...?"

She frowned. "Why I what?"

He shook his head. "Never mind. It's not important. I understand, Tiny. I get it now."

No, you don't.

"I'm glad." Tenzin slowly floated them back down to the

ground where a half-dressed Daniel was sitting on a rock, glaring at them.

"Nice of you to remember I'm still here."

Ben straightened. "We had things to discuss."

"And I have a shower to take please." He looked over his shoulder. "It's going to be dawn in a few hours."

"Did you feed?"

Daniel nodded. "Lovely herd of cows not far down the hill. Thanks for asking." He glanced at the ruined treasury. "Do you want me to cover it up?"

"No," Ben said. "I'm going to email Liya as soon as we get back. I'll fill her in on what we found." He looked at Daniel. "To be clear, there are no passages or chambers that you're sensing beyond what you uncovered here?"

"No." He shook his head. "This was thoroughly gutted at some point. I imagine there are still traces to be found, but nothing as large as even a small scroll. I'd be able to feel it."

Tenzin was still poking around the stonework. "I do think it is Aksumite, based on the layout and the stone work. Arosh and Saba probably looted it centuries ago. They wouldn't have left anything of value."

"Then let's head home." Ben glanced at the old-fashioned wristwatch he had taken to wearing. It needed to be wound once a day, but it had no electronics to kill. "We have about three and a half hours before dawn."

Tenzin nodded. "More than enough time."

They flew back through the night, and Ben tried not to notice Daniel squirming in his arms. At a certain point though, it became dangerous.

"Listen, I'm not going to drop you, but you could make it a little easier if you stopped wiggling so much."

"When *you* clear that much dirt with that much precision and spend that much time underground getting sand and pebbles in places you don't want to mention, then you can talk to me about squirming."

Ben bit his lip to keep from laughing. "Understood."

"When I told you I really needed a shower, I was not exaggerating."

Ben didn't have any response to that; he just flew faster.

~

THEY ARRIVED at the house in Lalibela a half hour before sunrise to find Giovanni and Beatrice sitting in the courtyard of the compound near the fountain. Beatrice was idly playing with the water, lifting it in the air and turning it in circles. Giovanni was staring right at them as they landed.

"How did it go?"

Tenzin stepped forward and splashed water on her face. "We found an old treasury, but it had already been looted. Daniel did well though."

"Thank you." Daniel took one look at Giovanni and Beatrice and continued, "You look like vampires ready to have a discussion, but I'm ready for a bath, so I'll say good night to all."

"Daniel." Giovanni didn't contradict him. "Rest well."

Ben and Tenzin exchanged a look, and Ben could see that they were both of the same mind.

Something was very wrong.

"Sadia and Dema were followed today," Beatrice said. "Doug and Zain were working on the cars, but they were only going out to find pizza for lunch, so Dema didn't think anything of it. It's a very quiet town."

Ben's heart had stuttered when Beatrice started speaking.

"Dema did everything correctly. She didn't tell Sadia what was happening, but she immediately flagged down a tuk-tuk and got them both inside. The driver spoke enough

English to get them back to the compound quickly. She even thinks the driver spotted the tail too and did his best to shake them. She got his phone number for future reference."

"Why?"

"Why do you think?" Giovanni folded his hands carefully. "You are in Saba's territory, searching for something that is not yours."

"Who was the tail?"

"Two human men. Dema thought they were Iranian, but she didn't hear them speaking."

"There's a Syrian refugee population in Ethiopia," Ben said. "We saw plenty of them in Addis. Maybe they heard Dema and Sadia speaking—"

"Have you seen a single Syrian in Lalibela other than Dema and Sadia?" Giovanni stood. "This is a small city, and almost everyone is local other than a few European tourists. These men were *not* tourists, nor were they Syrian. Are you doubting Dema's judgment?"

Ben felt chastised. "No."

Giovanni looked at him, then at Beatrice, who was still playing with the water.

She's fidgeting. Ben realized it when he felt the tense amnis vibrating off her.

"Never in a thousand years would I imagine that Saba or any of her people would target a child," Giovanni said. "Otherwise, I would never have brought her."

"It's not Saba's people," Tenzin sat next to Beatrice and took her hand. "They belong to Arosh."

Giovanni began to pace. "I thought the Fire King and I had reached a truce when I healed Kato." Kato was Giovanni's grandsire and purportedly Arosh's dearest friend. "But if he aims at my child—"

"Kato has met Sadia," Ben said. "He knows she's yours. Do you seriously think that Arosh would ever—?"

The water Beatrice had been tossing in the air fell back to the fountain with a crash, and Ben turned his eyes toward her.

She was vibrating with fury. "We are flying home tomorrow."

Ben looked at Giovanni. "Are you sure? What about the work you wanted to do with that one manuscript at the library here?"

Beatrice said, "You're only thinking of yourself and your cover story. But you're putting us all in danger, Ben." Beatrice looked at Tenzin. "And you. Did you actually think any of this would work?"

"As dangerous as Arosh already is," Tenzin said, "and you want him to recover this object of power? What are you thinking, Beatrice?"

"I'm thinking about my daughter!"

"There are many daughters in the world." Tenzin stepped toward her. "Are they expendable? Should they be subject to the whims of an unstoppable tyrant because you are afraid for *your* child?"

"Fuck you," Beatrice said. "She's not a guinea pig for your experiment."

"It's not an experiment," Tenzin said. "And you are endangering our mission here if you leave."

"I don't care," Beatrice said. "You and Ben are phenomenally powerful." She looked at Giovanni. "Let's just get it out in the open, shall we? You're far more powerful than we are. Even as young as Ben is. It's obvious, okay? You don't need us for this."

Ben looked away. He was embarrassed to even think it, but he knew Beatrice was right. Some instinct had told him the same thing months ago, and he still battled the feral instinct to consider Giovanni a threat.

"Powerful amnis is not a substitute for experience, training, and age," Tenzin said. "Obviously he's more powerful than *you*, but Ben still has many years before he would match Giovanni in combat."

Ben looked at his uncle, whose expression had shifted from worried to amused.

"Tenzin," he said. "There isn't going to be any combat." Giovanni walked to Beatrice and put two hands on her shoulders. "And I think we should stay."

Beatrice's jaw clenched. "Why?"

"Because Ben and Tenzin need us." He kissed her forehead. "And because Sadia is fine. She was only irritated that she didn't get her pizza. Didn't you hear her? She wasn't scared at all, and if Dema told her they were hiding from bad guys, she'd probably be excited."

Beatrice put her hands over his. "Gio, they *followed* her. They know who she is."

"They have always known who she is, *tesoro*. From the minute we set foot here, they have tracked us. But as Dema said earlier, now we know who *they* are. We are more prepared now, and Zain and Doug have agreed that one or both of them will accompany Sadia any time she leaves the house. If anything, this was a warning."

"Or a blunder," Tenzin said. "I suspect Arosh will not be happy with his humans."

Beatrice narrowed her eyes. "Why?"

"Revealing themselves reveals him," Tenzin said. "He's searching with Saba, but he's following *us*." Tenzin smiled. "This is more good news."

Ben said, "You don't think he knows where it is?"

"They went north, but they are keeping an eye on us here,"

Tenzin said. "I don't think they have a clue. I suspect we are far ahead of them."

Giovanni led Beatrice to the edge of the fountain and sat, pulling her next to him. He put his arm around her and hugged her closely. "Tell us about where you went tonight."

"It was the closest site that Liya pinpointed," Ben said. "But not the most promising. We are going to the second site tomorrow night."

"And what do you think is there?" Beatrice asked.

"We're hopeful," Tenzin said. "This is one of the sites that is more remote. There is no church nearby. Nothing but a small village on the side of a mountain. And according to Liya's report, local legends say there was once a palace at the top of the *adama*."

"*Adama?*"

"Like a mesa," Ben said. "Kind of. A flat-topped mountain. They were popular places to put castles, treasuries, storehouses."

"Prisons," Tenzin muttered.

They all looked at her.

"What?" she said. "There were a lot of royal princes in this country. They couldn't *all* become the king."

25

They spent the last minutes before sunrise reassuring Beatrice and Giovanni that they knew what they were doing, wouldn't put the family in danger, and had everything under control before they retired to their light-safe day chamber at dawn. Ben barely had time to take a shower before the sun hit the horizon and he drifted closer and closer to oblivion.

He heard Tenzin showering as he floated in the liminal space between waking and sleep. To his ears, the shower sounded like rain, and he flashed back to the night she had flown through a storm, carrying his body with a sword run through his midsection.

"I wish I could kiss you one more time. I really wanted one more dance."

"Shhhhh."

He remembered the sensation of pain in his midsection and the hot tears that wet his face as the storm raged around him.

"I didn't want to die yet."

"I know. You won't."

He didn't want to die, but he could only imagine eternity if she was in it. In the moments before he slept, he knew there was more. She'd told him about the sleep to distract him. There was something more stopping her from being his mate.

There was always something more.

Tenzin finished her shower and wrapped a towel around her body before she walked through the bedroom, but Ben was nearly out. He could only watch her, his lips moving silently as she floated around the room.

There is something more.

We are something more.

But all he saw was black.

FIRE EVERYWHERE, scorching his body, blackening his skin. He desperately looked at his surroundings.

Red rock everywhere, a long channel of carved stone dug into the earth. Moonlight reflecting on microscopic particles in the volcanic rock, the walls around him glittering like stars.

The heat came first, a dry suffocating heat like the desert night in the middle of August. The wind came second, sucking his breath as it concentrated around a shadowed form in the distance.

The fire came last.

It swept down the channel of rock, licked along the stone floor, and tumbled over him, seeking to devour.

"Benjamin!"

HE WOKE with a hand at his throat, sitting straight up in bed and gasping for air. Iron-hard fingers dug into the sides of his neck.

"Ben!" Tenzin pulled his hand away. "You're choking yourself."

He gasped. "Fire."

She let out a breath. "You were dreaming about Arosh again."

Yes. Yes, he was. Even her reassurances the night before hadn't changed his nightmares. "How can we beat him?"

She didn't say anything at first. Tenzin rose and went to the bathroom, returning with a washcloth she put against his throat. "The surest way to win a war," she said quietly, "is to avoid one."

"I don't understand what you mean."

"I mean we have to forget about Arosh. The bone scroll is in Saba's territory. All we have to do is convince Saba that the scroll is better in our possession than in Arosh's. If we do that, then we're in the clear. The Fire King won't be able to touch us."

"He's been her companion and lover for how many thousand years and you think she'll go for that?"

Tenzin pursed her lips. "Was Saba Arosh's lover? Yes. His companion? Also yes." She took the washcloth from his neck. "Also his rival. Also his enemy. Don't be too quick to classify what they are, Ben. It's very hard to explain it in human terms."

"I get that, but..." He still had a hard time believing the world's oldest living vampire was going to choose a known thief and assassin along with her newly sired partner as guardians of an ancient object of power and immortal ambition.

"I know." She sat back on the bed. "That's why we need Giovanni and Beatrice to stay."

"They make us look less like thieves?"

Tenzin lifted her shoulders in the world's slowest shrug. "I mean... I would like to disagree with that, but it's probably true."

He fell back on the bed, grabbing her around the waist so

she snuggled under his arm. "Tell me about your dreams," he whispered. "When you dreamed, was it about the past?"

Please don't let it be about the past.

"I dream about flying." She looked up. "I dream about you. So far, no nightmares."

His arm around her tightened. "Good."

Ben couldn't imagine sleeping after a century of consciousness. "How does it feel?"

"Peaceful. But I also worry. I went to Tibet after I left you in Penglai that last time. I felt safe there. I dreamed."

Ben played with a strand of her hair, sliding it between his fingers while he imagined what dreams must taste like after so long. "Does your father know?"

"No one knows but you." She looked at him. "No one needs to know."

"I would never tell." He kissed the top of her head. "Not a soul."

~

AFTER THE NIGHT BEFORE, Daniel asked for a reprieve in earth moving. "I'm not going to lie," he said. "It took more out of me than I expected. If I started again tonight, I might not be able to be as precise."

Tenzin was in favor of going without Daniel. Ben was not. After not a little bit of debate and one offer by Chloe to deep condition her hair, Tenzin relented and spent the evening in the compound, relaxing with Sadia and Chloe.

Daniel and Ben decided to relax by the fountain and enjoy a clear sky filled with stars.

"If I'm honest," Daniel said, "when Beatrice told me about this, I was tempted to invite you to Loch Ness to search for a great swimming monster as well."

Ben couldn't stop the smile. "Are people that skeptical that the bone scroll exists?"

"Skeptical?" Daniel shook his head. "Try incredulous. It's a mad idea, Ben. Our amnis can't connect to all elements; that's the nature of amnis. And the idea that a single vampire could have the ability and not find some way to take over the world is unrealistic."

"Maybe Ash Mithra decided to hide the scroll because he realized it was so dangerous."

"If Mithra believed that, then why didn't he destroy it?" Daniel asked. "According to vampire mythology, Ash Mithra was the most accomplished scholar of the ancient world and the most accomplished wind vampire. Greater than Ziri. Greater than Zhang. Why create an object like that and then turn it loose on the world?"

"Maybe he didn't mean to?" Ben said. "Maybe something happened to it, or maybe he thought it was destroyed and someone didn't do their job."

Daniel was still shaking his head. "Maybe it's wishful thinking, but a large part of me still believes we're running a fool's errand, my friend."

"Maybe we are," Ben said. "But the last thing anyone needs is Arosh getting his hands on it and having even more power. So if we can keep it from him, then we're not wasting our time."

THEY LEFT the following night for Amba Guba, another flat-topped mountain north of Lalibela. This site was well away from the human village and church, an isolated hilltop overlooking the human settlement in the distance. They landed in the middle of a rain shower, and Ben immediately looked for shelter. They would be able to do nothing while it was raining.

"There were caves on the side of the mountain," he said. "Let's fly down there until this passes."

Ben lifted Daniel and held the arms of the lanky vampire as they flew up and over the edge of the mountain, searching for an isolated cave. Ben could smell fresh smoke coming from one cave overlooking the human village, so they flew to the other side and found one that faced a narrow valley.

"Here," Tenzin said. "I don't smell any humans here." She glanced over the edge. "They'd have a difficult time finding this place."

"I've seen people make homes and churches on the side of cliffs in this country," Daniel said, shaking the water off his jacket. "I wouldn't assume anything."

Daniel's warning meant Ben wasn't surprised when he went to make a fire at the mouth of the cave and saw smoke marks on the ceiling. "Looks like Daniel was right."

"I'm always right." He settled against the cave wall, his jacket wrapped around him, and began to dig through his pack for snacks. "This is a good-size cave. Depending on how long this storm lasts, I'd rather spend the day here than try to fly back with all the rain."

Tenzin settled on the ground next to Ben. "I agree. This is an easily defensible position and a good prospect for a treasury according to Liya's information. It's worth spending the time here."

Ben shrugged. "Hey, I'm not going to argue. This storm looks pretty heavy, so the last thing I want to do is go flying around in it." He didn't hate rain as much as Tenzin did, but it was still uncomfortable to fly in it. "We can wait. And..." He looked up and around the cave. "I know I'm not an earth vampire, but Daniel may be able to poke around the mountain from here, right?"

Daniel sat up and his eyes were bright. "Not a bad idea at all, Benny-boy."

"Please don't ever call me that again."

"Right." Daniel rose, put his hands on his hips, and looked around. "This is typical sedimentary stone..." He muttered something about density and other geological stuff that made no sense to Ben. "I'm going to explore the back of this place a little more." He turned. "I'll let you know if I'm going in."

"I would say be careful for bears, but lions are probably a greater risk," Tenzin said.

Daniel spun around. "Lions?"

Her eyes were alight with mischief. "Don't they like caves?"

"I don't think there are any lions in the vicinity," Ben said. "There are lions in Ethiopia, Daniel, but I don't see any herds of zebras or gazelles around here, do you?"

"Right." The earth vampire nodded. "Excellent point, old man."

"Nope." Ben shook his head again. "Don't like that one either."

"Dammit, I need to figure some nickname for you. Calling you by your name just seems so formal."

"You could call him your life coach," Tenzin said. "I did that for a while."

"Did he like it?"

"Yes." Tenzin nodded. "Very much."

"No. I didn't like it. I didn't like being her yoga instructor either."

"Oh, no kidding? I didn't know you were a yoga instructor."

"I'm not." He glared at Tenzin. "Daniel, weren't you going to explore?"

"Right." Daniel started to undress. "Don't mind me. Just need less clothes to work my magic."

Tenzin and Ben watched Daniel disappear into the back of the cave wall; then Tenzin turned to Ben. "That's what she said."

"Nope." He shook his head. "Took too long to say it."

Tenzin sighed. "Humor is very complicated."

26

Tenzin watched Daniel melt into the rock wall of the cave. There was no other word for it from her perspective. He didn't tunnel, as she was used to seeing from his kind, and she forced herself to admit his amnis was far more subtle than his personality would seem to imply.

"How does he do that?" Ben's voice was incredulous.

"How do you make the air bend to your will?"

"Honestly, some days I don't know."

"It's instinct," she said. "That is something no one can measure before they embrace immortality." She thought about what the earth vampire had expressed at the previous site. "He loves the earth. That's part of it."

Tenzin could say she loved the air, but that didn't truly express what she felt for it any more than saying she loved Benjamin expressed what he was to her. The words were like a child babbling in the face of their first sunrise. Incoherent and inadequate at best.

He might think that her reluctance to accept him as a mate put a lie to that, but it was that acceptance of who he was to her that made her pause. He did not understand epochs. How the world changed and people with it. He did not understand the layered strata of feelings that shifted subtly over time like the inevitable rising and falling of the earth or the endless wind in the upper atmosphere. There were currents of feelings he could not imagine yet.

But he would. And with luck, she would be there to witness it.

"How long do you think he's going to be in there?" Ben asked.

"I imagine as long as it will take him to explore the mountain."

"So it could be a while."

"Yes." She settled into a crouch against the rock wall and picked up two stones, tossing them in the air in a rhythmic pattern that amused her.

Ben slumped against the opposite wall. "I should have brought a book."

She smiled. "You are so like him."

"Who?

"Giovanni." She met his eyes. "He was always impatient."

She never knew how her comparisons would strike him. Sometimes his erratic feelings were tiring, but mostly they amused her.

This time he smiled. "You know, I used to complain some-times when I was a kid that I was bored, and he'd always tell me, 'Ben, you should have brought a book.'"

"He's not wrong. When I want to be amused, I usually bring something to read. But sometimes I simply want to be." *You're too young to understand that.*

"I don't understand that." He shifted. "What do you do for fun in Tibet?"

She smiled. That was an unexpected question. "I have a garden that I love very much. It's nothing like the garden in

New York. Everything will grow in a greenhouse, but not much grows that high in the mountains."

"But a few things."

"Yes, a few things. And I enjoy tending them. Sometimes I'll fly down into the valley and work in the fields there. The humans always seem to like that."

"What?" He smiled. "You just go down and like... weed their gardens or something?"

"Yes. I enjoy that. Or sometimes there will be a shepherd out with animals at night and I'll talk with him. It's usually the boys. They like telling me about their school or their friends. In the past few years, they have had mobile phones too, and I don't like that as much. The boys on their mobile phones just play computer games."

"You like computer games."

"But I can't play on their phones."

A loud scraping sound came from the back wall, as if a gate had been opened. Tenzin turned her head to the darkness, but Daniel did not appear.

Ben continued as if they hadn't heard it. "So the boys in the valley, they don't ask where you come from?"

"No. Sometimes I wonder if I'm like a ghost to them or something like that, but none of them seem scared of me. So maybe I'm considered a kind of friendly spirit."

"A friendly spirit who weeds their gardens."

She shrugged. "If you're going to become something of a divinity to a village, you should at least be helpful."

He shook his head. "I'll have to remember that."

This time the scraping sound was louder and closer somehow. Tenzin turned and saw Daniel emerging from the darkness, and his face was a cross between grim and shocked.

"You two have to see this. I know what I want to do about it, but you're the ones who have to decide."

Ben looked at Tenzin; he looked as wary as Daniel. "What is it?"

Daniel waved them toward the dark tunnel he'd formed. "Just come and see."

Wonderful. Just what Tenzin always craved, a dark earthen tunnel with a mystery at the end.

"Lovely."

~

HE HELD her hand through the length of the narrow tunnel, which luckily smelled more like sand than dirt. Though he was in no danger from her anymore, Tenzin hated losing control, and there was nothing more likely to make her snap and lose herself than being buried in the ground.

Ben had seen it once with nearly deadly consequences.

"The tunnel slopes up," Daniel called from the front. "Watch your step."

The passage Daniel had formed was narrow and tall enough for his frame, which meant it was more than large enough for Tenzin and allowed her to keep focused on their mysterious errand.

The tunnel sloped up and then abruptly widened. As she stepped into the wider chamber, the glow from Daniel's penlight cast enough light with Tenzin's night vision that she was able to discern a structure that had been buried in the ground.

"Are those bricks?"

"Yes, but they're not structural." Daniel stepped toward a gaping hole in the wall where crumbled bricks lay in a messy pile at his feet. "The chamber was dug into the ground and reinforced with bricks. I dug around, trying to see what the construction was, but I'm certain it was originally dug into bedrock. The bricks are simply to keep the chamber from collapsing."

Ben was nearly salivating. "And inside?"

Daniel gestured toward the broken wall. "Take a look." He tossed Ben the penlight. "The ceiling feels stable to me. I don't think there's any chance of collapse."

Tenzin still decided to wait and let Ben into the chamber first. It was a giant hole in the ground, not exactly Tenzin's favorite environment.

"Tenzin." He nearly breathed out her name. "You have to see this."

Tenzin glanced at Daniel, who only nodded. She cautiously left the larger tunnel and stepped through the hole where Ben had disappeared.

And entered a completely intact ancient treasury.

The sheer amount of gold stole her thoughts for an extended moment.

Tenzin had always known the gold mines of ancient Ethiopia had been the source of the country's wealth, power, and dominance, but what was visible in museums and churches today was a drop in the sea of gold she was staring at.

The chamber wasn't huge, probably the size of an average human sitting room, and four pillars held up a ceiling that appeared to be sheer rock. The chamber was oblong, with one end slightly wider than the other, and all along the walls, bricks lined them and created niches where treasures were stacked.

Gold coins were scattered along the ground, spilling from wooden chests that had rotted with time and cracked open to reveal their treasure. Carved wooden crosses, gold crosses, ivory crosses, and various boxes wrapped in dusty silk appeared to make up the majority of the treasure. The floor was lined with wooden chests similar to the one that had split open, most still intact.

Which meant probably all of them also held gold coins.

Her mind immediately went to how they could move such a massive treasure trove to a safe location. Ideally, they could hire a truck, but who would accompany that truck until it could reach a safe exit point? Would this amount of gold pose a problem for Giovanni's plane?

She walked around the chamber in a slow circle, touching jeweled crowns, silver and gold goblets and plates, and miscellaneous household objects, some of which seemed utterly ridiculous. On one shelf there lay a golden headrest with rubies and malachite inlaid in intricate patterns. There, a child's cup in beaten gold. On a top shelf, Tenzin floated up to find a perfectly cast golden fish.

What was it for? No idea. Her fingers itched to slide it into her pocket just because.

"Tenzin?"

She turned toward Ben. "It's... beautiful."

He walked over to her and gently tilted her chin up. "It's not ours."

Her eyes went wide. "We found it."

"Technically, Daniel found it."

"So we'll share it with him," she said. "I'm not greedy."

Wait...

Ben snorted. "Tenzin."

"Okay, you're right, that is not an accurate statement. But I am fair, and he is the one who excavated it, so we are obliged by laws of honor to—"

"Tenzin, it's not ours." He looked around the chamber. "From the coins alone, I'm fairly positive this dates back to the Aksumite period, and this belongs to the people of Ethiopia. This is their history. Their inheritance, Tiny."

She hissed. "But we are the ones who found it."

"Yes. Do you want the national museum to give you credit

for the find? I'm sure that can be arranged." He slid an arm around her shoulders. "We need to have Daniel cover this back up, seal the chamber, and then we need to inform Liya that this is here."

She felt her heart fall to the floor and roll, ever so slightly downward toward the chest of spilled gold coins. "You're saying we can't keep any of it?"

"We promised Hirut in Addis—"

"But no one knows it's here!" She felt like whining but knew that would be beneath her. "This isn't a lost artifact. These are completely unknown artifacts. We could even keep a sizable amount here so that the chamber appears undisturbed."

"Or we could just leave the treasure intact, which is what we're going to do."

His voice was so flip that Tenzin rounded on him and bared her teeth. "Do you have any idea how long it has been since I've found—"

"We're not thieves!" he told her. "This isn't up for discussion, Tenzin. We made a promise."

"We are *recovery agents*," she said. "And this is a hell of a recovery."

"Agreed. This time our client is the nation of Ethiopia and all her citizens."

She rose to face him, nose to nose. "I don't remember getting a wire transfer."

"This is a pro bono case." Ben spun in a slow circle near the center of the chamber. "Trust me, Tiny, I feel that pull too. But we made a real promise, and I'm not willing to compromise that."

She would tear down the sky, crawl on broken knees, and beg for him. But in that moment, she hated him more than a little.

"Don't." His gaze was firm. "We cannot keep it."

Infuriating man! "Can we at least search it for the scroll?"

He walked over and kissed her forehead. "Of course we can."

"Don't try to mollify me like a stubborn child."

His pursed lips told her what his mouth didn't. *You're acting like a child, so I'm treating you like one.*

The sanctimonious, stubborn ass. She had already scanned the shelves but found no scrolls or manuscripts. This was a royal treasury, not a scholarly one. That left the wooden chests that lined the floor. She went to one end and Ben decamped to the other.

She opened the first chest and more gold coins spilled out.

Not mine, not mine, not mine. She slipped five of them into her pocket anyway.

Daniel chose that moment to poke his head in. "So what are you going to—"

"We're not keeping it!" Tenzin fumed. "Apparently it belongs in a museum." *And not in my safe in Morocco.* "Talk to Ben." Tenzin was too angry to humor the earth vampire.

"Oh, excellent. This will make your archaeologist friend's career, won't it?"

Slightly mollified that at least someone she liked would be getting something out of this extraordinary find, Tenzin shrugged.

"Yes, it will." Ben spoke from across the chamber. "Daniel, this is... I don't even have the words."

Neither do I! Tenzin opened the next chest and felt like crying. Gemstones winked from velvet pillows. Sapphires and rubies. Carved ivory scarabs from Egypt and finely polished lapis lazuli and garnets. She couldn't justify taking a single one, because they were all unique. Coins were one thing; one was basically like another. But these...

"Ben." Her voice was mournful. "There's an Egyptian scarab that—"

"Fine." His voice was clipped. "I will let you take an Egyptian scarab since it's not Ethiopian."

She perked up. "Really?"

"One, Tenzin. You get to pick one."

She spun, sensing an opening. "Can it be anything that's traded from another place?"

Ben turned and met her eyes. "You said a scarab, not—"

"I'm just saying if it's not native to Ethiopia, that probably means they looted it themselves, so it's already stolen." It was thin, but it might work. Might.

"Or they traded it, and evidence of trade is important to understanding history and will be significant to Liya." He held up a single finger. "The scarab, Tenzin. That's it."

Fine, if he was going to be like that, she'd pick the nicest scarab in the chest. She spotted one perfectly preserved carving in blue-green turquoise with an elaborate winged gold setting.

She smiled. Yes, that one would do nicely. "Okay, I'm only taking one." She pocketed it and moved to the next chest.

More coins. So tempting.

Another chest contained nothing but silver drinking vessels. Another one held only silver plates. Another one yielded rolled silk robes, and another one contained a folded silk tapestry that appeared to be Persian.

"Hey, Ben?"

"No," he grumbled. "I'm tempted too, but just no. You already got one piece, and don't pretend you haven't pocketed some coins too."

"I have no idea what you're talking about."

Two hours later, having scoured the entire treasury, they were both convinced that though this treasury was intact, it did not hold the bone scroll or any other ancient manuscripts or clues.

Tenzin stood in the tumbled doorway of the treasury, looking mournfully at the finest treasure cache she'd seen in over a thousand years.

Goodbye, my lovelies.

Ben pulled her away from the doorway. "You'll see it again. I'm sure there will be a special exhibit of international acclaim when Liya finds this."

I'll see you again behind glass. In a museum.

"Fine."

"You're pouting."

"I'm not pouting."

She turned and started back down the tunnel toward the cave as Daniel began carefully rebuilding the wall of the treasury so it would remain structurally sound until human archaeologists could "discover" it.

Ben took her shoulders in his big hands and guided her down the narrow tunnel toward a faint light that told her dawn was approaching.

"You're cute when you pout, Tiny."

"Shut up."

27

They took another day to regroup in Lalibela after their find in Amba Guba. Daniel wasn't as worn out from tunneling through a mountain, but he still needed time to recharge and feed his amnis, and Tenzin was openly mourning the loss of so much gold.

"There were gold plates and royal crowns—"

"Princess crowns?" Sadia was riveted to the story Tenzin was sharing about the fantastic find.

"Yes, I'm sure a princess could have worn many of the beautiful things in the treasury." Tenzin shot an evil eye toward Ben, who ignored her.

What did she think he was going to do? That treasury represented not only a massive amount of wealth but also a massive trove of historical information, along with treasure that would draw the attention of the entire world when Liya and her team were able to go in.

He'd already called the human archaeologist; it had taken some convincing to sway her, but after Ben dropped the phrase "career-defining find," she got into gear.

Ben had no doubt that with the fame and reputation this

treasury brought, Liya would be able to find as much funding for her Nile Basin excavations as she wanted, even without Tenzin's help.

Sadia ran over to Ben. "Tenzin says you hate her."

"Tenzin!" Okay, that was enough. This was getting ridiculous. "Where did she go, Sadia?"

"She said that she wanted to be by herself for a while."

Ben set down the book he'd been reading about the lost kingdom of Punt in East Africa. "Sadia, do you think I hate Tenzin?"

"No, you love her. And I've seen you kissing." She wrinkled her nose. "Just like Baba and Mama."

"Exactly. So just forget Tenzin being dramatic. We all know I do not hate her."

Sadia smiled. "Yeah, that's silly."

Silly? Yes, his partner was being very "silly."

"Okay, I'm going to go find her. Stay here with Dema, okay?"

"Can I get out a puzzle?"

"Ask Dema." And with that last dodge, he slipped out of the family room and into the cool courtyard where he could see Tenzin perched on a corner of the compound roof, watching the moonrise.

He floated up to her and sat beside her. The metal roof wasn't the most comfortable, but then, neither were the many conversations they were avoiding.

"You need to stop telling my baby sister that I hate you." He looked at her, but she was glaring at the moon. "I told you that we couldn't keep a priceless Aksumite royal treasury; I didn't say I hated you."

"It's the same thing, Benjamin." She sighed deeply. "It's the same thing."

"You're so emotional when it comes to gold."

"Because it's my favorite thing."

Dramatic much? Ben tried not to roll his eyes. "Do you like gold more than swords?"

She turned to him, and her expression could only be read as offended. "What kind of choice is that? I love them both."

"Okay, so if I find you a really kick-ass sword before we leave Ethiopia, will you feel a little bit better?"

She shrugged one shoulder. "Maybe."

"Okay, I'm going to find you a really great sword, and then we're both going to enjoy when Liya—who is the person who gave us the lead to Amba Guba in the first place—receives all the praise and accolades she deserves for her amazing work."

"Fine."

He nudged her shoulder. "Really fine? Or are you going to keep bringing this up for the next five years?"

Tenzin snorted. "Five? Ben, you're a vampire now. I'm going to be reminding you of this for the next five *hundred* years."

He nodded. "Great. Always good to have something to look forward to."

THE FOLLOWING night they headed north, farther north than they had before, deep into the heart of the old Aksumite kingdom in Tigray state. They crossed mountains and more river valleys, the human villages below sparse and spread apart. The flat-topped mountain they were looking for was a short distance from a human settlement, dominating the end of a fertile river valley where fields of green teff were already starting to sprout.

The rain had fallen during the day, but the moon had risen in a clear sky with only a few drifting cirrus clouds feathering the deep blue-black night. Countless stars shone on them as they approached the mountain that would mark the end of their "likely" sites; Ben was hopeful but not overly confident. Liya had given them a trail map, but after this site, they'd be heading into much deeper wilderness.

Tenzin pointed to the mountain in the distance, but they were miles away when they felt it: they were not alone.

"What is that?" Daniel asked.

"Amnis," Tenzin said. "Powerful amnis."

That kind of amnis was the kind that Ben felt when he approached a group of elders on Penglai. There were ancient beings of power on that mountain and definitely more than one of them.

Daniel said, "If we can feel them—"

"They can definitely feel us." Ben answered the question before Daniel could finish it. "Tenzin?"

"We can't keep hovering in the air with the digger."

"Hey!" Daniel didn't sound flattered by the label.

Ben ignored his offense. "You're right. Land as far away as possible on the mountain and introduce ourselves?"

"If they've already found it—"

"We have something to bargain with," Ben said. "Remember Desta's crown. We knew this was a possibility from the beginning."

"Who the hell is on that mountain?" Daniel asked. "Are you telling me—?"

"Saba," Tenzin said. "And Arosh. Possibly Ziri. And their entourage."

"Oh, fuck me," Daniel murmured.

As they approached, a spear of fire shot into the night, only a short distance from them. Tenzin lifted a hand and warded it off with a swipe.

"That annoying bastard," she muttered.

"Turn around!" Daniel yelled. "Turn around, Ben!"

"Nope." Unfortunately, they were going to have to fake some bravado. Lovely. "We're going down, Dan."

"Shit shit shit shit shit." The Englishman was panicking. "I didn't sign up for a battle, Vecchio. This is not what I was hired—"

"Shut it," Tenzin said tersely. "You think they can't hear you?"

Ben kept an eye out, but the fire didn't come again. Still, the air crackled with energy as they landed on the far side of the mountain. Silence lay like a blanket across the hilltop and no one moved, save Daniel, who wriggled out of Ben's hold and stepped behind Tenzin.

"You may be small, but I *will* use you as a shield," he muttered.

"Fine." Tenzin started forward and Ben followed, taking position just behind her left side. Daniel trailed behind them both.

"Son of Vecchio!"

The voice rang out clear in the night, speaking in English. Ben recognized the owner; it was Arosh, ancient Fire King of Central Asia, legendary warrior, elder of the Council of Alitea.

"Small daughter of Zhang!"

Tenzin curled her lip. "Ugh. This asshole."

Arosh's laughter rang through the night. "Tenzin, it has been too long since we have parlayed. My harem misses you."

Tenzin smiled. "You're welcome..." She let the pause hang. "...for our work retrieving the Laylat al Hisab. It truly was the finest blade I have ever seen. I am so glad that you and my father have finally put an end to your long war."

If you didn't know Tenzin, the sarcasm would be nearly undetectable. Ben did his best not to smile. His partner truly was the queen of courtly doublespeak.

"Ah yes. The Night's Reckoning. A fitting gift to end a war."

Was it though? "Interesting perspective," Ben muttered.

Tenzin and Arosh had been shouting into the darkness. While Ben could sense three strong immortals and two lesser ones, he couldn't see anything other than faint outlines from this distance.

"Harun was a friend of mine," Arosh said. "I have many of his blades."

Rub it in, why don't you? Ben saw Tenzin's lip curl. "Congratulations."

"Son of Vecchio, you are well grown in power."

"Son of Zhang." Ben corrected the elder. "Though I am still allied with my uncle, aunt, and their immortal lines." It was a subtle nod to his uncle's relationship with the fourth elder in Alitea, Kato of the Mediterranean, the elder who was not present that night. "How is my uncle's grandsire?"

"Not here," Tenzin said under her breath. "But probably the reason he hasn't tried to burn us yet."

"He hasn't tried to burn us yet?" Daniel whispered back. "What do you call that giant column of fire he shot at us five minutes ago?"

"A friendly greeting." Ben stepped forward and started walking toward the voices. "Arosh, sired to fire, king of the West, we have business on this mountain," he said carefully. "We seek an object of great wisdom."

"You seek an object of power," Arosh said. "Just as I do."

Ben was getting closer now, and he could see more of what was happening. An earth vampire he didn't know was moving the ground, faster than Daniel had worked, as Ziri and Saba sat on a large boulder some distance away. Arosh stood on the edge of the digging site, his hands braced on his hips.

Ben could sense a fifth vampire somewhere, but the way the amnis drifted, he knew it was a wind vampire like him and

Tenzin. The scent of her amnis was too diffuse, too ephemeral to be anything other than one of their kind.

He could sense the tension from Arosh, but what did he feel from Saba? His eyes turned toward her shadow in the distance. There was something there...

Amusement?

It couldn't be. That made no sense.

Ben tried not to react to any of the emotional currents floating in the air. "I see that you have already started excavation at this site."

"Leave, son of Vecchio," Arosh said. "I have no wish to harm the son of an ally."

Whether he was talking about Giovanni or Zhang, it didn't really make a difference.

"We can't," Ben said. "We have taken an assignment from a client to retrieve this object of great wisdom, and we cannot abandon a commitment."

"Children." A new voice called from the boulder. It was Ziri. "I beg you to reconsider this quest. Be wise."

Tenzin had cocked her head at the word *children*.

"Interesting," she whispered. "It's been some time since I've heard that."

"I imagine." Ben continued walking and raised his voice. "We have made a commitment to our client. We cannot stop looking."

"Interesting."

Movement in the pit had stopped, and a dark head peeked over the edge of the hole. "Arosh?"

"Keep digging, Gedeyon. These... visitors have no claim on this site."

"Do you?" Tenzin barked.

Saba rose, and Ben was once again floored by her sheer presence. She was a small woman with a massive energy signature, fitting for the oldest vampire known to human or immortal knowledge.

"Son of Vecchio," she said. "You are truly a beautiful sight."

Ben didn't know what to feel. He was unquestionably drawn to her amnis; it was nearly irresistible. But he also knew that this was the vampire who'd ended his human life and taken the choice of immortality from him.

And yet...

He couldn't bring himself to feel bitterness or hate. Frustration was his dominant emotion.

"Saba—"

"Don't." Tenzin reached for his hand and squeezed it tightly. "Not now. Not right now."

"Tenzin, I don't—"

"Open your senses," she bit out. "Don't you feel it?"

"What are you...?" He sucked in a breath when he felt what she was talking about.

Arosh stalked toward them, fire burning in the palms of his hands. His hair was braided into a long thick rope behind him, and dark markings on his face lent him a sinister air.

"Leave." It was a single command. "Leave this quest. Leave this land."

Shit.

Ben slowly shook his head. "Sorry. Can't do that."

Arosh cocked his head, incredulous that anyone would disobey his command. "Foolish child."

It stung, and Ben couldn't pretend it didn't. Here was a creature of immense power and years, telling him he was an ignorant kid. Still, Ben wasn't willing to back down.

"We have as much right to search for this object as you."

"Nonsense," Arosh said.

Saba laughed. "I want to hear his reason, my love. What right is yours, young Vecchio?"

Ben turned to Saba and addressed her only. "Mother, does your blood run through me?"

Saba looked at him with keen interest, her eyes bright in the moonlight. "It does."

"And is this land your territory?"

That question she took longer to answer. Saba's gaze turned inward, and she closed her eyes a moment before she opened them and stared into Ben's eyes. "This land has been mine, it is mine, and it will be mine always."

"So," Ben said. "I find myself in my mother's land." He turned to Arosh. "And you?"

The vampire's lip curled a second before the energy he'd been drawing to himself, energy Tenzin had sensed and warned Ben about, exploded like a bomb.

28

Daniel threw out his hands and shoved both of them back as he raised a giant wall of stone from the ground. The fire went on and on; pressed against the rock wall, Ben could feel the heat creeping toward them.

"He's melting the rock." Ben gasped at the sheer power of the fire. He'd felt his uncle's power, but it was nothing to Arosh's inferno. "What do we do? The instant we fly away, he'll turn it on us."

Tenzin was angry. "Who does he think he is?"

She reached out and gathered the air around her, spinning it into a whipping tornado that picked up the dust and rock on the top of the mountain. She spun it up and over the wall, catching the firestorm on the other side before she extended up and flung the fiery torrent off the edge of the cliff.

"My God," Daniel breathed out, still pressed against the rock. "Was that a fire tornado?"

Arosh sent another column of flame against them. "A clever trick!" he yelled. "But you cannot hide forever, small daughter of Zhang."

"It's just petty," Tenzin grumbled. "There's no reason to bring up my size."

"Maybe it's just how he remembers you," Ben said. "You're small and he's old."

"Can we maybe do something about the fucking fire that's turning this rock to lava?" Daniel said. *"And debate nicknames later?"*

"Fine." Tenzin called another whirlwind, but this time she caught the edge of Arosh's fire and drew it into the tornado like a ribbon into a fan. The Fire King kept pouring flames into the wind, and the firestorm grew in size until the column of the fire seemed to stretch into eternity.

Sparks flew out, singeing Ben's face and falling on his back. Daniel yelled when a large lick of flame fell on the back of his shirt.

"Ben!" He fell to the ground, rolling in the dirt. "Make it stop!"

Despite Daniel rolling on the ground, his clothes wouldn't stop burning. There was no water, no ready fire extinguisher available. He was pressed against a rock wall on the top of a mountain with a literal firestorm over his head.

So create a bubble without air.

Desperation charging his amnis, Ben reached out, imagining a field around his friend, and pulled the air away with a violent jerk. Daniel's hand went to his throat at the air was sucked from his lungs, but the sudden vacuum starved the fire that was burning his clothes and the flames died instantly.

Tenzin was watching the column of fire turn in her hands, her face alight with destructive fascination.

"Tenzin!" Ben tried to break through. "Do something!"

Her head cocked as she watched the column grow wider and wider. She spun it on the tips of her fingers like a trickster spinning a plate. A small smile played on her lips and she tossed it over the wall, flinging it back toward Saba and Arosh before she grabbed Daniel and Ben by the hand, launching herself off the rock wall and into the black night.

Ben heard a short scream and an angry roar.

Tenzin flung Daniel toward Ben and yelled, "Get him back to Lalibela!"

"What are you doing?"

She turned and waited, drawing a sickle-shaped sword from her tunic. "Waiting for Ziri. If he comes, I'll draw him away. Get Daniel back to the compound."

Every instinct in Ben told him to put Daniel down and help Tenzin, but two things stopped him.

His partner was far deadlier in air-to-air combat.

Daniel had burns all over his back.

Burns couldn't kill a vampire unless they completely destroyed them, but they could weaken them precariously and took a very long time to heal unless the immortal took in a substantial amount of blood and the surface wounds were treated with vampire blood too.

"Go!" she yelled. "It won't be the first time the old man and I have locked blades. If he comes, I'll be fine."

If he comes?

"Ben..."

Daniel's pained voice ended Ben's internal debate. He flew south, and he didn't look back.

Giovanni had Daniel stretched out on a bed in a light-safe room. He'd cut his own hand and poured the blood into the angry burns on Daniel's back while Beatrice rounded up every human servant in the house that was able to donate fresh blood to the wounded vampire.

"Ben?"

He turned from his station at Daniel's side to see Dema in the doorway. Her face was pale, and her lips were pressed together. She pulled up the sleeve of her tunic and bared her wrist. "I'll go first."

Ben nodded and let her kneel beside Daniel.

"Dema?"

"What mess have you started now, Danny?" Though her words were harsh, her voice was soft. She brushed a singed piece of hair away from Daniel's forehead with her right hand while she pressed her left wrist to his mouth. "Take it. You know I'm strong."

"I finally put my fangs in you and we have an audience?" His voice was still pained, but it carried an edge of his normal humor. "Just my luck."

"Shut up and drink, you ridiculous old man." Her fingers never stopped stroking his hair. "You're going to need more than me."

"This time it wasn't my fault, Dee. Promise." His mouth closed over her wrist, and Ben saw Dema's tiny flinch when his fangs hit.

Ben remembered that feeling, the mixed ecstasy of pleasure and pain from an immortal's bite. He'd only experienced it with Tenzin, and she hadn't always been gentle about it. Daniel was hurting. He would never purposely hurt Dema, but he could get a little lost in hunger, so Ben watched him and watched her.

Tenzin. Where was she? It had been over an hour since they'd returned and she hadn't appeared yet. He'd told Beatrice to tell him the minute she arrived.

Daniel released Dema's wrist, and she leaned over and kissed his temple. "I'm going to find someone else to donate."

"Forget it." Daniel's voice was rough. "I want your taste to live in my mouth."

"Romantic notion." Giovanni's voice was droll. "But you need at least three more donors. Dema?"

"I'll get them." She rose and, without another look at Daniel, headed out the door.

"She's an incredible woman," Giovanni said. "How did you manage to fuck it up?"

"Why are you assuming it was me?" Daniel asked.

Ben and Giovanni exchanged a glance but said nothing.

"Okay yes, it was me. It was about five years ago, and let's just say I wasn't the thoughtful and patient person that I am now."

"Thoughtful and patient?" Ben frowned.

"Fuck you."

Beatrice stuck her head in the door. "Ben, she's back."

He abandoned Daniel without a backward glance.

"I see how it is!" Daniel yelled. "See if I raise a rock wall for you the next time a fire vampire attacks us, Vecchio."

BEN STRODE out of the room and into the courtyard to see Tenzin sitting on the edge of the fountain, her blade sitting beside her and a spatter of blood across her face.

He ran to her and knelt down. "What happened?"

"It was a short fight," Tenzin said, instinctively reaching for her sword. "Inaya, not Ziri. She lived. I lived. It was amusing, but it mostly felt like a distraction."

"Do you think your firestorm hurt one of the elders?"

She cocked her head to the side as Ben took a handkerchief from his pocket and wet it in the fountain.

He started cleaning the blood off Tenzin's face. "Yours?"

"Inaya's." She pursed her lips. "Why didn't Ziri come himself?"

"I don't know. Are you insulted?"

"A little bit. Inaya and I parried for a short time, but it was... a distraction, as I said."

"Ziri was getting the others away."

She nodded. "Probably."

"You didn't say whether you think your fire tornado hurt anyone."

"I suspect if anyone was injured, it was the earth vampire who was digging for them."

"Expendable?"

"For them? Perhaps."

"Saba wasn't the one doing the digging," Ben said. "Why would they get someone else when the world's most powerful earth vampire is on your team?"

Tenzin snorted. "I'm sorry, were you expecting Saba to dig in the ground like a commoner?"

He raised his eyebrows. "I guess you're right."

"You really don't understand royalty, do you?"

"I'm American," he said. "And I don't even watch *The Crown*. I really don't get the fascination, to be honest."

Tenzin pushed his hand away. He'd cleaned up the blood and was just fussing over her. He knew that; it didn't make him want to fuss any less.

"They're searching for Aksumite treasuries," she said. "Just as we are."

"So neither Saba nor Arosh knows where the bone scroll is."

"No." Tenzin sat up straight. "What if it was destroyed?"

"How?"

"Saba and Arosh destroyed all the Aksumite treasuries they could find. They killed the princes who could claim the throne and even burned churches after they ransacked them. What if one of the things they burned was the bone scroll?"

Ben sat back on his heels. "So we're wasting our time?"

"No, that doesn't make sense. She would have taken anything of real value before Arosh started the fires." Tenzin shook her head. "I'm feeling lost, Benjamin. There is something we are not seeing, some purpose behind all this that doesn't make sense."

"Maybe you're just tired." Ben tucked her hair behind her ear and lowered his voice. "Take some of my blood, Tenzin. Get some rest. Maybe you'll think more clearly if you sleep, even for just a few hours."

Tenzin shook her head. "She knows where we are."

"She can't get to us during the day. Even Saba isn't immune to sunlight."

She turned her head. "Beatrice has discovered something."

Ben followed her eyes and saw his aunt waiting on the edge of the courtyard, leaning against a stone pillar. "What's up, B?"

"Come into the library," his aunt said. "I have a theory."

BEN WAITED in the library while Tenzin went to change out of her bloodstained clothes. He stared at the books his aunt had laid open, mulling over what Tenzin had said.

Saba and Arosh were searching for old treasuries too, but wouldn't Saba know where all of them were?

Unless she'd simply forgotten. It had been well over a thousand years since she'd sat on the Ethiopian throne.

Or perhaps there were treasuries that she'd missed; that was probably the most likely. The one they'd found in Amba Guba was obviously untouched, and it was definitely Aksumite. There could be more.

Saba could have razed the mountain they had battled on with Arosh. While the Fire King couldn't re-form the earth, Saba could. She pulled islands from the sea and remade the earth on a whim. She could have had the earth swallow them in one gulp if she wanted.

But she hadn't.

None of it made sense.

Beatrice spoke. "Tenzin said you saw Saba in Addis."

"Yes, in the garden with Hirut."

She shook her head. "Giovanni and I were there, Ben. Neither one of us saw her."

"I don't know what to tell you. I know it was strange, but I'm positive it was her. I remember..." His mind reached back to the first time he'd encountered the mother of the immortal race. "I remember her from Rome. The scent of her. The feeling of her otherness. I'm positive that the woman serving us coffee in the garden that night was Saba."

Beatrice shook her head slowly. "It was a human woman."

"No." Ben's eyes didn't waver. "It was her."

"Why would she... reveal herself to you and not to Gio and me?"

"I don't know that any more than you do, B. But I'm telling you, I know who I saw."

Beatrice frowned, but she said nothing else. "Tenzin is coming. I'll explain what I found when she gets here."

It annoyed him that Beatrice could often sense Tenzin before he could. Her sire had been Tenzin's mate, so the blood tie between them was unusually strong. Tenzin's blood mixed with Beatrice's sire was the likely reason that his aunt didn't sleep much. Of course, like fire vampirism, day-walking was also a genetic quirk that simply appeared in some vampires.

It often led to insanity and could be passed through the blood. Tenzin had told him once that many day-walkers didn't live very long and they rarely sired immortal children. Who wanted to pass on the curse of never-ending wakefulness?

His partner arrived seconds later and went to him, sitting next to him on the short sofa and snuggling into his side.

"Hi. Feel better?"

She nodded and rested her chin on his shoulder. "I took a shower. I had blood in my hair."

"I hate it when that happens."

"It's very annoying."

He kissed the tip of her nose. He couldn't help it; she was lethally adorable. "Beatrice has something she wants to tell us."

"Is it something that's going to lead us to this damn scroll? I'm starting to get sick of this search."

Beatrice said, "Yes, it might. And you're only saying that because Ben didn't let you loot that Aksumite treasury you found."

Tenzin scowled. "I knew you and Giovanni would take his side."

Beatrice smiled and picked up a book. "Give me a few minutes of your brain space and I think you might feel better."

29

"How did you first hear that Arosh had found the bone scroll?" Beatrice asked.

"Zhang came to us in New York and told us," Tenzin said. "Just the rumor of it was enough to put the elders in Penglai into a panic."

"The bone scroll could alter the entire balance of the immortal world," Beatrice said. "I'm not surprised Penglai was concerned. But how did Zhang hear about it?"

Tenzin cocked her head. "I don't know."

"I do," Ben said. "Lan told him." He shrugged when Tenzin stared at him. "I asked."

Lan Caihe was one of the more mysterious elders on the council. They appeared to be very young—no more than a child of eleven or twelve—and often roamed widely through the human world. No one questioned Lan's roaming because they often brought back useful information for the council, so it hadn't surprised Ben that the enigmatic elder was the one who'd shared the news about Arosh and the bone scroll.

"Lan is a fire vampire," Tenzin said. "I imagine they are particularly eager that Arosh doesn't retrieve the scroll."

"I imagine you're right." Beatrice set down her book. "I also imagine that Lan got that information from Saba's sources."

"Why do you say that?" Tenzin asked.

"Rumors, whispers, and political secrets," Beatrice said. "I hate them. I prefer to get information directly, and I have my own sources in Penglai." Beatrice picked up another book. "Lan was traveling in West Bengal when he got the news about the bone scroll. That news was shared by one of Saba's granddaughters, Anavi. Lan passed it along to the council, as I'm sure Saba's granddaughter knew they would."

"Okay," Ben said. "Where are you going with this?"

Beatrice set the book down and leaned on the table. "Saba's intentions toward anyone and anything are... mysterious, to say the least. It was hearing about her involvement in your turning that got me wondering about her role in all this." She looked at Tenzin. "I really wish you'd told us about that before a few weeks ago."

Tenzin rolled her eyes. "I am tired of apologizing, and I won't do it anymore."

"Shocking." Beatrice turned back to Ben. "She doesn't think like other immortals; we all know that. And Arosh having the bone scroll could, in theory, make him more powerful than she is."

Tenzin sat up. "You're right."

"It would fundamentally shift the power within their council," Beatrice said. "Right now, Saba is the queen of Alitea without question. She takes the advice of Kato, Arosh, and Ziri, but when it comes down to a final decision on anything, everyone knows that her wishes are the law. She also has an army of cured vampires to do her bidding. I cannot think of a single vampire in the world whose power even comes close to hers right now."

"But if Arosh could control all four elements..." Ben's mind was whirling. He'd been thinking of Saba and Arosh as a unit even though Tenzin had warned him not to. They weren't a unit. They were individuals with their own motivations and clans.

Beatrice continued. "Further, if Saba believes the theory that the scroll can *only* be used by a child of Mithra, then she's out of luck because she's no one's child. Why would she want to make Arosh more powerful than she is?"

"She wouldn't." Tenzin stared at Beatrice. "Saba doesn't want Arosh to get the scroll."

Beatrice slowly shook her head. "I don't think she does."

Ben frowned. "So what is all this that she's been doing for the past few weeks? She's been helping Arosh search for it."

"I think it's theater," Beatrice said. "A cover for her true intentions."

"Which are?"

Beatrice bit her lip. "I don't know for certain, but... Let's wait for your uncle."

He turned to Tenzin. "Do you think she wants to destroy it?"

Tenzin frowned. "No, I don't think she'd do that. The ancients can be destructive, but not about knowledge. Saba couldn't even destroy the Elixir manuscript after she knew it contained the recipe for vampire poison. She probably couldn't bring herself to destroy the scroll."

Beatrice said, "Ben, what was our original plan to search for the scroll in the north?"

"We were going to Bahir Dar and then Gondar. You and Giovanni were going to visit all the tourist sites with Sadia while Tenzin and I searched in the north."

"Exactly," Beatrice said. "Until Hirut asked Giovanni to consult with a priest in Lalibela."

"Which was far closer to our search area," Tenzin said. "So it worked out."

Ben understood immediately. "Hirut wouldn't have suggested Lalibela unless Saba wanted her to."

Tenzin said, "But the manuscript Giovanni is consulting on—"

"Is intriguing." Giovanni walked through library door and went to the table where Beatrice had her books spread out. "But the priests here don't need my help in the least. They're experts in Ge'ez manuscripts. I've been working with them, but I am the student here, not the teacher."

"So why did Saba want us in Lalibela?" Ben asked.

Giovanni and Beatrice exchanged a look. "Because your uncle is convinced that the bone scroll is here," Beatrice said. "And he thinks Saba wants you two to find it."

Dawn brought a halt to their meeting before they could go on, but Ben couldn't stop thinking about what Beatrice had said. "Why would she want us to find it?"

Tenzin was curled next to him, her arm wrapped over his waist as he drifted toward sleep. "As much as I hate her, maybe her aims are the same as ours. She has seen more of the world than any living being. She knows that no one immortal should have that much power."

"But why *us*?" Ben's eyes closed, and Tenzin's murmuring voice fell silent.

Ben dreamed of fire.

His eyes opened in the heat of a dark tunnel with blue flames licking along the walls. The tunnel wasn't the red volcanic stone of the Amhara region but dark and dripping limestone that smelled of green vegetation, seawater, and a child-hood lost before it could be.

He walked through the tunnel, but he was not burned, following the sound of a voice singing softly ahead of him.

Sadia sat on the floor of a mica-flecked grey cave with flames dancing around her. She looked up. "Ben!"

His heartbeat felt human again, raw and angry in his chest. "Sadia, it's not safe here."

She waved him closer, but he was afraid. He could feel the flames on his own arms, crawling up his clothing and creeping into his hair.

Sadia waved at him again. "Closer."

"It's not safe."

"Closer!"

He gave in to her demands, bending down until his face was right in front of hers. She put her chubby hands on his cheeks and looked at him. "Your eyes are like mine."

Ben blinked and she was gone. The cave was gone too, and he was standing in an open field where the stars shone like diamonds in the night sky.

Tenzin stood next to him, her hand over her heart.

"This is the place we truly worship."

Ben turned to look at her. "What?"

"This is the place we worship." She walked forward and bowed down, her head to the earth, as a figure walked toward them.

"Mother."

But it wasn't Saba, it was his human mother.

Ben felt a kick of revulsion at the hollow-eyed woman before him. Why was Tenzin bowing down to her? It was wrong. All of it was wrong.

But as he looked up, it wasn't his mother that he saw. There was another woman, her face similar, but instead of being hollow, her cheeks were full and glowing. Her hair was silver, streaked with ebony where it peeked out from an elegant pink head covering. Another face took its place, similar again in features, but also different and this time younger. Then another face and another and another, female faces old and young, morphing and slipping into the past until the woman before him was a stranger with familiar dark eyes, elegant arched eyebrows, and curling ebony hair that tumbled down her back and over her shoulders. She smiled, and he saw the fangs peeking out from her mouth a second before she lunged at his throat.

He woke, gasping on the floor of a red stone passageway. The sky above him was streaked with flames so dense that the stars could barely show through.

"Boy, you are faithful. Your time is now."

He turned and saw Saba resting on a stone bench, her back to the rock and her eyes on him.

"Mother."

"Destroyer." She stared at him. "There is no life without me; I give birth to death."

Ben shook his head. "I don't understand."

Saba looked up at the fire-stained sky, and when she looked back at Ben, his mother's face stared back at him. "My stolen son."

"No." He backed away from her. "You gave me up."

Her face was the picture of agony. "No."

He didn't trust it. She had too many faces.

"They stole you."

Ben blinked, and Saba stared at him again. Her smile was wide and her fangs were gleaming.

"Thief!" She laughed. "She taught you well."

Ben turned and saw a roaring fire tumbling and twisting down the passageway. He turned back to Saba.

"Thief," she whispered. "What are you waiting for?"

BEN WOKE with a start and felt the sun slipping beneath the horizon. Tenzin was beside him and turned when he gasped.

"What it is?"

"I was dreaming."

"You've been dreaming a lot. It's probably because of my blood. Instead of keeping you awake like Beatrice, it's allowing your sleep to cycle more like—"

"That was the weirdest fucking dream I've ever had." He turned to her. "Do you know where my mother is?"

Tenzin frowned. "What?"

"My human mother. Do you know where she is?"

Tenzin shook her head. "Do you want me to find her?"

No. No, of course he didn't. What was he thinking? Unlike his father, he hadn't seen his mother in years. Giovanni might know; he might have kept tabs on her, but he wouldn't have bothered telling Ben the details unless he asked.

Who was he kidding? The way she drank, she was probably dead.

"Why are you asking about your mother?" Tenzin asked.

He put his hands over his face and rubbed hard. "This... this dream."

"Explain it to me." She rolled to her side and gave him her full attention. "How much do you remember?"

Your eyes are like mine.

"Sadia was in it. I'm probably... It's probably because I'm afraid of her being here. Part of me really wishes that Dema would take her back to LA."

"Giovanni and Beatrice won't let anything happen to that girl," Tenzin said. "Neither will I."

"I know." He grasped her hand. "I know that. And I'm not powerless either, I just—"

"You're far more powerful than you realize," Tenzin said. "I'm trying to be patient with you, but it can be frustrating."

She taught you well.

"My mother was a thief," he said. "Did I tell you that?"

"Yes. But you said she tricked people and lied to them. She didn't steal directly."

"I mean, she did whatever she needed to get high and get enough vodka to make it through the day." Why was he talking about his mother? He hated even thinking about her. "I never met her family and I don't remember her ever calling them or anything, so I think they were normal. I mean... not like us. Not thieves. I don't think they even lived in the US. I think she was born in Beirut and emigrated. She told me once she was a ballet dancer who performed before the king of Lebanon, and a German count wanted to marry her."

"That's quite a story."

"I think..." Ben tried to think back to some of the few pleasant moments of his youth. Stolen moments when he remembered smiling. "I think she might have actually been a dancer. She loved dancing to the radio."

Tenzin laid her head on his shoulder and put a hand over his heart. "Did she dance to Louis Armstrong?"

He covered her hand with his own. "No, that's just for us. She'd put on classical music sometimes and dance. I think it was ballet, so maybe part of what she said was true."

It was the first time he'd remembered something positive about his mother in years.

"She was beautiful. My mother was beautiful." Had she studied dancing? What turn had she taken in life to leave her alone in New York with a kid and no one who gave a shit about her?

Why did he care?

Tenzin was quiet for a long time. "Do you want me to find her for you?"

"No." That part of his life had been dead since he was twelve. "She's probably dead anyway." And what did he feel about that thought?

Nothing. He felt nothing.

"The best thing she ever did for me," he said, "was give me to Giovanni."

"If she'd never given you to Giovanni, you'd probably still be human."

There is no life without me; I give birth to death.

"If she hadn't given me to Giovanni" —Ben tried to rid his mind of the crazy dream— "I'd probably be nothing. Just like her."

30

_____

Ben steepled his fingers and fought back the urge to break something—anything—to relieve the tension that had been his constant companion since nightfall. Images from his dream kept flipping through his mind.

Sadia in a burning cave.

Tenzin bowing down to his mother.

Saba whispering *thief*.

What are you waiting for?

He rubbed a frustrated hand over his eyes. "Why would Saba want Tenzin and me to find the bone scroll?"

Giovanni sat next to him in the library. Tenzin and Beatrice were across the table, and Doug appeared to be reading a magazine in the corner.

Giovanni said, "I think the obvious answer is that she doesn't want Arosh to have it. She can't bring herself to destroy it, but she doesn't want him to find it either."

"Why not just give it to us?"

Beatrice answered, "That would upset Arosh and damage the council in Alitea. You have to find it on your own and negotiate for it. Put her in a position where she has to grant you ownership of the scroll."

Giovanni added. "And do it in a way that Arosh can't criticize."

Ben wanted to groan. Fucking vampire politics. It was all lies, manipulations, and face-saving gestures. It didn't matter if it was Don Ernesto in Los Angeles, Zhang in Penglai, or Saba in Alitea. All of them were the same.

"Find the scroll and negotiate Saba into a corner until she is forced to 'give' it to us?" Tenzin actually used air quotes when she spoke. "Well, we've taken on more difficult jobs. This should be easy."

Ben looked at her. "I can't tell if you're being sarcastic or not."

Tenzin narrowed her eyes. "I'm not entirely sure either."

Ben shook his head and turned to Beatrice. "Why do you think the scroll is in Lalibela?"

Beatrice pointed at Giovanni. "Because Hirut asked for his help with the writings of King Lalibela."

"Who was a Zagwe emperor, right?" Ben asked. "But you two were sure the scroll was in the possession of the Aksumite dynasty."

"Ah," Giovanni said. "But in some accounts, the first Zagwe emperor was chosen by Yodit—"

"You mean by Saba?" Tenzin asked.

Giovanni nodded. "And that emperor was eager to reestablish the Solomonic dynasty that stretched back to the Queen of Sheba, so he married a noblewoman from an Aksumite royal family, Terde'a-Gabez. Most accounts say she was the daughter of the last Aksumite king and that she was instrumental in the establishment and acceptance of the new dynasty."

"So the Zagwe emperors became the heirs of the Aksum-

ites," Beatrice said. "It's not impossible that some of their treasure went with them."

Ben was nodding. "Okay, so the Zagwe emperors might
have had some Aksumite treasure, but that doesn't mean they
had the scroll."

"Except that Hirut asked me to help with this newly discovered manuscript," Giovanni said. "And there's no real reason for
me to do that. I am not an expert in Ge'ez scriptures. I didn't
understand why she would even ask me until the priest I'm
working with made a small note about a passage in this new
copy of the Gadla Lalibela that he hadn't seen in other
versions."

"Which was?"

"Mention of a scroll," Beatrice said. "This new manuscript
mentions that Lalibela's royal scribes had recently finished
translation of a strange scroll of wisdom that had been passed to
Lalibela by his mother. The scribe notes that the scroll was very
old, made of ivory, and came from Persia."

"Ivory?"

"But it was written in an unknown language," Giovanni
said. "According to this passage, an angel came and whispered
the translation to the scribes in their sleep. When they woke,
they could understand the language, and so they transcribed the
scroll into Ge'ez on the back."

"That's it," Tenzin said. "That must be the bone scroll.
What year was this written?"

"It would have been in the early thirteenth century,"
Giovanni said. "I'm not certain of the date."

"So the scroll was in the possession of King Lalibela," Ben
said. "And you think it's still here?"

Giovanni seemed to waver in his certainty, "*If* you wanted
to hide something, there aren't many places better than this
city. There are secret tunnels that no living person has ever

been in. There are ancient chambers dug into bedrock and hidden passageways. This city is full of secrets, and all of them are guarded by priests, monks, and nuns who cannot be bribed."

The optimism Ben had started to feel died a quick death. "Is that it? Okay, great, so it's here, but it's probably in a tunnel somewhere that no one even knows exists?"

Giovanni and Beatrice exchanged a look.

"Listen, we're just researchers," Beatrice said. "You two are the thieves."

Tenzin cleared her throat. "Excuse me—we are not thieves, we are retrieval specialists."

"Right." Beatrice nodded. "That's totally different."

"Obviously it is." Tenzin was staring at the wall. "None of the priests can be bribed?"

"No." Doug piped up from the corner. "I really don't think you should try bribery; that would not go over well. This is the second most holy city in the oldest Christian country in the world."

"Unless you ask the Armenians," Giovanni said quietly.

"I'm not touching that debate." Doug looked at Tenzin. "Please don't try to bribe priests."

"What about—?"

"OR influence them with amnis," he added. "There's no guarantee that any of them would know anyway. A lot of these passages may be lost to time. They're rumors, if anything."

"So..." Ben pursed his lips. "Daniel?"

Giovanni nodded. "Daniel seems to have a very real affinity for the stone in this place. I think he's your best option. And"—Giovanni glanced at Tenzin—"he was raised by a priest. He understands reverence."

She narrowed her eyes. "Are you trying to say I do not?"

Before Giovanni could speak and dig a brand-new hole, Ben

decided to pipe up. "What about a tour?" he asked. "Maybe we should start there. Just a general tour to get a lay of the land."

Beatrice and Giovanni both looked at Doug. "A night tour?"

"Is it possible?" Tenzin asked.

"It might be." Doug put the magazine away. "I think I know a guy."

~

THEY WAITED two nights so Daniel would be able to join them. Doug had arranged for a tour from a local guide whose brother was a priest and had good relationships with the church. He met them at the top of a hill overlooking the largest complex of churches.

"I have been given permission to allow you inside," their guide, Mula, said. "But you must understand that you may only go in the public areas of worship. I respectfully request you do not touch the altar while the priest is not there, nor may you ever cross into the holy of holies within the church."

"Of course." Ben took Mula's advice seriously. "Thank you for this. My friend's condition makes day trips impossible." He put a hand on Tenzin's shoulder. "But we're all very excited."

Tenzin looked up. "Yes. Very excited."

Her head was covered in a white scarf typical of Ethiopian Orthodox women. When Mula insisted that Tenzin's head would need to be covered to enter the churches, Ben thought she might protest, but when Mula pulled his own white wrap over his head, Ben saw her shoulders relax.

Their guide provided both Ben and Daniel with thick white *kuti* that mimicked his. They both covered their heads and cut the chill in the night air.

"I am glad we are able to accommodate you in this," Mula

said. "Douglas is a friend, so I am accustomed to some... unusual requests."

Meaning they weren't the first vampires to visit. Interesting.

As they walked from the hilltop overlooking Saint George Church, the massive monolith carved directly into bedrock, Ben was suddenly glad that flying was an option. The edge of the rock dropped into black nothingness even as the carved top of Saint George appeared in the moonlight.

"My God." Daniel crossed himself. "The centuries of love and reverence here..."

"Yes, this is a very holy place." Mula handed both of them long yellow rope candles that smelled of smoke and beeswax. "Very sacred. Take these. There is a ramp just over here that will lead us to the foot of the church. There you must take off your shoes. It is holy ground here."

Ben didn't consider himself particularly observant, but even he could feel the vibrant energy surrounding the churches. They walked down worn steps into an open trench that sloped down and cut around toward the front of the church. There was a tunnel ahead—one branch led straight and another cut off to the left, blocked by a wooden door.

"There are many tunnels in Lalibela," Mula said. "In fact, all the churches are connected by tunnels or passages."

"And how many churches in all?"

"There are eleven rock-hewn churches in the town," Mula said. "King Lalibela built them to create a New Jerusalem in Ethiopia." He stepped into the tunnel, but his hushed voice was easily audible to their vampire ears. "The churches are separated into three groups. The first group is the six churches that represent the earthly Jerusalem; the second group represents the heavenly Jerusalem."

As they exited the tunnel, Ben looked up and up, the red

facade of Saint George Church stretching into the night sky, framed by a halo of stars. "And this church?"

"Bêta Giorgis," Mula said, removing his shoes before he climbed the steep steps of the church. "The house of Saint George. This is considered the finest example of Lalibela's architecture, a church of three stories, carved from a single rock."

It was magnificent. Ben walked around the church, taking in the steep angles and simple decoration around the windows. Daniel walked behind him, his shoes removed and his amnis alive even to Ben's senses.

"It's extraordinary," Daniel said. "But I don't sense any tunnels or chambers below us."

"Keep walking," Ben said, running his hands along the walls. "I can sense empty space in here though."

"Oh yes." Daniel's hands followed Ben's. "These cliff walls are riddled with chambers and passages."

"Some of them are chapels," Ben said quietly. "I was reading about them."

"Some are monks' rooms as well."

"And there are mummies."

Daniel's eyes went wide. "Mummies?"

"Not like Egyptian ones," Ben said. "But there are tombs, and the air here naturally mummifies the corpses."

Daniel looked distinctly uncomfortable. "We'll try to avoid those chambers, don't you think?"

"Probably a good idea," Ben said. Mummies didn't freak him out; he'd seen too many of them from around the world. Still, if they could avoid human tombs, all the better.

"We'd better get back to Tenzin and Mula," Ben said. "God knows what questions she's tormenting him with."

But when they rounded the corner around Saint George

Church, Mula was staring into the distance and Tenzin was nowhere to be found.

Until Ben looked up. "Tenzin!"

She was floating two-thirds of the way up the church, peeking in the windows. "Ben, you have to see this."

Taking a short sweep of the area, he launched himself into the air. "What did you do to Mula? You are not supposed to use amnis—"

"On priests!" She held up a finger. "You said no amnis on priests. He's a tour guide. Completely different."

Leave it to Tenzin to find a loophole when it came to amnis. He looked into the dark window, holding up the yellow rope candle. "What are we looking at?"

"Look." Her smile was bright. "There are doves nesting here. Isn't that beautiful?"

The doves fluttered and cooed in the dim candlelight, clearly unhappy about having their rest disturbed, but Tenzin's expression reminded him of Sadia's the other day when she'd seen a butterfly. Delight and wonder, all because she saw a bird's nest.

Who are you, woman?

"I love you." He barely resisted the urge to pinch her cheeks. "We probably shouldn't wake them up though."

"I know." She peered into the window for a moment longer. "I don't think the bone scroll is here. This was the last church built. I think Lalibela, if he had the scroll, would have secured it someplace earlier."

"That fits with what Daniel said." He nudged her down from flying. "He says there are no passages beneath the church, just in the walls around it."

"What are we going to do if the scroll is in the holy of holies of one of these churches?"

"I don't think it would be," Ben said. "The priests go in and out of there regularly to get the tabot for ceremonies."

The tabot was a replica of the Ark of the Covenant, and every Ethiopian church used it for ceremonies throughout the year. It would be covered in elaborate, rich tapestries and paraded around the church while worshipers sang and chanted.

"That makes sense. It would be someplace more isolated. Like a treasury." She briefly touched Mula's hand, and the man woke up. "Thank you for showing us the church."

Mula looked confused for a second. "It is extraordinary, is it not?"

"Very."

"Mula?" Ben asked. "Was Lalibela known for his riches?"

"Oh no." Mula shook his head. "He was a priest as well as a king, and all reports from the time say he lived a very simple and humble life." He gestured up to the church. "Lalibela did not leave us castles or palaces as you see in Gondar. He left us churches."

Ben nodded. *Great.*

So no obvious treasuries.

"Fascinating." Tenzin's lips were pursed together. "What about books? Did he have a big library?"

"The manuscripts of the church are gathered in a library now," Mula said. "But traditionally, the books of scripture were also kept in the church." He motioned them back toward the old wooden door. "Come, there is much more to see."

Ben saw an old woman wearing the garments of an Orthodox nun sitting in a corner near the wall, staring at Tenzin with eyes the size of saucers. Her lips were pressed shut, but she slowly made the sign of the cross, never taking her eyes off them.

He decided not to alert Tenzin that she'd been watched. With any luck, the woman would think it was a vision.

"So Mula..." Daniel was following the human back into the darkness. "Tell us more about these tunnels."

31

"This is what I have so far." Daniel spread a large, poster-size piece of paper out on the table the following night. "These are the publicly marked tunnels." He pointed to passages indicated with solid lines. "These trenches connect the churches to each other in the first group. There are passages and some tunnels that go off the main trenches." He pointed to various tunnels and chambers marked in dotted lines. "But from what I can tell, they're pretty well traveled. Lots of human markers in all these places."

"What about Saint George?" Tenzin asked. "The rock around that felt like a honeycomb."

Daniel was impressed. "It was. The rock is thick, so I'm surprised you felt it so clearly, but there are a massive number of chambers around there." His finger moved to a different part of the map where only one church was marked. "Now, some of those are hidden or seem abandoned, but like you said, this was the last church built in the complex."

"We think Lalibela would have secured the scroll before then," Ben said. "I checked with Giovanni and Beatrice. They agree with me."

"That brings us to the second group of churches." Daniel re-centered the map on an area south of the river that cut through the town. "There are five churches in this group, and they're more spread out." Daniel raised a finger. "They also exhibit a distinctly more Aksumite architecture style than the rest of the churches."

"When were they built?" Tenzin asked.

"There's some argument about that, but they're earlier than Saint George. And this area?" Daniel spread out his hand. "This second grouping is a warren underground."

Ben looked up. "What do you mean?"

"There are tunnels on top of caverns on top of passages in this section," Daniel said. "Some of them are marked. More of them are not. There is also a monastery here, as well as a school where they teach a particular type of music that the priests sing. There's a bakery where they make the holy bread for the churches. There are also a number of architectural digs." Daniel straightened and put his hands on his hips. "I think if Lalibela hid a treasury chamber somewhere in this town, it's going to be in this section."

Ben nodded. "Okay. So this is where we focus."

"The problem is, it's a maze. When we went with Mula, we only saw half of these churches. I need to go back."

"So we go back," Tenzin said. "You're the one who said that they're farther away from the main part of town. It sounds like it'll be easier to explore without human attention."

"But a lot of the tunnels will also be closed," Daniel said. "We don't have the keys like Mula does."

Tenzin and Ben exchanged a look. "Dan," Ben said, "you do realize who you're exploring with?"

Daniel nodded. "Right. Thieves. So the locks on the churches and tunnels—"

"Not really a problem for us." Tenzin patted his shoulder. "Don't worry. We're not going to steal any holy relics."

"Are you sure?"

"I made a promise." Tenzin rolled her eyes. "The bone scroll only."

Daniel still looked unsure.

"What is it?" Ben asked.

"What if we're not meant to disturb it?" Daniel asked. "If you're right, it's been hidden here for centuries. No one has found it. It's become more rumor than anything else in our world. Why not just leave it alone?"

"Because Arosh is hunting it," Ben said. "And while I trust that King Lalibela put this scroll someplace safe, I don't think anything is safe as long as the Fire King is after it."

Tenzin ran her fingers along the map. "The people in this town don't know anything about the bone scroll, and they shouldn't have to. It's a foreign artifact, and one that would bring nothing but violence and evil to this place. Arosh would flatten this town with no remorse to gain power over all four elements. We have to get it out before he loses patience with the careful approach."

"The last thing we want," Ben said, "is for Arosh to have an excuse to unleash his anger when humans are nearby."

THE FOLLOWING NIGHT, they went deeper into the second group of churches, walking through a long, pitch-black tunnel connecting the churches of Bêta Amanuel and Bêta Merkorios. When they exited, it was near the partially crumbled church of Merkorios, whose irregular facade marked it as different from the other Lalibela churches, even the more unique ones in the second group.

Daniel said, "I read that they found shackles below this church in the sixties, during an archaeological expedition."

"Shackles?" Tenzin said. "Doesn't sound much like a church to me."

"There is speculation that it was an assembly hall at one point," he continued. "Or some kind of court."

"That would fit with shackles." Ben was staring at the church that seemed dug into the hill beneath the large shadow of the protective cover sheltering Bêta Amanuel. Daniel was right—there was something different about this place. "We need to get inside," he said. "I want to explore."

It was simple to break the lock securing the door to the churches, but Daniel pestered Tenzin and Ben until they had their heads covered and their shoes off.

"We're breaking into the church," the earth vampire said. "You can at least respect the traditions." He'd bought more of the rope candles that Mula had given them the first night, and he lit all three of them upon entering.

"Why not a flashlight?" Ben held the candle in front of himself, hoping none of the wax dripped on his toes.

Daniel raised an eyebrow. "Did they have electric light when these churches were built?"

"Obviously not."

"Daniel knows what he's talking about; the quality of light matters," Tenzin said softly, swinging the candle around the interior of the church. "Electric light is static. It doesn't create the kind of shadows that candles or fires do."

"And?" Ben was very tempted to reach for the penlight in his pocket.

"So sometimes you see things differently in fire." Daniel lifted the candle toward the wall. "There was fabric here."

Tenzin floated up and examined that section of wall more closely. "It covered the walls."

"According to the guidebook I read, there were tapestries attached to the walls in this church that were taken to a museum in Addis," Ben said.

"Museum," Tenzin muttered. "That must make you happy."

"It does, actually. Very happy."

Daniel looked at Ben sideways. "How long have you two been together?"

"Ten years," Tenzin said. "Or something like that."

Ben shrugged. "It's complicated."

"You bicker like an old married couple," Daniel said. "So I suppose you're doing something right."

"Thanks?" Ben's eyes caught on something near the front of the church. He looked at the holy of holies where a curtain separated the tabot from the church. Then he looked around the interior. "Daniel, do you have a compass?"

"I don't need one." He frowned. "What do you want to know?"

"Which way is east?"

Daniel thought for only a second before he pointed over his shoulder.

"Are you sure?"

"It's one of my strange quirks," he said. "I always know what direction it is."

"Even underground?" Tenzin asked, still floating along the ceiling of the church.

"Even in subterranean caves," Daniel said. "So yes." He pointed again. "That's east."

Ben said, "This church isn't oriented east to west."

"Interesting." Tenzin floated to the floor.

"Ethiopian Orthodox churches are generally oriented along an east-west axis." Daniel's eyes lit up. "Unless they used to be something else."

Thin red carpet covered the rock-hewn floor. Daniel and

Ben walked to the edges of the chamber and started rolling the carpet back as Tenzin hovered over them.

"Here." Daniel spotted the seam in the rock before Ben did. "I can feel it. There's a passageway beneath us."

It would have taken a pretty decent fulcrum and a long lever for humans to pry up, but Daniel popped the carved stone off like he was opening a soda can.

Ben could see the vampire's excitement taking over.

"Do you generally need help on these treasure hunts of yours?" the man asked.

Tenzin said no at the same time that Ben answered, "Fairly often."

"Well that's clear as mud." Daniel disappeared down a steep set of stone steps. "It's open."

Tenzin shot Ben a look as he started walking down. "You explore," she said. "Tell me if I need to follow."

Ben nodded. He followed Daniel to the chamber underneath the church, noting two areas of darkness where it looked like tunnels branched off.

"Tenzin not coming?"

"I asked her to keep watch in the church." Ben knew why Tenzin was avoiding the tunnel, but Daniel didn't have a right to her secrets. She'd already pushed herself to the limit that night, walking through the stone passageway that connected the two churches. It was rock instead of earth, but he could feel her uneasiness in his blood.

"There are storage chests down here," Ben said. "But they look fairly modern."

"Check them anyway." Daniel put his hands against the stone walls, searching for hidden niches. "I'll inspect the walls."

Their voices bounced off the stone cavern, making the chamber feel bigger than it was. In fact, it was probably no bigger than fifteen by thirty feet.

Ben opened a storage chest, but the only thing he found were old ceremonial clothes, more rope candles, and a simple wooden cross. The next chest revealed a collection of books, but they were new, printed within the past century if he had to guess. The last chest was a collection of old ceremonial instruments and more candles.

"Nothing in the chests."

"And no hidden niches," Daniel said. "Let's take the first tunnel."

They started with the one the earth vampire said ran under the holy of holies. Ben had no idea how he did it. Without the sky overhead, he felt completely lost. He was starting to understand Tenzin's reluctance to be underground when Daniel came to an abrupt halt.

"There's another set of steps."

Ben looked around and saw the short set of steps that seemed to lead straight into rock. "Can you push it up?"

"Yes, but we have no idea what's on the other side," Daniel said. "Can you feel anything?"

Ben put his hands on the wall and searched for a feeling of emptiness on the other side, but the stone was thick and there was no sense of air seeping through the rocky seam.

"I can't feel anything other than space. A lot of space."

Daniel looked at him and raised an eyebrow. "Wish me luck. If this ends up leading into a nun's bedroom, I will not apologize for my scream of terror."

"Are nuns scarier than Arosh?"

Daniel began to steadily push the stone up. "I'll have to consider that one carefully."

Ben had been braced for anything...

Except a narrow wash between two hills with banana plants and palm trees in the distance with a clear sky overhead.

"Well," Daniel said, kicking back some of the loose soil he'd disturbed when he lifted the stone portal. "That's rather anticlimactic, isn't it?"

"Should we search the other tunnel?" Ben pointed to the stairs.

"It doesn't seem quite as scary now, does it?" Daniel grinned. "When you know it's probably just a way the altar boys escaped when they grew tired of Sunday service."

Ben climbed back into the tunnel. "Let's just hope the other tunnel leads somewhere slightly more interesting."

They made their way back to the main chamber under Bêta Merkorios. Ben popped his head up into the church to check on Tenzin. He could feel an odd sensation from her. Not exactly concern, it was curiosity tinged with impatience with just a hint of worry.

The worry made him smile. "Tenzin?"

She was leaning against a wall, staring at a burning candle. "Did you find anything?"

"A nice escape route, but nothing scroll related. There's another tunnel, and we're checking it now."

She never looked away from the candle. "Okay."

Her obvious fascination gave him pause. "Please don't set anything on fire."

She looked up. "Inside the church?"

Ben opened his mouth. Closed it. "Why don't we wait to set any fires until we get back to the compound?"

She shrugged one shoulder. "If you like."

With that less than reassuring concession, he ducked back underground.

"Let's not take too long on this one," Ben said. "She's getting bored."

"Is that dangerous?" Daniel started into the second tunnel.

"It can be."

32

The second passage beneath Bêta Merkorios proved to be as fruitless as the first, though it did lead to another tunnel that Daniel hadn't mapped yet. By the time they returned to the compound that night, Ben was mentally exhausted.

And Tenzin was bouncing out of her skin.

"How many more churches are in the second group?" she asked. "Three more? It was three, right?"

"We checked Amanuel and Merkorios." Ben sank into the couch in the living room of the main house. "Daniel wants to check Abba Libanos tomorrow night. He says there are quite a few tunnels he can feel in that area that aren't on any maps."

Giovanni poked his head in from the kitchen. "Warning, Sadia is awake and wandering, and so apparently, is Arosh."

Ben sat up straight. "Arosh?"

"Doug received information from someone he won't name that Arosh and his people are approaching Lalibela."

"For?"

Giovanni's grim expression was the only answer Ben needed.

"So our theory isn't as niche as we thought," Ben muttered. "Great."

"I'm not surprised," Tenzin said. "Arosh isn't an idiot." She raised her shoulders. "A bit overconfident in his sexual prowess, but not an idiot."

Ben stared at her. "I'm... I don't know how to respond to that."

She frowned. "Why do you need to respond? It wasn't a question."

Okay, he couldn't argue with that.

"Just wanted to make you aware," Giovanni said. "I'm going to try to get Sadia back to sleep. She's escaped her room again."

"Are you sure?" Tenzin looked ready to go hunting.

"Dema is searching outside even though the guards say she didn't leave via any doors. I know she's around; I can smell her somewhere in the house."

Tenzin relaxed and Ben allowed his mind to wander.

Arosh in Lalibela.

Saba *allowing* Arosh in Lalibela.

Saba knew they were already here. Did that mean she was confident they would find the scroll before Arosh? Had they missed it in their search? Were they completely delusional and mistaken that Saba wanted Tenzin and Ben to have it at all?

Ben still had questions swirling in his mind when he felt a small hand on his shoulder. He turned, not surprised that Sadia had managed to sneak up on him. She had on what Ben referred to as her "grumpy pixie face." She was tired and cranky, but still so cute he had trouble taking her seriously. "What's up, buttercup?"

Sadia didn't answer, but she walked around the couch and wordlessly crawled up into his lap. "What's a buttercup?" She rested her cheek on Ben's chest. "I'm tired."

"So why aren't you in bed?"

She shrugged but didn't say anything.

Tenzin sat across the room, watching the small girl with an indulgent expression while she balanced effortlessly on the back of an armchair. "You should be asleep, little one."

"I'm not tired though." Her voice held the hint of a proper whine building up.

Tenzin narrowed her eyes. "But you just said—"

"That's okay." Ben put a hand on Sadia's head, pressed her closer to his chest, and wordlessly shook his head at Tenzin. "Why don't you just rest here, Sadia?"

Her voice was garbled. "Don't have to sleep?"

"Noooo." Ben stroked a hand over the braids Beatrice had put in Sadia's hair before she went to bed. "You don't have to sleep; just rest your eyes a little bit."

"Okay." She took a deep breath and relaxed into Ben's chest. "Your heartbeat is funny now. Like Baba's."

Ben's heart probably beat even less than Giovanni's. He wasn't surprised Sadia had noticed. "Oh yeah?"

"But Tenzin's heart doesn't beat at all." Sadia yawned. "She's the quietest one."

He looked at Tenzin, and a smile touched his lips. "Her heart beats sometimes."

"Nu-uh, never." The little girl rubbed her eyes. "Where were you guys tonight?"

"Looking at the churches."

Tenzin watched the little girl with unhidden affection. "We are looking for a lost scroll."

Sadia snuggled closer into Ben. "Like Baba."

Tenzin nodded a little. "Something like Baba, yes."

Her eyes were drooping. "My mama and baba find lost books. And my brother finds lost paintings."

Ben shifted her a little bit as she began to droop more. "Yeah, that's a pretty good summary."

"Except Ben and I try to avoid paintings," Tenzin said softly. "Especially after the incident in New York."

"Can we not?" Ben asked. "Maybe can we just drop that whole—?"

"Paintings are crim-niminal." Sadia interrupted Ben with a broad yawn. "They're kind of make-believe because paintings are just..." She paused to yawn again. "Canvas and oil and pictment."

"Pigment," Tenzin murmured.

"Yeah, pigment." She looked up at Ben through hooded eyes. "Paintings aren't worth your time."

"Really?" Ben shot a look at Tenzin. "Where on earth did you hear *that*, Sadia?"

Tenzin's eyes went wide. "What? She clearly has good instincts about the intrinsic worth of specific artistic mediums."

"She came up with all that herself?" Ben asked. "Really?"

"Benny?" Sadia's eyes were completely closed. "I liked the angel churches. Well, they aren't churches really, but I liked the paintings in them. If paintings aren't expensive, can you get big angel ones like that for my room?"

Ben's brain locked on his sister's sleepy statement. "What do you mean, the angel churches aren't churches?"

She groaned a little and squirmed in his lap. "Just... they aren't."

Tenzin leaned forward. "What do you mean by that, Sadia? Did someone tell you that those churches aren't churches?"

Ben's mind flew to a mental picture of the twin churches carved into the side of a small cliff. They were in the mazelike second grouping of Lalibela churches, accessible only by a wooden footbridge that connected to an open cavern that led to another tunnel.

Sadia was beginning to doze.

"Sadia?" Ben squeezed her a little. "What do you mean that they aren't churches?"

She groaned a little and opened her eyes. "I told the guide that they didn't look like churches to me, and he said I was right. He thought I was a dumb little kid though."

Tenzin floated over to sit next to Ben, which woke Sadia up. "Tell me why you don't think they're churches."

"I don't know. They're just not shaped like the other churches. And they're way high up! Why would they make a church that normal people can't get to? It's like they wanted to keep people *away* from the church and make it hard, and that doesn't make sense. All the other churches have lots of stairs and lots of people."

Tenzin didn't take her eyes away from Sadia. "Is there anything else about them that you think is different?"

"Yeah, because where the curtain part is was different in the angel churches too."

Ben suspected she was talking about the curtain that separated the church interior from the "holy of holies" where the tabot was kept.

"What else?" Ben asked.

Sadia blinked her eyes and sat up straighter, suddenly aware of her audience. "Well, they have a door between them, and that's different. Because it's not just for the boys like some churches."

There were some rooms in Lalibela churches reserved for monks to pray, and female visitors didn't go into them, but Ben knew Bêta Rafael wasn't like that even though it connected to Bêta Gabriel via a carved doorway.

"And... and they're, like, *way* high up." Sadia raised both arms. "But then where you get the water is allllll the way on the bottom. At Saint George Church, it was really high, but it was carved all the way inside. But not the angel churches. It was like the people who made them didn't finish them." Sadia shrugged broadly. "Maybe they forgot or something."

Or maybe his baby sister was completely right.

Maybe the "angel churches" weren't churches at all.

Isolated.

Elevated.

Inaccessible with a protected water supply.

Ben looked at Tenzin. "Get Giovanni."

She reached out. "I'd rather hold Sadia."

"I realize that, but I'm not waking her up because you don't want to chance walking in on Giovanni making out with Beatrice."

She made a face. "Every time they're in the same room. Like rabbits."

Ben couldn't stop the smile. "You're pretty insatiable yourself, Tiny. Remember nightfall?"

"That time when we were completely alone and not flinging ourselves at each other in front of other people?" Her expression said she was not impressed. Tenzin was highly affectionate, but she was not demonstrative in front of other people.

In fact, if Ben had to guess, half their business associates had no idea they were romantically involved.

Need to change that.

Once they were mated, that would change. Once they were mated, she would smell of his amnis and he would carry hers. No one would mistake their connection once that happened.

"Can you just get Giovanni please?"

Tenzin disappeared and returned shortly with Ben's uncle.

"Ah." Giovanni smiled. "I figured the two of you would be able to get her back to sleep."

"What?" Ben looked down at a limp Sadia. "Oh right. Gio, what's the deal with Bêta Gabriel?"

Giovanni leaned against the doorjamb and put on what Ben referred to as his *professor face.* "What are you asking?"

"Sadia says they're not churches."

"That's a popular belief," Giovanni said. "Many scholars are convinced that the churches of Gabriel and Rafael were originally part of a palace complex or had some nonsacred purpose."

"But they were carved by King Lalibela?"

Giovanni shrugged. "We don't know. Not really. That's the popular belief, and he speaks of them in his hagiography but doesn't speak of building them. At least not in what I've studied so far. They could have already existed."

"What does he say about them?"

Giovanni frowned. "I can't remember exactly, but there was something about outsiders not disturbing the church. So he did refer to them as churches."

"What does that mean?" Tenzin asked. "To not disturb the church? Who would disturb the church?"

"I don't know," Giovanni said. "But even in the thirteenth century, thieves existed." He looked pointedly at Tenzin. "Or so I've heard."

Ben said, "But maybe the angel churches aren't churches at all. Or they weren't churches. If they were treasuries, that could be why Emperor Lalibela wanted to keep outsiders away."

"Lalibela wasn't known for his riches," Giovanni said. "He was widely hailed as a humble king who lived very similarly to his people. He left no castle or palace. The churches are considered his greatest achievement."

Tenzin raised one eyebrow. "So maybe he was guarding something else besides treasure."

Giovanni was slowly nodding. "Like a powerful object hunted by immortal powers?"

"Maybe," Tenzin said. "According to Sadia, Bêta Gabriel is not a typical church."

"And that's exactly what we're looking for." Ben squeezed his little sister tight and placed a kiss on her forehead. "Brilliant baby."

"Thanks," Tenzin said.

Ben stared at her.

"Oh, you're talking about Sadia." Tenzin pulled her legs up to her chest. "I knew that."

~

THE FOLLOWING NIGHT, Ben, Tenzin, and Daniel climbed up a hill where a rocky outcropping was shaded by towering eucalyptus trees. Ben was walking with the earth vampire while Tenzin flew ahead, irritated by even the idea of the ground.

Ben could feel her tension and knew she was reaching the end of her patience.

Not unlike a certain ancient vampire who was approaching Lalibela.

"Do you think Arosh is already in the city?" Daniel looked suitably worried. "I really don't want to create stone walls in the middle of populated areas."

"I think he's going to have to behave if Saba is with him."

"She was with him last time." Daniel ducked under a low-hanging branch, still following stairs cut into the side of the hill. "You think she'll have more respect for the humans than for us?"

Tenzin flew toward them, hovering in the dark night. "In short? Yes. She considers humans like little children, unable to defend themselves and thus off-limits to truly powerful predators like her. It's not that she cares more for humans than vampires, but she would consider the fight uneven."

"Like it was when she razed the Aksumite kingdom and tried to wipe out the Solomonic dynasty?"

Tenzin raised a finger. "To be fair, that prince murdered her favorite daughter."

"Not humanity's finest moment." Ben veered toward the right when he saw a deep channel cut into the side of the mountain. "We're here."

Tenzin came to settle on the narrow stone bridge that started at the base of the hill and grew narrower and higher toward the churches. "The bridge of heaven." She skipped up the narrow path. "Symbolizing the journey of a devout, earthly life."

"Narrow." Daniel looked down at the steep drop off the right side. "And precarious for a human."

"They don't allow the humans to climb this way anymore." Tenzin pouted. "Pilgrim safety or something like that."

Ben suspected that a drop from the top of the bridge really did mean a quick trip to the hereafter. It was well over three stories high at the peak.

"Are we sure about this?" Daniel asked. "Are we really taking advice from a five-year-old?"

"She's six," Ben said.

"Oh, that makes it completely different," Daniel said. "What was I worried about?"

Ben paused and turned to Daniel. "We were planning to search this church anyway. We're just moving it up the queue."

"When Arosh's arrival is imminent?"

"Hey, you didn't disagree with Sadia's assessment."

"I don't, but if King Lalibela was the one to hide the scroll, I simply think it's far more likely to be in a church, not a strange building with more questions than answers."

"The angel church." Ben looked ahead and began to climb next to the earth vampire again. "What if Sadia was right in more than one thing? She's the one who was wondering if angels were really just wind vampires that humans didn't understand."

He looked over his shoulder; Daniel was following them. "What do they say? Out of the mouths of babes?"

Daniel spoke under his breath, his eyes fixed on the dark outline of the churches in the distance. "Surely He said to those around him, 'Out of the mouths of babes and nursing infants, you have perfected praise.' The Son of God didn't say anything about wind vampires, my friend."

"Maybe I have faith anyway. Saba wants us to find this scroll," Ben said. "The closer Arosh gets, the more I'm sure of it."

Minutes after they had started the climb, Ben stood staring across a gulf at the shadowed facades of Bêta Gabriel and Rafael. Tenzin had already flown across the span of the steep drop and tested the door, which was locked. Then she flew to the carved base of the churches two stories down, inspecting the wells and cisterns carved into the rock, wells that had no logical point of access for anyone other than a wind vampire or an earth vampire who could scale walls.

"There are handholds." Daniel peeked over the edge. "Difficult for a human free climber, but not impossible."

"For an earth vampire?"

He shrugged. "A mildly amusing exercise. Nothing more challenging than that."

Tenzin flew along the sheer walls of the space, her hands pressed against the rock beneath the wooden bridge that connected the cavern to the front of the church.

"We need to get inside." She turned and her eyes were nearly glowing in the darkness. "I can feel something."

"What?"

"Space." Her voice was nearly a whisper as she spread her arms and hugged the wall. "So much space."

33

They entered the church in silence, their shoes left on the rock platform outside. Daniel's eyes swept across the pitch-black church, and he reached for a long yellow candle, lighting it before he swung the light over the space.

Tenzin's immediate impression was that Sadia had a keen eye. The church was odd, different on a level she had trouble articulating, though she'd spent time in hundreds of Orthodox Christian churches in the span of her life. The interior space was broken into three rooms, an altar placed almost directly in front of the doorway in the main room with another smaller space going off to the left. In the far corner, she saw a black cut in the rock that led to the church of Rafael.

The air moved around her, curling and teasing her with secrets. It had whispered its mysteries to her from within the rock walls outside, beckoning her to discover the corners where it lived.

"Sadia was right." She turned in a circle, looking up at the high ceilings. "This wasn't always a church."

"A palace?" Ben took a long rope candle from Daniel, lit it, and began exploring. "You said there was space beneath us, Tenzin. I can't feel it though."

"Kick back the rug," the earth vampire suggested. "Feel the floor."

The earth vampire was smarter than he appeared.

Daniel rolled back a corner of the rug near a wooden door on the back wall and pressed his hands to the earth. "There's a solid meter of rock beneath us, but then there's a chamber." He shook his head. "I want to look for a tunnel; there has to be one."

There was one. In fact, there were several.

Her eyes were drawn to a door high on the back wall of the church with stairs leading upward. "That doorway smells of bread."

Daniel looked at her. "Yes, there's a sacred bakery beyond it."

"What makes bread sacred?" Ben asked.

Tenzin ran a hand along the walls and felt for the space within the rock. "There are many cultures in which bread is sacred. You're familiar with the Eucharist ceremony, but bread is considered sacred by Wiccans and many pagan cultures as well. Egyptians considered bread essential to life."

Daniel said, "The bakery here feeds the priests and the monks mostly."

"Gotcha."

A whisper of movement captured her attention. "Stop and listen." Tenzin raised a hand and closed her eyes. "Feel where the air is traveling."

Ben walked to Tenzin and pulled back another corner of the rug, moving a large drum that was placed in a corner of the church that wasn't a church. He bent down and placed his hands on the ground. "I still can't feel anything."

"Trust me?"

He looked up and met her eyes. "Always."

"This way." She followed a tendril of wind that drifted toward Daniel. The earth vampire had already spotted where that air was traveling even though she hadn't said a word.

She spoke to wind, he to earth. And that earth had shown the vampire a rounded square hole cut deep into the rock and covered by a wooden door closely fitted to the stone passage and secured with a heavy iron lock.

"Can you open it?" Dan asked Ben.

"Give me a little room." Ben knelt down and took the lockpicks from his pocket. They looked delicate against the dark iron, but within minutes, Ben had the lock open and removed from the door.

With Daniel, Ben slowly pulled up until the heavy wood door swung up and over to reveal a wide, round hole dug into the bedrock of the mountain.

"It's a hole in the ground," Ben said.

"No." Daniel leaned forward. "It's a doorway."

"There's no door."

"You are mistaken, my friend." Daniel put his hands on the bottom of the pit and dug his fingers into the rock as if it were no harder than clay. "It's designed to be opened from the bottom, or there's some mechanism we can't see."

He lifted the rock straight up, revealing a finely cut slab angled slightly so it wouldn't fall through the passageway it revealed.

"Give me that candle." Daniel held out his hand, and Tenzin passed him a long lit rope candle, which he lowered into the passageway before he looked up. "There are footholds carved into the side."

"Is it damp?" Tenzin forced her voice to remain steady. Something within the rock called to her even though she despised being underground. She saw the candle flicker as the air moved over it.

It's not damp. The earth is not close to my mouth. Feel the space between the rock.

"It's dry." Ben looked up. "And the air smells fresh. There has to be an outlet on the other end, Tenzin. It's not a closed passageway."

She nodded. "Daniel goes first."

"No objection," Daniel said. "I'll call when I reach a floor or if I get into trouble." The man handed the candle to Ben, then slowly lowered himself into the passageway before he reached up and took the light again. "It's tight. We better hope there's a better exit, because I think I'll have to widen the rock if we try to go back up this way, and that would be noticeable."

"Okay." Ben was watching the darkness as Daniel disappeared. "So we look for an alternate exit. Got it."

"The air movement would indicate that there is another exit," Tenzin said.

Daniel didn't speak for a long time, but minutes later, he called up. "Ben? Tenzin? I think... you better come down here."

"How big is the space?" Ben looked at Tenzin.

"Once you get through the tunnel, there's space." A long silence. "Quite a bit of space."

Ben stared at Tenzin, but she had nothing to add.

"We go down," she said. "Like you said, it's not a closed passageway."

He jumped up and went to close the door of the church. "We're probably not coming back this way."

I certainly hope not.

Tenzin knew there was something waiting for them. She knew it the same way she knew her father feared her and Ben never had. "We go down." She moved to the passageway. "I'll go first."

～

ALL THREE OF them stared at a wooden chest standing roughly four feet high on a platform in the center of the cavern and covered in rich purple cloth and animal skins. It was nearly four feet long and about three feet wide. Near the base of the chest were two long, reinforced poles, one on either side.

"Is it?" Daniel's voice was small.

"I... Maybe?" Ben shuffled closer to her side. "Tenzin?"

Tenzin cocked her head and stared at it, her mind racing. The object under the heavy veils positively oozed with power, more than she'd ever thought possible. It was similar to amnis but carried a different flavor when it reached her mind.

"It's powerful." That was all she could say about it. All she knew for certain.

Power. Massive, massive energy.

Still, the power felt familiar. She saw the currents twisting around it, as if suspended and pushed by an upwelling of air. She felt the connections between the rock and the air, the space between both. The power emanating from the chest was something far closer to amnis than any other force she'd felt in the human world.

Ben reached for her hand and knit their fingers together; in the wash of reflected power, Tenzin felt her blood brimming within him, moving in his veins, the life within him battering her with the sudden realization that she was a fool.

An utter fool.

He was already marked by her and she by him. While vampire biology might not have caught up yet, there was no way she could walk away from him. It was as impossible as the object pulsing in front of her eyes.

He was her mate. They would have to deal with it one way or another.

Not the time, Tiny.

She could almost hear the disapprobation in his voice.

Focus, Tenzin.

Daniel was still having trouble speaking. "I mean... That is, the dimensions are... accurate. If it is... You know."

"I'm not fluent in Old Testament measurement conversions," Ben said. "But I'll take your word for it." He cocked his head. "Those... could be wings. On the top, I mean."

"The replicas I've seen pictures of would indicate—"

"How accurate are the replicas? I mean, are we actually going to believe—?"

"Do you want me to look?" Tenzin reached out her hand, her fingers almost touching the edge of the decorated silk.

"No!"

She wasn't actually going to poke it, but the panic in their voices was highly amusing. Daniel grabbed her hand inches from the rich gold and purple coverings that draped the chest while Ben grabbed her by the shoulders and physically pulled her against his chest.

"Tenzin, are you nuts?" Ben asked. "Even *I* know you do not touch that thing!"

"Am I nuts?" She mulled over the question. "I mean... am I tempted to touch the very holy magical object rumored to cause the death of anyone who even looks at it? Yes. Yes, I am. It's supposed to be covered in gold. I love gold. But *will* I touch it? No. I may have unusual neural patterns and stilted social skills, but I'm not stupid." She wasn't even getting close to that thing. She'd learned long ago that some fires weren't worth experimenting around.

Daniel could barely speak. "It's the... Ark of the Covenant. The real... I mean, I always thought—"

Tenzin narrowed her eyes and turned to Daniel. "The Ethiopians have claimed for thousands of years that they hold the Ark. Are you really that surprised?"

"But no one ever saw it."

"The high priest saw it."

"But he wouldn't let anyone check that it was actually there."

"Of course he wouldn't. If they looked on it, they would die." This seemed like very obvious logic to Tenzin. She wasn't sure quite why Daniel was having such a hard time with it.

"That's why no one would believe him," Daniel said. "Because they couldn't confirm what the priest said."

"Clearly they had reason." Tenzin crossed her arms. "If the real Ark is here, it must be a replica in Aksum."

Daniel blinked. "I mean... Are we even sure..." His hand drifted toward the chest as if pulled by an invisible magnet.

"Sure enough." Ben grabbed Daniel's hand and pulled it back.

"But archaeologists—"

"Don't know everything," Ben said. "Otherwise this debate clearly would have been over a long time ago."

"Well." Tenzin was still staring at it. Oh, she wanted to see it. She was so tempted it was painful. "That definitely explains why King Lalibela told everyone to leave this chamber alone."

"And they just did it." Daniel spoke with quiet awe. "For nearly a thousand years."

"Yeah, until a bunch of foreigners broke into the church and blew those good intentions out of the water," Ben said. "Speaking of that, we should probably try to ignore that this thing is even here."

"Good idea." Forcing her eyes away from the suspiciously shaped chest covered in royal cloth, Tenzin examined the rest of the room.

Though everything was covered in dust, the air did smell fresh, and Tenzin knew Ben was right. This chamber and passageway had an outlet somewhere.

A hint of smoke in the air.

Tenzin turned to the candle Daniel was holding. The scent was no more than traces of a candle, she was certain of it.

But all the same, there was no need to linger.

"That box may be off-limits," Tenzin said, "but the bone scroll isn't. If Lalibela stored one secret and powerful object down here, then he may have stored another. Let's get searching."

There were more chests to open, but these were definitely older than the ones Ben had described beneath the church of Bêta Merkorios. These were heavy-lidded and made of solid acacia wood, often detailed with bronze rivets.

"The period looks right," Daniel muttered. "I've been studying up on my woodworking."

"Watching *The Repair Shop* is not the same as studying up," Ben muttered as he opened a heavy chest with leather straps that fell apart in his fingers. "Oh my God, didn't Giovanni say that Lalibela wasn't known for his wealth?"

Tenzin turned to look at Ben, who was lifting a handful of gold coins from a chest.

"He wasn't known as a flashy monarch," Tenzin said. "That didn't mean he didn't inherit a lot of wealth."

"He locked it under a church," Ben said. "Why?

"Maybe it wasn't always a church." Daniel dug his hands into another chest filled with gold coins. "Maybe Sadia was right. This wasn't a church, it was a treasury. Lalibela consecrated it as a church to keep rivals from his wealth and protect the secret of the Ark."

"That makes as much sense as anything." She felt a tug toward a chest on the far edge of the room. "We need to hurry."

Ben frowned. "Why? We have plenty of night left."

Tenzin couldn't tell him, just like she couldn't tell him why she knelt in front of the single chest in the storeroom that wasn't marked by some kind of royal seal or marker. There was no lion on this chest, and the box wasn't finished with brass or bronze, but a series of leather straps that crumbled away when she tried to move them.

Gotcha.

Whispering voices filled her mind as she reached into the chest and withdrew a round object a little over a foot long wrapped in leather.

"Ben."

Tenzin carefully unwrapped the leather, and her heart gave a hard thump when she saw the faded silk marked with Persian designs.

Embroidered pomegranates marked the edges of the silk while Huma birds chased each other across the blood-red scroll cover.

"Tenzin?"

She carefully unwrapped the silk from the heavy weight in her palm. She could feel the power of it even before she laid eyes on it.

"Tenzin?" He was at her shoulder now. "My God."

"Not any god you know," Tenzin said. "But maybe one you never expected." She held it in her hand, marveling at the weight and the heft of it. Bone wasn't as light as she'd antici- pated. Oiled sinew was strung and stretched, woven through the polished human ivory of Ash Mithra, connecting the work of his eternity into one piece.

"The bone scroll." Tenzin held it in her own hand, and she didn't want to let it go. In one instant, the world and all its power opened to her, laying itself at her feet as she realized that this mythical object belonged to her.

It belonged to her.

In that moment, not a single vampire in the world was her equal. Not Zhang. Not Arosh. Not even Saba. None of them could do what she could. None of them held the power that she did.

Not four elements. Five. There had never been only four. A foolish presumption of the infantile West to only consider four. The potential of five elements sparked in her mind.

Wind.

Water.

Fire.

Earth.

AMNIS.

Call it the ether or the void. The space between, which was Tenzin's true home. She held the potential for all of it in the palm of her hand, her fingers curling over the etched markings that whispered their secrets.

Take me.

Use me.

I am yours.

"Tenzin." Male arms came around her, and a stubble-roughened cheek brought her back to the cave. "Hey, Tiny."

Her voice felt rough and unused. "Benjamin."

"Hey." His voice was achingly casual, painfully easy. "Why don't you wrap that back up to keep it safe until we can get it back to Giovanni?"

Her fingers curled over the scroll.

No. It was hers.

"Tiny?" His cheek pressed to hers. "Wrap the bone scroll in the coverings. Please. We don't want it to get damaged, right?"

In a swift moment of clarity, she wrapped the pile of bones in leather and silk, turned, and shoved it into Ben's chest. "Take it from me. Don't ever let me touch it again."

34

Ben held the scroll in his hands, refusing to even look at it. He didn't know what kind of trance had overtaken Tenzin in the chamber, but as they walked farther into the tunnel leading away from the Ark chamber, following the smell of fresh air, Daniel kept turning to him.

"Anything?"

"Nothing." Ben had held the scroll with bare hands and tried to use amnis to manipulate the earth around them or draw water from the canteen they'd brought, but nothing happened. Whatever secrets were held by the bone scroll must have been in the contents of the writings and not the physical scroll itself.

"I can feel that thing," Daniel said.

The earth vampire had already earned a handsome commission, but Ben was tempted to hire him on full time. He'd opened two doors that Ben hadn't even been able to see, the rock was cut and set so finely. Without Daniel's help, Ben knew they'd have been crawling back up through the church.

Ben frowned. "What are you talking about?"

"I don't know." Daniel almost seemed to shudder. "Just...

Can you stay back a little bit? There's something very *wrong* about it."

Ben reached for the backpack he'd brought to the site and took it from his shoulder. "Should I put it in my bag?" He didn't understand what the big deal was. Maybe it was because he was so young, but nothing about the scroll felt any different to him. It was a bit heavier than similar scrolls made of bamboo he'd encountered in Asia, but the construction was similar.

"Don't put it away," Tenzin's voice was low and almost a little strained. "Keep it in your hands."

Daniel nodded. "Yeah. It feels duller somehow when you hold it."

"Okay, I guess." Ben frowned. What was up with the two of them? "Daniel, can you tell which direction we're going?"

"North, but that's all I can tell. The path is relatively even."

As they walked, tunnels broke off and branched in different directions. Ben was depending on Daniel's inherent sense of direction to get them where they needed to go.

It was pitch-black except for an old flashlight Ben had taken from his backpack and pointed at the ground. It had enough light that it illuminated the tunnels nicely with the enhanced vision that came with immortality. Daniel had more candles, but Tenzin had objected to them; she didn't want the smoke or the scent, adding that she needed to keep her senses clear.

For what, Ben had no idea.

He heard nothing in the heart of the earth. He smelled nothing but stone, a little bit of damp, and every now and then a touch of frankincense. The silence around them was more than deep; it was profound.

Before him and behind him, however, he could feel his companion's tension.

"It's the scroll that's making you both edgy?"

Daniel shook his head. "For the life of me, I cannot understand how you're carrying it like that. Something about it makes me want to grab it and run away, but it also makes me want to cry."

"Cry?"

The vampire's shoulders shuddered slightly. "Something about it is very unnatural, Ben. That's the only way I can describe it."

Feels like a fucking scroll to me. He resisted the urge to put the damn thing away. He kept bumping into corners, and it would be nice to have both his hands back.

"The path leads up," Tenzin said quietly.

A moment later, the slope started upward.

Ben looked over his shoulder. "How did you know?"

"I felt the air."

It was going to be a long, long time until he felt as connected to his element as Tenzin was. For her, the air around her was a living organism, a true extension of herself.

For Ben, controlling the air sometimes still felt like trying to nail Jell-O to a wall.

"There's light," Daniel said. "Just ahead. It's indirect, so we could just be entering a cavern that leads to another tunnel."

Halfway toward the light, Tenzin stopped dead in her tracks. "He's here."

Ben didn't need to ask to know who Tenzin was talking about—he could feel the shift in his bones. "They found us."

"How?" Daniel asked. "We're returning by a completely different route than we—"

"If Saba always knew the scroll was here," Ben said, "then she likely knew roughly where the king had hidden it. Maybe she didn't want to enter a church. Maybe she just didn't want to go crawling around in tunnels." Ben looked at Tenzin. "We were wrong. She was just using us as errand boys."

In the distance, a shadow partially blocked the outline of the doorway.

"Son of Vecchio," the vampire called down the passage. "Bring Mithra's scroll to me, and I shall spare your life and the life of your companions."

Ben heard something at the back of his mind, a tangled rush of whispers that drifted into his mind and slipped away before he could grab them.

Take it.

You are more than he...

The blood of Mithra—

Fly.

We are more than...

FLY.

"Daniel." Ben's voice was barely audible. "All these branches in the tunnel—?"

"I have no idea where they lead," the earth vampire said. "But I guarantee they're a better option than the vampire barbecue that Arosh has planned for us."

"That's what I thought." Without a word, Ben turned, grabbing Tenzin's hand, and ran back the way they came.

He could hear Daniel following them; Ben ducked into the first dark corridor he found.

"Son of Vecchio!"

Ben could feel the heat coming.

"Foolish child." The low voice behind him rumbled with displeasure. "Now you will taste my wrath. It no longer matters what Saba approves."

The voice was coming closer and Ben ran faster—leaving him no time to examine that particular riddle. He clutched the scroll to his side as if carrying a football and pulled Tenzin with the other hand. "We have to get out of here!"

"We're vulnerable in these tunnels," Tenzin said. "Arosh's fire will eat us alive as soon as he has the scroll."

Of course. That was why he hadn't struck already. The bone scroll was old, and the sinews holding it together were brittle. Bone could burn; no doubt Arosh knew that firsthand.

"As soon as he gets it," Daniel panted, "we're toast. Literally, he will toast us."

Ben curled into an alcove and pulled Tenzin to his chest. "Daniel, you lead."

"Oh, now you want my advice?"

"Shut up and find us a way out of here!" Ben shoved him ahead and Daniel moved, his legs pumping up and down as he ran down the corridors, faster than what should have been possible.

Earth vampires.

Ben ran after him, Tenzin behind him and clutching his hand.

"Wait." She tugged her arm away and turned. "I can at least slow him down."

She spread her arms as wide as she could, and Ben felt the cold wind from underground caverns sprinting toward her. The rush of cold air sent a chill down his spine, and he pressed his back to the tunnel wall as a roaring river of air swept through them and down the black corridor where the smell of smoke was rising.

Seconds later, there was a faint "ugh!" from the darkness. Tenzin smiled and turned to Ben. "It won't stop him, but it will irritate him."

"And we want that?"

She shoved Ben toward Daniel's retreating form. "Of course we do."

Ben continued to follow Daniel, trusting the earth vampire to lead them to some kind of opening. Everything was blackness around him, and the scroll lay in the curve of his arm like a contented child.

"Where are we going?" Tenzin asked.

"Just follow him," Ben said. "We don't have time to ask."

The air remained fresh, but Ben could feel them sloping down, going deeper into the earth.

"You feeling okay?" He squeezed Tenzin's hand.

"I'm fine. Focus on keeping that scroll away from Arosh. I want to grab it for myself and also throw it at him to keep him away, even though I know that is a very bad idea."

Ben frowned, barely keeping his eyes on Daniel, who was an elusive shadow that darted to the right and into another tunnel. "It's not like you to be so emotional about an object."

Particularly one that wasn't gold.

"I don't have rational thoughts about that scroll, Benjamin. My urges are pure instinct." She took a second to meet his eyes. "Do *not* give it to me. No matter what I say."

"I won't."

Daniel pulled his arm, jerking him into another cavern, but this one was wider than the last and looked vaguely familiar.

He glanced around. "Have we been here before?"

"Not exactly." Daniel walked to a wall of rock.

"What are we doing?" Tenzin asked, looking over her shoulder. "He's coming."

"Is Saba with him?" Daniel felt along the wall with his fingertips.

"I don't think so." Ben watched as Daniel pressed his fingertips into the wall and began to pull. "What are you doing?"

"There's a door here." Daniel grunted. "I could create a new tunnel and hide all of us, but doing it slowly would take too much time and doing it quickly could collapse everything down on top of us. This ground is riddled with passageways."

The wall was slowly sliding away to reveal an oblong doorway.

"Tenzin." Daniel nodded toward the door. "Go."

Tenzin eyed the narrow sliver of blackness with suspicion. "No."

"I'll go first." Ben reached for her hand, squeezed it, then headed for the door. "Just give me a minute to check it out."

"I'll close it behind us once you do." Daniel's voice was strained, but Ben knew it was more nerves than exhaustion.

Ben caught Tenzin's eyes. The time underground was wearing on her. "Hey. We'll get out of here soon. Taste the air, okay?"

She was silent but nodded. Ben turned and slipped through the narrow passageway, raising the flashlight to check out the room he was entering. He smiled with relief when he realized it was familiar. "Tenzin, I think we're back under Bêta—"

A loud crash behind Ben spun him around.

The passageway was closed and a small woman stood in front of the door, pressing her hand to the rock. Ben saw the seams in the rock knitting together as Saba slowly turned to face him.

"Son of Vecchio." Her eyes glowed. "I think your time is now."

35

The rock crashed shut, and Tenzin spun on Daniel, knowing exactly where he was even in the immense darkness underground.

"What did you do?"

Daniel lifted his hands away from the rock. "I didn't do anything!"

She reached over, put her hand around his neck, and lifted him in the air, baring her teeth. "Open the door, digger."

"Hey!" Daniel frowned. "*I didn't do this.* Do you understand me? The rock was... It was like someone pulled it from me and sealed the door shut. I cannot do shit like that. Don't you understand?"

Tenzin dropped him to the ground, her mind racing. "Saba."

"No," Daniel said. "Arosh."

Tenzin shook her head. "No, Arosh can't control earth like that. He only—"

"Arosh!" Daniel lit one of the long ropelike candles he'd slung around his neck. "The Fire King is coming, Tenzin. And we're sitting ducks."

Tenzin swung her hand toward the door. "So make a tunnel there."

"And risk collapsing the chamber? I don't think it would kill him, but he might lose a few limbs for a couple decades."

No, that wasn't acceptable. She heard Arosh walking leisurely toward them in the distance and wanted to scream.

But she didn't.

She did notice a narrow chamber in a corner of the cavern that looked like it might lead somewhere. "What is that?"

"I think it's part of the ventilation system," Daniel said. "I've seen them in a few larger rooms now. The underground cities in Cappadocia have something similar. Do you want me to—?"

"Break through one for me." She walked toward the vent. "We're going through."

"What?"

"Our options are not good." She walked to the round shaft and smelled the fresh air flowing into the room. "This is why the air is fresh everywhere."

"Yes. Tenzin, you may fit through these ventilation shafts, but I don't think there's any way—"

"We couldn't do it with Ben." She examined the earth vampire, who was built in far more slender proportions though his height was substantial. "His shoulders are much broader than yours."

"You shameless flatterer." Daniel had his hands on the wall, shifting the stone to create a channel large enough for Tenzin to fit through. "Whatever will Ben say?"

"He'll say nothing, because he's with Saba."

"Wait. That was Saba back there?" Daniel was gobsmacked. "I thought you were talking about who was following... How did she get—?"

"You think she doesn't know these tunnels?" Tenzin shoved

Daniel to the side as soon as the shaft was clear. "Give me your hands. We need to get out of here and back to Bêta Merkorios."

"Why?"

Tenzin climbed into the ventilation chamber and floated there, taking a deep, longing breath of the fresh air and the promise of sky. "Just give me your hands."

Daniel glanced down into what looked like an endless hole. "If you drop me..."

"I'm not going to drop you!" she hissed. "He's almost here."

Daniel tossed the rope candle into the black hole where Tenzin was hovering.

It fell, and it kept falling.

"Fuck me..." Daniel groaned. "Tenzin—"

"We do not have time for any other options." She could smell the smoke of Arosh's amnis and knew they had to hurry. She hung upside down and reached for his hands. "Saba has Ben isolated with that scroll. The night sky knows what she's doing to him or saying to him. Just before the door closed, he said we were back under Merkorios. We have to get under that church and get him away from her."

Daniel thrust his arms into the empty shaft; Tenzin grabbed his wrists and jerked him into the stone hollow just as a lick of fire crept around the doorway of the cave where they'd been hiding.

"Tenzin!"

She ignored the Fire King's enraged voice as she held Daniel's wrists in her hands, pointed her feet upward, and closed her eyes.

"What the hell are you doing, Tenzin!" Daniel was panicking.

"There's not enough room for us to fly side by side." She closed her eyes and asked the wind to guide her. "And I can't turn around in this space. Don't look down; just trust me."

She had to hold on to his wrists and back them out, wiggling through the narrow parts of the passageway and pulling Daniel behind her. She could feel him subtly shaping the rock to clear the passage in the tightest spots.

"Do you smell that?"

Tenzin hadn't been paying attention to anything but the shape of the air around her, the expanse and shape of the void, and the nascent bond she could feel from Ben's blood in her system. "What?"

"It smells like bread."

"The sacred bakery?" She reached out with her amnis, searching for heat and the scent of bread. "I think I can get us there."

"Just don't land us in the middle of an oven or something."

"Don't be ridiculous." She twisted through the last of the passageway until she felt her feet hitting stone. Above that stone, there were footfalls that spoke of humans walking back and forth above her. "Daniel?"

"Yes?"

"I think I feel a door of some kind, but it's stone."

"Is there air around it?" he asked.

"Yes. It's not a perfect seal."

"Then you can get it open." He squeezed her hands. "You don't know stone, but you know air, right?"

"Right." Tenzin felt the fine tendrils of air that whispered along the seams of the rock and focused on them, pushing more and more air into those crevices until she heard the rock move.

"Yes. You're doing it, Tenzin."

"With my feet."

"With nothing, you brilliant woman." The smile was in his voice. "Keep going."

"Can you widen it?"

"If I widen it, it will fall and probably give us a very nasty bump on the head, darling. I think your way is far more promising."

"Okay." It was slow, but it was working. She felt the stone creak as it gave way, and small pebbles and particles rained down on them, falling into her nose and eyes.

Daniel coughed and sneezed when the dust reached him. "Almost there."

Almost there.

Almost to Benjamin.

And if Saba had harmed him, Tenzin would be going to war.

36

Ben stalked around the room, which smelled of earth and decay, his eyes locked on Saba, who sat on a stone bench, waiting with an enigmatic smile.

She'd placed candles around the room, so he could see her clearly, and his teenage memory hadn't done her justice.

Objectively, she was the most beautiful woman he had ever seen. Her features were dramatic, and her jawline and cheekbones looked as if they'd been sculpted from marble. Her skin was the color of dark mahogany, and her eyes were so dark they appeared to be solid black. Her eyelashes were thicker than average people's and curled around her eyes, framing them like kohl.

She wasn't tall, but she was well proportioned and powerful with straight shoulders and a regal bearing.

Which made sense for the mother of the immortal race.

"Saba." He finally spoke her name.

"Benjamin Amir Rios Vecchio," she said, her voice resonant in the earthen chamber. "You are everything I wanted you to be." Her eyes fell to the scroll. "Does it call to you?"

Ben had almost forgotten about the wildly dangerous object

he was carrying around like a football. "No. It's a scroll. I don't think it has any of these rumored magical powers people are so excited about." He was trying to keep focused, but he couldn't keep from blurting out, "You ordered me injured so badly that I would have to turn."

Saba sat back, her shoulders resting against the wall. "Yes."

Ben nearly sputtered he was so angry. "Just... Yes. Yep! Sure did. You wanted to end my fucking life, so you did. Is that who you are? A murderer? I thought that you were... I don't know. Greater somehow. Above all the stupid shit that modern people worry about. I thought you were *wise*. What the fuck did I ever do to you, Saba?"

She cocked her head and frowned a little. "Are you angry?"

Ben finally paused in his pacing. "Um, am I angry that you ordered a fucking sword put through my body so that I would have no choice but to become a vampire? Yes, I'm a little angry about that."

She nodded. "But just a little."

Ben rubbed a hand over his face. "Oh my God, you're worse than she is about the literal stuff."

"I was repaying a favor, Benjamin Amir Rios Vecchio." She folded her hands on her lap.

"To who?"

"To you."

Ben blinked. "What are you talking about?"

She smiled, and it was so beautiful Ben felt like crying. "You saved the life of my last living child, Benjamin. Lucien had given up; he'd surrendered to the sun, but you risked fire in order to pull him to shelter. You gave him your own blood. After such a gift, how could I leave you to a life of slow disintegration as a human?"

Ben couldn't take his eyes away from Saba. He leaned his

back against the wall and let out a long-held breath. "You were repaying... It was a *favor?* To me."

"Of course." She nodded to the object cradled in his arm. "You were nothing to me at the beginning. An honorable human and a good servant. But later... Something made me look closer, Benjamin Amir Rios."

She'd left off the Vecchio on purpose, Ben knew it.

"What?" Ben shrugged. "I'm nothing. I was a nobody, exactly what you said, a pretty decent human and a good servant. Why would you—"

"The blood of Mithra," she murmured, "is a complicated thing."

Ben fell silent.

"I have known for many years where the scroll of Mithra rested. I gave the scroll to Mararah with my own hands when I guided him to the throne." She drummed her fingers on her leg. "He did not have the blood of Mithra, of course."

"Because he was human," Ben said. "Only wind vampires carry his blood, right? So it has to be a wind vampire who—"

"Do you think..." Saba smiled. "You think *any* wind vampire could carry Mithra's scroll?"

Ben lifted it. "I'm carrying it."

Saba smiled, her eyes dancing. "I can see that."

"And Saba..." Ben's mind pushed past the confusion and focused on the job they'd come to do. "Tenzin and I did not come empty-handed. We know that even though the scroll isn't Ethiopian, it's still in your territory and so we're prepared to offer you—"

"Have you read it yet?" Saba was staring at him with unwavering eyes. "The scroll. Have you read it?"

"Uh, no. One, I don't read Ge'ez, and two, we've kind of been running for our lives from your homicidal boyfriend."

Saba's eyes danced. "I'm going to tell Arosh that you called him that. He will be so amused."

Oh dammit, what had he gotten himself into? "Please don't. What do you want?"

She leaned forward and rested her chin in the palm of her hand. "Isn't it obvious, young Benjamin? I want to know if it works. I want to know if Mithra truly did what he claimed. I never believed him in life. But then after I met you, I began to wonder. Was it possible? Could Mithra have actually—?"

"I don't understand!" Ben was losing patience with the riddles and the double-talk. "If you've known all along where the bone scroll was, you could have had any wind vampire you were allied with—Ziri, Inaya, a *thousand* others—any of them could have—"

"Don't be ridiculous." Saba frowned. "Do you still not realize who you are? Why the serendipity of Giovanni Vecchio's finding you was so very extraordinary? Why you hold the scroll of Mithra with such ease? All of this was meant to be. Who am I to interfere with fate?"

Ben shook his head. "I *am* utterly ordinary. Just like this scroll. The only thing that makes me special is Zhang's blood, Saba, and I'm not even sure—"

"Has anyone ever told you, Benjamin, that your eyes are quite special?"

Ben blinked. "They changed color. That happens when you turn sometimes, and Tenzin said—"

"You have Persian eyes." Saba smiled. "Benjamin Amir Rios. Son of Horiya Haddad, daughter of Qamra Saliba, daughter of Dina Azimi, daughter of Ardeshir Azimi, son of Javid, son of Hasan Khani, son of Farideh, daughter of Zana—"

"Stop!" Ben held up a hand. "Stop it. I... I don't know any of those people. I don't know what you're talking about."

"Those are your ancestors, Benjamin. I could go back further if you like."

"No, they're not... They can't be—" Ben's mind was swimming. "I don't know *any* of those people. You don't know what you're talking about. My mother's name wasn't Hori... whatever you said."

"Horiya Haddad," Saba said. "It was the name she was born with. An honorable name from a prominent family in Lebanon whose roots go all the way back to a Sasanian governor who ruled Sidon a very long time ago, even for a vampire."

Holy fuck. If Saba was right, his mother hadn't been lying about everything. Ben was frozen in shock, but what Saba was revealing...

"What are you saying?" he asked. "Be very clear." A memory surfaced from weeks ago, sitting in Giovanni's library thousands of miles away in Pasadena.

"But if the bone scroll can be used by someone with the blood of Mithra, that could mean a lot of people... In theory, his human descendants could have had lots of children. They could be thousands and thousands in the modern world, right?"

"You are one of many." Saba folded her hands together. "And yet you are unique. In so many ways, Benjamin Amir Rios, son of New York, you are singular."

"You're saying that I carry the blood of Mithra," Ben said. "Not only as a wind vampire but as a human."

Saba smiled. "An exciting prospect, isn't it? You would think that in all my years of life, I would have tracked down another descendant of Mithra's and made sure they turned to the air, but I often lose track of things." She frowned. "Time especially. I forgot about the bone scroll for centuries until Arosh brought it up some time ago." Her smile turned sly. "So convenient that you'd fallen in with a wind vampire, and one whose own sire owed an obligation to the Fire King."

A hundred tiny puzzle pieces fell into place around him. The revival of a rivalry thousands of years at rest. A sword lost to the sea. An impossible decision and a wrenching separation.

"You've been playing with us." Ben heard his own voice, and it was tinged with bitterness. "All along, you've been playing with Tenzin and me as if we were nothing more than pawns."

"Have I been playing with you?" Saba cocked her head. "I suppose from your perspective, that could be correct. But you and your partner are far from pawns in this game."

"My life" —his anger rose— "was not a fucking game!"

"If we are using your metaphor, you and Tenzin are the king and queen of this chessboard. Don't you see?" She spread her empty hands. "I've just admitted to you that the scroll is useless to me. And indeed, Arosh doesn't know this yet, but he could never wield it." She smiled smugly. "As if I would allow him to gain such an upper hand; I dearly love my prince, but I have not forgotten who he is."

"You don't feel a single regret," Ben said. "Do you?"

"For what?"

"For taking my human life from me. For forcing Tenzin to give me to her father. For playing your *game* with our lives."

Saba's chin rose. "No. Regrets are useless, and I don't waste my time on them."

"You think you're smarter than everyone, don't you?"

"Smarter? That is a different matter entirely. But wiser?" She smiled. "Who in our world could be wiser than me? What child can claim to be wiser than his mother?"

Ben held out the scroll, which suddenly seemed to weigh a thousand pounds. "So what keeps me from destroying it right now, *Mother*?" Anger began to burn in his chest. "What is stopping me from crushing it in my hands?"

37

Tenzin emerged from the floor of the bakery, a dusty mess of a woman with red stone dust all over her clothes, her hair a tangle, pulling an earth vampire through a hole in the floor no bigger than a large loaf of round bread the humans were pulling from the oven.

She looked around the bakery, alive in the predawn hours. The priests who had been baking were frozen and staring at her and Daniel. "Uh... Bêta Merkorios?"

Their eyes went wider.

"Have you picked up any Amharic?" Tenzin murmured.

"Nothing more than yes, no, and thank you." Daniel looked down at his bare feet. "We look a bit of a mess, don't we?"

"I imagine so." She nudged the stone back into the hole with a loud thunk. Then she walked toward the open doorway, feeling Daniel following her.

"Bêta Merkorios?" one of the humans asked.

Tenzin spun around. "Yes. *Awo*. Bêta Merkorios." She nodded hard.

The old man dressed in white walked them silently out the

door and down the hill, pointing toward the massive metal cover that sheltered Bêta Amanuel in the distance.

"Thank you." She took his hand and had to resist the urge to kiss it. "Thank you."

Daniel shook the man's hand as well and thanked him in Amharic. Tenzin walked down the hill, itching to take to the sky but knowing the humans were watching.

"The cavern Saba pulled Ben into," Daniel said. "I'm sure it's part of the complex under Merkorios. There was a scent that was familiar and there was more water. It smelled damp."

"We have to get to Ben and make sure he's safe," Tenzin said. "And we also need to make sure he secures the bone scroll. We have leverage, and he better not reveal it until the right time." She picked up speed, floating just over the ground to avoid the clumsy earth. "Daniel, are they still—"

"We're far enough away," he said. "I really don't think they can see. The moon isn't very— Oh my God!"

She'd already grabbed him by the back of his collar and yanked him into the air, speeding over flowing hills and round houses to land in front of the church they'd explored the previous night.

Someone had put a brand-new lock on the old door, but Tenzin didn't have time for subtlety. She yanked the padlock off the door, twisting the metal in her fingers, the fire of Ben's blood burning through her veins.

Her mate wasn't panicking. Now that her head wasn't swimming from being underground, she could feel him. He was angry. Worried.

Not frightened.

Should he be?

It was a question she had no way of answering until she found him and looked into his eyes. Ben's bravado could drive her absolutely out of her mind. Male egos were infuriating. She felt him though. His blood hummed with contented energy in her veins, happy that Tenzin had finally recognized it.

The humans who cared for the church had replaced the carpet, but Daniel tore it up again, which Tenzin was grateful for. She had no patience for—

"Small daughter of Zhang!"

"Fuck!" Tenzin bared her fangs and turned to snarl at the voice of the fire vampire who was determined to make her kill him.

"Go deal with him." Daniel was already moving the stone back from the floor. "I'll try to find Ben."

She grabbed his arm just before he walked down the stairs. "Daniel, if he returns safely to me, I will owe you a favor."

It was no small thing among their kind, and Daniel knew it. "He's my friend, Tenzin."

"He's my mate." She leaned closer when Daniel's mouth fell open. "Do you understand me?"

The vampire nodded silently and slipped into the stone passageway.

As soon as he was gone, Tenzin walked out of the church, dirt and stone dust covering every inch of her, her hair sticking up at odd angles from being tugged and pressed in the ventilation shaft.

Arosh stood across a wide gulf carved into the rock that surrounded the church of Merkorios. Between them, a two-story drop threatened to make life very painful for anyone who happened to fall into it at night.

"Tenzin."

She tucked a chunk of hair behind her ear. "Arosh."

He still looked immaculate. His hair was braided and shining. His skin had a healthy glow gained from the rich oils he used on his body, and his leather leggings and billowing white shirt reminded Tenzin of a pirate in a movie. She couldn't stop a smile from touching the corner of her lips.

"Do I amuse you?"

"You amuse many women," Tenzin said. "But not me." She gave him a small salute. "I consider you a valuable competitor, however." She shook her finger at him. "Your women had very high standards, and I think you should consider that a compliment."

He narrowed his eyes. Arosh hadn't known for sure quite how Tenzin had "enjoyed" staying in his harem, but he might have been starting to get an idea.

"The boy—"

"Is a man now, Arosh." Tenzin scanned the surrounding area, but she found only one other vampire mind hovering nearby. It wasn't Ziri—nowhere near powerful enough. Inaya maybe? "You do know Ben is a grown man, don't you?"

"Do you?"

She smirked. "Oh yes."

"Ah." He shrugged. "I wish you happiness, but despite my new peace with your father, I must take the bone scroll from you."

"No." She shook her head. "That will not be happening. Ben is the one who found it. He is its caretaker now."

"But it is a treasure from Saba's territory." Arosh paced back and forth along the edge of the rock. "He has no right to it."

"He does if he bargains for it," Tenzin said. "You know your queen is amenable to a fair trade. Especially if that trade nets her a token from her most beloved daughter."

"Desta?" Arosh's face went blank. "You have something that belonged to Desta?"

"What else could compel her?"

Tenzin saw the moment Arosh realized he might lose.

His upper lip curled back and he snarled. Then he lifted his arms and sent a blast of pure fire directly across the trench, heading straight toward Tenzin's face.

—————

38

"Y ou won't damage the scroll," Saba said. "You are Giovanni
Vecchio's son."

He began to pace back and forth, feeling trapped by Saba,
her expectations, and the painful revelations she'd dumped on
him. "Some things should not exist. This is one of them."

Even as he said it, he knew she was right. He could never
destroy an artifact so ancient. His uncle would never forgive
him. *History* would never forgive him.

Saba smiled again. "Have you read it, Young Vecchio?"

He stopped pacing. "No, I told you I don't read—"

"You will learn," Saba said. "And only after you have read
the scroll of Mithra should you make a decision about its value.
It is the only logical course of action."

He was angry, afraid, and confused. *Why did Saba keep
making so much sense?*

Ben held the scroll close to his body. "You're just giving me
this superpowerful object? Why?"

"I told you," she said. "I'm curious."

Ben felt like screaming. "I don't think that's what Walt
Whitman intended."

Saba frowned but said nothing more.

"And if it does work?" Ben stepped closer to Saba and looked down at the calm vampire sitting on the bench. Her calm stoked his anger. "Say it does work, Saba. It will make me more powerful than any immortal on earth. More powerful than even you."

There was her infuriating smile again. "Do you think so?"

"I will control all four elements. I would be able to conquer nations. Steal territory. Rule over cities where you hold sway." He held the leather-wrapped scroll in front of her face. "What is to say that I won't figure out the secrets of this scroll and—"

"You're Giovanni Vecchio's son," she said softly. "The same man who risked burns to pull an ancient vampire from the sun's killing rays. The man who sacrificed his innocence to protect a pregnant woman. The man who handed power back to an ancient instead of claiming it for himself. You are the hope and the legacy of your family line, son of Giovanni and Beatrice, brother of Sadia, mate of Tenzin."

Despite the import of the moment and the kindness of her words, Ben felt a stab of pain in his chest. "She's not my mate."

"Of course she is." Saba rose and took his chin between her fingers. "If you could see who she has become with you, compared to who she was." Saba shook her head softly. "My most reckless and rebellious daughter. The one who has survived. I could never tell her anything; she would not accept it. But I smell her blood in your veins, Benjamin Vecchio. I see her mark on your heart. She is your mate."

Saba moved toward a blackened passageway. "Come. It is time to stake your claim."

As soon as she moved, Ben smelled the acrid smoke drifting down the passageway. "Arosh."

"And Tenzin." She shook her head. "The two of them, so arrogant."

~

TENZIN SENT another wave of wind across the chasm, directing the fire into the side of a hill. "Does Saba know you're burning churches?"

"We've done it before." His eyes were alight with destructive joy. "It will hardly be the first time."

"You aren't going to get the scroll. We won't let you have it." Tenzin rose in the air and dove down, drawing Arosh's fire from a line of early-morning pilgrims she saw walking toward the church. There were children in the group, mothers with infants. The bastard Fire King wasn't going to kill any more innocents, not while she was alive.

Arosh aimed another stream of fire at her, but she stopped it, sucking the air from the flames before they could do any damage.

The pilgrims walking toward the churches turned and ran, their cries echoing in the predawn light.

"The scroll is mine!" Arosh screamed. "I am the blood of Mithra. I am the inheritor of his power. I am—"

"You don't know who the hell your sire was!" Tenzin yelled back. "I've heard the stories." Tenzin watched the door of the church. Surely Daniel would emerge soon with Ben in tow. Then she could finish off her fight with the mad bastard who didn't even realize the sun was less than an hour from rising. "You woke in an empty black cave, Arosh. You probably killed your sire before they realized what you were."

"I am the blood of Mithra," Arosh shouted from a rocky ledge.

"Repeating it doesn't make it true." Tenzin darted through the air, no longer caring about stealth. She had to keep an eye on the church doors, another on the horizon, and still dodge the spears of flame Arosh kept sending toward her.

Where the hell was Benjamin?

She drew a long throwing dagger from her tunic. She had no desire to kill Arosh—she didn't need the political headache—but maybe she could scare him enough to stop raking the earth with flames.

Part of her desperately wanted to end the man—she had a feeling she could take him in combat—but that would shift the balance of power. She had no intention of taking on Arosh's responsibilities on the Alitean Council or his territory, so as much as he irritated her, she had to let him live.

She tested the edge of her dagger, then flung the blade toward him, shifting the air around it until she saw the quick flick of hair that flew up when the edge of the knife caught the Fire King's ear.

"Tenzin!"

The vampire flew into an even greater rage, a column of fire forming around him, the flames making his hair fly in a torrent of heat and wind.

Dammit. He was losing control, forgetting their location and the people around him.

She needed Ben and his diplomatic words. He always seemed to be able to temper situations and avoid violence.

He would probably not have advised throwing the dagger.

Plus, when he was with her, their power built on each other. Their amnis reinforced the other. In the dry, crackling air of the Ethiopian mountains, Arosh was at his most powerful. She couldn't pull enough air from around him to kill the flames. She could suck the fuel for his fire away for a second, but then he lit it again.

And again.

And again.

Taking shelter behind a wall, Tenzin looked at the horizon, then back at the church. The sky was growing lighter; she needed to get Ben away from this place and safe in their compound. She needed Daniel to emerge. She needed Saba—

"My love."

Tenzin flew up when she heard Saba's voice.

The most ancient one put a gentle hand on Arosh's shoulder. "What are you doing?"

Tenzin's eyes flew around the church compound. Arosh was cornered on a ledge across from the church where he'd leaped to mount his attack on her.

Where had Saba come from?

It was as if the earth just spit her out wherever she wanted to go. Tenzin hovered over the chasm between the church and the path, watching Arosh and waiting for Ben.

"The human has the scroll." Arosh growled.

"He is no longer human," Saba said. "And he has my favor." She stroked a hand over his long beard, then turned toward the growing light. "Come, my prince. We will take shelter for the day and continue this discussion tonight."

"Discussion?" Tenzin couldn't stop the snark.

"Not helpful, Tiny."

His voice brought a rush of inexplicable joy to the center of her being.

Tenzin looked behind her and saw Ben and Daniel standing at the door of the stone church, a leather-wrapped bundle still cradled in Ben's arm.

Tenzin looked back where Saba and Arosh had been, but they were gone, swallowed into the earth like the myths they were.

With only minutes to find shelter, Tenzin flew down and grabbed Daniel by the collar. Then she tugged Ben into the air, and her heart felt whole again.

"Come on." She wouldn't panic. Panic produced nothing useful. "We only have a few minutes to get home."

Ben wrapped his arm around her waist in midair and moved them so fast Tenzin knew that humans on the ground, looking up into the morning sky, wouldn't believe what they were seeing.

He was stunning and powerful, a creature of immortal grace so elegantly dangerous that her heart gave two thumps just from looking at his profile. He turned and smiled at her; he'd heard the sound.

"Almost home," he mouthed, the sound of his words whipped away by the streaking wind around them.

"Always home." She gripped his hand. "With you."

Minutes before dawn, they landed in the compound and took shelter from the deadly rays of the sun. Minutes after that, both Ben and Daniel were passed out in the middle of the entryway in the main house.

Beatrice came down and saw the two vampires sprawled on the floor, one of whom was clutching a bundle roughly the size of an American football. "I'm almost afraid to ask."

"Is my hair burned?" She inspected the ends she could see, certain she'd smelled Arosh's flames singeing her.

"I don't think— Oh, there's a little spot in the back." Beatrice patted her head. "Hardly even noticeable."

"That bastard." She looked down at the men, then at the windows that would eventually expose them as the sun rose. "Why are they so big?"

"Don't lie, you like his height and his muscles." Beatrice bent down and grabbed Daniel by the ankles. "I'll drag this one into the library if you want to hide in the closet with Ben."

"It's not ideal." She glanced at the bone scroll. "But I have a lot to think about, so I guess that will do."

"Good luck." Beatrice was still lugging Daniel toward the light-safe room. "Sadia is going to be awake in an hour, maximum. And I have a feeling she's going to have a lot of questions."

Tenzin opened the closet door and pushed and pulled Ben into its safety. "Maybe today is a good day to pretend to be sleeping."

39

B en sat at the library table with his uncle at his shoulder, examining the scroll that had caused so much drama.

It was over five feet in length when it was stretched out, with the bones split, polished, and woven delicately with sinew that had grown stiff with age. Giovanni had used subtle heat with his fingers and palms to unroll the scroll to its full length without damaging it, but it still needed some restoration work.

The writing on the scroll was both carved and inked, meaning that even in places where the ink had faded, the writing was still intelligible. The leather casing in the cool, dry cave had protected it beyond what Ben could have imagined for anything so ancient.

"Do you recognize the language?" Ben asked.

His uncle stared at the scroll for a long time. "No," he finally said. "I recognize the Ge'ez on the back, of course, and this language is in an old cuneiform writing system that was in use in Persia prior to the first century BC, but the language itself?" Giovanni shook his head.

"So there's no way of knowing what the original language is saying?" Ben asked. "The Ge'ez translation on the back—"

"Will definitely be helpful, but I need to take pictures and take them to a classical Persian specialist. This may simply be a dialect of Old Persian I'm not familiar with, but I'm not recognizing any words at all. An expert in the writing system should be able to transcribe the language somewhat accurately, and then we might be able to decipher it or link it to something more familiar."

"Or we could depend on the expertise of the Aksumite scribes who translated it on the back." Ben flipped up the top edge of the scroll to reveal the writing system still commonly used in the Horn of Africa. "That's probably going to be the easiest."

Giovanni looked at him with annoyance. "Easiest? Possibly. Most accurate? There's no way of knowing. Translations from the original script are necessary."

"Okay, you go ahead and work on that." Ben rolled the top of the scroll down so he could see the blackened marks where the ancient scroll had been translated. "But I'm going to do what Saba suggested."

"Which is?"

"Learn to read Ge'ez," Ben said. "Read the scroll. Try to understand it and what Ash Mithra was attempting to preserve."

"I admire you." Giovanni leaned on the library table. "I cannot lie—the energy coming from this scroll is unsettling. You really feel nothing of the sort?"

Ben shook his head. "I mean, I definitely feel kind of in awe of anything that's survived for this long, you know? And it's weird as hell to have a scroll made from human bones. But I don't feel uncomfortable or hypnotized or anything like what you and Tenzin have described."

"Interesting," Giovanni muttered. "The blood of Mithra indeed."

"Gio, we don't even know—"

"We do." Giovanni set down his magnifying glass and looked up. "She wouldn't have lied about something like that. She knows I can confirm it."

Ben blinked. "You can confirm it?"

"I can confirm your mother's true name," he said softly. "And Saba would know that—should you want to explore it—I could do a complete ancestry." Giovanni slid his hands in his pockets. "If you want."

Did he want? Ben shook his head. "I know who my family is."

"There's nothing wrong with wanting to know," his uncle said. "With wanting to understand her."

"I understand that—whatever shit happened in her life— she had a kid," Ben said. "And chose not to protect him. I lucked out when she gave me to you. If she hadn't, I'd probably be dead."

Giovanni shook his head. "I don't believe that. I have no doubt that whatever you chose to do in life, you would have been successful at it. Your character was already rooted when I adopted you."

"Rooted, maybe." Ben shrugged. "But you're the one who raised me. Taught me how to be a man. Taught me what family was supposed to be."

Giovanni's hand spread and hovered over the scroll. "What-ever this is. Whatever power or knowledge it may hold" —his uncle looked up and met his gaze— "know that I will never fear you. Never, Benjamin."

How had he known the dread Ben hadn't even been able to articulate? "Giovanni—"

"And I agree with Saba. She couldn't have given it to the keeping of a better vampire."

Ben voiced the question that had been haunting him since

he spoke to Saba in the cave. "Do you think she turned me because of this?"

Giovanni frowned. "It's hard to say. As twisted as it may seem to us, she saw herself as repaying a great favor when she engineered your human death. I think the fact that you're a human descendant of Mithra was convenient and exciting to her, but I don't know that—even if you were not—she would have allowed you to have a typical human life or death. Remember, Saba cares about humans, but she doesn't see them as equals. The man who saved her son deserved immortality. At least in her own mind."

In the distance, a loud BOOM reverberated. Giovanni and Ben rushed to the door and saw a distant puff of smoke far in the hills on the north side of Lalibela.

"Is that near the airport?"

"No," Giovanni said. "I am going to guess that explosion is a fire vampire having a small temper tantrum."

"Small?"

Giovanni nodded a little. "Knowing Arosh... quite small."

"Great." Ben stuffed his hands in his pockets. "This meeting should be super fun."

SABA SAT in the middle of the leather couch in the living room like a queen, nodding graciously as blood-wine was opened for her, frankincense was lit, and coffee was roasted. No one accompanied her but a single vampire of her line, Gedeyon, who stood behind her at attention.

Tenzin sat in the chair across from her, trying her best to remain civil after everything Ben had shared earlier that night.

Ben had shrugged and moved on, but Tenzin still felt the

scrape of her knees against stone in a courtyard half a world away.

Saba looked up, her eyes piercing in their brightness and clarity. "You're angry with me."

"Is it that obvious?"

"Yes." Saba sipped a glass of blood-wine. "What were you forced to give, daughter of Zhang?"

"That is not for you to know."

"Isn't it?" Saba's eyes never left hers even as she drank the blood in the goblet. "I know the answer already. You were *forced* to give nothing. Everything you offered was given willingly."

"I would have given anything to keep him alive."

Tenzin heard silence fall around them, and all the polite murmurs of company fell away. Perhaps some immortals wouldn't want to speak of such personal things among others, but Tenzin knew she wasn't saying anything that Ben, Giovanni, Beatrice, Sadia, Dema, and Chloe didn't already know.

They were her family.

Saba smiled softly. "You bare your secrets in your actions, daughter, even as you keep the truth in your heart."

"I don't know what you're talking about."

"Of course you do."

"Tenzin." Ben put his hand on her arm. "Learning to love it, remember? I'm not angry anymore. Let it go; we can't change the past."

She finally looked away from the arrogant queen and to her mate. "You are more forgiving than I am."

"Anger..." He shrugged. "I've learned that it doesn't accomplish much."

Tenzin turned back to Saba. "You have given the scroll to Benjamin as the blood and immortal heir of Mithra."

"I have."

Ben leaned toward Saba. "I know you told me to learn to read Ge'ez—and I will do that—but you should know more than anyone else." He gave her a level look. "The scroll... is it real?"

"You've held it in your own hands," Saba said. "You've felt its power."

"But that doesn't tell me if it actually will let me control all four elements," he countered. "Do you know—?"

"I told you, I do not know if it works." She spoke carefully. "I do know that Mithra spent two thousand years writing the scroll. I know that he *claimed* to have mastered the discipline of a practice that would give him control of all four elements."

"He claimed?"

"Mithra was... an interesting friend." Saba's eyes drifted away from Ben. "If anyone could train their mind to master the four elements, it would have been him."

Tenzin wondered what kind of obsessive vampire would choose to spend thousands of years trying to master all four elements.

She was a little bit afraid she was going to find out.

Ben persisted. "So this isn't a... spell? Or some magic—"

"It is a map, Benjamin Vecchio." She glanced at Giovanni. "I believe you have learned to read maps, have you not?"

"I don't think I've ever had a map quite like this."

Her eyes returned to him. "Oh no. You definitely have not. But as Tenzin stated, I have named you as Mithra's heir. The scroll is yours to study for as long as you may need to study it to discover its secrets."

Ben sat back in his seat. "That sounds like the project of a lifetime."

"Indeed," Saba said. "Of many lifetimes. Which you have now."

Tenzin was still focused on practical matters. "You have

named Ben the heir of Mithra. And have you have made this clear to your fellow elders?"

Saba nodded. "Arosh and Ziri are on their way back to Alitea. They have matters to attend in court that have no bearing on my personal territory."

And Arosh hadn't told Saba anything about Desta's belongings. Apparently.

This presented an opportunity in Tenzin's opinion. An excellent opportunity.

"Being that the scroll was in your territory for centuries," Tenzin said, "and left in the safekeeping of your human kings, it is yours to give. And you have done it." She turned to Ben and smiled. "So she has no need of an exchange."

Ben's expression told her he didn't approve. "That's not what we agreed to, Tenzin."

"My daughter has told me of the recovered items you gave to her," Saba said. "On behalf of my people and their history, I thank you."

"Good." Ben was still staring at Tenzin. "That's great to hear. Tenzin, did you want to add anything to that?"

She shook her head slowly. "I think we're settled. Like you said, let it go."

Ben pursed his lips. "I don't think that's what I meant."

"Literal meanings can be so limiting, don't you think?" She glared at him. *Think of the pretty crown. Think of the beautiful book.* "I think if you consider everything we returned to Hirut, we've given far more than we've *been* given, and that's always a good place to be." Tenzin tried to make the most virtuous expression she was capable of.

She wasn't sure she succeeded, and Ben was clearly not convinced.

"A better place to be is a place without secrets." He turned to Saba. "Saba, Tenzin and I have found Desta's crown."

Damn it!

Well, it was almost worth giving up the beautiful crown to see the shock on Saba's face. Almost. Tenzin offered her a smug smile as Ben explained more.

"We also found one of her illuminated books in a private collection in San Francisco," he said softly. "We confirmed the authenticity of the book with Lucien. He says he remembers his sister painting it. I promise you, I would not claim these things if we weren't sure we had the right pieces; that would be cruel."

Saba still hadn't spoken. She opened her mouth, then closed it.

Tenzin looked away. She'd enjoyed surprising the unflappable queen of the vampires, but the sheer maternal longing in Saba's expression was too intimate to view.

"How can you be sure?" Her voice was hoarse.

Tenzin glanced at Saba's red-rimmed eyes and looked away again. "We matched the crown to a sketch that Lucien gave us. It was found in the secret collection at the British embassy in Addis."

"We think it might have been part of the treasure looted at Magdala," Ben said. "It had been kept with—"

"Show it to me." Saba stood and her chin rose. "I will tell you whether it was Desta's or not."

They led her to the library, where Giovanni and Beatrice stood behind the large library table. Giovanni opened a velvet-lined box with Desta's polished crown while Beatrice placed the devotional manuscript on a padded wedge and opened it.

Saba stared with a frozen expression, saying nothing. Tenzin could see the stories flashing behind the ancient woman's eyes and tried to imagine what she was seeing in her mind.

Was she remembering the daughter she had chosen and

nurtured for centuries honored with riches and glory? The gifted artist, her talent a cry of joy to the God she worshipped?

Or was she seeing the ashes and hearing the screams of a beloved child's death?

"The manuscript in particular," Giovanni said softly, "is a testament to Desta's obvious talent as well as her training. While she painted this devotional in the style typical of iconic Ethiopian artists in the late Aksumite period, the depth of color is, I think, most telling. It lifts the manuscript beyond what were the normal standards of Orthodox iconic art into pieces that are truly profound." Giovanni flipped the manuscript to a page where the Virgin Mary held the infant Jesus. "I believe she used your face for the inspiration to this piece."

Saba nodded but still said nothing.

Ben reached for the manuscript and slid it toward Saba. "You must have been very proud of your daughter."

Saba reached for the crown and held it between fingers that had clung to survival far longer than Tenzin could even imagine. She turned it in her hands, examining every part of it.

Saba turned and met Tenzin's eye. "When they took her from me, I was inconsolable."

"You ended an empire to avenge her death."

"I wanted to do worse." She closed her eyes. "I would have done worse. Love is a dangerous gift."

"And yet you survived." Tenzin nodded at the manuscript. "As did your daughter, in her own way."

Saba looked at Ben. "The bone scroll is ash and dust to the gifts you have given me. I find myself in your debt again, Benjamin Vecchio."

"There is no debt." Ben smiled a little. "Maybe just... try to let me live my life from now on. No more chess games."

Saba narrowed her eyes, then looked at Tenzin. "He doesn't understand."

"No, but that's part of what makes people like him. It frustrates my father too."

Ben looked between them. "What are you talking about?"

Tenzin continued, "I will consult with Zhang and send something official from Penglai."

Saba nodded. "Very well. I'll expect your messenger." She opened the box where Desta's crown had rested, placed the manuscript inside, and set the crown on top. Then she handed the box to Gedeyon, who was also looking at it tenderly.

"Desta's legacy is going home," Saba said. "I will give the crown to Hirut, who is of my daughter's line. The manuscript I will keep for myself."

Ben said, "We're very happy to be able to bring them back to you."

Saba spoke to Tenzin. "Where are the men who stole these things from our country?"

"Dead," Tenzin said. "Long ago. We stole them from their ancestors."

"Good." Saba nodded. "That is good." She looked at Beatrice and Giovanni. "I wish good fortune on your family, son of Kato."

"I thank you," Giovanni said. "Good fortune on your people, Saba."

"A self-serving wish." She looked around the room, and a smile touched her lips. "You are all my people. Every single one of you." And without a backward glance, she walked out of the room and out of the house.

The front door shut and Saba was gone.

EPILOGUE

The flight back to New York was quiet. They'd left at the end of a long day, stopping in Addis to refuel before they headed to Dublin, where they would drop off Daniel and Chloe, who was meeting Gavin in the city. Then they'd stop in New York to leave Ben and Tenzin at home.

The scroll that had caused so many problems would be joining the archives in Italy for a while. After much deliberation, Ben had decided to let Giovanni and his librarians try to reconstruct the unknown language of the original text while Ben did his own work learning Ge'ez and coming to grips with what could be a centuries-long task of exploring Mithra's work.

Since the mother of the vampire race had given the scroll to Ben, Giovanni didn't think that he or the scroll would become a target for opportunists. That and the general incredulity about the artifact itself were the best protections they could hope for.

Giovanni and Beatrice had briefly entertained the idea of staying in New York for a couple of weeks, but Ben's reaction must have persuaded them that over three weeks of family togetherness was quite enough.

Ben wanted Tenzin to himself. He was starting to understand her need to escape from the world. He didn't want to see anyone. He wanted to wave at Arthur—who'd been good enough to feed their birds and water their houseplants—and then not see a living soul other than Tenzin for a month.

She lounged against him, a tiny powerhouse bursting with manic energy from being on a plane for so long.

He tugged her hair. "How do you travel to Tibet?"

"Not in a damn plane," she muttered.

"No, tell me. It's really far to fly over the ocean. Do you go north?"

"Yes, I travel to Alaska and then across that way. That way I avoid ocean storms too. I have found a quicker route over the Pacific, but it's not as comfortable."

"It sounds cold though."

"It is."

His eyes were drooping shut. "I think we're headed into the sun."

She nodded and brushed his hair off his forehead. "Let's go to our room."

"Sounds good."

They entered one of the narrow bedrooms that had been added to the plane when it stopped being just Giovanni's plane and became a family vehicle. Ben lowered the bed and folded it out from the wall. It was a tight squeeze, but then again, vampires weren't exactly restless sleepers.

While Ben was getting the bed ready, Tenzin engaged the lock and used the small basin to wash her face. Then they both slipped into comfortable clothes to sleep.

Ben pulled Tenzin into his arms. The temperature in the plane was cool, and Ben knew she'd start complaining about the overly filtered dry air soon.

"Guess what?" he asked.

"You're not really tired," Tenzin said. "You just wanted to have sex."

"You're very perceptive." His fingers found the edge of her shirt.

"Well, you are very transparent."

Tenzin lifted her arms, and Ben pulled the shirt up and over her head, his eyes already fixed on the gentle rise of her breasts and the tattoos rising to frame her hips.

"You are so beautiful." His voice was barely over a whisper, but she heard it.

"Benjamin—"

"Take off my pants."

Her hand was already in them. "I don't know. My hands are nice and warm in here."

"I'll make you warmer." He kissed along her temple and down her jaw, teasing kisses under her jaw until she was squirming and her grip on his erection tightened.

"Careful." His voice was tight. "You're going to want to play with that later."

Tenzin's hand slid out of his pants and around to the small of his back as she used her feet to hook around his waistband and push his sweatpants down.

"So fucking flexible." He kicked off his pants and rid her of the panties that were interfering with his view. "Tenzin—"

"Ben." Tenzin lay on her side, their bodies aligned as she placed a long, soft kiss over his heart. "I realized something when we were in Lalibela."

"That I'm your mate?"

She looked up. "What? How did you—?"

"I can feel you, Tenzin. Even though we haven't been sharing much blood, it's there. I feel everything about you." He slid his hands down to cup her bottom. "I can feel when you're happy. When you're irritated. When you're kind of wary, like you are right now." He pressed his forehead to hers. "If that's not mating, I don't know what is."

She was frozen in his arms.

"Your secrets are safe with me, Tiny. They always have been. Always."

Her mouth dropped open, as if she was going to say something, but after a moment her mouth spread into a broad smile, her curving fangs glinting in the low light of the cabin.

"Ben?"

"Yes?"

She nuzzled along his throat, licking the warm skin over his heartbeat. "I think we finally figured out what to call you."

Mate. He pressed her face into his neck and smiled. She would call him her mate. "Yes."

She pulled away from his neck and looked into his eyes. "Yes?"

"Yeah." He smiled, and every part of him felt alive. More alive than he could ever remember feeling. "I want your teeth."

"Good. I definitely want that too." She didn't make him wait. She rolled on top of him, her legs straddling his hips as he surged up, grinding into her heat.

Tenzin bent down and bit.

Her fangs slid into his neck and her lips pulled against his skin. He could feel it again, the twisting amnis that spread through his bloodstream, curling around his own elemental energy until the air in their small cabin whirled and whipped them into a frenzy, knocking bottles from the shelves and tossing books and papers around the room.

Tenzin pulled her mouth from his neck, licking the blood from her lips and pulling him up until his mouth was just over the rise of her breasts. Tenzin pushed his face toward the soft flesh and held him there. Ben cupped her in his hand, pushing her flesh up and teasing the nipple until she was twisting in his arms. Then he bent down and sank his fangs into the delicate skin.

She gasped, and he pushed his hand against her mouth to quiet her. She gripped it and bit down on his wrist. Hard. Ben had to stifle a groan when he entered her.

Their joining was fast, desperate, and as silent as they could make it. Ben sincerely hoped that the ambient noise in the aircraft masked the muttered curses he made as he came. Tenzin had turned his arm bloody, trying to mask her cries.

She collapsed on his chest, and her fangs grazed his nipple.

He flinched, his body overly sensitized by the violent crash of their elemental energy and blood sharing.

Tenzin's face was glowing. "How much time before we land in New York?"

"Over twelve hours." Ben glanced at the clock. "But I'm going to be passing out pretty quickly here. We're headed into the sun."

She pouted. "Oh, I forgot that was real and not just an excuse to be alone."

"Right." He was already feeling the afterglow turning into languor. He settled Tenzin against his side, stroking the nape of her neck and the fine hairs on her skin. He could feel everything.

Everything.

"Hey, Tenzin?"

"We need a humidifier," she muttered. "Don't get me wrong; I'm not a water vampire, but air this dry isn't natural."

"Isn't the air dry in Tibet? We should go to Tibet."

"It's dry, but it's a natural dry. And we should definitely go to Tibet."

"Right." He kept stroking her skin. "Tenzin?"

"Yes?"

"There's something on the floor in my... pants. In the pocket of my pants," he said. "I have something shiny for you."

He could feel her excitement when she reached down to find it, then her confusion.

"Ben?"

He smiled, just waiting for her to start protesting.

"What is this?"

He glanced down; her eyebrows were furrowed, and she was glaring at the beautiful gold piece he'd found in an old jewelry store in Addis.

"Don't you like it?"

She scowled. "It's a ring."

"Yep." He smacked a kiss on her forehead. "It's a ring."

"I don't believe in marriage, Benjamin. We've spoken about this before, and I thought you understood—"

"Did I ask you to marry me?"

Her eyes were still suspicious. "No."

"No." He closed his eyes. "Do you like it?" It was a gold ring and it was far simpler than most of the jewelry she collected, but he liked it because he thought it was something she'd actually wear. The crown of the ring mimicked a small circular shield, and the center was dominated by a deep red ruby. "It's a shield," he said. "With a ruby."

"I know what it is." She was still frowning. "And I like it."

Of course she liked it. She had a fondness for rubies, though she claimed to love all gemstones equally. But Ben could tell she loved her rubies the best. "So if you like it, wear it. It should fit on your left hand."

"I thought this wasn't a marriage ring." Her tone said *gotcha!* "Why the left hand?"

"Do you usually carry a weapon in your left hand?" He yawned a little. "If you do, then put it on your right."

"Oh. I suppose you're correct."

You suppose? Ben opened his eyes a crack and watched her slide her new ring onto the third finger of her left hand.

Exactly as he'd planned.

He closed his eyes, feeling the pull of the sunrise. "Does it fit?"

Of course it fit.

"Yes." She sounded surprised. "It does."

"Oh good." He kept his voice casual. "I found it at an antique store, you know? But I figured we could always get it sized to fit you if you liked it." *Ha!* Yes, he put a ring on her. Ben knew she didn't want marriage, but at least this way he could stake a small claim.

Small. A minor thing really. It was just a ring. For his mate.

He smiled as he drifted off to sleep.

"I know this is not just a ring." Tenzin pinched his chin. "I'm letting you get away with it for now."

Because you love me. He smiled but kept his eyes closed. "I don't know what you're talking about."

"Just a ring," she muttered. "You think you're so smart."

"I know I am." He cuddled her closer. "It's okay, Tenzin. We've got forever to argue about it."

"No, I am not agreeing to that." Ben was irritated and trying to not let it grow into hurt. "I can't believe you'd even suggest it."

"And I can't believe we're still arguing about it when I offered a perfectly reasonable explanation—"

"You agreed—I heard you!—that we had forever."

"That was a figure of speech." Tenzin turned to him from across the kitchen. "I was trying to use more colloquial English, and now you're using it to trap me." She let loose with a tirade in her language, and Ben felt his temper spike.

"You are teaching me that language, or I'm filing a formal complaint with Zhang."

Tenzin lifted her chin. "You need to learn Ge'ez."

"I'll *multitask*, dammit."

Ben was standing in the doorway of Tenzin's house in Tibet, a truly strange habitation perched on the edge of a mountain and consisting of three rooms, two caves, and the world's narrowest garden. It was a house that only a wind vampire could love.

Because the only way to get there was by flying.

Ben watched her as she heated a bag of blood in boiling water on the wood-fired stove that heated the house. "I cannot believe after everything we've been through— Tenzin, we're mated! Your amnis is literally inside my body. You think that it's just going to disappear after a while?"

"I am not going to promise you forever." She poked the bag and turned to him. "You have no concept of what eternity means. What forever is. We could turn into completely different people, and then promises made with the best intentions become prisons, Benjamin."

"And I'm not agreeing to a hundred years!" He stood and braced himself in the doorway. "A hundred years is going to pass like the blink of an eye for you, and then what? We're done? Just... *done?*"

She took the pot off the stove. "I never said we were done. I'm just saying that we agree to renegotiate—"

"Our relationship is not a sports contract, Tenzin."

"We agree to honestly evaluate how we feel about each other, and then we can extend... You know."

"Our contract?" God, she was so infuriating. If he didn't know it came from a place of love and concern for his age, he'd want to strangle her.

Who was he kidding? He still wanted to strangle her sometimes.

"A thousand years," he said. That was twice the length of his uncle's entire immortal life, and it was a substantial chunk of Tenzin's.

Five hundred was what he was going for, and Tenzin loved to bargain.

She narrowed her eyes and considered it. "Two hundred."

Gotcha. "That's ridiculous. I'll consider eight hundred."

"Three hundred."

"Five, and that's as low as I'm going, Tiny. You try to negotiate *our relationship*" —he leaned down and got in her face— "any shorter than that, and I'm walking away from this conversation."

She stuck her hand out to shake. "Five hundred."

"Fine. Five hundred years together, and then we can sit down and have a conversation and make sure it's still working for both of us."

Tenzin nodded. "That seems fair."

"Good." He shook his head. "You drive me up the wall sometimes. You really do."

Her curving fangs flashed in the lamplight when she smiled. "Then I supposed it's a good thing I taught you how to fly."

She forgot the blood and grabbed his hand, leaping off the edge of the cliff and dragging him down toward the dense forest of birch trees that blanketed the river valley below her mountain.

Ben flew through the birch grove, darting among the trees before he flew to Tenzin, following the path of the river lit by the light of a full moon. He dipped his fingers down to trail in the water, splashing Tenzin as she soared above him.

She laughed and reached for him, drawing his body to hers as the wind led them over the forest and through the mountains, holding them as she pressed their bodies together and her mouth took his in a possessive kiss. Her lips were honey, and his blood sang when her fangs found his neck.

Ben held her as she drank him in, pressing Tenzin to his heart as his soul rose with the wind. He heard the music in his mind as his arms encircled his mate. The air held them in its gentle embrace.

And they danced.

THE END

(for now)

~

Continue reading for a first look at Martyr's Promise, the next book in the Elemental Covenant series.

Brigid and Carwyn are two elemental vampires finding the lost and righting wrongs, searching for meaning in an endless stretch of immortality.
And trying not to blow things up, but that might be more aspirational.

FIRST LOOK: MARTYR'S PROMISE

Summer Mackenzie watched the waves slowly recede from the ash-grey pebbles tucked against the sweep of the foggy California coast. She turned to her right, keeping an eye on the trail where her boyfriend Dani had detoured to look for a campsite.

Low tide wouldn't be for another six hours, which meant the current leg of their route was impassible until early morning. They'd need at least five hours to finish the stretch of trail that took them closest along the beach, and they needed daylight. Summer had learned long ago that you didn't go into the forest at night.

She'd grown up in Appalachia, and even though she might have been away from those ancient rolling hills of North Carolina for three years, she knew better than to disrespect the woods.

Summer heard Dani before she saw him. Daniel Uriarte might have been an incredible athlete—with the soccer scholarship to prove it—but he wasn't a woodsman.

Dani smiled when he saw her. "I found the perfect spot. Come, you should see this."

"Oh yeah?"

"Definitely." He held out his hand. "You are going to love this one."

Summer was tempted to leave her pack near the beach, but if Dani had really found a prime camping spot, she didn't want to backtrack and there was no way they were staying that close to the water; the waves along California's Lost Coast had a mind of their own.

Summer hoisted her bag over her shoulder and followed Dani between two pines. "So what's so special about this spot? There's a clear camping area up on that last bluff that was all leveled off."

He turned, his smile still vibrant. "Trust me. I know you think I don't know anything about camping, but—"

"I have never said that," Summer protested. "I just know you didn't grow up in the woods like me. Your knowledge of soccer—"

"Football."

"Football." She rolled her eyes. "Your football trivia is expert level. I'm just saying that when it comes to what bugs you can eat in a survival situation, I have skills."

Dani laughed and grabbed her hand. "Summer, stay with me so you will never eat bugs again."

She couldn't hide her smile. "So romantic."

"Just follow me, mi sol, and you will see."

When Dani had first moved from his high-rise in Mexico City to the rainy streets of Seattle, Summer knew he would have laughed at the idea of camping, much less backpacking for six days along the Northern California coast.

Summer followed Dani as he led her along a slightly worn path leading into the trees, his broad shoulders carrying a bright orange pack as if it weighed nothing.

Since they'd met, Summer had turned Dani from a total city

boy into an outdoor enthusiast. They fished, they hiked, and they'd even backpacked a little. He loved boats, and his family had more than one.

Or maybe they were more like yachts?

Ugh. Rich people vocabulary was confusing.

"How far back is this site?" She looked at the brush that was giving way to denser forest.

"Not too far."

Summer couldn't even imagine the level of wealth that Dani's family enjoyed. In truth, it was starting to become a Thing They Didn't Talk About. They had been dating a year, but she hadn't met Dani's parents and he hadn't met hers. When any of their mutual friends happened to bring up family stuff, they both changed the subject.

Summer had been raised by a high school math teacher and a musician in rural North Carolina. Her father had taught her how to hunt and fish—along with her times tables—and her mother had taught her the guitar and how to cook anything out of everything. They were a traditional clan who took pride in hard work, loyalty, and self-sufficiency.

She had no idea how they'd react to their daughter dating the heir of one of the largest tile empires in Mexico. Half the time, she didn't know how to react herself.

Dani walked between another set of trees, stopped, and spread out his arms. "Voilà!" He glanced at Summer, whose mouth was agape. "You see, I knew you would love this."

Love... wasn't the right word. Summer turned in a circle, her eyes scanning the obviously man-made clearing in the middle of the woods.

A nearly perfect circle of tall pines soared into the sky, their tops obscured by a layer of marine fog. As she stood in the center, she looked up and saw the sun disappear behind a cloud.

Dani was crouched in the center of the clearing, kneeling

beside the old stone fireplace in the middle. "It's perfect, yes? Some local family must camp here."

No, this was not a family campground.

The dense forest suddenly felt claustrophobic, and Summer felt eyes peering at her through the trees. There was something out there. Something was watching them.

Don't stare into the trees unless they know your voice. Her grandmother's whisper tugged at her ear, warning her to leave the clearing.

Summer walked over, grabbed Dani's shoulder, and tugged. "Come on. Let's go back to the trail."

Dani stood and frowned. "What are you talking about? This is the perfect spot! The area around the campfire is so clear and level. I checked for poison oak." He pointed at the fireplace. "See? There is even some wood left over from the last people who stayed here."

It wasn't even a firepit; it was a full-out, dressed-stone stove with grates in the bottom for wood and braces on either side to hang pots over the flames. This wasn't natural, it wasn't even foraged.

This was a lure.

"Dani, just trust me, we shouldn't stay here." Instinct told her they were being watched. "I think we should head back to the coast, okay?"

Dani pointed toward the ocean. "We're not far from it. You can see the ocean from here." He turned and faced the coast. "I bet you could even see a fire from the marked trail. And people come back here." He pointed to the trail that had led them into the circle of trees. "See?"

She couldn't explain it, and she loved that he'd found what to any sensible eye seemed like a great spot. "It just... it feels very visible. Everyone can see us."

Dani set his pack down and sat on a piece of log that circled the fireplace. "Summer, everyone we've met on the trail has been so cool. We have to camp until the morning, right? We might as well camp in a clear camping spot with a firepit that someone has already prepared."

Was she just being stubborn? Paranoid? Granted, her family made it hard to discount the mythological, but she was probably overreacting.

Dani stood and held out his arms. "Listen, even if you are right and people can see us, so what? They can see us just as easily from the bluff on that last hill. We're the only human beings out here, we have our bear repellent, and I am tired." His arms dropped. "Please. Can this one thing be easy?"

She looked over her shoulder at the marked trail, then over at the worn path through the brush, the forest, and into the clearing. This was obviously a well-used spot on the trail, and the rangers did request that they keep to used camping spots instead of creating their own.

"Okay." She kept her voice small. "But we're pitching our tent right by the fire. I don't want to be near the edge. If something gets into this clearing, I want some advance notice."

THEY'D STOPPED FAR SOONER than they usually did, so they had plenty of time to cook a full meal with the supplies they'd brought along with some sea lettuce and large limpets that Summer had foraged on the nearest beach.

After they'd eaten, Dani pulled out a bottle of whiskey and poured a little into both their camping cups. "We're going to sleep well tonight."

"We are." With the tents set up and the coals glowing,

Summer was starting to feel as if she'd been paranoid earlier. Sure, they hadn't seen anyone else on the trail since the day before, but it was September and tourist traffic was pretty low.

She leaned back against Dani's chest as he propped himself against a fallen log and stared into the fire. "Did you pack up all the food?"

"Yes." He patted his pack, which held the bear canister they were required to take. "I'll hang it from one of the trees before we go to bed."

Summer was full from a hot dinner and the whiskey that warmed her throat. She felt herself drifting, and the sounds of the forest at night settled around them. Crickets hummed, and a few night birds started calling. She heard an owl start to hoot in the distance, and the faint sounds of the sea crashing on the rocks below them lulled her into sleep.

She woke when Dani moved.

"Come on," he said. "Tent time."

She groaned but forced herself up to sitting and rubbed her eyes. She reached for the portable motion sensor that her father had bought for her and set it within range of their tent door; then she went inside to find the small remote and set it.

"Your burglar alarm." Dani smiled as he entered the tent. "Do you think the bears will be scared away?"

"I just like knowing if I need to wake up." She smiled and tucked the remote into a mesh pocket in the tent. If anything tripped it, the remote would beep. Not loud enough to wake Dani, but Summer had always slept light.

"You're worse than Ignacio." Dani stripped off his flannel shirt and shuffled into his sleeping bag, wearing only his pants and a thermal shirt. "There is less wind here than by the beach."

"I know. It might be warmer." Nevertheless, Summer kept her pants and socks on. If a bear—or anything else—attacked the tent, she wanted her shoes on in seconds, not minutes.

Dani rolled toward Summer, put his arm around her waist, and tugged her sleeping bag toward his until she could feel his warm breath near her neck. "Sleep well, Sunshine."

Summer smiled at his affectionate nickname and closed her eyes.

In minutes, she was asleep.

~

THE BEEPING WAS INSISTENT. Summer's eyes flew open and her heart was already racing.

"What is that?" A low voice whispered outside the tent.

She sat up, put a hand over Dani's mouth, and nudged his shoulder until his eyes flew open. He frowned and moved to pull her hand away, but the voices spoke again.

"A phone maybe?"

"There's nothing out here that can get signal." The voices were matter-of-fact. Bored even.

Summer shook her head and put a finger over her lips as she removed her hand from Dani's mouth. He nodded, understanding the need for silence.

Their tent was a typical backpacking tent, small and compact. Easy to pack and set up, but there was no room to move around without being heard.

Something shook the top of their tent, and Dani sat up.

"Wakey-wakey," the voice said, amusement coloring the words. "Come on out, neighbors."

Summer knew these were no friendly woodsmen. Dani took the canister of bear spray from his pack as Summer removed her hunting knife from its sheath. They both slipped out of their sleeping bags. Summer shoved her feet in her hiking boots, and Dani did the same. She eyed her jacket in the corner and took the calculated risk of setting her knife down for a second to put it on. Dani did the same.

Don't move. Make them come to you. Waste their energy, not yours. Her father's voice was the one whispering to her now. Her father, who'd been raised by monsters, knew what he was talking about.

A flashlight beam moved around the tent, and Summer concluded that there were two men stalking them. Well... two somethings. Humans were the most obvious, but not the only choice.

Dani whispered, "Summer—"

"Shhhh."

"Oho." A man outside chuckled. "I think the city birds are awake."

"Come on out, little birds." The flashlight moved to the tent opening and didn't move. "Don't make us come in there to get you. That'll just irritate me."

Where were the voices from? Summer tried to decipher an accent, but she couldn't. It was flat California speech with just a hint of surfer.

Dani's hand gripped Summer's, and he kept the bear spray aimed at the exit of the tent. If he let it off in an enclosed area, they'd be weeping and sick, but hopefully whomever Dani hit with the spray would get the nastier end.

The zipper on the tent started to move. "Come on out now."

Fingers were visible at the entrance now, fat callused fingers with black curly hair on the backs.

Dani looked at her with panicked eyes. Summer took a deep breath and tried to breathe through the rush of adrenaline that was starting to course. She held up a hand for him.

Wait.

She motioned to the bear spray and then the tent flap.

Spray them when it opens.

Dani nodded.

Summer pointed her knife at the back of the tent and made a slashing motion. If Dani sprayed the person trying to come into the tent, she'd rip open the back and they could escape away from the sprayed men.

Dani nodded again and took another deep breath.

"You going to be stubborn, are you?" The voice was losing patience. "Fine, I'm coming in. No funny business; I don't want to hurt you."

Bullshit.

The tent zipper was ripped open, and a bright light glared in their eyes.

"Now!" Summer shouted before she took a deep breath.

Dani leaned forward and let the bear spray stream into the intruder as Summer slashed through the back of the tent, ripping down and away twice to open a flap large enough to let them both out. She scrambled out of the reeking canvas, her eyes already flooded with tears.

Dani had thrown the bear spray canister at the men coming into the tent when they started screaming, and he scrambled out after her.

She clutched her jacket around her and tried to make her steps wide enough so she wouldn't trip over her untied boots.

"Back to the trail." She was coughing and sneezing at once, her body desperate to rid itself of the toxic fumes they'd used to escape. She heard Dani running behind her, wheezing from the bear spray.

Summer used her adrenaline to jump over logs and rocks, heading toward the ocean and the open expanse of coastal bluffs. She could see a light in the camping area on the last bluff they'd passed. If they could just make it there—

"Summer!"

She turned and saw Dani on the ground a few yards behind

her. She ran back to help him up and saw a black-handled knife sticking out of his shoulder.

"Shit!"

"Go." His voice was a painful rasp. "Run!"

She looked up and realized it was too late. Three men were running after them, and none of them were laughing anymore. Summer rose and held her hunting knife in front of her.

The largest one leaned down and grabbed Dani by the leg, pulling him toward them as if he weighed nothing. They were great, hulking shadows in the darkness, three men with broad shoulders and square heads.

Another one of the men yanked the knife out of Dani's shoulder, and he groaned in pain. Summer's knife rose, but she didn't move. The men had Dani; she couldn't leave him.

"Drop the knife please." The largest shadow spoke calmly. He wasn't crying like the other men, nor did he move the same way. Something about him was... different.

As soon as she felt the ground beneath her move ever so slightly, she knew exactly why this one was different. "I know what you are." She lowered the knife.

Know when to run and when to wait.

She'd never outrun him, never overpower him. Any human attack was a waste of her energy and would only endanger her more. "We're the wrong prey for you."

"Oh?" A slight hint of amusement.

"They'll look for me if I disappear."

The vampire stepped out of the shadows and into the light of the full moon. His fangs gleamed in the darkness as he smiled.

"They all say that."

～

Preorder today for October 26, 2021,
And grab the first book of the Elemental Covenant series,
SAINT'S PASSAGE,
from all major retailers right now.
Available in e-book and paperback.

AFTERWORD

Dear Reader,

You've reached the end of Ben and Tenzin's journey!

Or have you?

This has been a HUGE debate in my reader group and even with myself, because I have been very clear that THE BONE SCROLL was the last planned book in the Elemental Legacy series.

Last *planned*.

But I have to tell you, **even though I've spent three novellas and five novels with these characters, I'm actually... not sick of them yet?** I know. That's pretty weird for me. I usually write three or four books about a couple of characters and I nearly want to destroy them with an errant asteroid by the end.

But it's true. I really do love these two, and I feel fortunate that they're the type of characters who are dynamic by nature, which means that *even though this is the last planned book and definitely the finale of a character arc for them,* Ben and Tenzin will very likely come back for an encore or several.

Meaning: I definitely envision writing more Elemental Legacy adventures.

There are still more treasures to find and more mayhem to manage, so if you're a fan of the series, don't despair! These two will be back.

I may take a break for a bit, since my writing schedule has been pretty hectic, but until then, you can enjoy the new Elemental Covenant series, another paranormal mystery series featuring Carwyn and Brigid from the Elemental World series. I included a preview of their second book at the end of this one, and I hope you check it out.

All the best to you vampire lovers. It has been such a privilege to tell the stories of these two amazing characters. Thank you for joining this wild ride.

Best always and thank you for reading,

Elizabeth Hunter

ACKNOWLEDGMENTS

Spending the end of spring and beginning of summer in Addis Ababa was exactly the kind of refreshment I needed to make *The Bone Scroll* everything I wanted it to be.

By the beginning of 2021, I was struggling. Though I had outlined books and had made plans, finding inspiration and motivation had become increasingly harder. I was worn out. Spiritless. It was the first time I had realized as a writer how much I depend on the world around me for motivation and inspiration.

When my husband I were able to be fully vaccinated, traveling to visit family in Ethiopia became a possibility. It provided exactly the kind of new scenery that I needed as a writer, and it provided me the opportunity to develop and research this book with a depth I couldn't have otherwise had. So, when I think about all the people I want to thank for their help in writing this book, I'd like to start with...

Brilliant German scientists, **Ugur Sahin and Ozlem Tureci**, researchers and heads of the company that developed the Pfizer/BioNTech Covid 19 vaccine. Every time I have heard either of these two scientists speak, I have been humbled and awe-struck by the brilliance of their minds and their dedication to world health. As recipients of the Pfizer vaccine, my family is so grateful for your work, your wisdom, and your dedication to the pursuit of scientific advancement in the field of vaccine therapy. You'll probably never read this, but it doesn't matter. Thank you so much for everything you've done.

My husband! My best guide and interpreter. From finding me the perfect living and office space (with miraculous wifi!) in Addis Ababa to translating for me daily to coordinating tours and research trips in rural areas, I am so grateful. Also, thank you for making me remember to eat and not get too wrapped up in my work that I forget the world around me. David, I absolutely adore you.

My incredible guide in Lalibela, **Mulugeata Fentaw**, who I cannot recommend enough. Mule was a tour coordinator, guide, and translator all in one. And though I'd visited Lalibela before, he added a depth of understanding and specificity about the churches and town that made a huge difference. **If you're traveling to Lalibela, he can be reached at mulugeata230fentawa@gmail.com or via Telegraph at +251 935438503.** I don't usually include contact information for guides, but Mule said I could this time, so there you go!

My best friend, K, and my son, who held down the fort while we were gone far longer than originally planned. I am so grateful that I have such good friends and such an incredible son. I am so proud of the young man you are becoming, C. Love you so much.

My whole publishing and publicity team, who worked with me while I was overseas during the release of *Fate Interrupted*, and who deftly managed when I did *not* come back on time. **Jenn and Catherine at Social Butterfly PR, Amy**

Cissell, my content editor, **Anne and Linda at Victory Editing,** all of you are ROCK STARS, and I could not publish my books without you.

All my friends in Addis who were so supportive, gave me car rides, found doctors (long story) and generally helped me and David to navigate life in the city. Melke, Tedy, Bire, Tedy (yes, there are several), Didi, Akli and Elsa, Bisi and Tedy, Fisho, and I'll just mention Melke again because he's the best. We love you all so much.

And finally, to all my readers who have been so incredible with their love for this series and these two very unusual characters, thank you for loving these weirdos so much. I adore them, but I wasn't always sure readers would get who they were or what I was trying to do.

Since the beginning of Tenzin and Ben's journey, one question has returned to me over and over again: What does "happily ever after" look like to a five-thousand-year-old immortal being? How would Tenzin even wrap her mind around forever? How could Ben hope to understand? I hope that, by the end of *The Bone Scroll,* you see both the struggle of those questions and the resolution for what it is, an ongoing work of love-in-progress.

Love is always a choice, one I hope to make every day. It's a choice that colors everything in my life and drives who I have been and who I am becoming as a person and a writer. Thank you for going on this journey with me.

Thank you for loving these characters.

And thank you for reading,

Elizabeth

ABOUT THE AUTHOR

ELIZABETH HUNTER is a *USA Today* and international best-selling author of romance, contemporary fantasy, and paranormal mystery. Based in Central California, she travels extensively to write fantasy fiction exploring world mythologies, history, and the universal bonds of love, friendship, and family. She has published over forty works of fiction and sold over a million books worldwide. She is the author of the Glimmer Lake series, Love Stories on 7th and Main, the Elemental Legacy series, the Irin Chronicles, the Cambio Springs Mysteries, and other works of fiction.

ElizabethHunterWrites.com

ALSO BY ELIZABETH HUNTER

The Elemental Mysteries
A Hidden Fire

This Same Earth

The Force of Wind

A Fall of Water

The Stars Afire

The Elemental World
Building From Ashes

Waterlocked

Blood and Sand

The Bronze Blade

The Scarlet Deep

A Very Proper Monster

A Stone-Kissed Sea

Valley of the Shadow

The Elemental Legacy
Shadows and Gold

Imitation and Alchemy

Omens and Artifacts

Obsidian's Edge (anthology)

Midnight Labyrinth

Blood Apprentice

The Devil and the Dancer

Night's Reckoning

Dawn Caravan

The Bone Scroll

The Elemental Covenant

Saint's Passage

Martyr's Promise

Paladin's Kiss

(Spring/Summer 2022)

The Irin Chronicles

The Scribe

The Singer

The Secret

The Staff and the Blade

The Silent

The Storm

The Seeker

Glimmer Lake

Suddenly Psychic

Semi-Psychic Life

Psychic Dreams

Moonstone Cove

Runaway Fate

Fate Actually

Fate Interrupted

The Cambio Springs Series

Long Ride Home

Shifting Dreams

Five Mornings

Desert Bound

Waking Hearts

Linx & Bogie Mysteries

A Ghost in the Glamour

A Bogie in the Boat

Contemporary Romance

The Genius and the Muse

7th and Main

INK

HOOKED

GRIT